PROTECT & SERVE

PROTECT & SERVE

The Adventures of Maxwell Heath

The Menagerie
Book 1

CARTER CHRISTENSEN

Carter Christensen

This one's for NJD

All the dead bolts, pulled shades and hidden knives in the world couldn't protect you from the truth.

Wally Lamb

Contents

Prologue

There are moments in life that leave an indelible impression, a mark so deep it feels permanent: a first kiss, the birth of a child, or the first time you kill another person.

If you're aware enough, you can almost feel your DNA change. Colors, lights, sounds, are all different. You feel alien to yourself, like a stranger has taken over your body. You're sure the whole world can see that you're somehow altered, that you are no longer who you once were.

But as you grow older you realize that a kiss is just a kiss and there will be many more in your lifetime that are better, deeper, wetter, different. And childbirth, for all its wonder, is just biology. It's been happening since the cavemen…and will continue long after we've all passed on.

But that first kill…the suddenness of the strike, the shocked look of recognition in your victim's eyes when they finally understand what's happened to them, the sound of the gun as it goes off in your hand and the exquisite recoil that follows, the energy jolt that travels up your arm, that lights up all of the nerve centers in your brain. That moment, that singular instant, will never be replaced no matter how many more may follow, as monumental as each one may be.

Murder is a drug. It's an unquenchable thirst and an insatiable hunger. Once you have that first taste, you crave the next hit, search for it until you find it. But you know from experience that the satisfaction is only temporary, the euphoria won't last long. No matter what you tell yourself, or others, there's no quitting. Once it gets into your veins, it takes hold and doesn't let go. You're a killer. It defines you. No one is ever an ex-assassin, you're just lying dormant until you're called on for your next assignment. You can lie low, tell yourself you've left it behind. But you haven't. The urge never dies, it sleeps. And sooner or later, something will wake it up. It always does.

Maxwell Heath

Chapter One

I never knew my Grandpa Pete. He dropped dead from a stroke a couple of years before I was born, not long after Momma and Pa got married. He was a pig farmer just like his father, and grandfather, before him. His family had worked the land we lived on for almost a century. It was his legacy. One of them.

His name wasn't spoken much in our house, for what I'd eventually learn were obvious reasons. Pa called him *that sonofabitch,* while Momma didn't mention him at all, except on the anniversary of his death, which she treated more like a celebration than a day of mourning. His death became a slow-burning fuse wrapped around all of our necks, setting off random explosions throughout our lives. Grandpa Pete did his damndest to kill each of us from beyond the grave.

As a kid, I didn't understand what he'd done that was so bad. After all, we owed the farm to him. Momma was an only child, so it passed to her the day he died, which I'd later realize probably wasn't her dream. But it gave us a lot. And there are worse things in life than a successful farm, especially in Choctaw, Oklahoma in the early nineties. I grew up thinking we were lucky. I was wrong.

It was years before I learned about the other women Grandpa had in his life, before and after Grandma died. The only one that mattered though, as far as Momma was concerned, was Becky Ann Hollis and her bastard son Grandpa had fathered.

Maybe it was the child, or maybe it was Becky Ann's lack of shame in not hesitating to name the boy after Grandpa, it didn't really matter, Momma was not turning the other cheek or finding it in her heart to extend any sort of Christian love and kindness towards Becky Ann. It was war.

Momma always tensed up when we'd run into Becky Ann at the bank or the Piggly Wiggly, even though I knew they'd gone to school together. They never acknowledged one another. Momma would tighten her grip on the shopping cart handle and we'd suddenly veer off down the cookie aisle, even though I knew we weren't buying cookies that day. We never did. I didn't know what the problem was, only that there was a big one.

Eventually I learned what it was. Becky Ann had threatened to go public about who her son, Petey's, father really was, unless she got a piece of Grandpa's estate. Backed into a corner, Momma and Pa took out another mortgage on the farm to buy her silence. That was the start of it but the gauntlet had been thrown. The feud between our families had begun.

The farm I thought was a blessing, my parents saw as a weight around their necks, a costly reminder of Grandpa's betrayal. They kept that part from us as long as they could. All we knew was Pa hated the farm. He wanted no part of it.

"I'm not a fucking pig farmer," I heard him say more than once. Whether that's why he became a cop, or if that had been the plan all along, I couldn't say. But he kept his word. He had nothing to do with the farm.

Grandpa died out by the south sty, falling dead next to the fence. His body caught on the crossbeam so it looked like he was just hunched over, gazing into the sty, watching the pigs go about their business. Roger Oldham, who helped Grandpa run the farm, found him around dinnertime, well beyond saving.

Roger's first thought was that he was out of a job. He'd only been working there a year. His wife, Molly, was pregnant, and Grandpa's death was more unexpected than the pregnancy. But when Momma offered him the job of running the farm, he jumped at it. The Oldhams moved into the quarters at the far end of the property, about a half mile from our house.

That was the world I entered. We lived on the farm, Pa was a cop in town, and the Oldhams were more like family than employees.

I don't remember Evan being born, I was barely a year old, but as far as I knew, he'd always been there. My partner in every little crime, my alibi when I needed one, and vice versa. When we were old enough to explore the farm on our own, Bobby Oldham joined us. We played baseball, climbed trees, and ran wild from sunup to dinner, until Bobby started school. Then it was just Evan and me. And before long, it was just Evan.

I remember Momma being pregnant during those years, but somehow, we never got a new brother or sister. There were arguments. Then silence. We were sent to our room a lot. There was crying. I'd pull Evan under the blankets we used to build a fort and tell him stories, pirates, princes, whatever came to mind, until the house got quiet again. That usually happened after Pa slammed the front door and sped off, tires spitting gravel against the siding. I never knew where he went. I only knew that when he did, the silence stayed behind.

When I was five, Jasper was born. Clara came two years later. The year after that, Pa was shot in the line of duty.

I was the one who answered the phone that night. Momma was giving the little ones their baths, and Evan was at the kitchen table, bent over his spelling workbook. The man on the other end of the line kept insisting he needed to speak to Momma, so I went upstairs to watch Jasper and Clara in the tub, making sure neither of them slipped under the water.

I heard the phone hit the floor first. Then I heard Momma follow. I wanted to run into the hall, but I couldn't leave the kids. So I scooped up their slippery, naked bodies and ran down the stairs, heart pounding, arms full.

Momma was collapsed on the rug, completely still. I nearly dropped Jasper. Clara started wailing.

I looked toward the kitchen. Evan was frozen, staring back at me.

"Help me," I said. Just those two words. But it was enough to pull him out of whatever place he'd gone in his head. I put the kids in his arms and called the Oldhams.

Mr. Oldham was at our door almost before I hung up. Mrs. Oldham and Bobby arrived soon after. Momma had only fainted, but when she came to, she blurted it out without thinking: "Walter's been shot."

Mr. Oldham took her to the hospital. The four of us stayed with Mrs. Oldham for a long time.

Pa wasn't the same after that. He was worse.

He couldn't, or wouldn't, go back to work, so he lost the only job he'd ever wanted. Most days, he just sat in one of the high-backed chairs in the parlor, staring out the front window at nothing. He was angry all the time, quick to lash out at us for breaking the new rules he never explained but expected us to know.

He demanded silence. That meant no playing in the house, or near the house, or at all, really. If you displeased him, you'd feel the back of his hand before you ever saw it coming. He was like an ornery snake, striking fast. Sometimes it was a slap across the face. Sometimes it was a boot to the ass that left you sprawled on the floor. For worse offenses, he'd remove the belt from his pants.

It was old, black leather, cracked and stiff, and it tore the skin on my bare ass and the backs of my thighs when it made contact. Depending on what I'd done, I might get four or five strokes. Other times, like when I threw a baseball too high for Evan to catch and it smashed the kitchen window, I got twenty. I thought he might kill me that time.

Still, I often took the blame for things Evan had done, trying to spare him the fate I'd already resigned myself to. Evan wasn't as strong as I was.

Pa called me worthless. Told me I was an embarrassment and deserved every lash he gave me. I hated him for it. I wished that bullet hadn't missed his heart.

I don't know what was worse: that Evan and I had memories of Pa from before the shooting, or that Jasper and Clara never would. They'd only know the monster he'd become. But for reasons never explained, he spared them his wrath. They never got the belt. Never got the back of his hand. That wasn't going to last forever though.

As we got older, Evan escaped into his books. He'd disappear into the woods with one of his fantasy novels tucked under his arm, reading alone, where it was safe. I started spending more and more time with the Oldhams. Bobby had moved on to high school, so I didn't see him much during the day, but in the afternoons he helped his Pa on the farm. I'd race home from junior high to join them.

Even though Bobby was sixteen and probably had better things to do than hang out with a fourteen-year-old, we were still best friends. When the pigs were fed and penned for the night, Bobby and I would find something to get into. He taught me how to make a whistle out of a blade of grass. How to drive the tractor. How to shoot his Pa's rifle.

The three of us, me, Bobby, and Evan, became obsessed with hunting the small animals that roamed the woods and ran through the fields. We made up contests to see who was the better shot. Bobby usually won. Evan was a close second. I got better with time, but never good enough to make it a real contest.

When I turned sixteen, Bobby taught me how to drive a real

car. It wasn't so different from the tractor, but it *felt* different. Having a license meant freedom. One step closer to escape.

When Bobby graduated, he didn't leave like the other kids who ran off to Stillwater or Norman. He stayed on the farm, working full time with his Pa.

And I started to see him differently.

It seemed to happen overnight, but I'm sure it had always been there, just under the surface, waiting. One minute we were in the back field, shooting at rabbits, and the next I was wondering what it would be like to kiss him. What his lips would feel like against mine.

It was exciting and terrifying all at once. I knew it was taboo. I knew I shouldn't act on it. I couldn't. And I knew there wasn't a single person I could talk to about what I was feeling. My best friend was also the object of my affection. I kept quiet. Said nothing. Did nothing.

The other boys at school started talking about girls they liked, girls they wanted to date, whatever that meant at our age. I played along, always picking girls who I knew would never look twice at me. I was safe that way. But I knew I couldn't keep it up forever, so I started pulling back, withdrawing from those conversations. Isolating myself.

I got quieter. More afraid. More unhappy.

I had a secret. And I knew I had to protect it, no matter the cost. I couldn't let the other boys find out. And I *definitely* couldn't let Bobby know. If it changed things between us, I didn't think I could handle that.

Every day, I went to school, then rushed back to the farm to help Bobby with whatever he was working on. By the time I got there, he'd be sweaty and covered in dirt, and even in the colder months his shirt would cling to his chest under his work jacket. When the weather got warmer, he'd shed layers with the heat. By summer, he was down to just his overalls, no shirt underneath, his skin a deep brown from the sun. His chocolate-colored nipples peeking out from behind the bib whenever he turned. My feelings ran deep for Bobby Oldham.

"Why don't you have a girlfriend?" I asked one afternoon after we returned to the barn.

He shrugged. "Just don't have the time, I guess. Plus, there's no one around here who interests me."

"No one?"

I don't know what I was expecting him to say. He sure as hell wasn't going to profess love for me. Even at seventeen, I still felt awkward and scrawny next to him. I was a boy, and he was a man. A real one. Strong. Sure of himself. I told myself friendship had always been enough, it would have to stay that way.

But I still thought about kissing him.

Autumn brought senior year. Questions about the future that didn't have any answers. I could apply for loans. Go to college, or at least community college. I could learn a trade. Do something, *anything*, that would get me off the farm for good.

The only problem was: I wasn't sure I *wanted* to leave anymore.

Leaving the farm meant leaving Bobby. I could almost stand another year or two in the same house as my father if it meant working side-by-side with Bobby every day. By then, Evan would be out of the house. Safe.

Throughout the winter, I dodged Mrs. Griffin, my guidance counselor, and her endless questions about college applications and possible majors. More and more, the only thing I wanted to study was Bobby Oldham's body.

It was getting worse, not better. I was daydreaming about him in class. Dreaming about him at night. Waking up with erections I couldn't ignore, awkward since Evan and I still shared a room.

I moved through my days carefully. Quietly. While the other kids were picking out tuxes and talking about the winter formal, I was coming up with excuses about why I wasn't going.

I kept my secret safe, held tight. I was only fooling myself.

It was February, and I was walking through town after school on my way to the store for Momma. I was distracted, as usual, wondering what it would be like to ask Bobby to the Valentine's Day dance, when I heard someone call my name.

Then: "Queer."

I turned. It was Petey Hollis.

For a long time, I hadn't known that Petey, the bully who was a few years older than me, was actually my uncle. I'm not sure he knew either. But eventually, we, and everyone in town, found out. Secrets don't stay buried long in a place like Choctaw. If two people know something it's only a matter of time before the whole town does, unless one of them dies first.

The story of Grandpa Pete knocking up one of his daughter's classmates was just too ugly to stay buried forever. And Petey hadn't taken the news well.

I don't know what Becky Ann told him about his father, but when the rumors started flying, he acted like I'd personally done it. Like I aired the family dirty laundry. I almost felt sorry for him, until I remembered I had an old sonofabitch for a father too. That put us back on even ground.

I got used to the shoves into the lockers, the casual trips in the hallway, the names. I'd lived with Walter Heath for years, Petey Hollis was nothing by comparison.

But then Petey got held back and didn't graduate with the rest of his class. Becky Ann's beauty shop, the one she opened with the money my parents paid to buy her silence, struggled to stay open. Things got bad for the Hollises. Momma was thrilled. Petey was not.

His bullying turned meaner. More personal. The names got uglier, and the way he looked at me sometimes made my stomach knot. That's when I knew I needed help.

"I need to learn how to fight," I told Bobby.

He looked at me hard. "What's going on, Max?"

So I told him. Everything. About Petey. About how I needed to be able to defend myself if it ever came to that.

Bobby didn't hesitate. He started teaching me to fight. We shadow-boxed. He hung a makeshift heavy bag in the barn, and we'd take turns wailing on it. We punched at it until we were drenched in sweat, our knuckles red and raw.

Then Bobby showed me wrestling moves, how to get free if someone dragged me to the ground. That was harder. The contact was constant, intimate. His breath was hot against my neck. His arms locked around me. His weight pressed down on me.

When he pinned me, part of me never wanted to get back up.

I wasn't sure what kind of fighter I was becoming but I knew one thing: my crush on Bobby was turning into something I could barely contain.

In the end, I didn't need to fight Petey Hollis. He either forgot why he wanted to pound me or he just moved on. He graduated and vanished, like so many others. I stopped thinking about him.

Until that February day, walking down that street.

The sound of his voice raised every hair on my body. Part of me wanted to run. But another part, bigger now, had had enough.

I was sorry he was angry that my grandfather had knocked up his mother. But that was between the two of them, not me. If he wanted to scream at Grandpa's grave, I'd give him directions.

But I wasn't going to be his punching bag anymore.

I turned to face him and tried to look dangerous, like I'd seen in movies.

"What did you say to me?"

"You heard me, gay boy…"

The heat rose up in me. Maybe it was because he was too close to the truth. Or maybe it was just his time.

Either way, I knew what I had to do.

It became an out-of-body experience. From somewhere above, I watched myself take action. I was out of control. I knew I couldn't stop myself, even if I tried.

I turned toward Petey, walked straight at him, peeling off my gloves as I moved, letting them drop to the sidewalk without looking. Before he knew what hit him, *I* hit him. A right cross, hard and clean. I knocked him off balance, his feet tangling beneath him. He went down like dead weight.

When his head hit the sidewalk, it made a sound I'll never forget, like the hollow thump of the melon I once dropped in the Piggly Wiggly. Echoing. Sickening.

I bent to pick up my gloves, my right hand still stinging from the impact. Petey was trying to get up, but he couldn't seem to figure out how his limbs worked. I pushed him back down with my boot.

"Don't ever speak to me or anyone in my family ever again. Or I'll fucking kill you."

Then I walked home, forgetting all about the store. I couldn't wait to tell Bobby about everything his training had done. For the first time in my life I'd won.

My eighteenth birthday came the same week as graduation. I wasn't looking forward to either.

I knew Momma wanted me to go to college, to start a life that didn't involve pigs or Oklahoma. I knew Pa just wanted me gone. And I, I didn't know what I wanted. The unknowns of my life stretched out in all directions, like a dark chasm I was never climbing out of.

I couldn't imagine leaving Bobby. He meant everything to me. And I knew I'd be lost without him.

But I couldn't say that. Not to anyone. Certainly not to Bobby.

So I kept quiet that whole week. Barely spoke at school. The only person I saw outside of class was Evan, but he seemed just as lost as I was. His fear of my leaving him was palpable and created even more turmoil for me.

My last exam fell on my birthday. I should've felt proud. Relieved. Instead, I just felt...numb. In two days I'd be free of Choctaw High, as if that was some kind of accomplishment. My birthday went unnoticed at home, same as always, except for Evan, who wished me a quiet 'happy birthday' when we woke up that morning. There was no pie, no card with five dollars inside. Nothing.

I couldn't remember why I wasn't itching to get out of there.

But then, I always remembered.

"Max," Momma called after supper. "Run this box of old clothes over to Molly. She wants to try her hand at a patchwork quilt."

"Yes, Momma."

I hoped Bobby wouldn't be there. I didn't want to see anyone, not even him. I just wanted to drop the box off and go home. Alone.

But fate had other plans. Bobby opened the door wearing his favorite cutoffs and an old T-shirt that clung to his body. When he raised his arms, I saw the dark trail of hair on his stomach disappearing below his waistband.

"Hey, Max. Ma said you'd be coming by." He took the box from me, our hands brushing. That familiar jolt of something sparked beneath my skin. "Where you been all week? You haven't been around."

"Busy. Finished school today…"

"Wanna hang out? My folks went into town for dinner."

"I can't. I gotta get back. I gotta…" But there was nothing I *had* to do, and I couldn't even come up with a convincing lie.

"At least come out to the barn. We can spar for a few minutes. Gotta keep those skills sharp, man."

It was pointless to argue. And truthfully, I discovered I *did* want to be with him.

We cleared a little practice space in the back of the barn. No breeze, just stale air and the hum of summer coming on. We stripped off our shirts and laced up our gloves, already sweating before the first punch was thrown.

"So what are you gonna do now that school's over?" Bobby asked between jabs.

"I'm not out yet."

"Close enough."

"Dunno. Get a job, I guess."

"Don't you wanna get out of this place?"

"Don't you?"

"I got my reasons for staying. What're yours?"

"No place to go, I s'pose. Why do you stay?"

That stopped him.

He froze mid-step, then pulled off his gloves. Just like that, the sparring match was over.

I'd somehow asked the wrong question.

"Sorry. I don't mean to pry. You don't have to tell me. It's OK."

For the first time in years, I felt like a stranger in his space. Maybe his family couldn't afford for him to leave. Or maybe he was embarrassed that all he ever wanted was to be a pig farmer. Either way, it was fine. I didn't know how to tell him that without making it worse.

I took my gloves off and tossed them into the corner of the barn beside his. When I turned back, Bobby was standing inches from me.

Before I could react, his hands came up to my face. He leaned in and kissed me.

I closed my eyes. I was in a dream.

It was sweet. Gentle. He tasted salty from sweat. His lips were soft. His stubble scratched my cheek. It was heaven. And it was over too soon.

"Sorry," he said. He dropped his hands and turned away.

"Wait."

I felt like I was shouting, the blood in my ears pounding so hard it made my head spin. I reached for his hand, but he was already out of reach.

"I shouldn't've done that, Max. Sometimes, though…sometimes I feel like if I don't kiss you, I might explode."

"How long have you…"

"I don't remember a time I *didn't* like you. I mean, well, you know."

"Bobby…"

I was trying to speak words I'd only ever used inside my head, and now they were going to come out in the wrong order.

"Really, Max. I'm sorry. Forget I did that. It didn't mean anything."

"It *did* mean something. It meant something to me…"

Now I was whispering. I didn't want the world to hear me say I liked Bobby Oldham. I wasn't even sure I wanted *him* to hear it.

"I think about you all the time, Bobby."

He took a slow step toward me.

"Really?"

His hand reached out, and I held my breath until I felt the soft graze of his fingers across my shoulder. They trailed down my arm, and I shivered.

I gripped his waist and pulled him gently to me. I wanted to feel his lips again.

We were magnets, finally connecting. I didn't know what I was doing. Bobby was the first person I'd ever kissed, the only one I'd ever *wanted* to kiss. When he opened his mouth, I opened mine. When I felt his tongue, I gave him mine. My hands wandered through his hair, down his bare back, and when I found the courage, I let them explore lower. His body had tempted me for so long, and now he was giving me silent permission to touch it.

Somewhere, I heard someone saying his name and I realized it was me.

He broke the kiss, pulled back. His eyes were wide, locked on mine.

"We should stop," he said.

"I don't want to." I felt like I would start crying if we stopped.

He took my hand and placed it on the front of his cutoffs. I felt him, hard, huge, and my eyes widened without meaning to.

"Max, we don't have to…"

I started to rub him and he shut up. He closed his eyes. I saw the bob of his Adam's apple as he swallowed.

I gathered every ounce of courage I had and started to undo his shorts. This was it, the moment every dream had led to.

And then: headlights. Sweeping through the barn. Tires crunching on gravel.

We froze.

"It's OK, Max," he whispered. "I'm not going anywhere."

He squeezed my hand and did up his shorts while I scrambled to find our shirts. He kissed me once, fast, before we heard his parents' voices outside the barn door.

"Max," he said, "you should know...I stayed because of you."

That was all I needed to hear. I'd stay in Choctaw forever if Bobby was staying too.

"Will I see you tomorrow?" he asked.

I smiled so hard it hurt.

"And the next day. And the next day..."

He kissed me again.

"Oh, and happy birthday."

I couldn't speak. I just smiled.

"G'night, Bobby."

I stepped out of the barn to walk home across the field. Our hands separated. Our fingers waved goodbye.

My heart was pounding the whole way home. I could still feel his lips, his tongue, the heat of his calloused hands. The darkness that had weighed on me all week was gone. The world felt new. I didn't feel scared anymore. I didn't feel ashamed.

I didn't know what tomorrow would bring, but I finally knew what it felt like to be wanted. To be loved.

I swung open the screen door and stepped into the house without slowing down, letting it slam behind me with a loud crack. Pa would have something to say about that, I was sure. But I didn't care.

Nothing could touch the way I felt.

Then, flashes of light. A collage of frozen images:
Momma lying dazed on the living room floor.
Evan sobbing in the doorway.
Pa's face, deep violet, twisted with rage.
And the shotgun.
The blast came seconds later.
Pa lay on the carpet, dead.
And just like that, my life changed yet again.

Chapter Two

I left the Dewey F. Bartlett Youth Detention Center almost two years to the day after I went in. I could've done longer if I'd had to, but the judge was lenient. I guess I was lucky he'd known my pa, known the man he'd been and the man he'd become. He believed the Justifiable Homicide plea my lawyer presented. The court sealed my record. My past, officially at least, was locked away.

I was twenty years old when I got my freedom back.

I walked out in the same clothes I went in wearing: jeans, a T-shirt, work boots. I'd been given a hundred-dollar bill, which I'd stuffed in my pocket, and a Greyhound voucher to get me back west to Choctaw.

I wasn't ever going back there though.

When the judge handed down my sentence, I cut ties with everyone in Choctaw. I didn't want visits. I didn't want Momma bringing the little ones to see me, or leaving them with Evan while she came alone. I didn't want letters about how much they missed me, or phone calls full of silence because no one knew what to say.

And that included Bobby.

I wasn't going to ruin his life by dragging his name through the dirt with mine. I wasn't who he thought I was. He needed to forget me. He deserved a better life, and I realized I wasn't meant to be part of it anyway.

Still, I'd spent eighteen months trying to forget him, and failing miserably.

I should've told him I loved him, had always loved him, when I had the chance. But I was glad I didn't. That wouldn't have been good for either of us.

The Heaths were cursed. Grandpa Pete's raging infidelity. Pa's terrifying anger. That's the DNA I carry.

I cashed in the westbound bus ticket for one heading east. It would only take me as far as Memphis, but at least I'd put the Mississippi River between me and Oklahoma.

That'd have to be enough, for now.

We arrived in Tennessee by early evening. I watched the other passengers collect their luggage from the belly of the bus and was reminded, yet again, that I had nothing but eighty-seven dollars and some change in my pocket. I needed a plan, and I needed it fast.

I walked slow circles around the depot, scouting, getting my bearings. There was a restaurant nearby that would probably throw food out at the end of the night, and a park close enough where I could sleep. Not ideal, but it'd get me through the first night. I'd figure out the rest in the morning.

I was roused by a cop nudging my side with his nightstick. The sun was barely up, but I'd made it through. First thing I did was check my pocket. I still had my money. My shoes were still on my feet.

I apologized, not because I thought I'd done anything wrong, but because I didn't want trouble. If I ended up sleeping on that bench again, I didn't need him remembering my face.

Don't be more conspicuous than you have to be. Don't create a problem where there isn't one.

Those were lessons Dewey Bartlett had taught me.

I found a water fountain, stuck my face under the spout, and brushed my teeth with my finger. I ignored the hollow ache in my stomach and started walking again, widening my circles block by block, scanning every storefront and light pole for signs of work. I needed a Job that didn't care about my past or where I slept at night.

Eventually, the city thinned out into neighborhoods. Bigger lawns. Quieter streets. I didn't know what I thought I'd find there, but after a few blocks, it felt like a waste of time. I turned around to head back when a pickup truck marked *Delgado Lawn & Landscaping Services* pulled up across the street. Three men were riding in the back.

They started unloading equipment, and I crossed over. I approached the driver and asked, I nearly begged, if he'd take me on, just for the day.

Carlos Delgado was my first bit of luck after a very long streak of anything but. He was down a guy and behind schedule. I was desperate and I knew how to work. The farm had taught me that.

We shook on it. He'd buy lunch, and I'd get paid in cash at the end of the day with the others.

I stripped off my shirt and pulled on the Delgado L&L Services one he handed me. Then I got to work.

I played follow-the-leader. I knew there was a right way to do everything, you just had to watch someone else who knew. So I watched. I learned.

Everything went smoothly until one of the mowers gave out. The guy who hadn't shown up that day was apparently also the best mechanic, and no one else knew how to fix it.

I grabbed a wrench and a screwdriver and went in like I was performing surgery. I'd been around enough temperamental tractors on the farm to know a few tricks. Before we lost too much of the day, the mower was up and running again, and I had a permanent job with Delgado L&L Services.

When the last yard was done, we climbed into the bed of the

truck and Carlos drove us back to the office, which wasn't much more than a trailer tucked at the back of a near-empty lot.

He peeled off twenties from a wad he kept in the glove box and handed them out. My cut was smaller for only working half the day, but twenty bucks was more than I'd had that morning, and I was grateful for it.

Once they were paid, the other guys scattered. I stayed behind, clearly with no place to go. Carlos picked up on it fast.

"You know a cheap place to get a room for the night?" I asked. "I just got to town yesterday…"

"There are some boarding houses around," he said, "but it might be too late to show up without notice."

"Oh. Right. OK." I turned and started walking, already resigning myself to another night on a park bench.

"Wait up, Max," he called. "My wife and I have an ADU behind the house that's empty right now. I'm sure Connie won't mind if you use it for a few nights, till you find something permanent."

I didn't know what an ADU was, but I didn't ask. It sounded like it had a roof and maybe running water and a mattress. That was enough for me. I said yes, and for the second time that day, Carlos Delgado had come to my rescue.

The ADU turned out to be his converted garage with a few upgrades. It looked like heaven to me. The windows were bare, and there was only a single chair. A toilet stood in one corner, and a bare mattress in the other. It reminded me a little too much of my cell from two nights ago, but it wasn't a park bench and I didn't have to worry about being attacked or arrested in my sleep.

It was enough. A place to catch my breath.

I asked Carlos to thank his wife before he left me for the night. Then I stripped down and washed up in the utility sink on the back wall, unable to abide by the sour funk of my own body any longer.

Sleep came quickly, in spite of the bare mattress and the lingering smell of oil and exhaust. But it was quiet. No Tyson wheezing beneath me. No night terrors echoing from down the block. I let myself sink into the dark, into silence, into a kind of oblivion I hadn't known in years.

Almost too soon, it was morning again. And with it, a new offer from Carlos.

"I told Connie about your situation," he said, "and we both agree, you should stay in the ADU as long as you need. No charge. In return, help me fix it up on the weekends."

I stared at him. "Carlos, that's too generous. I couldn't…"

"Don't be stupid, Max. I'm a good judge of character. This helps us both. Just don't tell the other guys. I wouldn't want them thinking I'm giving you something they're not getting. They could all use more, but I don't have enough for everyone. It's just easier if we just keep this between us…"

I said yes immediately.

Suddenly, Memphis, meant to be just a temporary stop on my way to someplace else, had started to carry weight.

Carlos handed me a small amount of cash at the end of each day. I used it to buy clothes, supplies, a knapsack to hold everything, even a secondhand bike for independence. On weekends, I helped him finish out the garage: we built walls around the toilet, a counter for the hotplate and new microwave, a frame for the mattress, a small table to eat at. After a couple of months, it wasn't just an old garage anymore. It was a home.

By early July, the heat had settled in, thick and relentless. The humidity clung to everything. I slept with the windows and the door wide open, a fan barely pushing the air around. Carlos kept promising to get an air conditioner, but the money never quite came through. We'd spend evenings in the backyard drinking Connie's sangria over ice.

"I don't mean to pry," Carlos said one night, and every muscle in my body tensed.

What had he found out?

Was this it, the end of my time in Memphis?

I hadn't thought far enough ahead to give him a fake name. Anyone who cared to look could find out almost everything about me. I waited.

"I don't mean to pry," he said again, "but have you thought about applying for public assistance?"

I blinked at him. "What's that?"

"Government help. Money to live on. I pay you in cash, you don't pay taxes, so they don't know about it. You'll qualify. They'll send you a check every month. A lot of people do it."

I frowned. "And I just tell them I live in your garage?"

"Use the house address. They won't check. If they do, Connie and I will say you're a nephew or something. Just a thought, trying to help you get ahead."

I told him I'd think about it.

Truth was, I didn't know how long I planned to stay in Memphis. It didn't feel far enough from Choctaw. I felt pulled to keep going toward something I couldn't quite name.

But a few days later, I asked for his help.

A few weeks after that, the first check arrived.

Carlos came down to the ADU with a pitcher of sangria and an envelope addressed to me. I tore it open. I couldn't believe it. Someone was actually going to pay me that much money every month, and I didn't have to do anything for it except cash the check?

"We can set you up with a bank account tomorrow," he said. "Money won't do you any good sitting in an envelope."

What harm could a bank account do?

Didn't mean I had to stay forever. I could close it as easy as I could open it.

I drank the sangria like I was the king of the world. Everything was finally going my way.

Then came Labor Day, and with it the realization that the lawn business would soon slow to a stop for winter.

I started thinking maybe that was my sign. Time to move on.

Between work and the government checks, I'd saved a decent amount of money. Enough that I wouldn't need to sleep on a park bench anytime soon. I just didn't know where to go. East, definitely. South, maybe.

I still had some time to figure it out.

I told Carlos what I was thinking. He and Connie had been so good to me, given me so much, that I wanted to give him time to find a paying tenant for the renovated ADU. I also wanted to make sure he had someone lined up for the crew before spring rolled around.

He took the news well. Just nodded, like he'd always known this day would come.

Carlos wasn't old enough to be my father, but he was the kind of man I wished my father could've been: steady, supportive, quietly looking out for me.

"Well," he said, raising his glass, "I hope I can find someone who works as hard as you and appreciates a good Friday night sangria."

I raised mine too. I hoped I wasn't making a mistake, but deep down, it felt right.

Still, Bobby kept slipping back into my mind. No matter how many times I thought I'd buried him, something would pull him to the surface. If I was ever going to go back, now would be the time.

But I couldn't let that door open up again. I couldn't let him in, not even the idea of him. I hoped he'd moved on. Found someone who could love him the way I once did. Still did.

Whatever we'd had, it was over. I had to force myself to believe that.

The other guys were sorry to hear I was leaving, but none of them seemed surprised. I got the feeling I wasn't the first to pass through Carlos's crew for just a season. It was that kind of job.

That Friday, we finished our three usual lawns, but Carlos stayed in the truck the whole time, said he had a migraine. He still looked off that evening when he came down to the ADU with our weekly pitcher of Connie's sangria.

"Here's to one more week," I said, lifting my glass and savoring the fruity burn. I noticed he wasn't drinking.

"If you're not feeling it," I said, "we can call it for tonight."

"No, drink up," he replied. "I'll catch up in a minute."

He started asking questions, about my plans, about whether I'd ever reached out to my family, what I wanted to do with my life. His voice was calm, but there was something off in it. He was careful, measured.

I'd never told Carlos much about my family, just that we'd had problems, that I hadn't been in touch with them in a long time. That was still true.

I told him I would leave my bike behind. It had given me freedom this summer, but I wouldn't need it where I was going. I'd figure out about forwarding my mail later, what little there was.

The sangria was hitting harder than usual. I couldn't remember if I'd eaten lunch. I got up to take a piss, but the yard spun around me. Or maybe I was the one spinning.

The ground came up fast. Everything went black.

Then there was yelling.

Was it Pa? Was he about to take the belt to one of the others? No, it couldn't be. But I couldn't move. My limbs weren't responding. Something was digging into my wrists.

My head felt foggy, wrong. I smelled the sour aroma of vomit.

It was mine.

The pressure on my arms wasn't Pa's hands. It was rope.

It was dark. Cold. Concrete under my back. Loud voices overhead.

Carlos. Connie.

"You were supposed to finish it," she said.

"He hasn't signed it yet," Carlos replied.

"We've worked too hard…"

"I know. But I need…"

A loud crack.

The sound of skin on skin.

Someone had just been slapped.

I shook my head several times, hoping it would help. I wasn't sure what was happening, but I knew one thing for sure: I was in danger, and I had to get out of there. Fast.

The ropes were tight. Too tight. It was too dark to see if there was anything nearby that might help me to escape. I wanted to close my eyes, pretend it was just a bad dream.

But I couldn't, because it wasn't.

I was in Carlos's basement. I could smell it: the damp air, the mold. The ADU never got this dark.

I tried to picture the layout: back door to the driveway, backyard beyond that, stairs up into the house. But none of it mattered if I couldn't get my hands or feet free.

I clawed at the rope. Bit into it until I tasted blood. Nothing loosened.

Time was running out. I didn't know how long I'd been unconscious, but whatever Carlos needed from me, whatever was keeping me alive, he'd be coming to collect it soon.

One thought pushed all the others out: *I'm going to survive this night.*

The click of the back door lock jolted my mind into focus. Every nerve in my body went electric.

A voice surfaced from somewhere deep inside: *Set your body free. Absorb what is useful. Reject what is useless. Have faith in yourself.*

Zhang Zichen.

The third cellmate I had at Dewey Bartlett. Like the others before him, we hadn't hit it off right away. We kept to our own corners for weeks. Until the day I watched him take down Thor without a single guard noticing.

Thor was an asshole and he deserved everything that came his way that day. He'd tried to provoke me on numerous occasions, each attempt growing more and more vicious. He was trying to get me to fight back so he could really attack, claim self-defense. Instead, I'd spend nights in the infirmary thanks to him.

To see Zi quickly and efficiently dismantle the ugly giant within seconds was like watching as artist create a masterpiece.

"How the fuck did you do that?"

It was the first thing I ever said to him. He looked surprised, but it opened the door.

Over the next year, Zi added a whole new layer to what Bobby had taught me. Defense wasn't just about the body, it was also about the mind.

It was *his* voice I heard in that basement.

The open door barely changed the light, but I could make out Carlos's shape as he stepped in.

His walk was different now, slow, deliberate. He loomed over me. The warmth I'd once known in his face was gone.

"You gotta sign the bank form, kid. Then we can let you go."

Liar.

I didn't know what he was talking about, but I knew he wasn't letting me go.

My eyes adjusted. I tried to scan the room.

"Whatever you need, man. Just let me go," I said, making my voice soft, scared. "I won't tell anyone…"

I'd always been even-keeled with Carlos. I needed to keep him thinking I was helpless.

He shoved a pen into my hand, held a piece of paper in front of me.

"I can't see it," I said. "I don't know where you want me to sign…"

"Fuck."

He grabbed my wrists and dragged me into the moonlight streaming through the open door.

"There!"

I pointed behind him. "I dropped the pen…"

When he bent over, I struck, just like Zi taught me.

29

I swung my legs hard, catching him off-balance and sending him crashing to the floor.

In one motion, I folded my body, sprang to my feet, and launched myself at him. My fists pounding into his solar plexus, fast and brutal. He gasped, stunned, breathless.

I grabbed his throat and slammed his head against the floor. The crack echoed in my ears. My arms vibrated from the violence.

It wasn't enough to kill him, I didn't think, but he'd be out long enough.

I reached into his front pocket where I knew he kept his knife. Got it.

I had to move quickly. If Carlos didn't return soon, Connie would come next, and she'd probably be armed. I was sure she'd have a story to tell about my dead body. She'd be well rehearsed, telling the cops about how I'd tried to rob them, and how lucky she felt to be alive.

The rope came apart fast. With each unraveling strand, the whole summer snapped into focus:

The secrecy about living there.

The probing questions about my family.

The push to open a bank account.

The checks in my name.

They never cared about *me*.

I wasn't a tenant. I was a mark.

I flexed my hands and feet, forcing blood back into them. My head was still spinning, but I knew what I had to do: cross the gravel drive and the backyard to the ADU. Grab my duffel. My cash. My identity. It was the only way I'd survive.

The moonlight, once a comfort, now felt like a spotlight.

Where was Connie? In the yard? In the ADU? I didn't know. But I had to risk it.

I ran.

I reached the ADU just as Connie screamed Carlos's name.

I knew she'd be coming for me and I reached for the closest weapon I could lay my hands on.

I'm sure Connie never expected to be hit full force by a Cannondale Super X carbon road bike, but that turned out to be the best hundred dollars I'd ever spent.

I hit her full-force. She collapsed, the handgun she'd brought skidding across the floor.

I grabbed it. Grabbed everything.

And ran.

My duffel bounced at my side, every step a punch to the ribs.

I didn't trust myself to make thoughtful decisions so I didn't make any. I just ran until I couldn't anymore.

Then I walked.

When I couldn't walk, I slept for an hour or so in a copse of trees by the side of the highway. When I awoke, I buried Connie's gun and kept going.

I didn't know which direction I was headed until the sun came up.

But it didn't matter.

Once again, I was lost.

Chapter Three

I didn't stop moving. I remembered reading once that sharks had to keep swimming, always forward, or they'd die. I understood that now.

I stayed off the roads as much as I could. In my worst fears, Carlos had slipped past the police and was hunting me. I couldn't let him find me. I couldn't let anyone find me. I was just as afraid of the police. If they caught me, I didn't think they'd believe me. I'd end up back behind bars, adult prison this time, and I wasn't going there.

I followed the sun. I circled wide around cities. I stopped at the emptiest diners I could find, ate fast, and kept my head down. I tried not to do anything that might draw attention, but I knew it was only a matter of time before my appearance gave me away.

My beard grew long. My hair turned wild and matted. Dirt worked its way into my skin. When I caught glimpses of myself in car windows or the backs of spoons, I didn't recognize the person looking back. I guess that made sense. I didn't feel like him anymore either.

It had been a few weeks since I left Memphis, and mountains

were beginning to rise in the distance. I thought I might be in North Carolina, but I didn't ask. I didn't want to know for sure. It didn't matter. The nights were getting colder, and my aimless wandering needed to end soon. I just had no idea what that ending might look like.

Every day since leaving Carlos's house, I'd beaten myself up over how easily I'd been fooled, how I'd let myself get conned, nearly killed. Before I left Memphis, I'd called the police from a payphone and told them what I could. I gave them the address, told them about Carlos and Connie, and where they could find the gun Connie tried to kill me with. I didn't know if it was enough. It was all I had to give. I was sure I wasn't their first victim. They were too practiced, too confident. That setup had been used before. I figured if the cops dug deep enough, they'd find bodies in that yard.

I kept thinking about the mountains ahead, what lay beyond them. Ocean, maybe. I'd never seen the ocean. I decided the coast was as good a destination as any. There'd be work, probably. Maybe I could settle down for a while. I kept telling myself I hadn't done anything wrong, even if I felt like a fugitive. It was fear, not guilt, that kept me hiding. I didn't trust other people, and I didn't trust myself around them. Every choice I'd made for as long as I could remember had been the wrong one. Nothing had gone the way I thought it would.

I'd been playing chicken with the terrain, skirting the base of the mountains, but eventually they called my bluff. I stepped onto the road and stuck out my thumb. If I was going to get where I wanted to go, I'd need help. This was the only way I knew to ask for it.

I figured my odds were less than fifty-fifty that someone would stop. After a couple hours, those odds felt worse. Still, I kept at it. I told myself that once the sun started going down, someone might take pity on me. Not that I felt I deserved pity. I didn't.

The sun was getting low behind me, headlights flicking on as dusk settled in. I decided to give up for the day. I needed to find a place to sleep before it got too dark to see where I was going. I lowered my arm in defeat just as a pair of headlights pulled up behind me. I turned, shielding my eyes from the glare, trying to look friendly. Hopeful.

The pickup slowed and stopped a few feet away. The sunset behind it made it hard to see inside, but I caught the outline of a single figure in the cab. A man, I guessed, not a big one. I swallowed and took a chance.

As I walked up, the passenger window lowered. The man inside said, "Where ya headed?"

He looked to be in his mid-twenties, maybe not much older than me. He gave me a quick, easy smile that threw me off. I stumbled for a second.

"I, uh...just...to the coast, I guess."

"You don't sound too sure. But I'm headed almost that far if you want a ride."

I sized him up. He didn't seem dangerous. And I figured if it came down to it, I could take him. I tossed my duffel in the bed of the truck and climbed in.

"Name's Bear," he said. "I'd shake your hand, but..." He held up his arm, wrapped in a cast from elbow to fingers.

He didn't look like a Bear. More like a Tim.

"I'm Max," I said. "What happened to your arm?"

"Me being stupid. Lesson learned. Can't do shit with this hand for another two weeks."

"That sucks."

"So what brings you to the North Carolina coast in October, Max?"

"Just never seen the ocean before. Figured now was as good a time as any."

We drove in silence for a while. Twenty minutes or so. Then Bear took an exit and pulled into a truck stop.

"I'm starving," he said.

And I had to admit, the idea of food, and maybe not having everyone stare at me while I ate it, sounded pretty damn good.

The burger was thin, the fries were greasy, and the soda was flat, but I devoured it like I hadn't eaten in weeks. Across the table, I caught Bear watching me a few times. He looked half-amused, half-impressed, awkwardly trying to manage his own burger with just his left hand.

He'd taken his hat off when we walked in, probably a habit drilled into him by his momma, and now, sitting across from him in better light, I got my first real look. His dark hair was cropped close, like he'd gotten a fresh cut not long ago. His thick black eyebrows framed a pair of dark eyes that I bet didn't miss much. A patchy beard couldn't quite hide his baby face or the sharpness of his square jaw. I could maybe see why people called him Bear.

"So," he said, "what are you gonna do once you get to the coast?"

"Find a job, I hope. Just looking to settle somewhere new."

"What was wrong with the somewhere old?"

"Pretty much everything," I said, and took a sip of the flat soda. I was starting to regret giving him my real name. His questions were casual, but they came quick. "Where are you headed?"

"Back north. New York. Took a break after doing this", he lifted his cast like it didn't belong to him, "but it's time to get back to work."

"What do you do?"

"I work for a guy. Sort of an assistant, sort of a problem solver, computer geek."

"Sounds…interesting, I guess."

"Oh, it is. He's rich. We travel all over. He takes care of me, I take care of him."

"Until you somehow break your arm."

He grinned. "Like I said, that was just me being stupid. Finish up. We need to get back on the road."

It felt good to be sitting down and still moving forward. The hum of the truck, the vibration of the tires, and my full stomach all worked on me at once. I hadn't realized what the last few weeks had done to my body as well as my mind. Tense had become my default. But now, as that tension drained into the old fabric seat, my eyes began to lose focus. My thoughts drifted, climbing the mountains and spilling out toward the ocean, toward whatever possibilities might be waiting there.

Bear didn't seem threatening, but I still kept my guard up. I scanned the cab for anything that could be used as a weapon, listened closely to his words in case they turned sharp. He told me he was from the Midwest, same as me, and hinted that he'd left for some of the same reasons, never quite fitting in, getting into trouble. I didn't ask for details. I didn't offer any of my own. I mostly listened.

Eventually, he turned the radio on, low and static-filled. I drifted off to sleep.

I don't know what woke me, Bear's shouting, the tires screaming against the road, or the sickening crunch of metal on impact. In my dream, it all happened at once. But when I opened my eyes, I realized it wasn't a dream.

It was dark.

Bear was pounding the steering wheel with his good hand, cursing, over and over. The front of the truck was a wreck of crumpled metal, and there was blood on the cracked windshield. I twisted around, trying to see what we'd hit.

On the shoulder of the road, a large buck thrashed in the gravel, too injured to get up, but not dead.

"What the fuck happened, Bear?"

"He came out of nowhere," Bear said, breathing hard.

We weren't on the highway anymore. No other cars in sight. Just darkness all around. One of the headlights was out, or gone entirely.

"Fuck, fuck, fuck," Bear muttered, pacing beside the truck. "Fuck. I do *not* need this…"

"Hey," I said. "We're both okay. We'll figure it out."

But I got it. I really did.

His eyes shifted suddenly toward the road. "I've gotta do something about him, man. He's suffering."

I stepped out of the truck and followed his gaze. He was right. The deer was still alive, barely. At least two of its legs were broken, and the pool of blood beneath it was spreading, inching into the road. We could wait for the inevitable, but that didn't sit right. Life on the farm had taught me the difference between cruelty and mercy.

Bear appeared at my side. "I can't do it," he said, lifting his useless arm.

"You have a gun?" I asked.

He looked at me like I'd just asked if he had three dicks.

"No. I don't have a gun. All I've got is a hunting knife in the glove box…"

It would have to do.

I pulled the knife from its sheath and approached the buck slowly, stepping around the blood, keeping clear of the antlers. It watched me with wide, terrified eyes. With one swift stroke, I slit its throat. The blood poured out in a rush, steaming in the cold air. I rested a hand on its flank as the life drained out of it.

"Peaceful journey," I whispered.

When it was done, I walked back to Bear. My hands were slick with blood, dripping onto the pavement. I grabbed a towel from the bed of the truck and cleaned the blade before sliding it back into its sheath.

"You'll want to clean that better when you get the chance," I said. "We'll need a tow. Do you know where we are?"

"There's supposed to be a town just up ahead…" He leaned into the cab, pulled out his phone, and checked for a signal. A moment later, he called 911.

While we waited for the tow truck, we moved the buck off the road and into the tall grass. Nature would take care of the rest.

"You're pretty good with that knife," Bear said. "Should I be worried?"

"I just did what needed to be done."

The road felt colder now. The quiet heavier.

The tension had crept back into my body like it had never left.

The tow driver brought us into town, but the news wasn't great. It'd be a few days, at least, before the truck was drivable again. He kept telling us how lucky we were. The truck wasn't totaled. We weren't dead. And there were worse places than Pine Ridge to be stuck for a few days. He gave us directions to a bed and breakfast, then drove off.

It wasn't even ten yet.

I'd only met Bear a few hours earlier, and already my plans were off track again. I thought about ditching him and heading out on my own, but I knew the accident hadn't been his fault. Deer on country roads were just a fact of life, and he'd been the only one to stop for me all day. Leaving now felt wrong. And it's not like I was on a schedule. The ocean would still be there.

Steve and RuthAnn at the B&B didn't blink at the blood dried on my hands and clothes. They just showed us to the laundry room, pointed out the low water pressure in the shower, and handed Bear the keys to two rooms at the top of the stairs. The shared bathroom, we discovered, was right between them.

"I'll let you shower first," Bear offered. "I can wait."

I tried to be quick, mindful of the hot water, but no amount of scrubbing seemed enough. Weeks of grime and blood circled the drain in a muddy whirlpool. When I stepped out and wiped the mirror clear, I barely recognized my own face. Fifteen minutes and a dull razor later, the beard was gone.

I pulled on a pair of sweatpants and stepped into the hallway, towel slung over my bare shoulder.

"Goddamn," I heard Bear mutter from his doorway. "I thought

I was gonna have to call the fire department to haul your ass out of there."

"Sorry, man."

"Looks like you did a hard day's work in there. You look like a different person."

"I almost feel like one." I paused. "You might want to give it a few more minutes for the water to heat back up."

"While I wait, can you help me with something?"

"What do you need?"

He pulled his t-shirt off and handed me a plastic bag and a roll of tape. "I've gotta keep this dry," he said, holding up his cast. "Can you? It's been a bitch doing it myself..."

I nodded, but my brain stalled for a second.

His shirt had hidden the kind of body that made you forget whatever sentence you were about to finish. Tight abs. Solid pecs. Dark, round nipples peeking through a soft mat of chest hair. Jesus.

And a tattoo of a bear's paw trailing vicious claw marks down his left side.

"Yeah, sure," I said quickly, and knelt to wrap his arm. I taped it off tight and got the hell out of there.

I shut my door firmly behind me.

The bulge in my sweats gave me away.

My sex life ended before it ever began. I could still taste Bobby on my lips when the police pulled up and I surrendered. He and I were over before we'd had a chance to do anything more than kiss. All our hurried plans disappeared the second that gun went off.

I saw Bobby only a few times after that day, and always from a distance. He sat in the back row of the courtroom gallery, far enough away that I couldn't do him any more harm. He looked at me like he was trying to piece together the Max he thought he knew and the Max who was now about to be sentenced for murder. He must've figured it out, or maybe he just gave up trying, because one day, he wasn't there anymore. And I never saw him again.

In juvie, I learned fast that sex was a commodity, something you traded for better treatment from guards or for protection from the other inmates. I'm not proud of anything I did in there, but I did what I had to do to survive. Who was I to think I deserved better?

Eventually I figured out how to separate myself from it. The act. The body. There was never emotion. Never feeling. They were just using me. My heart was safe. I'd given it away back on the farm.

There was something about Bear, the way he stood in the doorway asking for help. Maybe it was the look in his eyes. Or maybe it was how he waited until I'd left the bathroom before taking his shirt off. Whatever it was, it hit me low in the gut, hard and sudden.

I shut off the light and slid down my sweatpants. My cock sprang free, and I gripped it tight. I listened to the faint sound of the shower running down the hall, imagined Bear standing under the hot spray, naked, water tracing the lines of his chest, his stomach, his thighs. I came fast, into my hand. I cleaned up. I got into bed, alone.

I didn't dream of Bobby that night. I didn't dream of Bear either.

I dreamt of the ocean.

The vast open space. The wild crash of waves. The sheer power of it all. I woke more certain than ever that my future wasn't behind me in Oklahoma, it was out there, waiting, just over the mountains.

Bear and I stayed in Pine Ridge for three days while the truck got repaired. A few times, Bear told me I didn't have to stick around. I could take a bus, be on the coast before he was even out of the driveway. A few times, I told him I'd wait.

It wasn't because I thought something might happen between us. I was pretty sure Bear was straight, and that was fine. He never mentioned a girlfriend or a wife, but the secret phone calls, the lowered voice, the way he stressed about getting back to New York on time, it was clear someone else held his leash.

I didn't care. It just felt good to be around someone who didn't want anything from me. Not my body. Not my secrets. Not my soul.

He just let me be.

Bear was only twenty-four and had already lived more life than I could ever hope to. His work had taken him all over the world. He'd done things I'd only read about. My dream of seeing the ocean felt small next to everything he'd seen. Still, he sparked something in me, something new. Something bigger.

By the time the truck was fixed and we were back on the road, I impulsively told him I wanted to go with him all the way to New York.

"What about the coast?"

"New York has a coast, doesn't it? The whole fucking country has a coast." I tried to sound casual, like the idea had just come to me because it sort of had. "You've got me dreaming bigger now. Maybe your boss could find something for me, if you put in a good word..."

He didn't answer right away. I could see him working through something. I'd gone too far. Fuck.

"Sorry," I said quickly. "I'm not trying to put you in a rough spot. You can drop me anywhere. It's not..."

"Max," he cut in. "It's not about you, or me. I was just thinking about how Dixon would take to you."

"Take to me? What do you mean?"

Bear kept his eyes on the road. "Dixon's a man with very specific needs. He's powerful. And to stay that way, he works constantly. Demands a lot from the people around him. If you're open to new experiences, and willing to do *anything* to meet the end goal...then yeah, I think he could find a place for you."

I didn't say anything.

"But know this," Bear continued. "There's no dipping your toe in. He doesn't do halfway. He'll demand full commitment. And he won't accept less."

"I can give him that," I said. "I've got nothing holding me back. And with a little coaching from you..."

Bear let out a quiet laugh. "I don't think I can teach you much. You've already got the basic skills he looks for. The rest comes down to instinct, *his* instinct. How he sees you fitting in. You get me?"

I wasn't sure I did. Not completely. But I nodded anyway.

We arrived in New York two days later. On the way, Bear made a detour to the Jersey Shore so I could step into the ocean for the first time. The water was freezing. The force of the waves nearly knocked me off my feet. I felt small, completely at their mercy. I let them shove and pull me, let them show me how little I actually controlled in my life.

But the ocean wasn't the most powerful thing I saw that day.

Manhattan was something else entirely.

The sidewalks flooded with people walking fast, not looking around, each on a mission. The buildings glowed with a million lights, bright enough to make the city feel like it was stuck at noon. Cars moved like they were part of a single machine, shifting lanes, adjusting speed, fluid and rehearsed. Bear slipped into it like he never left.

He changed, too.

He pulled a pair of glasses from the glove box, ones I'd never seen him wear, and slid them on like a costume piece. Like Clark Kent. He became someone else. Not unrecognizable, just...different. Sharper. More serious. The city had power over him, and I could see him letting it take hold.

My world had expanded past anything I could process.

"Jesus, Bear, how do you even..."

"Relax and breathe," he said. "It's big, but it's manageable."

I wasn't sure I believed him. But I believed in him. He wouldn't let anything happen to me, not on purpose. He'd already told me I could crash in his spare bedroom until I found something else. It didn't feel anything like Carlos's offer back in Memphis. This wasn't about control.

When we pulled up to his building, Bear handed the keys to a man in uniform, who slid behind the wheel of the pickup and drove it off without question. The doorman welcomed him back from his trip, asked if it had been restful, and said he hoped the cast would be off soon.

The lobby looked like it belonged in a magazine, brand-new furniture, polished stone floors, art on the walls that should've been under glass in a museum. The elevator rose in total silence to the seventeenth floor.

Bear didn't need to scam welfare checks to afford this place.

The only thing I couldn't figure out was:

Why the hell was he driving that old truck?

He must've read my mind, or seen the question written on my face.

"Dixon owns the apartment," Bear said, "and everything in it. He owns the whole damn building, actually. Very little of what you see here is mine, except the truck. Dixon prefers it that way."

I was starting to see a fuller picture of the world I'd just walked into. Dixon wasn't someone to take lightly. Getting in with him could change everything for me. I just had to make sure he liked me, *if* I ever got the chance to meet him.

I dropped my duffel in the spare room, *my* room. It was twice the size of the one Evan and I shared growing up, with a massive king-sized bed, a treadmill, and a rack of free weights that looked like they actually got used. The window overlooked a dark stretch I assumed was the park we'd passed on the way in. I felt like I was still dreaming.

When I came back to the living room, Bear was finishing a call.

"I really think you'll like him…Friday it is. Thank you, sir." He ended the call and tossed the phone into an expensive-looking bowl on the glass coffee table.

"That was Dixon," he said. "I arranged for you to have dinner with him on Friday."

I must've looked panicked, because Bear quickly added, "Don't worry. It'll be casual. You might even fit into one of my suits…"

"A suit is *casual?*"

"Well, no tie."

"Oh, *that* makes more sense."

I'd never owned a suit in my life. In Choctaw, you only wore one to get married or buried. So far, I'd avoided both. I was locked up when they put Pa in the ground.

"We've got a few days," Bear said. "We'll go shopping. Get you whatever you need."

"I wasn't expecting any of this. I'm not even sure what I *was* expecting."

"Listen," he said, his voice lowering a little. "Dixon's a serious man. He works hard, plays hard, and he takes care of the people who take care of him. I don't want to mislead you about all this," he waved a hand around the apartment "he expects a lot from us. It's not always easy. But he trusts us. And we trust him."

"We? How many people work for him like this?"

"Maybe a dozen, I'm not sure. We're not all in New York. Here in the city it's just Kit and me. But Dixon's got places all over. If he likes you, he might want you somewhere else. Could be anywhere in the world."

It was hard to wrap my mind around that. The possibilities felt endless, and totally out of reach.

"So what do you actually do for him?" I asked.

"Kit and I are problem solvers," he said. "That's how I look at it. When one of his companies runs into trouble, competitors, management issues, internal stuff, and they can't handle it, we step in. Our job is to make the problem disappear. Dixon gives us full control to do whatever's necessary."

"Sounds intense."

"It can be."

He walked over to the window and pointed out into the night.

"When I first got here, I lived with two roommates in a one-bedroom walk-up. So far from here, you couldn't even see it on the horizon. I never imagined living like this. Didn't even think it was possible. But Dixon made it happen. I owe him everything. And I'd do anything for him."

"Anything?" I echoed.

"Anything," he said. "Without question. And that's the way it has to be."

I let that settle. The words didn't feel like a warning. They felt like a truth he'd accepted long ago.

And I still trusted Bear. He hadn't given me a reason not to. It didn't feel like he was trying to con me. He had nothing to gain, I had nothing left to take. Everything I'd ever had was already gone.

This was where I'd rebuild.

If that meant pledging myself to a man who could offer me a future, I couldn't see the downside.

Over the next couple of days, we spent thousands of dollars I didn't have, and knew I could never pay back, on clothes, haircuts, gym sessions, and spa treatments. A woman gave me a spray tan and offered to wax my butthole. I declined. Still, I quickly transformed into someone entirely different, at least on the outside. The old Maxwell Heath was gone.

By the time I stepped out of the bedroom that Friday evening, I was laser-focused on one goal: making Dixon St. James like me.

"Let me see," Bear said, giving me a once-over.

The new navy-blue suit fit like it was made for me. The crisp white shirt made the tan glow just enough to make me look expensive. Bear reached over, undid another button on my shirt, exposing more of my chest.

"There," he said. "Looks more casual now."

I felt like a kid playing dress-up.

I was meeting Dixon for drinks and dinner at *Papillon*, the private restaurant he owned on the top floor. I took the elevator down to the lobby to catch the express up.

"Mr. St. James is expecting you, Mr. Heath," the man at the desk said. "Last elevator on the left, sir."

He pointed. I nodded and thanked him.

I was still getting used to how everyone somehow knew who I was, but *Mr. Heath* had always been my Pa. I wasn't sure I liked the way the title tried to settle onto me now.

I pressed the button. The elevator climbed fast, leaving a hollow pit in my stomach.

"This is going to be okay," I muttered aloud. I wasn't sure if I believed it. I didn't know if I was walking toward an opportunity… or a mistake I wouldn't be able to undo.

The doors opened.

A maitre d' stood waiting. "This way, sir."

Of course Dixon had a private dining room. We didn't step into the main space. Instead, we moved through a dim hallway until the maitre d' pulled back a heavy curtain.

And there he was.

Dixon St. James.

I wasn't sure what I'd expected, exactly. But I knew I'd been expecting *more*. More age, maybe. More drama. More obvious menace. Based on Bear's stories, I thought he'd be older, seventy maybe. A kingpin. A relic.

But he was only about fifty, older, but not distant. More father than grandfather.

He stood to greet me.

He was trim, no gut, his suit fit without effort. His short dark hair was cut close, greying just at the temples. He smelled clean, not cologned, something subtle and probably expensive. His grip was firm. His handshake didn't last longer than it needed to.

But it was his eyes I remembered most.

Crystalline blue. Bright. Focused. They caught the ambient light like glass and held it there, pinning me in place.

"Maxwell, it's a pleasure to meet you. I'm Dixon St. James. Bear has spoken quite highly of you."

Whatever nerves I'd brought with me to this dinner, the fear I'd say the wrong thing, the dread that I didn't belong, they vanished. For a man of such power, Dixon had a warmth that made me feel like I was the only person in the world. Which, of course, I was. At least in that room.

"Please, sit," he said. "Let's have a drink, get to know each other. Would you like a glass of wine? Cocktail? I'm having a dirty vodka martini…"

As much as I wanted to ask for a beer, Bear had coached me on this part. Sophisticated, practiced, not too complicated.

"An Old Fashioned, please. Orange, no cherry."

Out of the corner of my eye, I saw a waiter, previously hidden in the shadows, slip away to fill the order. Only then did I really take in the rest of the room, wondering who else might be just out of sight, watching.

"So, Maxwell, what brings you to New York from…?"

"Oklahoma, sir. That's where I was raised. There just wasn't anything left for me there. I hadn't planned to come to New York, not until I met Bear."

"Yes, he told me about your chance meeting. And the unfortunate deer that delayed his return to work."

"It wasn't his fault…"

"Oh, I know," Dixon said, a slight smile touching the corner of his mouth. "Even clumsy Bear couldn't hit a buck like that on purpose. But you haven't told me why you were leaving Oklahoma so suddenly…"

"It wasn't all that sudden," I said. "It was just time. Time to go."

"I see. And what was the plan when you got to…wherever you were headed?"

My drink arrived. I took a long sip. The whiskey burned my throat, settled warm in my gut, and gave me just enough courage to push through the rising tension.

"I didn't really have a plan," I said honestly. "I was keeping my options open. I like to think I'm smart enough to pick up whatever work interests me."

Dixon tilted his head. "And does working for *me* interest you?"

"It does, sir."

"Please," he said. "Call me Dixon. And what about the position appeals to you?"

I paused, choosing my words carefully. I knew this wasn't just small talk, every answer mattered. I looked him in the eyes, those impossibly clear blue eyes, and for a moment I forgot what I was going to say.

Then I remembered.

"Dixon," I said, steadying myself, "I come from nothing. My family owned a pig farm. My Pa was a small-town cop in a place I'm sure you've never been. The idea that I might one day be sitting here in a New York restaurant, wearing a real suit, talking to someone like you? That idea didn't even exist in my mind until a few days ago."

I took another drink.

"But these past few days…they've opened my eyes. To what's out there. To the dreams I didn't even know I was allowed to have. And they're big. And they're exciting. Spending time with you, learning from you, assisting you, that's appealing. Seeing the world beyond Oklahoma? That's very appealing."

I thought of what Bear had told me.

And then I said it, steady and true:

"And I would do anything for you. Without question."

Dixon finished his drink, placing the empty glass at the edge of the table. A fresh one appeared almost instantly, condensation catching the candlelight like glass in a storm.

"*Anything*, Maxwell?" he said. "I'd like to believe that. And yet, you won't even answer my questions truthfully."

It landed like a slap.

"I'm a man who does his homework," he continued. "I wouldn't meet with just any hitchhiker Bear brought home unless I knew everything there was to know about him."

His voice was even, unbothered. Mine had fled.

"I know you shot and killed your father. I know you did time for it. I know why you don't want to go back home."

Whatever bravado I'd come in with drained out of me. I felt like a kid again, caught lying, back straight, bracing for the belt.

"So why did you want to meet with me?" I asked, my voice thinner than I wanted it to be.

"Because none of that matters to me, Maxwell. I'm sure you had your reasons. I'm not here to judge. In my experience, everyone's running from something."

"Even you?"

He smiled faintly. "Of course, *even me*. The question isn't whether we've sinned. It's what happens if we get caught…and how bad the damage is."

"I'm sorry I didn't tell you everything," I said. "I'm not proud of what happened. But I served my time. I'm trying to leave it behind me. And I know, *I know*, it won't affect the work I can do for you."

"Oh, but I *hope* it does." Dixon leaned forward, eyes gleaming. "I hope that fire's still alive inside you. That passion. That capacity to *act* when it counts. Everyone in my little circle has been tested, burned, reshaped. That's what makes them valuable. When the moment comes, I need to trust that you'll find that fire again. That you'll rise to the occasion. That you'll do whatever's necessary."

"I've always done what's needed in the moment," I said. "For better or worse. I don't think about what it costs me. I just do it. That's who I am." I held his gaze, firm and open. "And I'd do the same for you, Dixon."

I meant every word. He knew it, too. His eyes scanned mine, searching for the lie. I didn't flinch. I couldn't have lied to him if I tried.

"Thank you, Maxwell."

He reached across the table and laid his hand over mine, casual, confident, calming.

"I believe you."

Relief unspooled inside me. I hadn't realized how tightly I'd been wound. The night had exhausted me in ways I didn't expect. But I understood why it had gone the way it did. Dixon was powerful. Careful. He didn't surround himself with amateurs. And I was, on paper, still just a dressed-up hitchhiker with no references, no past worth speaking of.

I needed to prove I was worthy of his trust. That I'd follow through on *anything* he asked.

Dixon set his napkin on the table. "Let's have dinner brought down to my suite," he said. "I think a change of scenery is in order."

I didn't argue.

He gave a slight wave, summoning the waiter and murmuring instructions. Then he stood and moved toward a shadowy doorway I hadn't noticed before. Halfway there, he paused, looked back to make sure I was behind him.

I was.

Just a few steps behind but keeping up.

We walked down a short flight of carpeted steps to a landing, where Dixon opened a door and ushered me in ahead of him.

I should've known, just from seeing Bear's place, that Dixon's apartment would be in another league entirely. It wasn't just luxurious, it was expansive. The entire floor of the tower, surrounded by floor-to-ceiling windows on all sides. The darkness outside turned the glass into mirrors, and I kept catching my own reflection, though I wasn't entirely sure it was still me I was seeing.

Huge pieces of art lined the interior walls. A fire burned low in the hearth. It all looked staged, yet lived in. Controlled.

While Dixon made drinks at the bar, I wandered. When he handed me mine, he guided me toward the terrace. The cold autumn air whipped through the open door, but before I could step back, he turned a knob on the wall and heaters around the perimeter began to glow, slowly pushing back the chill.

His hand rested lightly on the small of my back as he steered me toward the edge.

"This is what I work for, Maxwell," he said, his voice quiet. "This is what I need to protect."

I looked out over the lights of the city, glittering and endless.

"But protect it from who?" I asked.

Dixon didn't hesitate. "Whoever tries to take it from me."

His hand slid down until it rested casually on my ass. This was my first test.

"You're a very attractive man, Maxwell." His voice was low, almost inaudible. I could feel his warm breath on my ear, smell his scent. "Would it shock you if I told you I wanted to fuck you? Right here, and now?"

His breath lingered at my neck, hot against the cool night air. I couldn't tell whether it was fear or adrenaline that made my skin prickle. Maybe both. I'd told him I was willing to do anything, and now I was being asked to prove it.

"I'm not shocked," I said, quietly. My voice didn't shake. That surprised me.

Dixon didn't press further right away. He simply stood behind me, hand still resting at the base of my spine, drink in his other hand, like this was just another business deal being considered over the New York skyline.

"This isn't a demand," he said after a moment. "It's an offer. A door. One you can step through, or not. But it will tell me a lot about you either way."

I needed to pause. Everything had been moving so quickly, I hadn't had time to think. This was my Rubicon and to cross it meant there was no going back.

I nodded again. Not out of submission. Out of clarity. This was my choice. The night wind stirred my hair. Below us, the city pulsed with life, lights blinking like stars turned inside out.

"Then I'm stepping through," I said.

He stood behind me, close enough that I could feel his substantial cock pressing into me. One arm wrapped across my chest, his hand slipping beneath the fabric of my shirt. The touch was purposeful, claiming, not gentle. When his fingers found my nipple and twisted, I gasped, startled by the intensity.

I reached out instinctively to steady myself, setting my drink on the terrace rail before it could slip from my fingers, and before I could follow it over the edge. The wind whipped around us, the city roaring quietly below.

Dixon pressed even closer, the weight of him was undeniable. Controlled. Measured. His hand moved with confidence, unfastening my belt, loosening the clothes that made me feel like someone new. He stripped them away with ease, and I let him. I didn't flinch. I didn't resist. Suit pants and designer underwear dropped to the terrace, exposing the real me, baring my soul and my body.

Anything for Dixon. Anything for a new life.

The skyline stretched out before me, lit up like a promise. I gripped the railing tighter. This wasn't about romance, it was about power. Trust. Surrender. This was a test of loyalty and I was choosing to pass it.

Whatever came next, I had already said yes.

Dixon guided me into position, his hand firm on my back, controlling every movement with precision. The night air pressed against my bare skin, made sharper by the glow of the terrace heaters and the distant hum of the city below. I gripped the rail as he entered me, steadying myself, bracing not just for what was happening, but for what it all meant.

It wasn't about pleasure. Not mine, anyway. I was merely his vessel.

This was a performance of trust, of obedience. A transaction in the currency Dixon understood best: power.

I kept my eyes on the skyline, on the glittering promise of a life I never thought could be mine. I told myself I was ready for this, whatever *this* was asking of me. I let go of control, of shame, of the old version of myself who would've run from all of this.

Now, I stayed. I endured. I gave.

Anything for Dixon.

Anything for a new life.

Despite the urgency at the start, Dixon didn't rush. He stayed in control, every movement deliberate, measured, every thrust, generous, as if he were proving a point. I could feel it in the way he handled me, in how little effort it took for him to bend me to his rhythm. I held on, breath shallow, heart pounding. I couldn't see him, but I could picture him perfectly: the greying hair at his temples, the tailored lines of his body, those glacial blue eyes that had seemed to see straight through me.

I thought of everything I wanted to say: *I'm yours, I'll do anything, just don't stop.* But the words stuck somewhere between surrender and reverence.

Instead, I pushed back onto him, listened to the sounds of our flesh meeting. I tightened my muscles around him which excited him even more. I met his pace, gave him everything I had.

The city lights blurred in my vision. Heat rose up through my chest, flooded my limbs. Somewhere deep in my mind, something cracked open. I wasn't the same person who'd stepped out onto that terrace.

And maybe that was the point.

His pace quickened, his breath grew heavier behind me. One hand slid up my damp back, beneath the shirt clinging to my skin from sweat and heat and nerves. I wasn't ready for it to be over, not because I wanted more, but because I didn't know what came next.

Then, with a sudden gush of warmth deep within me, it was done.

A sudden, quiet shift.

He slipped free of me without a word.

The night air hit me hard, sharp against my skin. I felt emptied out. Not just physically, but in some deeper, quieter place I hadn't realized was open. His hands lingered on my hips, still steady, still in control. My body was trembling. I tried to stand, to pull myself upright, but my knees wouldn't cooperate. I stayed bent over the railing, breathing shallow, unsure of what I'd just become.

And yet, I didn't regret it.

Not yet.

"Thank you, Maxwell."

He pressed a single kiss to the back of my neck, brief, deliberate. The only exchange between us. It wasn't affection. It wasn't tenderness. It was closure.

He didn't want romance.

He wanted satisfaction.

He wanted control.

I didn't know if I was supposed to say something in return. I stayed silent, pulling up my underwear and pants, tucking myself away as best I could. The cold air clung to me even after I was dressed. I felt like a man returning from somewhere far off, a version of myself I didn't yet understand.

I found my drink and drained what was left, then followed Dixon inside.

Dinner was already set at the long dining table, silver domes over polished plates, candles flickering, everything perfectly timed. The thought hit me all at once: someone in the restaurant must have seen us fucking. Staff. Waiters. Security cameras. The terrace hadn't exactly been private.

The shame came fast. Hot. Unwelcome.

But Dixon? He didn't even flinch. He walked in like nothing had happened. Like that was just...part of the night.

Was this my new normal?

We sat in silence. The wait staff poured wine and served us

steak with roast vegetables. I could still feel Dixon's cum as it slowly seeped out of me. I worried about the upholstery but Dixon ate with the appetite of a man without worry.

"Maxwell, I'd like for you to manage my yacht. *The Menagerie II.*"

I almost choked on my filet.

I hadn't known what kind of offer to expect, but it wasn't *that*. A yacht? I didn't even know what 'managing' one really meant. But I saw the shape of an opportunity in the words, and I knew I couldn't, wouldn't, turn it down.

I swallowed, then reached for the wine, taking a long drink of the heavy red.

"Of course, Dixon. Whatever you need."

"It's currently moored in Marseilles," he said, casually. "I'll need you to fly over and get it ready to sail. I think I'll be spending the winter on board."

Everything was moving fast.

"Kit has all the details," he added. "Have you met Kit yet? He used to manage these things, but I have other plans for him…"

I had a dozen questions, but dinner wasn't the time to ask them. None of this was up for discussion anyway. This was my chance. I told myself there were no hidden strings, no lurking agenda. Just loyalty and reward. Just give yourself fully to Dixon, like Bear had, like the others must have.

After dinner, he asked me to spend the night.

I said yes.

I knew what was expected. I knew I didn't have much choice.

He fucked me again, slowly and methodically.

This time, he let me finish.

We fell asleep with his arm draped across me.

Was it protection? Possession? Did it matter?

I felt safe.

The next morning, I pulled on the same suit I'd worn the night before. It had laid crumpled on the floor while Dixon slept soundly beside me, his breathing slow and measured, like nothing had changed.

Before I left, I looked around the apartment in daylight. The space looked different, sharper in the morning light, less like a dream and more like an **IMAX** movie, large and bold. His staff moved through the rooms quietly, cleaning away the remnants of the night without acknowledging the young man walking barefoot out of their boss's bedroom.

I didn't know exactly what I was now, but I knew who I belonged to.

Chapter Four

FIVE YEARS LATER

I walked into the squad room on that first day, determined and focused. I scanned the space, took everything in quickly, and found my desk. The Post-It on the monitor read **HEATH**. I sat down.

"Hey," said the officer across from me. "Tristan Caine."

"Maxwell Heath. Max." I tossed my keys into a drawer and powered on the computer. "Are we waiting for roll?"

"Yeah, Cap'll call it soon. Stick with me, rookie. I've got you."

"Thanks, man."

Just like that, my police career began. It was that simple, and it would become the hardest thing I'd ever done.

I thought about my Pa most of that first day. What would he make of me in uniform, taking orders? He always claimed I had a problem with authority. That's why he was such a tough disciplinarian, he said. But I didn't have a problem with authority. I had a problem with *his*. His punishments never fit the crime.

Thinking of him didn't mean I missed him. It meant I was proving him wrong.

"Caine...my office! And bring the rook..."

I looked across the desk. Tristan cocked his head toward the booming voice and said, "Let's go."

I nodded, pretending I knew exactly what was coming.

Captain Leo Harris was exactly the man I'd expected. More like my Pa than not. He looked like someone who'd been on the force longer than he'd wanted to, who'd seen more than he'd ever be able to forget. I wondered if he took it home with him too, if his family feared his moods the way Walter Heath's had.

"I trust you two have done your 'good mornings.' Caine, Heath's riding with you for the foreseeable. You know the drill. Teach him what you know. Rook, listen close. Follow Caine's lead. He's got ten solid years on the job, and he's seen about all a good cop can see. You're lucky he's available."

"Yes, sir," I said, dutifully. I understood the message. And that was it. Dismissed. No questions, no further direction. I was at Caine's mercy.

We sat through the morning briefing, grabbed our radios from their charging stations, and headed for our assigned car. Day one was officially underway.

"Let's hit the range," Tristan said. "I want to see your skills before I put my life in your hands, rook."

I didn't argue. The streets *were* dangerous. You never knew when you'd need to draw, or who the real threat was. The line between victim and perpetrator blurred fast, and in that blur, trust had to win out over chaos. There was no better way to earn trust than to prove you could handle your weapon.

Still, I knew better than to show him up. He needed to be the Alpha. If he landed five chest or head shots, I'd hit two or three, even though I could put them all dead center if I wanted. I'd had plenty of practice.

When our target silhouettes came whizzing back, I watched his reaction. The way Tristan nodded, just slightly, told me what I needed to know. He was satisfied with my skills and with the fact that he could still think of himself as the man in charge. I was fine with that. I'd disposed of my ego years earlier.

We climbed back into the squad car, and that's when our partnership really began. The hours of mind-numbing small talk, bad bodega takeaway coffee, petty disagreements that didn't last long. All of it ahead of us. So were the nightmarish calls no one talks about. The ones that stay with you.

But it all started there, in the car. Tristan at the wheel, driving lazy circles around the precinct while I scanned the sidewalks for anything out of place. One stretch of city block at a time. One boring story of Tristan's after another.

I heard about his weekend golf game. About the women he picked up at clubs and screwed in the backseat of his car. It wasn't hard to understand why his two marriages had lasted less than three years, combined.

We fell into our roles quickly, or at least I did. Tristan was the wheelman in the car, the lead when we patrolled on foot. I was the rookie, fetching coffee, keeping watch, typing reports. I kept my head down. Took it all in. Didn't make waves. Didn't call attention to myself.

I was Officer Maxwell Heath, rookie. Reporting for duty, sir.

Until the day everything changed.

"Something's about to go down at Mr. Lee's," I said as we passed by, unnoticed.

Tristan was driving north on Third, more focused on the woman in the car next to us, the one giving him *come fuck me* eyes, according to him, than on the rest of the neighborhood. Typical. We'd circled these blocks a thousand times in the five months we'd been partnered, and by now, I knew every routine by heart. I knew when people put their garbage on the curb, when they rolled down or cranked up the security grates on their storefronts. I knew what normal looked like.

And what I'd just glimpsed through the window of Mr. Lee's bodega wasn't normal.

"Pull around the corner and let me out," I told Tristan. "I'll duck in the back."

I didn't give him time to argue, not that he would've. For all his bullshit, Tristan was a good cop. I trusted he'd radio it in, note our stop for probable cause, and have my back. But I also knew I needed to move fast before someone got hurt.

Mr. Lee was kind, proud, and stubborn. That last one would work against him if he was facing someone with a gun and something to prove. He'd been robbed before, before my time in the neighborhood, but he never stopped fighting to protect what was his. He always greeted us with a smile and a jab about doing better at keeping the area safe. He made a mean cup of coffee and didn't mind busting our balls. But he also refused to lock his back door during business hours, a habit I'd warned him about more than once.

Today, that unlocked door gave me safe passage.

The store seemed empty as I moved in, carefully edging past each aisle. Voices echoed from the front, loud, frantic. Two men. Hoodies. Handguns. Short fuses.

Mr. Lee was refusing to open the register. His voice, usually so warm, was tight with fear but still holding firm. The men were getting more agitated, and I knew it was about to take a turn. Daylight robbery like this? That meant desperation. Probably drugs. Their judgment was already gone.

I got eyes on both of them.

"Drop your guns!" I shouted.

One turned without hesitation and fired before I even finished the sentence. I returned fire and dropped him with one shot, center mass, head. He was dead before he hit the tiled floor.

The other panicked and bolted toward the door and right into Tristan's raised gun.

It was over before it really began. Except for the dead guy. The one who challenged me to a duel and lost.

Mr. Lee's became a crime scene. Investigators came. Statements were taken. Word spread fast: the local cops weren't fucking around.

I was pulled from duty while they cleared me. Standard procedure. They ruled it a clean kill. I'd been fired on first. Witnesses backed me up, including the one still breathing.

But I knew the truth.

I was going to kill that man whether he fired or not. It was instinct. It was decided the moment I saw the gun in his hand.

The captain commended me the next morning at roll. Said he'd never seen a rookie in a shooting so early in his career, let alone one that ended in his favor. The neighborhood treated us like heroes. Tristan soaked it up. Free lunches, dinners, coffee, you name it. People would've offered the shirts off their backs if we'd asked.

It was too much. It was more attention than I wanted.

I'd changed back in my street clothes after shift one evening and was headed toward the backdoor to catch my train uptown when I passed the conference room and noticed the new sign on the door. Handwritten in black felt-tip marker:

OPERATION FALCON TASK FORCE

I ducked in, uninvited, and slipped into a seat in the back, hoping to go unnoticed.

I read the notes on the whiteboard and started piecing it together. The focus of Operation Falcon was Cesare Donato and his son, Spencer, names I already knew. You didn't have to be a New York lifer to know the Donatos. Their name was on office buildings, hospital wings, a Broadway theater, even a few parks. Their philanthropy was highly regarded, heavily courted.

I remembered reading their fortune came from shipping. Cesare had supposedly started on the docks downtown and built his empire from the ground up. Nothing had been handed to him. Now he was wealthy beyond reason. But money like that always raises questions and judging by the tone of the room, not many had ever been answered.

At the front, I recognized Raquel Diaz, the new DA, speaking to the assembled task force. Cesare hadn't been seen publicly in years. The family hadn't said anything about his health, so the assumption was he'd retired quietly to his estate in Connecticut. Spencer Donato now ran the empire, maybe alongside his sister, Paloma, but the details were quite murky.

Intel pointed to illegal shipments: guns, drugs, possibly human trafficking, all traced back to Donato-owned ships. But they were experts at covering their tracks. Every attempt to seize their cargo had either failed or come up clean. Someone on the inside was likely tipping them off.

Spencer had been impossible to get close to. He was considered bulletproof. And recent attempts to reach Paloma hadn't gotten far either. Few friends. Fewer lovers. No clear routine. She'd all but disappeared.

The new focus? Their younger brother: Grayson.

I leaned in.

According to Diaz, Grayson wasn't involved in Donato Enterprises. He was head chef at *Joshua*, the ultra-exclusive restaurant in TriBeCa. No known ties between the business and the family. He was squeaky clean. So clean that there was speculation of a family rift. Grayson now went by Grayson Dunne and hadn't been seen publicly with the Donatos since high school. Still, he was the best shot at getting anywhere near Spencer.

"So what, you want a female officer to work her magic on the little brother and spin her web around Spencer too? This is just a honeypot," someone blurted out.

"Not quite," said DA Diaz. "Grayson Dunne is homosexual."

That got the room buzzing. The usual posturing started up. Macho cop bullshit. Someone muttered something about a "back-door route." I rolled my eyes at the predictably juvenile response.

I raised my hand before order could be restored.

"I'll do it," I said.

I wasn't entirely sure what I was volunteering for. I didn't even know if they were looking for volunteers. But I saw an opportunity, and I took it. I wanted to make it clear to the rest of the room that I was game for anything.

Captain Harris's head lifted, his eyes locked on me.

"Heath, you shouldn't even be in here," he started, but DA Diaz cut him off.

"What's your name, officer?"

"Officer Maxwell Heath, ma'am."

"And why are you volunteering for an operation you know nothing about?"

"I could tell you were going to have a hard time selling it to the rest of the room, ma'am."

Silence.

I knew I hadn't made any friends, but I didn't care. If they wanted to clock in and out, fine. I was here for other reasons.

"Captain, may I speak with you and Officer Heath in your office?" the DA asked.

Harris didn't look thrilled. Inside his office, he told Diaz about the bodega shooting. Said I had promise but he wasn't convinced I was ready for an undercover op, especially one involving the Donatos.

Diaz disagreed. I fit the profile perfectly. An older cop wouldn't get anywhere near Grayson Dunne. And Spencer would smell the stench of a seasoned undercover cop a mile away. A rookie? A fresh face? That had a lot of potential.

She turned to me with a list of questions:

Did I have a wife or girlfriend who might object? ("No, ma'am.")

Would flirting with another man make me uncomfortable? ("It would not, ma'am.")

Did I think I had the courage to be knowingly placed in dangerous situations? ("I do, ma'am.")

And so on.

Then she asked me to step outside while she conferred with the captain.

Even with the door shut, I could hear the tone of their argument. I knew Harris was doing his best to keep me out of it. But Diaz had the leverage. As long as I was willing, her authority would win out.

When the door opened, I didn't need to hear a word. I saw the look on the captain's face.

And I knew I'd won.

We spent the next hour talking through timelines and scenarios. I'd embed with the undercover unit, develop a cover identity, move into a new apartment, start working a cover job. A lot had to happen before Operation Falcon could officially launch. If this was going to work, the Donatos had to believe every part of my new life. One missed detail could blow the whole thing, or get me killed.

The department kept several apartments scattered around the city. I moved into a third-floor walk-up off Tompkins Square Park, on Avenue B in Alphabet City. Records would show I'd lived there for the past three years. I began training at a pet clinic in Chelsea, again with employment files to match a long tenure. For four months, I prepared and waited, until finally, all the pieces were in place.

It was time to bait the trap.

I'd been working with Christian for about a month, rehearsing our scene until we could hit our marks without thinking. He was a thirty-year veteran of the force and would be the fly to lure Grayson Dunne into my spider's web.

At eight o'clock sharp, Christian and I walked into *Joshua*, his arm locked dominantly around my waist like he was afraid I might bolt. The fireworks began almost immediately

Christian complained, loudly.

The table we were led to? *Completely unacceptable.*

"I did not wait a month for a reservation to be seated this close to the goddamn kitchen!"

I stood nearby, quiet, gaze turned slightly away, letting him play his part. To anyone watching, we looked like a May/December gay couple with a crumbling dynamic. That impression was exactly what we wanted.

We ordered cocktails and Christian's went "wrong."

"I *specifically* asked for a lemon twist," he snapped, sending it back. He hadn't.

Then came the appetizers. Disaster.

Christian refused to eat what he'd ordered, said something "smelled off."

"It's fine," I said just loud enough for nearby tables to hear. "It's delicious, Christian."

But he waved me off and shoved the plate toward the edge of the table, nearly dumping it at the waiter's feet.

"Take this away," he hissed.

"Christian, please…we waited a long time to eat here," I said, trying to keep the peace.

He ignored me.

"You're not the one paying, *Maxwell*, now are you?"

Dismissive. Cold. Perfect. I was shamed.

I could feel the other diners watching. Their pity drifted my way; their disgust was aimed squarely at Christian. They bought it. We had them.

The main course brought the final act. Christian sent his food back, again, and this time, demanded to speak to the chef.

I gave a well-practiced look of mortified apology.

Then Grayson Dunne stepped out from the kitchen. Game on.

He wore a starched white coat, open at the collar to reveal a fitted v-neck T-shirt beneath. A dark plume of chest hair curled over the edge. The descriptions hadn't done him justice.

Seducing Grayson Dunne, it turned out, would be my pleasure.

"Sir, I'm so sorry you haven't enjoyed your experience here at *Joshua* this evening. I'm Grayson Dunne, the head chef…"

"I am so overwhelmingly disappointed with this entire evening, young man."

I tried to make myself smaller in the seat. Most of the dining room had turned to watch by now, eyes locked on Christian's performance. He was hitting every note. For a straight man, he was playing the role of Bitchy Old Queen like he'd studied under legends.

Grayson was doing his best to salvage the situation. "Is there anything I can do to…"

"No. In fact, we'll be leaving as soon as I pay for this disaster of a meal."

"Please, sir," Grayson said, composed, "there will be no charge for you and your guest this evening."

He finally looked at me. I met his eyes with every ounce of quiet apology I could summon.

"Again, I'm sorry we didn't live up to your expectations."

"Come along, Maxwell. We're leaving."

And like a chastised puppy on a short leash, I followed him out of the dining room, casting one last sheepish glance behind me.

Grayson was watching.

We kept up the act until we turned the corner and flagged a cab. Act One: complete. A smashing success. Now it was time for an intermission.

A few hours later, with the restaurant winding down for the night, I returned. Time for Act Two.

I walked in with my most contrite face and approached the hostess, who looked me over with a mix of suspicion and thinly veiled disdain.

"I'm really sorry to bother you, but is there any chance I could speak to the chef again?" I asked.

She didn't move. "I'm sure he's busy, but I'll see if he has a moment," she said, voice cool. A perfect gatekeeper but just another domino that had to fall out of my way. I smiled politely. I already knew he'd see me.

He emerged a minute later, not as buttoned up this time. His chef's coat hung open and I could see just how tight the t-shirt underneath was. The flush from the kitchen hadn't yet faded, and a sheen of sweat dotted his hairline. He looked tired and he appeared to have sprouted a full five o'clock shadow in a mere couple of hours.

He was even more handsome now.

I expected a guarded reaction. Maybe even hostility. Instead, he greeted me with a warm handshake. I wasn't prepared for the heat of his palm or the way he held on, just a second too long.

"Thanks for seeing me. I'm Maxwell, Max, VanDoren," I said. He was still holding my hand, and it threw me a little. "I really wanted to apologize for my friend earlier. I was mortified. It was...inexcusable. I thought the meal, or at least what I had, was incredible."

I was rambling. I knew I was. But he wasn't stopping me. He wasn't brushing it off. He was just *watching* me, studying me like I might be part of some elaborate prank.

At last, he let go of my hand. I missed the warmth instantly.

"Thank you for the apology, Max. It wasn't necessary, at least not from you."

"That may or may not be true," I said. "But I should've done more to stop him. He can be...a little high-strung."

"A *little?*" Grayson chuckled. "I'd hate to see *a lot.*"

I smiled, more relaxed now. "Yeah, he can be a handful. But...I owe him a lot. I know, it's fucked up. Or, it *was.* I actually ended things with him earlier. Not that you need to hear any of this."

"Oh, wow. I'm, uh, sorry. Jesus, I hope it wasn't because of my cooking."

"NO!" I said too quickly, before realizing he was joking. His grin caught me off guard. I let out the breath I hadn't realized I was holding.

"Anyway," I continued, "I just wanted to say you didn't deserve to be called out in your own restaurant."

"A restaurant, and its chef, lives and dies by its patrons. I've developed a thick skin over the years."

"Still. Let me make it up to you. Let me do something nice for you."

"There's no need, Max."

"I know. But I *want* to. Sometimes you need to release good karma into the world to balance out the bad. It would mean something to me."

He paused. I saw the hesitation flicker behind his eyes, but it was softening. I remembered the surveillance photo, Grayson exiting the small Buddhist temple in the West Village. The karma line had struck the right chord.

"Listen, it's late. Let me think about it. Leave your number with Shannon at the front."

I gave him a pleading smile, one that I hoped would be impossible to refuse. "I'll do that. I hope you call, Grayson."

Three days later, he did.

And just like that, Operation Falcon was on.

Chapter Five

"You're a brave man, Max VanDoren."

"How do you figure?"

"There aren't many men who'd think taking a chef out to dinner is the smartest move."

"So I'm brave, but not smart? Ouch."

"I guess what I'm saying is that I appreciate bravery over brains, if I had to choose."

"Good to know, but I'd like to think I'm a healthy mix of both. Besides, I didn't say where I wanted to take you to dinner..."

The conversation flowed easily, light, effortless, and surprisingly comfortable. I would've thought Grayson would be more guarded, more hesitant, but he agreed to dinner without much convincing. His only concern was that I might be about to make the fatal error of taking a Michelin-star chef to a much lesser competitor.

Oh, ye of little faith, I thought to myself.

"Listen, I have to get back to work. I'll pick you up at five on Friday..."

"Five? We're eating dinner at five? Are you taking me to a Denny's?"

"I'm braver than that, and you should be too. Dress code is casual. I'll see you then." I hung up before he could say another word. I knew a few things about Grayson Donato/Dunne, but not everything. I just had to hope he liked what I had planned or Operation Falcon would be over before it began.

I was surprised he'd agreed to meet me on a Friday night. I thought the demands of his restaurant would've pushed us to a Monday or Tuesday when *Joshua* was probably quieter. I guess if you want something bad enough, you make sacrifices. Interesting thought. Or, at least, it was until he called me Friday afternoon to say he'd been called into the restaurant to handle an issue with one of the specials. I guess when the fish goes off, date night gets postponed.

"Do you need to reschedule?" I asked, making sure to sound just the right amount of caring and disappointed.

"No, no, not at all." He almost sounded as disappointed as I'd pretended to be. "I'll have it sorted in no time. But can you meet me at the restaurant instead of my place?"

"Not a problem," I told him. "As long as Shannon lets me back in the front door."

"I'll let her know you're coming on an apology tour. Maybe I'll hide the sharp objects, just in case."

I stepped into the near-empty restaurant right on the dot at five. The wait staff were busy prepping tables for the first seating, and Shannon was already at the maitre d' station, giving me an icy glare that could've cut through steel. I'd been bracing myself for it, so I ate as much shit as I thought I needed to make her, if not like me, at least tolerate me, at least for now. I offered my hand in truce, bowing deeply to the keeper of the door. Who knew how much influence she had with Grayson, but I assumed every little bit would help my cause.

With Shannon sufficiently thawed, I asked if Grayson had managed to resolve the dinner issue. I told her I didn't want to stress him out. I knew work came first, even if he wouldn't say those exact words to me.

"Grayson's a genius," she said, her voice almost reverent. "You need to understand that. There's nothing he can't do if he sets his mind to it."

"Good to know," I said, flashing her my best conspiratorial smile. I wanted her to think we were both on Grayson's side.

She picked up the phone and dialed the kitchen. "Grayson, your, uh, friend is out front whenever you're available."

I wouldn't call us friends, more like hunter and prey, but I'd know better by morning.

Almost immediately, Grayson appeared, running a hand through his messy black curls, trying to smooth out the dents left by his chef's hat.

"When I said 'casual,' I wasn't expecting this," I said, smirking.

Grayson had emerged wearing khaki cargo shorts, black tank top, and a very loud, very colorful, Hawaiian-print shirt, complete with flowers and a large parrot on the chest. On anyone else, it'd have looked horribly cheesy, but on Grayson, it looked effortless and cool. The shirt was unbuttoned. The shorts were tight enough to accentuate the firm, bubble butt his chef's pants had unfortunately hid during our first meeting.

"This is my 'day off' drag," he said, grinning. "I can change if you want."

I sensed this was a test, and I wasn't about to let him win.

"Nope. You'll fit right in where we're going," I said with a mischievous smile, winking at Shannon, which might've finally won her over. "Shall we?" I gestured toward the door and our awaiting adventure. The next few hours would either make or break Operation Falcon. No false moves allowed, but I loved a good challenge.

"Where's the car?" he asked as we stepped outside onto the sidewalk.

"Okay, the first thing you're going to learn about me is that I can't afford car service everywhere I go."

"I don't take cars everywhere," he protested. "I just thought…"

"Nope. Think again," I said, taking his elbow and turning him toward the subway. "Come with me," I added, letting the innuendo hang in the air.

In spite of what most people think, there are relatively few surprises remaining in New York City. The D train is one example. Long before you reach your final destination, you know exactly where you're heading, the end of the line. Coney Island.

As it loomed in the distance outside the grimy train window, the parachute jump towers rising up into the skyline, Grayson muttered to himself, "I haven't been here since I was a kid." I caught him grinning out of the corner of my eye.

It was past six by the time we stepped out onto the platform and into the late-June warmth. The difference in the air from Manhattan was immediate. A breeze off the Atlantic, salty and faintly fishy, but not wholly unpleasant.

I wanted to take Grayson's hand right then and there, but I knew patience would be better in the long run. I didn't want to seem over-eager. This was just a casual get-to-know-you evening. An apology for Christian's rude behavior. I wasn't sure if Grayson thought it was a date or not, so I had to play it cool.

We walked into the park with the rest of the crowd from the train. The sky was turning orange, and the boardwalk lights were slowly flickering to life. We passed the arcade, its games beckoning us to waste our money for a chance at a cheap prize. Grayson had already won his cheap prize, he just didn't know it yet.

I guided him past the barkers and into the hustle of the boardwalk.

"I want to walk in the sand," he said, kicking off his well-worn loafers.

"OK, let's do it." I untied my sneakers and stuffed my socks inside, realizing I was no longer in control of the situation but willing to go wherever Grayson wanted to lead.

I stepped off the boardwalk and into the sand, still warm from the early summer sun that had been beating down on it all day. My feet sank into it, toes wrapping around the grains. I remembered my long-ago quest to step foot into the ocean, a journey interrupted by a random pickup and the accidental killing of an innocent deer. This was the feeling I had been searching for, I just hadn't known it at the time. The warmth creeping up through my feet and into my body. It somehow made me feel safe, protected.

I looked over at Grayson, who seemed to be having a similar experience. His eyes were closed, and a small smile played at the corners of his mouth.

"I haven't been here since I was a kid," he said softly. "My mom would bring us…"

Of the little I knew about Grayson's family, there was almost nothing about his mother. Marie Donato seemed to disappear from the family history when Grayson was four or five. No one knew if she left voluntarily or was forced out by other means. But Grayson clearly still had fond memories of her.

"It must've been fun, growing up here," I said, trying not to pry too much into his past too soon.

He didn't answer right away. "Where did you grow up, Max? You've got a faint twang to your voice…"

"Damn. I've worked hard to drop that," I said with a half-laugh. "Oklahoma was where I was raised." Christian and the others on the force had coached me to stick close to the truth. Fewer things to remember, fewer chances of getting tripped up in a lie. "But I left there years ago."

"For the big city?" he asked, trying to make it sound intimidating but failing. It just sounded goofy coming from him.

"Something like that. I had dreams of making a name for myself on Broadway, my name in lights…"

"Really?"

"No, not really!" I gave him a slight shove. "I just wanted to get

73

as far from Oklahoma as possible, and New York seemed like the best place to start."

"I've lived abroad, but New York has always been home. I always seem to come back," he said, beginning to walk slowly toward the ocean. I followed in his footsteps like a disciple. "Everything I've ever loved has always been here."

We stopped at the water's edge, waiting for the next wave. It hit, icy cold, and I took a step back, but Grayson stood firm in the wet sand, waiting for the next rush of water.

"You're crazy," I said, hoping he wasn't planning on going in any further.

When the second wave hit, it seemed to break him out of his reverie. "So, what are we having for dinner?" he asked.

"Let's walk," I said, heading down the beach.

We walked in silence for a moment while I planned my next move.

"Did you live abroad for cooking school?" I asked, already knowing the answer.

"Paris was where I really learned to cook, but I'd loved it my whole life. I went to prep school in Geneva for five years, too."

"That must've been hard, being so far from your family."

"I'm the youngest. My brother and sister were off at prep, too, England and France. I guess it's just what we did. It didn't seem weird at the time, but I can see how it looks now."

"The hick from the sticks who barely got out of Oklahoma…"

"But you knew what you wanted, and you worked for it. There's nothing wrong with that. I did the same thing, just slightly differently."

"I don't mean to imply you've had it easy in any way. I'm sure you've had to work hard to get where you are, too. No one becomes a Michelin-star chef before they're thirty on their good looks alone." I glanced at him to see how the compliment landed and saw that same small smile from earlier.

He suddenly pulled me up the beach just as a large wave came crashing in.

"Oh, you saved me," I mocked. "I owe you my life..."

"I'll happily collect at a later date," he said, finally letting out a full smile.

We walked in silence for a few minutes before I stopped and pointed.

"We're here."

"How did I know..." he said, glancing up at the boardwalk.

Nathan's Famous hotdogs. The pride of Coney Island.

"I hope you brought your appetite, Chef."

"Well, I loved them when I was a kid. You're really hitting all the big nostalgia buttons tonight, Max."

"I told you I was brave."

"Yes, yes you did."

We grabbed a couple of dogs each and two root beers to wash them down. We sat at a table on the boardwalk, watching the mix of New Yorkers and tourists walk by as we continued the easy conversation we'd been enjoying all evening. I told him a little about the farm, which went over better than I expected, and he told me about his favorite place in New York City: the Frick Gallery on the Upper East Side.

"It's an old turn-of-the-century mansion, so it's not impossible to see everything in just a few hours. It's the perfect, quiet day, and I don't get many of those."

"I've never been," I admitted, "but I'll have to check it out sometime."

"Maybe we could go together someday."

"Maybe," I said, adding "I'd like that" for effect.

We wadded up our paper wrappings and started walking the boardwalk again. The sun was almost set, and the park lights had blazed to life.

"Isn't the subway back the other way?" he asked.

"We're not going back so soon. Did you think I'd bring you all the way out here just for a hotdog?"

He threw his hands up in surrender and laughed. "My mistake. Lead on, kind sir."

As famous as Nathan's might be, the giant Wonder Wheel was even more iconic and definitely not to be missed.

"Oh, I don't know about this, Max."

"You're not scared, are you?"

"Kinda," he admitted. "My brother used to try to swing the car when we were up high. It left an impression on a certain four-year-old."

"I'll protect you. Remember, I'm the brave one…"

We got a car to ourselves, and as the wheel jerked into motion, Grayson grabbed my leg reflexively. He didn't remove his hand as we continued to circle higher.

"The view is pretty amazing from up here," I said.

He looked at me. "Yes, it is." Then he leaned in and kissed me.

It took me by surprise, actually, a lot by surprise. I thought I'd have to make the first move, but I was glad I hadn't had to. I leaned into the kiss, letting him know I was perfectly fine with the impulse. When he pulled back, he looked almost shy, like a schoolboy caught looking at a dirty magazine. I took his chin in my hand and kissed him quickly in return. The mood had definitely shifted to the romantic.

We walked along the boardwalk, holding hands like excited kids. We rode a couple more of the rides, but Coney Island had lost its allure, so we decided to head back into Manhattan.

"I'm calling a car," he said. "Forgive me if I don't want to spend another hour on the D train today."

"I suppose I'll allow it," I smiled.

"Eighth and B," I told the driver. Grayson didn't say anything, but I could tell by the way his body stiffened that he was thinking, probably expecting, that I'd go back to his place with him. That wasn't going to happen. That wasn't the plan.

As we made our way back into the city, I told Grayson how happy I was that he decided to take me up on my apology offer and that I hoped he'd had a nice time.

He placed his hand back on my leg. "Max, I've had a great time."

When the car pulled up outside my dingy walk-up, I grabbed the door handle, but Grayson grabbed my arm.

"I do want to see you again, Max."

"Good. I want to see you too." I gave him a quick kiss before opening the car door and stepping out into the close, nighttime city air. The freshness of the ocean breeze already felt like a distant memory.

"Good night, Grayson." I shut the door before he could protest.

The car pulled away, and I headed into my building without looking back.

Inside my apartment, I dropped my keys and wallet into the ceramic dish on the table by the door. I poured myself a glass of water and checked the time on my phone. I paced across the floor. I sat on the sofa and flipped through a magazine. I checked the time again. Only ten minutes had passed. I paced some more. I looked out the window, scanning the street below for anything that might take my mind off the evening. I nervously drank another glass of water. After twenty minutes, I picked up the phone and dialed his number.

He answered, but before he had a chance to say anything, I blurted out, "I think I might've fucked up."

"Hi to you too, Max."

"Sorry. Hi, Grayson. I think I fucked up."

"Why do you think that?"

"Because I pulled the plug on a date that was going really well, and two seconds after I closed the car door, I knew I'd made a huge mistake sending you off alone."

"It was kind of abrupt, but I don't want to pressure you into doing something you're not ready for. That's not me."

"I'm just stupid, I guess."

"You're not stupid…"

"I feel like there's a 'but' coming…"

"No but, maybe an offer…"

"An offer?"

"Would you like to come over?"

"Now?"

"Yes, Max, now."

"Are you sure?"

"I wouldn't have offered if I wasn't. I'll see you in twenty minutes?" And then he hung up.

I gave him enough time to get home, not wanting to catch him still in the car. I didn't want him considering a drive back to my place. I needed the invite to his TriBeCa loft. It needed to be his idea.

I took the cab fare from my wallet, the wallet with the tracking device sewn inside, and left it sitting by the door. We knew Grayson didn't pose a physical threat to me, so no official back-up was awkwardly tailing us on our date, but I was still being tracked electronically. I didn't think the surveillance team needed to know I was about to go off script.

There had been a lot of discussion about how to handle the physical side of dating Grayson, with the general consensus being to delay it as long as possible and then be creative about what we did and how we did it. Everyone was so concerned about protecting me. I didn't need anyone's protection.

I left my traceable phone sitting next to my wallet (if asked, I'd tell him "I was in such a hurry, I forgot it") and headed out to hail a cab for the crosstown ride to TriBeCa.

The buildings we passed on North Moore Street were outdated, industrial-looking, and seemingly abandoned. When we pulled up to Grayson's, it looked no different. I knew, though, that behind the rusted facades and cracked, peeling paint were some of the most expensive properties in all of Manhattan. Grayson may not have been publicly in touch with his family, but he was certainly in touch with their money. His residence was not what you'd expect from a young chef, Michelin-star or not.

I rang the buzzer for unit nine, and without a word, I heard the click of the front door unlocking. Without fanfare, I'd been allowed entry into Grayson's world.

There was no doorman, no sign of any security at all. I called the elevator, rode it to the top floor, and it opened directly into the loft. I paused to take it all in. The giant expanse of open space was seemingly divided into 'rooms' by different clusters of furniture or seating. Grayson hurried over from the far end of the loft, taking long, loping strides. He seemed lighter than when I'd left him less than an hour ago, an easy smile on his handsome face. He was clearly more comfortable in his own space, the ruler overseeing his kingdom greeting his visitor.

He'd changed into a well-worn, faded olive t-shirt with a deep, stretched-out V-neck and a pair of loose basketball shorts. Helen Keller would've noticed that he wasn't wearing underwear underneath. The bounce of his cock was more than noticeable, and it was goddamn distracting.

Grayson pulled me into a tight embrace, and I realized this was the first time we'd really made physical contact. I hadn't felt his body up against mine like this before. I hadn't fully taken the measure of the man I was trying to seduce, or who might be seducing me.

We were almost the same height, but he had a few extra pounds of muscle that I didn't. His shoulders were broad, tapering down to a narrow waist, with strong, hard thighs that were pressing against mine.

Before he broke our embrace, he kissed me like he wanted to devour me.

"I'm glad you called," he whispered in my ear.

"I'm glad you answered," I replied, smiling to myself.

"Come in..."

I kicked off my shoes and left them by the elevator, suddenly feeling overdressed. I untucked my shirt from my shorts and followed Grayson into the loft. The space was enormous, with high ceilings that made it feel cavernous. Art hung on the walls, an Andy Warhol series on one, a large Pollack on another.

Grayson plopped down onto the overstuffed sofa, or maybe he just sank into it. When I sat next to him, it was like being enveloped in a cloud. The sofa seemed to swallow me up, and Grayson's arm wrapped around me as I melted into him.

I knew for sure then, I wasn't the one doing the seducing.

He leaned in and began kissing my neck, biting at it, his lips warm and his touch deliberate. I closed my eyes, trying to steady my breath. This was the moment I had been expecting, though it was happening in a way I hadn't anticipated. The hook was set; I needed to reel him in slowly.

Our hands were everywhere. I ran mine under his shirt, finding the solid, firm warmth of his hairy chest. I traced his nipples with my fingers, twisting them until I heard him moan softly. His body was a contrast of strength and warmth, and I started to wonder when he had the time to work out before he grabbed my hair, pulling my mouth back to his. Our tongues met in a fiery kiss, and, for a moment, my mind went blank.

He laid back onto the sofa and pulled me with him so I was laying on top of him, my mouth not leaving his. I could barely breathe.

I settled between his spread legs noting how perfectly we fit together. I could feel his hard cock pressing into mine. I ground into him with a primal urgency, a need I knew he understood by the way he ground back.

His hands grabbed my ass and pulled me into him even tighter than I thought possible while still fully clothed.

"I want you, Max," he groaned into my ear. That was obvious.

With a swift movement, he rolled me off of him as if I were weightless, only saving me from hitting the floor at the last second.

He took my hand, gripping it tightly as if he were afraid I might run off. "Come with me," he said, his voice low, almost possessive.

I followed as he led me to the back of his loft, through the maze of makeshift 'rooms'. We passed the kitchen, a dining area, a video game setup, and the master bath before finally reaching the farthest corner, where his huge bed awaited us.

Shirts were pulled over heads, shorts were dropped, bodies were exposed and admired. I knew Grayson was a beautiful man, but seeing him naked and erect took my breath away.

Fur covered his chest and tapered down his belly until it exploded into a forest. A thick, veiny cock jutted out, upwards toward the ceiling. It begged to be grabbed, stroked, sucked, ridden.

"You're so beautiful, Max," he said, sinking to his knees, kissing my chest, licking my stomach. He took me into his mouth before I had a chance to respond.

It was intense. *He* was intense.

His hands worked in unison with his mouth and tongue, stroking, licking, sucking, fingering.

My head spun. My knees were weak. I struggled to keep myself upright. I grabbed his head, weaving my fingers into his messy, dark curls, trying to steady myself.

"Fuck, Grayson, fuck…feels…amazing…" I panted, wondering how I even managed to find those words.

He pulled me in, took me as deep as possible into his throat. My shaft lightly grazed his teeth and shockwaves shot up my spine.

I was afraid I would come right there. He must've been thinking the same thing. He pulled off and leapt onto the bed, laying back and spreading himself open for me.

I didn't need further encouragement.

I got between his legs, his knees over my shoulders. I pinned him in place. His cock danced before me, pearls of precum dripped onto his belly. I let my fingers play in the pools before licking them off one by one. Grayson watched. He tasted sweet on my tongue. I was greedy. I wanted more.

I took each of his balls into my mouth and rolled them with my tongue, their aroma was heady, uniquely Grayson. Sweat. Soap. Hints of the ocean we'd just left.

I licked the length of his shaft, felt every vein as I worked my way up to the engorged velvety head, dipping my tongue into its leaking slit, searching for the delicious nectar that spilled forth. I spit on his cock and watched it run down the shaft, down to the base.

He squirmed beneath my exquisite torture.

I couldn't wait any longer. I swallowed him to the base, opening my throat to accommodate all of him. I let him rest inside me, letting my throat caress him, before withdrawing and beginning again.

Euphoria swept through me.

My fingers danced around his furry hole, rubbing it, teasing it. He lifted his hips, silently begging me to go further.

So I did.

One finger, then two. His hands gripped at the bedcovers. His head twisted from side to side. My free hand reached up and stroked his chest, wet with sweat.

"Jesus, Max, just fuck me, I want you…"

Before he'd finished his thought I'd flipped him over onto his stomach, exposing his near-perfect ass. He arched his back. I spread him open with both hands. My tongue invaded him. I lapped around the rim, slowly, teasingly, before I probed deeper. It was warm. The sweat of our night at the beach created a tang that sat on my tongue. It was delicious.

Grayson let out a moan from deep within.

"Stop teasing me, Max…fuck me. Jesus, please fuck me…I want your cock in me…"

I obeyed his command. He pointed to the bottle of lube on the nightstand. He *was* ready for me.

I crawled on top of him, nestling my straining erection between the furry mounds of his ass. I pushed in slowly, inch by inch.

Grayson gulped air, concentrated on relaxing his muscles, letting me in deeper. When I couldn't go further, I paused for both of us to acclimate.

I kissed his neck. I licked behind his ear while my cock pulsed inside of him. More moans of satisfaction.

I flexed my hips, slowly withdrawing myself before slamming back into him.

He yelped but he didn't tell me to stop. And I didn't.

I gained momentum. His hips rose further to meet me. He was desperate to get every inch of me inside of him.

We were both sweating, my body slid across his back. My hands pinned his wrists to the bed.

"Get on your knees," I commanded.

I grabbed his hips and thrust back into him, hard, watching his muscular ass quiver with the force of my penetration. Again. Again. Again. His head thrashed. He bucked like a stallion. His hand disappeared to stroke himself. I reached forward and took his throat in my hand and choked him lightly.

"Harder," he begged.

We both worked towards our climax, each lost in our own pleasure yet still intensely aware of the other. I was oblivious to everything else. Operation Falcon was a distant thought. The Donato crime syndicate faded away. In that moment, it was just me, in that loft, with that man, for one reason only.

I tightened my grip around Grayson's throat, feeling the way he leaned into my movements, desperate for more. We were both teetering on the edge, caught in the raw urgency of the moment.

I don't know who came first.

I released myself into him while lights flashed in my head and inhuman sounds came from my throat. Similar sounds were coming from Grayson. His arm flailed as he jacked himself off.

The world slowly righted itself, and with it, I regained some semblance of focus. My cock slipped out of Grayson, I collapsed onto his back, and he fell forward onto the bed, dropping into the pool of his own cum.

We shifted, positioning ourselves so we were looking into each other's eyes. I kissed him, or maybe he kissed me. It didn't matter. The connection had been made, and it was solidified. Grayson Dunne was mine. And I, I feared, was his.

Chapter Six

DA Diaz and Captain Harris were pleased with my work, and during our weekly meetings they asked precious few questions about the methods I was using to get close to Grayson. But I knew that no matter how far I'd come with him, it meant nothing if I didn't get closer to his brother, Spencer. Gaining Spencer's trust would take time, but it was time we were all prepared, and willing, to devote.

Fucking Grayson was easy. Getting to really know him was the challenge. From the first night we talked, I knew there were deep feelings he kept hidden, especially when it came to his mother. He shared stories of his past, his time at boarding school and coming out while living in Switzerland, falling for a boy named Hans, who of course, broke his heart, the way all hearts are broken at that age. But now, he could smile about it. I didn't tell him I wasn't as lucky. He told me he wanted to open his own restaurant, to build on his success at *Joshua*. That was his future.

After that first night, we quickly became inseparable. Grayson would swing by the clinic to take me to lunch, and I'd meet him at his loft after *Joshua* closed. North Moore Street became my home.

His bed became mine. I knew every inch of his body, but not what went on inside his head. His family secrets stayed locked up tight.

Six months had passed. We were still in the bloom of new love, and with the holidays approaching, I started asking seemingly innocent questions, questions I knew would provoke a strong reaction.

"Do you want to go Christmas shopping this weekend? Maybe see the tree at Rockefeller Center? Ice skate in the park? I think I might want to see you on skates…"

His mood shifted in an instant. "Ugh. The crowds. I deal with tourists all week long. I just want to stay home with you this weekend."

"But don't you have to get gifts for your family?"

"Not really, just you…"

I sat next to him on the couch, casually reaching up to play with his hair, tracing gentle circles on his head the way he liked. It calmed him when he was upset.

"Gray, you never talk about your family. We've been together this long, and I don't know anything about them except that they exist."

"I don't know much about your family, either, Max."

"I don't really have one. I've got my brother, Ethan, and I've told you about him. We're not close. My parents are gone. That's about it."

"I've got nothing in common with anyone in my family. They don't approve of any of the choices I've made."

"Being gay?"

"It goes way beyond that. My father and I butted heads long before I came out."

I leaned over and kissed the top of his head, pulling him into my chest where he could hear my steady heartbeat. "I'm sorry. It's none of my business."

"I don't mean to be mysterious about them. I just don't know what to say. I haven't seen them in a long time. They didn't even come to the opening of *Joshua*. They don't call on my birthday. They're just not a part of my life anymore..."

I kept holding him, stroking his hair to calm him.

"...everything changed after my mom..."

Grayson had never mentioned his mother since our first date on the beach. I knew she was the most painful subject, and the one thing I wanted to understand most.

"What happened to your mom, Gray?" I asked softly, but he didn't respond. I wasn't sure if he'd even heard me. He'd gone quiet, probably lost in thought as he often did. I'd learned to give him space when he went into one of these moods. I started gently rocking him back and forth.

"She left us," he said suddenly. "One day, she was just gone. I never saw her again."

"Oh God, Gray, I'm so sorry. That's awful." I pressed my lips to his head, feeling the weight of his pain. "We don't have to talk about this. I'm sorry I brought it up."

"It's OK, Max. I'll tell you about her someday. It's just hard. I love you..." He looked up at me, his eyes brimming with tears. "Let's go to bed."

We quietly turned out the lights in the loft, undressing in the dark. In bed, I pulled him close, wrapping my arms around him, and held him until morning.

In the morning, it was as if nothing had happened. Neither of us mentioned the conversation or its effect on Grayson. But I knew I'd made a small crack in his tough outer shell. And from experience, I knew those cracks only grew with time.

I kept working at the clinic and maintained the apartment in Alphabet City, even though I was hardly ever there. Max VanDoren was trying to carve out a life for himself, not the kept boy Grayson had originally met with Christian. And I was, at least until I wasn't anymore.

After the new year, Grayson asked me to move into the loft with him. Then he got me a job as Assistant Manager at *Joshua*.

Each day, I sank deeper into his world. And the line between that version of me and the real one became blurrier with every passing moment.

I was falling in love with him.

That wasn't part of the plan. Grayson was supposed to be a means to an end, a pawn in a much larger game. But his impenetrable walls weren't the only ones with cracks.

He was an innocent, a good, caring man who, in my quieter moments, I knew didn't deserve what was headed his way. My feelings for him were genuine, surprising, and I knew they had to stay buried. I had a job to do. The city of New York, and others, were depending on me. I couldn't afford to let anyone down. But the longer I stayed with him, the harder it became to hold onto that resolve.

In February, we went to Rio for Carnival and to celebrate Grayson's thirtieth birthday. Four days away from the city, the loft, the restaurant. Grayson, completely out of his comfort zone, with all his safety nets gone. Even though it had been his joking idea, it took some convincing once the reality of leaving set in. To him, leaving *Joshua* was like leaving a baby at home without supervision. He felt like a bad parent, something we both knew something about. He was torn up about it until we locked the loft door and were on our way to JFK. When we were finally settled into our first-class seats and the handsome Brazilian flight attendant handed us champagne, Grayson and I both exhaled deeply, clinked our glasses, and vowed to not think about New York until we were back on the JFK tarmac in a few days.

"Cheers to a fun and happy birthday celebration," I murmured in his ear before lightly tracing my tongue along his lobe. His deep sigh was all the answer I needed. The crew sealed us in.

The hours passed quickly, or at least the first few did. As the crew cleared away the dinner trays and our fellow travelers reclined into their seats, I tried to get into a book I'd picked up three times already. But I wasn't in a reading mood.

I raised the armrest between us and leaned into Grayson. He hardly noticed, too engrossed in the movie on his screen. I pulled the blanket around me, planning to nap, but my hand had other ideas. It made a beeline for his crotch. For a brief moment, he must've forgotten where we were. He let out a low moan as he shifted in his seat, allowing me more generous access.

His cock began to swell to its full hardness beneath my hand.

"Not here," he whispered, aware finally of his surroundings.

He unfastened his seatbelt and got up, pulling his shirt from his shorts, attempting to hide his erection as best he could. He headed to the lavatories that separated first class from the rest of the plane. I waited five seconds before doing the same.

It was a tight fit for the two of us, but neither of us cared. He maneuvered himself to the least uncomfortable position while I squatted to the ground, taking his shorts and boxer briefs with me. His cock sprang free and grazed my stubbled cheek sending a charge through Grayson, His whole body shivered.

I wasted no time sucking him off.

My hands stroked his furry belly while his engorged cock pounded the back of my throat. Spit leaked out of the corners of my mouth, tears streamed down my face. It was glorious.

Drawing deep breaths through my nose, inhaling Grayson's unique aroma with each one, I knew he was close. I grabbed his ass and pulled him in tight, forcing him to shoot his cum down my throat. Wave after wave he came until I started to choke on his semen. I pulled off of him and covered my mouth. I didn't want to spill any of his sweet juice.

I swallowed repeatedly before standing up and giving him a deep, sticky kiss that was heavy with his own cum.

"Happy early birthday," I said.

Grayson pulled his underwear and shorts back up, a sly grin spreading across his face.

I tried not to look like someone who'd just blown his boyfriend in an airplane bathroom as he slid the lock back and cautiously opened the door. We made our way back to our seats and had just settled in when our handsome flight attendant came by with two more glasses of champagne.

"I thought you might like something to, um, wash everything down," he said with a smile and a wink.

I slept soundly for the next four hours, waking only when the pilot announced our imminent arrival at Rio's Galeão International Airport.

We shuffled through the maze of immigration, waiting for our luggage and clearing customs before finally settling into the back of a taxi to our hotel. We were exhausted, unsure whether to feel happy or annoyed that it was only noon.

"I just want to crawl into bed with you," I whispered in Grayson's ear, unsure how the Brazilian cab driver would feel about my right to fuck my boyfriend into the mattress.

"It's only an hour's time difference from New York, and you slept half the flight…"

"It was a third at most," I retorted petulantly, feeling a mood shift I needed to fight off. I hated being denied by Grayson. I turned to look out the window at people going about their day, the sun beating down, baking everything in its path.

"Are you here for Carnival?" the driver called from the front seat.

"Isn't everyone?" I muttered, half-heartedly.

The Copacabana Palace was every bit as stunning as I imagined. Grayson had nailed the reservation, as I knew he would, and I could feel my mood lift as we pulled onto the front drive. The white marble structure glowed in the Rio sun. I looked at Grayson, and for a moment, I felt myself glow, too. I felt lucky to be with him. But then reality hit and I remembered it wasn't real. One day, sooner than I wanted it to be, Grayson would learn the truth, and this fantasy would be over. My mood turned dark again.

The bellman took our bags and immediately ushered us to our

room. They'd been expecting us, but I hadn't expected the sheer grandeur of our penthouse suite.

The expansive living room, decorated in creams and tans, seemed to pull the colors of Copacabana Beach into the space. Splashes of aqua and cerulean mirrored the ocean just beyond. I'd been in many beautiful places since leaving Choctaw, but this one literally took my breath away.

I wandered into the main room while Grayson showed the bellman where to leave the bags. On a table next to a small basket of sunscreens, aloe lotions, and a uniquely-shaped bottle of coconut-scented 'personal lubricant,' there was a huge bouquet of fresh flowers. The hotel had provided everything.

There was a card hiding in the flowers that I delicately plucked out.

Mr. Grayson Donato and Guest

Grayson and I had been together for eight months, and this was going to be the first deep gash into his armor. I knew I needed to exploit it, even though part of me began to hate my idea.

I heard him tipping the bellman and closing the door to our room. It was time. I couldn't not do it.

"This is interesting," I said, my voice steady, but I could feel my pulse quicken.

"What's that, babe?"

"Who's *Grayson Donato*?"

He didn't even try to hide the shock that spread across his face. It was instantaneous. He was quickly trying to figure out what was happening and how to explain who he really was.

"I'm not sure what you're thinking, Max, but it's not that, I swear."

"I'm thinking that I thought I knew you, but I don't even know your name? You're a Donato? One of *the* Donatos?" I tried to keep my voice from sounding hysterical. I needed him to feel bad, not think I was completely losing it.

"Max, Max, calm down." He reached for me, trying to pull me close, but I fought him off.

"This is just weird, Gray. Why haven't you told me this before?"

"I've told you I'm not close with my family…"

"A lot of people aren't close with their families, they don't go by a different name because of it."

"My family is different."

"No fucking kidding." I turned and walked out onto the terrace, staring at Copacabana Beach, my back to the door. I counted the seconds before Grayson followed. It took ten.

"Max. Sit down. Let me tell you about my family."

Success.

He spoke carefully, telling me things I already knew: the family's questionable businesses, the rift with his father, and the strained relationships with his brother and sister. He stopped short of mentioning the actual racketeering, smuggling, or murder his family was involved in. And, of course, he avoided talking about his mother. He still wasn't ready to go there. But this was a huge leap forward for Operation Falcon.

I relaxed a little, my body visibly calming as Grayson stroked my leg the way he liked. I apologized for becoming irrational. He kissed me, the heat of it matching the Brazilian sun that beat down on us through the French doors.

"You could've told me this a long time ago," I said, my voice soft but still tinged with frustration. "You should've…"

"I didn't know how," he replied. And I believed him. How do you tell someone you're trying to build a relationship with that you come from a family of monsters? I knew I couldn't do it.

I kept him off balance, never letting him question the card or where it came from. That would stay my secret. But I felt guilty for what I'd just put him through. He wasn't his father. Or his brother.

He used a different name to distance himself from them, and I couldn't hold that against him.

"I want to take a shower," I said, standing and walking back into the living room before turning around. "Are you coming?" I hoped to ease the tension, get our trip back on track.

A smile crept onto his face as he stood, and we began silently undressing. Clothes were discarded in a trail across the room, and by the time we reached the shower, we were both naked. Grayson stopped me before I stepped in.

"I'm sorry, Max. I love you. I wouldn't do anything to knowingly hurt you. I swear."

His earnestness sent a jolt through me. My body responded, my desire for him growing. I kissed him, unable to make the same promise in return.

"I love you too. I guess you're just a mysterious man. My mysterious, sexy man…" I caught a glimpse of myself in the bathroom mirror and had to look away.

I pulled him into the shower, letting the steam engulf us, the scent of eucalyptus filling the air. His body pressed against mine, our arms and legs tangled, our hard cocks rubbing against each other.

I washed his body, savoring the feel of his sensitive skin beneath my fingertips, finding pleasure in giving it back to him. He returned the favor, scrubbing me raw. His fingers traced the black bird tattoo on my shoulder.

"Someday, you have to tell me the story behind this…"

Never, I thought.

Since I started working at *Joshua*, I'd seen Grayson in his true element: the kitchen. His hands moved fast, he directed the other chefs, he kept the surprisingly complicated operation running smoothly. But with me, at home, he was different. He was submissive, docile, like a kitten, purring at my touch, begging me to control him, use him however I wished. Our desires often aligned, but something felt different now. Grayson was about to change, even if he didn't know it yet.

It was obvious he wanted me to fuck him. The way he moved, the way he stood, opening himself up for me. Normally, I wouldn't have hesitated to bend him over and take him right there, but not today. Not now. What had transpired between us earlier, our conversation, my hurt, needed to linger between us for a while longer. The seed had been planted, and it needed time to grow. He needed to know that things had shifted, even if only slightly, and even if only for a moment. I wasn't ready to go back to business as usual, not yet, even if my own hard cock wanted something completely different.

"Let's put on our suits and go to the beach," I said, shutting off the water and breaking the mood.

"I thought you wanted to crawl into bed?"

"I changed my mind…second wind, I guess." I grabbed two towels, tossing one to him. Normally, I might have toweled him off myself, worshipped his body, kissed his skin, traced my fingers through his hair. But not today.

I walked into the bedroom, hurriedly unpacking my bag. I slipped into a black Speedo, pulled on a pair of loose shorts, and threw on a casual short-sleeved shirt. All I needed were my sandals, and…

"Are we OK?"

His voice sounded hurt. When I turned to see him standing in the bathroom doorway, still naked, holding his towel by his side, I saw the sadness in his expression. It made me hate myself even more.

I paused, took a breath, and said, "I think we'll be fine. I just need to process everything that's happened."

He slowly got ready for the beach: white Speedo, gym shorts, a tight t-shirt, and tennis shoes. He looked sexy in anything he wore. I wanted to fuck him, but I knew I couldn't.

The beach was loud and crowded. Even the private hotel area

was teeming with guests, eager to be part of the Carnival spirit. But in our cabana, it was just the two of us, quiet, withdrawn. Exactly what I needed. I wanted him thinking, processing. I wanted him motivated. I knew he loved me, and I knew he'd do whatever it took to get us back on track. He just needed to understand that sharing his secrets, sharing his family, was the key.

I thumbed through my book, unfocused. I ordered us caipirinhas, but Grayson didn't touch his. I was restless. He was pensive. His brow furrowed every time I glanced over at him. I finally gave up.

"I'm going up to the room..." I said.

"'K," he replied, monosyllabically. I paused, wondering if anything else would follow, but when nothing did, I grabbed my beach bag and walked away. I didn't like it, not at all. But I knew it was all necessary.

Dinner in the hotel restaurant was eaten in near silence, and we returned to the room immediately afterward. Whatever Grayson was thinking, he wasn't ready to share. I had a glass of port on the terrace and watched the lights twinkle up and down the beach, the dark, ominous silhouette of Sugarloaf Mountain looming in the distance. I waited for Grayson to join me, but he never did. When I walked back into the suite, it was quiet, nearly dark. I found him in bed, already asleep.

I undressed and slipped between the sheets, curling around him, my arm draped over his chest, my legs tangled between his.

"I'm sorry, Grayson," I whispered into the stillness. "I love you."

Sleep finally came, though it was restless, filled with thoughts I couldn't shake. Through it all, I never loosened my grip on him. I needed to give him strength to face the uncertain future that was waiting for us.

Dawn broke, and immediately, it was clear that the new day had brought at least one change with it.

He was kissing my collarbone, his tongue swirling in the hollow just above it. My sacred spot. It tickled me as much as it turned me on, and Grayson, of course, knew this. He grabbed my hair, pulling my head back as he licked his way up my sensitive neck. My body responded, unwilling to fight the pull.

He wasted no time taking my swelling cock into his hand, gripping it firmly. It felt good. Really good.

At some point in the night I had somehow convinced myself that we'd never fuck again. I had pushed him too far. We'd break up when the new day came. He'd see me as more trouble than I was worth. I'd never been so happy to be so wrong before. I moaned with pleasure.

I was fully hard and waiting for Grayson to straddle me, slowly ride me like he loved to do in the mornings, but he had another surprising idea.

Wordlessly, he rolled on top of me, spreading my legs open with his body. He nestled himself between them and kissed his way up my body. By the time his lips reached mine he had me opened wide as if...he was about to fuck me for the first time.

In the eight months we'd been together, we'd never deviated from our chosen roles. Grayson on bottom, me on top. I'd never asked for anything different and neither had he. But something had finally awoken in Grayson and he wasn't asking for my permission.

He fumbled a little. It can be a little like trying to thread a needle in the dark, but I let him find his way. Before long I could feel his swollen cock head pushing into me. The next seven inches of his cock swiftly followed. Searing pain, intense pleasure. My fingernails clawed down his back.

I grabbed my ankles and arched my back. My hips rose to meet him. I was all his. He could do whatever he wanted to me.

He was tentative at first before acclimating himself to each new sensation. He withdrew and thrusted, picking up momentum, fucking himself into me. I responded with pleas for more.

His eyes were shut tight in concentration, his sweat dripped on me from above. I felt like I was free falling off a cliff. My body, my mind, were not my own. I wanted to quit everything and run off with Gray and never look back. I wanted to grow old and die with him.

"Fuck, Fuck, Fuck me, Grayson! Harder…"

He pounded me relentlessly. I fisted the expensive bedsheets, attempting to anchor myself, to offer him whatever resistance I could. His power overwhelmed me.

My brain was on fire. I felt heat on my chest and realized I'd come without touching myself.

Grayson's eyes had gone blank. I was on the verge of passing out when Grayson's gyrations became more erratic. He was tiring. His climax was nearing.

I braced myself and soon felt the warmth of his cum spreading deep inside me. He growled triumphantly into my ear. I had unleashed a demon. He was a dominant force I'd have to carefully nurture and somehow also contain.

He collapsed onto me, gasping for breath. I wrapped my tingling arms and legs around him, holding him as tightly as I could, bringing him back to me. His weight threatened to suffocate me, but I didn't care.

A knock at the door broke the spell.

"That must be breakfast," he said rather casually, and I reluctantly loosened my grip on him. He grabbed a robe from the closet and headed for the living room, but then turned abruptly, coming back to the bed. He kissed me, his lips lingering as he whispered, "I love you, Max VanDoren. Don't ever forget that," before leaving the room to let the waiter in.

The words hit me like cold steel, sharp, sudden, and unexpected. They landed between my ribs, twisting. It almost felt like a threat. I couldn't shake it. I thought about it for the rest of the day.

We lay naked in the sun on the terrace, the privacy and the view from the penthouse a welcome escape. We ate fresh fruit, made cocktails from the fully stocked bar. Later, we had another round of energetic sex, Grayson taking me from behind, on our knees, on the living room carpet. The rocky start to our vacation seemed far behind as we basked in the warmth, ready to celebrate both Carnival and Grayson's birthday.

Grayson's charm, and his Michelin star, got us a dinner reservation at *La Capitale*, bypassing the months-long waitlist I couldn't crack. He was in his element, quietly critiquing each course, making mental notes about flavors and dishes he wanted to try at *Joshua*. We left the restaurant high, all of our needs satisfied.

We immersed ourselves in the crowd of revelers dancing the samba in the street. We drank cocktails made by passing vendors, sang songs we didn't know the words to at the top of our lungs. Our clothes were plastered to our bodies with sweat, our throats sore from screaming. Block after block, we partied until we were deep in the heart of Rio.

The crowds grew thicker, the music louder, and the street more packed. Then, suddenly, it was nearly impossible to move. The crowd pressed in, a single, tightly packed entity.

Grayson grabbed my hand, pulling me towards him, but the undulating surge of bodies separated us. I saw him only feet away before he was swallowed up by the mass, lost among a sea of dark, curly-haired men. I tried to call his name, but my hoarse voice only croaked. The crowd spun me around, and I lost all sense of direction. Bodies pressed in, making it hard to breathe in the stifling heat.

For the second time that day, I thought I might pass out. But this time, fear gripped me. I couldn't let myself go. I fought my way through the crowd, desperate to find a way out. I saw a street sign being pulled down by the surging crowd. Cars were trampled. Panic flooded me.

A woman in front of me tripped and fell. I stumbled trying to move around her, but others stepped on her, uncaring, as they pressed forward. It turned ugly, riotous. The music cut off. The crowd swelled again. More people went down, disappearing into the darkness. An abandoned float lay tipped over at the edge of the street.

I scrambled, my feet slipping, until I managed to climb onto it. There, I had a moment to think while it was rocked by the crowd. There was a fire escape above me, maybe eight feet up. If I could somehow reach it, I could stay there until the chaos passed. I leapt.

I missed.

I fell into, or rather onto, the crowd. They carried me like a rag doll, pawing at me, ripping my clothes, until they lost interest and tossed me aside. I hit the pavement hard, grabbing whatever I could to push myself up. Both of my shoes were gone. My wallet and phone were nowhere to be found.

The crowd began to thin. I looked up and saw a park ahead, people were flowing into the gate. I peeled off to the side, escaping into an alley. Blood and sweat ran into my eyes. I was lost, but I was safe.

I stumbled further, finally reaching a street where normal traffic passed, oblivious to the deadly chaos just a few blocks away. I flagged down a taxi, a small miracle, considering my condition, and directed the driver to the hotel. I had no money, but I'd figure that out when I got there. My thoughts were on Grayson. Jesus. Not Grayson. He had to be OK.

The Copacabana Palace loomed ahead. The adrenaline I'd been running on drained from my body, replaced by exhaustion, relief, and fear. I fell out of the taxi in front of the hotel, and when I came to, I was on the sofa in our suite, a blanket wrapped around me.

Grayson sat beside me, his eyes shut tight, tears on his cheeks, holding my hand to his murmuring lips.

"Thank God, you're OK," I rasped, my voice barely a whisper.

His eyes flew open, and before I could react, he pounced on me, kissing me frantically.

"Ow, ow, ow," I gasped. Pain jolted through me with each breath.

"Sorry, baby," he murmured. "We think you might've cracked some ribs…"

"We?" I managed.

"Hotel doctor. He tried to examine you a few hours ago…"

"Hours?"

"Shhh…don't talk. You'll be fine. Just banged up a little, a lot. You had me so scared…"

"Me too," I said, my hand reaching for his face. It was the last thing I said before closing my eyes again.

I didn't leave our room for the rest of our stay. Grayson nursed me, took care of my every need, never letting me out of his sight.

Chapter Seven

We returned to New York, our relationship in a new place. I had managed to empower Grayson, but in doing so, I felt like I was losing control. His persona outside the restaurant now reflected who he truly was at *Joshua*: confident, assertive, in control. He wanted to go out more, be seen more. He wanted to own his image, present himself to the world with me, as a couple. And while part of me reveled in it, another part of me recoiled. I could feel it, the inevitable shift was coming, and I was terrified. I'd set everything in motion, and now I wanted it to stop. I wanted Grayson to walk away unscathed. I had no idea how I'd live with myself when the final pieces fell into place.

June was approaching, bringing with it the anniversary of our first date. Diaz and the Captain were getting anxious for the operation to wrap up, but I knew I couldn't rush Grayson, hell, I didn't want to rush him. I wanted to savor these last precious days with him.

Then Paloma showed up at the restaurant, unannounced.

Shannon called me in the office to say someone claiming to be Grayson's sister was at the front, asking to speak with him. She didn't know he had a sister, so she was hesitant to bring him out for what could just be a fan wanting an autograph, or worse. It was New York, after all.

I told her I'd let Grayson know and to make his guest comfortable in a booth near the kitchen. Another domino was about to fall.

As I passed from the office into the kitchen, I saw her. She was sitting alone, ramrod straight, looking as if she'd just stepped out of a salon. I could see the family resemblance, the dark hair and those beautiful eyes. But I could also see the differences immediately. Grayson's easy casualness versus Paloma's crisp perfection.

I stepped into the kitchen to find Grayson huddled with his sous. I waited for a moment until he looked up, and then waved him over.

"Your sister's out front, table seven. She'd like to speak with you."

He hesitated for a moment, then nodded. The old Grayson would have avoided her, probably had Shannon send her away. But this new Grayson, he removed his apron, his eyes became focused and determined. I smiled to myself as he passed by me. Not because of what I'd done, but because of who Grayson had become.

I left the kitchen and headed to the bar, hoping to overhear their conversation. Their voices were too low, but their body language spoke volumes. They didn't greet each other with hugs or even a handshake. Grayson took a seat across from her, while Paloma sat with her hands folded neatly in front of her, her gaze avoiding his. It wasn't a reunion; it felt more like an obligation she was there to fulfill, like she was delivering a message because she'd lost a bet.

Her cool demeanor never cracked. I could tell Grayson was irritated. His finger jabbed at the air as he emphasized whatever it was he was telling her.

And then it was over. Grayson stood up quickly, rushing past me without so much as a glance. He retreated to the kitchen. Paloma gathered her purse and jacket, standing with graceful poise as she smoothed her skirt. She paused for a moment to look around the restaurant, perhaps admiring what her little brother had accomplished, or maybe assessing it for a possible takeover, or arson. It was impossible to tell what was behind those Donato eyes.

She glided past me, her perfume lingering in the air like a cloud. She didn't acknowledge my presence either. In the world she inhabited, I didn't exist. I was fine with that. It worked to my advantage. It allowed me to observe, to see all of the cracks. Like the delicate scar that ran the length of her otherwise flawless cheek, from ear to chin. She'd tried to hide it, covering it with foundation and rouge, but it was there. The one imperfection she couldn't control, possibly the one thing that made her human. I couldn't stop wondering how she'd gotten it even when all that was left of her was the scent of her perfume.

Grayson was late getting home that night. I was asleep on the sofa when I heard the elevator doors open. Without a word, he helped me into our bed. When he kissed me goodnight, I could taste whiskey and cigarettes on his lips. His sister's visit had clearly affected him, but any discussion would have to wait.

He slept restlessly. Every time I tried to hold him, he roughly pushed me off. At one point, I heard him get out of bed and pace through the loft. I wasn't surprised to find him still asleep long past his usual internal alarm.

I got up and threw on a pair of gym shorts and one of his old t-shirts. I started the coffee brewing before heading out to get him a bagel from his favorite deli, hoping it might put him in a talkative mood. When I returned, I found him propped up on one elbow, staring at me. The sheet was pushed down low, barely covering his naked body.

"Come back to bed," he begged.

"I have coffee and your 'Everything but Capers' bagel…and you need to talk to me about what happened yesterday. No more secrets, right?"

I hated forcing him into this corner, but I couldn't let him fall back into his old ways. I'd worked too hard to get us here, and as much as I didn't want this life to end, I knew we had to move forward.

He took a sip of his coffee, then set the mug down on the nightstand beside the untouched bagel. He got up, silently walking to the wardrobe to grab a pair of pajama pants to cover his nakedness before returning to the bed where I sat, patiently waiting.

Another drink of coffee, another jolt of courage. He looked at me, then away, his gaze drifting to the industrial windows that overlooked lower Manhattan.

"Before yesterday, I hadn't seen my sister, Paloma, in five years or so. She lives uptown, but there's been no contact. I used to text her, but she'd barely respond. Leave me on read for days, sometimes weeks. To say we aren't close is an understatement. I told you, none of my family came to the opening of *Joshua*. 'Other commitments,' or whatever excuse they used. It was fine, probably better without them. I learned to think of myself as an only child. It was fine. I was fine. I had *Joshua*. And now I have you. So when she showed up, just like that, I knew there was a reason behind it. And it had nothing to do with me. She doesn't care about me unless she wants something. Spencer's the same. And she was there as his envoy. Plain and simple."

He paused to take a bite of his bagel, clearly gathering himself, trying to navigate a painful past without ripping open old wounds that had, perhaps, finally healed.

"Spencer is…a bully. Always has been. Always will be. Not just to me, but to everyone. He's been angry about something my whole life. He blamed me for Dad divorcing his mother. It was bad, bitter. Spencer and Paloma, they were caught in the middle of it. Dad had gotten my mom pregnant. I didn't know that when I was a kid. But Spencer was ten when they split, and at ten, you think you know everything. You don't. You don't know about the things people hide in their marriages. My mom wasn't the first woman Dad cheated with, and she wasn't the last. My mom learned the hard way about dreams coming true. But none of that mattered to Spencer. From the moment I was born, I was his sworn enemy."

I could see he was starting to get lost in the past, the pain of his childhood rising back up, and I reached for his leg, rubbing it gently to remind him that he was safe. He was with someone who loved him.

"He convinced me that I was the reason my mom..."

"What?!" I blurted out before I could stop myself. I was shocked at how far Spencer Donato could sink, even as a child.

"I was only five. It wasn't hard."

"My God, Gray. That's horrible..."

"I carried it for a long time. Still do, I think."

"But now...Where...?" It had been twenty-five years. Why hadn't his mother taken him with her? I assumed Cesare and his wealth had been part of the reason. But what about now? Where was she? He didn't answer my questions.

"Paloma wasn't much better, but she was afraid of him too. Spencer didn't care who he hurt." His hand moved unconsciously to his cheek, and suddenly I understood. I understood how Paloma had been hurt, or at least by who.

"So why did she come to see you? Why now? What could they possibly want?"

"My father's ninetieth birthday is coming up. They want me to go to the manor to honor it."

"Why? Why would you? You don't have to go there, even if you wanted to..."

"Oh, I'm sure Spencer has other motives. He always does."

"So don't go. Don't put yourself through that."

"That was my first thought, too. But...I keep thinking about Rio. I could've lost you. One second you were in my hand, and then you were just gone. Life changes so fast, Max. I'm not sure I want to leave things unfinished with my family any longer. I've run from them as much as I could. I changed my name to distance myself. But I'm not that scared child anymore. I think I need to go."

I squeezed his hand. "Grayson, I'll support whatever decision you make. You know that."

"Good. Because I'm going to need you by my side. That scared child isn't entirely gone."

It was playing out perfectly. All I needed was an introduction to the reclusive Spencer Donato. The rest would take care of itself.

"Are they going to be OK with a stranger crashing their celebration?"

"They're going to have to be. It's not negotiable."

"Then, of course, I'll be with you...discretely in the background..." I smiled mischievously at him. "...waiting in your childhood bed for you..."

I pulled him toward me, onto me, and wrapped my legs around him. He kissed me, hard, his hand caressing my ass through my shorts.

I held his face in my hands, pulling it away so I could see deep into his eyes. "I love you, Grayson. Don't ever forget that."

"I love you too, Max." And his mouth was on mine again, his tongue pushing in eagerly.

The words were true. But I knew deep down, they wouldn't be enough to keep us together forever. Love was never meant to be permanent. Not in my life. Not for me.

Gray tugged my shorts down. I'd planned on going for a run after breakfast, so all I wore underneath was a jockstrap. In an instant, I was exposed and vulnerable.

His pajama pants vanished, and before I had time to prepare, he was inside me. The pain hit hard, sharp, but I gritted my teeth and endured it. He was desperate, like an animal in heat. He'd never been this rough before, but I understood, this wasn't about me. This was about the familial monsters he was battling inside.

I rode out the frenzy of his movements, waiting for the moment when he came, pulling out of me without a word.

It wasn't about love. It wasn't about pleasure. It was about dominance. Grayson was putting on his warpaint, gearing up for whatever fight lay ahead. This, in some twisted way, was what I had silently asked of him in Rio.

I lay there on the bed, still recovering, watching Gray get ready as if nothing had happened, as if it was just another ordinary morning.

"When is your father's birthday?" I asked, trying to bring normalcy back to the air.

"End of June."

"So's our anniversary," I said quietly.

"Well, we may be celebrating it in Connecticut this year, I'm afraid."

"Oh. Alright." It was fine. I didn't want him to feel bad about it. "We can go away on our own after it's all over," I suggested, though I knew that trip would never come to be.

Grayson left for the restaurant, and I told him I'd meet him there later. As soon as I heard the elevator doors glide shut, I dialed DA Diaz to update her on the developments of the last 24 hours. Operation Falcon had its first major breakthrough in a long time. She was pleased with the progress, but there was an underlying concern in her voice.

"You've been under for a long time, Max. Are you sure you're OK? This would be a tough haul for a seasoned officer…"

"I'm fine. Don't worry about me. I know what I need to do…"

"OK, Max. I trust you. When you check in next, we'll talk about what happens when you meet Cesare and Spencer Donato. Spencer won't be an easy man to get close to, even if you are dating his brother."

"I know, but I'm looking forward to the challenge, Ma'am." The words came out with false bravado. The truth? I was dreading the trip to Connecticut and everything that would follow. I wasn't OK. I hadn't been for a long time.

I got ready for work, but something felt off about the day. It wasn't just Grayson's confession about his family or the rough way he'd fucked me afterwards. It was something else. It was loss. When I looked around the loft, I saw the life Gray and I had woven together. There were pieces of me everywhere. What had started as a ruse had slowly turned into something real. And now, with the truth looming over us, I could feel the clock ticking, counting down to when everything would vanish. When the truth came out, there was no way Grayson would ever look at me the same again, or forgive me. I had fallen in love with a time bomb.

I walked into *Joshua* with the same sense of impending doom. What would happen to everything Grayson had built when the lies were exposed? What would happen when the truth of who he really was became known?

Grayson was in command in the kitchen, as always. The staff moved around him with practiced precision, a well-choreographed dance. I watched him from the doorway. His imposing frame dominated the space, and the energy of the room seemed to shift in his presence. Larger than life. My chest tightened, the weight of everything I'd been carrying these past months pressing down on me. I had to be strong. Everything depended on it.

I loved him. And I had to figure out how to protect him from the fallout, if that were even possible. Even if he never spoke to me again, I needed to try to shield him from the storm coming his way. But so much depended on his father and brother.

Grayson looked up and caught my gaze. A smile broke across his face that nearly shattered me. I gave a small wave, then turned and headed to the office to update the accounts. I needed to think about the position I'd put myself in.

We spent the next few months not talking about the date circled in red on the calendar. It crept closer and closer, like a predator stalking its prey, until one day it was upon us, pouncing seemingly without warning.

Gray called the garage and told them we'd need the car at noon. The drive to Connecticut was only about an hour, but the day passed in slow motion. We loaded our bags into the trunk and drove up the West Side Highway, leaving the city behind. I wanted to scream at Gray to turn around, to forget all of this. We could go to the airport, catch a flight to Paris, or Guam, or anywhere but the Donato estate. But when I looked at Grayson, I saw only determination. So, I took a deep breath, rested my hand on his thigh, and let my head fall against his shoulder.

"No matter what happens, remember how much I love you, Gray." Even if I said it a million times, it would never feel like enough.

He thought I was being supportive, and I was, but I was also saying goodbye. If everything went according to the DA's plan, I wouldn't be coming back to New York, to my life with him. When the weekend was over, so were we.

The fence marking the property line began long before we could even see the house. We drove for what felt like ages before we came to a break in the road where we could turn in. Still, no house was in sight. "Isolated" didn't begin to cover it. This was why Cesare and Spencer were rarely seen. They could live full, secret lives, hidden from the scrutiny of the public eye here.

When we finally reached the house, we pulled in next to a silver Lexus with New York plates.

"Must be Paloma's," Gray muttered under his breath.

We grabbed our bags from the trunk and walked up the front steps, hesitating at the door. Grayson wasn't sure if he should ring the bell at his own house, and I realized this was as unfamiliar to him as it was to me.

The tension broke when the door opened, revealing a liveried butler.

"Mr. Spencer is in the library, sir. He's expecting you."

I slipped my hand into Grayson's, holding on tight as he led me down a darkly carpeted hallway lined with dimly lit art. The atmosphere couldn't have been more different from our bright, open loft on North Moore Street.

When we reached the door, Grayson gave my hand one last squeeze before letting go. He was about to walk into battle alone, and I would be on my own, too. How he interacted with his brother and sister in the next few minutes would determine the course of the weekend. I watched as he turned the knob and pushed open the heavy oak door.

I reminded myself that Captain Harris had back-up not far away, and there was a tracker sewn into my jacket. I refused to wear a wire. Nothing that would be said over the weekend needed recording. Everything was going to be fine. The cops would only get in the way.

Spencer and Paloma sat in matching wingback chairs, a small round table separating them. They looked like royalty holding court.

"Grayson! And you must be Maxwell..." Spencer strode across the room with big, bold steps, hand outstretched to me, arms wide open for his baby brother. It wasn't the reception I'd expected, and I had to remind myself that Spencer Donato was a killer, and we weren't here under the best of circumstances, despite his warm greeting.

Gray stiffly returned the hug, then leaned down to kiss Paloma, who had taken her time walking over. She wasn't interested in me.

"Nice to meet you, officially, Paloma. I saw you briefly at the restaurant when you stopped by..." She'd turned back to her chair before I finished speaking. She didn't acknowledge me, too busy settling into her seat.

"Come, sit. You must be stiff from the drive. Cocktail?" Spencer was playing the host with ease, though I doubted it was a role he often played.

We made small talk, awkward, strained. The fact that they hadn't seen each other in almost a decade was left unspoken. I wondered where Cesare was. I had no idea how his health was, but I assumed he must've been bedridden somewhere in the mansion. No one mentioned him, and it certainly wasn't my place to ask. So I sipped my drink and let the Donatos dance around each other.

"Dinner will be at seven," Spencer announced, standing, signaling the end of our brief encounter. "You'll be staying in the green room, Grayson. Maxwell, your bag is in…"

"He's staying with me, Spencer. I'm not sure why you'd think otherwise."

It was the first real crack in their interaction.

"Of course. I just thought he might like the adjoining room for some extra space. But the green room is plenty spacious, I suppose."

As we walked upstairs, I noticed Grayson's body begin to relax. He had made it through the opening salvo, and we had a couple of hours to prepare for round two.

The green room was beautiful, though surprisingly not green. It clearly hadn't been used in a while. We opened windows to let in fresh air, unpacked, hung up our suits, and then laid down on the bed. Grayson was quiet, too quiet. I propped myself up on an elbow and looked over at him.

"Can I ask where your father is? We are here to see him, after all. Will he be at dinner?"

Shock crossed his face.

"Max, my father's dead. I thought you knew. I thought I'd said…"

I didn't know what to say. Nothing in our research mentioned his death. It had never been announced, in fact, it must've been specifically covered up. The empire would've been vulnerable if it had been known Cesare Donato wasn't running the family anymore. Spencer was formidable, but Cesare had been the man made of iron holding everything together.

"I didn't. When? How?"

"Six years ago, maybe more. He was old, unwell. It wasn't a surprise."

"So why are we here? I'm confused."

"Some sort of memorial service in the family chapel tomorrow. I told you, it's one of Spencer's shows."

"So it's just the four of us? Or does Spencer have a wife and kids tucked away in here to surprise us?"

He chuckled. "Not that I know of, but it's not out of the question. I'm sorry. This must seem like a lot to you. If you want to take the car back..."

"No." I laid down into the crook of his arm and wrapped my arm across his chest. "I'm not going anywhere without you."

I must've dozed off because the next thing I knew, I was lying on the bed alone and heard Grayson in the shower. I got up, stripped off, and slipped in with him, wrapping my arms around his body from behind, my hands resting on his chest, my cock nestling between his ass cheeks.

We stood there silently, pressed together, letting the water pour over us. Both of us were lost in our thoughts. Finally, Gray reached out and turned off the water.

"We shouldn't be late."

We dressed quickly and headed to the dining room. The long walnut table had four settings gathered at one end. Spencer stood at the head, Paloma to his right. Gray and I took our seats to his left. The atmosphere was formal, intimate, and terrifying all at once.

The questions started almost immediately. Where was I from? Did I have family? How did Gray and I meet? Innocent enough, but I knew I was being tested. There was no way Spencer Donato hadn't had someone look into me. I had to hope that DA Diaz and Captain Harris had done airtight work in creating Max VanDoren or I was going to end up as dessert.

Paloma was mostly silent, watching. I almost feared her more than Spencer.

She didn't try to hide the long scar that marred her otherwise flawless face. Maybe she wanted Spencer to be reminded of what he'd done to her. He'd see it every time he looked at her, but he didn't seem bothered by it in the least.

"The service tomorrow is at three," Spencer said. "If you want to go riding in the morning, just let Xavier know. He'll have the horses saddled. Or there's the pool, the sauna, or the gym... Grayson knows his way around. You remember, don't you, Grayson?"

"We'll manage," Grayson replied curtly.

With that, we said our goodnights and separated, going off in our own directions.

We undressed and climbed into the king-size bed from opposite sides, meeting in the middle. The sheets were so crisp, I was afraid we might break them if we moved too much. Sex didn't seem like an option, so we just wrapped ourselves around each other and fell asleep.

I woke in the morning on the far side of the bed. The rest of the expanse beside me was empty. I listened for sounds from the bathroom, but all was quiet. I got up and looked out the window, hoping to see Gray out riding or maybe burning his brother in effigy. But all I saw was land, endless land.

I dressed and set out, hoping to find either breakfast or my boyfriend, or, ideally, both.

The dining room was empty. How naïve of me to assume breakfast would be served in the same room as dinner. My Oklahoma roots were showing, bursting through painfully, as always. Of course, there was a breakfast room. Somewhere.

I wandered, opening doors to rooms that clearly hadn't been used in years. Stuffy air and dust motes swirled through several. Then I came upon what was unmistakably Spencer's office. Dumb luck, but I'd take it.

I quickly stepped inside and scanned the room, making mental notes of the layout, the furnishings, any cameras, and possible exits. I didn't want to linger. If anyone saw me enter, they needed to see me exit quickly if my cover story of "looking for breakfast" was going to hold.

I peeked into the hallway, exited, pulling the door shut behind me, and walked quickly down the corridor. After a few turns, I began to hear voices and smell coffee. I entered the room unannounced, and the scene around the table was almost jovial, a stark contrast to the tension of last night's dinner. Paloma looked relaxed. Spencer was at the stove, making eggs. Grayson was smiling. I felt like I'd stepped into the Twilight Zone.

"Hey, Sleepyhead," Spencer called out. "We were about to send Xavier up to wake you."

I checked the clock on the wall. "It's not even seven-thirty. And I've been wandering around lost for about an hour, it seems."

"Grayson should've drawn you a map," Paloma said, the friendliest thing she'd said to me yet.

"Babe, there's coffee and juice on the sideboard. I think Spence will have eggs and bacon up shortly...or never. It's fifty-fifty at this point. He seems to have forgotten that his little brother is a master chef."

Who was this man? What had they done with the Grayson I'd arrived with?

I poured twice as much coffee as I usually drink and settled in, preparing myself for the show that was unfolding.

"Max, Grayson says today's your anniversary. I'm sorry you have to spend it here with us."

"Don't be. We'll celebrate it in a few days," I replied warily.

"That's what I told him, babe. Father's memorial is important too."

I agreed, just as the food arrived at the table, focusing on that instead of trying to make sense of what had caused the shift in everyone's behavior.

"So, I thought Max and I might take the four-runner out to the lake for a picnic before the memorial."

"There's a lake out there?"

"A small one," Spencer said, though I had a feeling his definition of "small" and mine were miles apart.

I was right. It took us a half hour to reach the lake on the four-runner, driving across Spencer's vast property, what I was sure he called his 'yard', and through a patch of woods that seemed to appear out of nowhere.

"This was my favorite spot to escape to," Grayson told me, and I could see why. The water was calm and clear, and there was nothing for miles around to disturb the peace. I could imagine Grayson spending a lot of time out here when things at the house got rough.

"I'm trying to picture young Grayson…"

"Awkward, gawky, shy, angry…"

I ran my hand through his hair and pulled him toward me for a kiss. "I'm sorry," was all I could think of to say. I meant it for everything: for what had already happened to him and for what was about to unfold.

Grayson had packed a picnic hamper, and we spread out the blanket not far from the lakeshore. The early-summer sun was warm, so I pulled off my shirt to let it soak into my skin.

"Let's go swimming," Grayson said, already up and stripping off his clothes before I could even think about it.

The sight of him, nude and wading slowly into the lake, disappearing inch by inch, made my heart pound. *Don't leave me*, I silently begged. *Don't go.*

I tossed my shorts and boxers onto the grass and hurried to join him. But as I splashed into the water, Grayson was already swimming further out, pulling away from me.

The cold water shocked me. My feet sank into the silt. I dove in, hoping to freeze time. When I came up, I saw Grayson had paused, watching me. I swam toward him, eager to close the distance between us.

I caught up to him, and he grabbed me by my slippery waist, pulling me into him. Our bodies slid against each other, our legs kicking and tangling. My hands found his shoulders, and I braced myself against him. We flailed, spun, kissed, and splashed, laughing like we were kids with no cares in the world.

Eventually, we worked our way back to the shore, emerging from the water like two sea gods born anew. I raced him to the blanket, and we tumbled onto each other, a tangle of limbs and laughter.

"I love you, Max."

I couldn't answer him, not with words, because his mouth was on mine, his tongue twisting with mine. But he knew. He had to.

He rolled beneath me, parting his legs so I could settle between them, laying my head onto his wet chest. I could feel his heartbeat, matching the rhythm of my own.

My cock was uncomfortably hard, begging to release itself. Grayson reached over his head into the picnic hamper, doing the best he could to blindly find what he was looking for, finally producing the bottle of lube he'd so thoughtfully brought along.

"I need you, Max," he groaned, slicking my cock and his desperate, wanting hole.

I hovered over him, pressing into him, feeling the warmth and tightness between us. Water dripped from my hair, tears from my eyes. My love. My love. Long, insistent strokes. Grayson's hands gripped my ass, pulling me closer, silently begging for more.

He was so beautiful, lying there, open to me, just as he had been a year ago when I first showed up at his loft, now our home. He trusted me. And I, in return, had been nothing but deceitful.

I quickened my pace, pounding harder and harder, trying to turn back time, wishing I could find a way to make things right.

I came in a burst of ecstasy and resignation. The die had been cast and I knew it.

I watched as Gray shot his load onto his chest, completely lost in the moment. He called my name like it was his own.

I collapsed beside him, both of us breathing heavily, perfectly spent.

"This wasn't exactly how I had planned this," he said, sitting up and digging into the hamper again. "But now seems like the perfect time."

He pulled out a small box, and my heart dropped, heavy in my chest.

He opened it slowly, revealing two silver rings nestled together on blue velvet. Side by side, they sat there, waiting for us.

He stared into me. "Max. You mean everything to me. This past year has been the most special of my life. You've loved me and changed me in the best possible ways. I almost lost you in Rio, and I can't imagine what that would've meant. I want to spend the rest of my life loving, and being loved by, only you." He paused, and I could see the tears pooling in his eyes. "Max," he choked, "will you marry me?"

All I could do was stare back at him. I knew the words I had to say, but I also knew the cost of saying them.

I sat up, cupping his face in my hands, hoping my tears would be mistaken for joy and not what they truly were.

"Yes, Grayson," I choked out. "Yes, I will marry you."

His hands shook as he placed one ring on my finger, the other on his own. He kissed me, and then, with a smile, produced a bottle of champagne from the picnic hamper.

"You were pretty confident, weren't you?" I teased, trying to lighten the air.

"I don't think I've ever been so sure about something in my life. I believe in you, in us."

We drank straight from the bottle, champagne running down our chins, onto our bodies, and we licked it off of each other. He fed me strawberries, and I sucked his cock, until it was time to get dressed and pack everything away. We had to return to the rollercoaster before it plummeted into uncertain depths again.

We rode back to the house, my arms wrapped around Grayson from behind. I tried to imagine abandoning Operation Falcon, quitting the force, and becoming Max VanDoren for the rest of my life. Diaz would have to find another way into the Donatos. Grayson was off-limits. He was mine.

We showered and dressed for the memorial, walking with Spencer and Paloma to the chapel, more of a large family mausoleum. Stepping into the cold, marble building, I was over-whelmed by a sudden wave of dread. Was Grayson expecting us to be lying here one day, spending eternity with the rest of the Donatos? There was certainly room for all of us. My throat went dry.

And then I saw her. Marie Therese. Grayson's mother.

She left, he'd said, not 'she'd died'. Or was she gone? He couldn't bring himself to say the words, but I'd always assumed abandonment, not death. The date on the tombstone was Grayson's fifth birthday. *Jesus.* Spencer had convinced a child that he was responsible for his own mother's *death.* I could've killed him right there, left him to rot with the rest of his fucking family. Monsters, all of them.

I glanced at Grayson, who was avoiding his mother's grave. I squeezed his hand, and he squeezed mine back.

The memorial for Cesare Donato was, as Grayson had predicted, nothing more than an act on Spencer's part. He spoke for a few minutes, and then we were filing out of the crypt, heading back to the house for whatever 'light fare' Xavier had prepared for us. The service wasn't the reason we were there. My senses were on high alert now.

Spencer opened a bottle of wine and filled glasses for everyone, though I noticed Paloma set hers aside. Whatever was about to happen, she wanted to keep a clear head.

Spencer stalked around the dining room, never staying in one place long, keeping us all off-balance as we tried to follow his move-ments. A second bottle of wine was opened, then a third. Finally, Spencer turned to Grayson.

"Let's take a walk to my office. There's a matter to discuss." The moment of truth.

Grayson stood tall, his gaze steady. "Whatever you have to say, you can say in front of Max. You should know, I asked him to marry me today."

Spencer's face twisted like he'd swallowed something sour. Something was going wrong for him, and I could see it in his eyes.

"That's…" he started, pausing to find the right words.

Paloma picked up where he left off. "…lovely, Grayson. But there are certain business matters to handle before that can happen." She spoke with a calm authority, taking control of the situation. "Or have you forgotten?"

It was clear from Grayson's face that he had no idea what she was talking about, or maybe the wine was taking its toll on him.

"Little brother, it's simple," Spencer said. "When you turned thirty, your trust opened. You now own one-third of Donato Enterprises outright. No more trustees, no more advisors when you need money. But since you've chosen to have nothing to do with the family business, Paloma and I are prepared to buy your shares."

There it was. It always came down to money with these people. Always.

Grayson's face twisted in fury as he turned on Spencer.

"You son of a bitch. All that talk this morning about being a family, about burying the past, this is what you were leading up to?"

He pointed at Paloma. "And I should've known you were only here for one reason. You used our dead father as bait. You paraded me past my mother. Fuck both of you."

He stumbled as he stood, needing to grab the table to steady himself.

"Let's go, Max. We're leaving."

I knew we wouldn't be leaving the estate. The wine was definitely part of Spencer's plan. But we headed upstairs to our room, and Grayson slammed the door shut hard when we got there.

"I'm so stupid. I should've known, I did know, but I looked past the red flags…Jesus, Max. FUCK!!"

It took an hour to calm him down, to convince him to sleep and that we'd go back to the city in the morning. Neither of us were in any condition to drive at that moment. He took a long shower and eventually came to bed.

"I'm sorry, Max."

"Don't apologize," I said, my voice firm. "You have nothing to apologize for. They're the assholes. You may not want to be a part of the business, but it is your birthright. Your father wanted you to have a part of it."

He nodded, his voice quieter now. "Today, when we were alone, everything was perfect. We were so happy, and then my family had to do what my family always does."

I looked down at the ring on my finger. It did look perfect there.

"I will never equate the two events in my mind," I told him. "After tomorrow, they won't exist in our lives anymore."

I kissed him, long and deep, while he closed his eyes. The wine, the hot shower, and the adrenaline that had been coursing through him finally took their toll, and he slipped into a deep, troubled sleep.

I, on the other hand, began pacing the floor. I still had a job to do. And we weren't leaving until I'd completed it.

The clock in the hallway struck midnight, then one, then two. I took a deep breath and turned the doorknob, glancing back over my shoulder at Grayson, still lying unmoved, lightly snoring.

"I love you, Grayson. I honestly do," I whispered, my voice thick with the weight of it, "but Spencer is a bad man, and I have a job to do."

I moved quietly, retracing my steps from earlier, until I reached Spencer's office. I had to collect whatever intel I could on the Donatos. After tonight, Operation Falcon would be over, at least for me. There'd be no coming back.

I closed the door behind me and crept toward his desk, switching on the flashlight on my phone. It wasn't much, but it would be enough to illuminate the surface without alerting anyone to my presence.

Drawer after drawer, I searched. No one but Spencer was ever in the house, so nothing was locked. I sifted through the folders, focusing on anything related to the shipyard, taking pictures, as Diaz had instructed.

I was scanning a file marked "Grayson's Trust" when I heard the door open. Fuck. Caught.

The lights flicked on.

Spencer and Paloma stood in the doorway.

"I knew we'd catch our little mouse," Paloma said, suddenly emboldened, taking charge. "Max, VanDoren? Is it?"

I stayed silent, weighing my options. There might still be a way out, one way or another.

Spencer chuckled darkly. "It's not Maxwell VanDoren, that much we know, don't we, Paloma? Good forgery, but not great. Who are you really? Another gold digger after the Donato money?" His eyes flicked to the trust file on the desk, and the conclusion was clear in his mind. "Does my brother know?"

He started moving toward me, but I stepped around the desk, putting it between us. Now I was trapped between him and Paloma. I trusted Paloma less than I trusted Spencer at that moment, but neither of them was good news.

Spencer reached into the credenza behind him and pulled out a gun. He pointed it at me.

"Robbery? Does that give us motive to shoot him, Paloma?"

"I'd risk it," she said, almost with a smile.

I finally spoke. "You kill your brother's fiancé and think you'll get away with it just because you found me in your office? You're dumber than I thought." I leaned in, my voice low, "Both of you."

"Shoot him, Spencer."

"You know she's gonna let you take the rap, don't you, Spence?" I said, trying to provoke him. "She's not going to get her hands dirty..."

"Shut up. We're actually doing Grayson a favor. He'll see it eventually. And who said anything about getting the cops involved…"

"Shoot him now, Spencer…"

He started to move around the desk, clearing his view of me. I could see it in his eyes. He had killed before. He didn't need Paloma's encouragement to pull the trigger.

It was Grayson's gasp that saved me. That split-second distraction gave me the opening I needed. I lunged for the gun, wrestling with Spencer for control. I focused on him, but out of the corner of my eye I saw Paloma and Grayson moving through the room. Only one of them was coming to help me.

The gun went off. Once, then a second time. I heard crashing behind me. The recoil shot up Spencer's arm, giving me a brief moment of control. I bent his arm back into him, and, in that instant, I fired twice more. The bullets flew upwards, through his gut, into his chest. He was dead before he hit the carpet.

The smoking gun was in my hand. I looked over at Paloma, too late. She was already lying in a pool of her own blood. The hole in her chest was too large, her vacant eyes staring up at the ceiling. My mission was accomplished.

Grayson stood frozen above his sister, his face twisted in shock at what he'd just witnessed.

My legs buckled, and I collapsed onto the floor, the pain from the bullet in my own stomach hitting me like a freight train. I reached down, feeling the blood pumping through my fingers with each of my pounding heartbeats, spreading across my body, staining the new ring I had only been wearing for a few hours.

I knew I only had moments before I lost consciousness. I grabbed the phone cord beside me and yanked it toward me, thankful that Spencer still had a landline. The phone hit the floor with a crash, but I managed to dial 911 with my blood-slicked fingers.

"I need an ambulance. The Donato estate. And the police. Officer down."

The phone slipped from my bloody hand as I fell back onto the rug.

The room spun, but I could still hear the sharp intake of Grayson's breath, the way it caught in his chest as he looked at the scene in front of him. His eyes, those eyes that had trusted me, the ones that had finally seen me for who I truly was, locked onto me, wide with disbelief. The love I had seen in them just hours before, that warmth, was now gone, replaced by something else. Something cold. I couldn't place it. Hurt, confusion, rage.

"Max..." he whispered, but it came out strangled, like he couldn't say my name without it tearing him apart.

I tried to speak, to apologize, but the words wouldn't come. The weight of what I'd done pressed against my chest, and the blood from the bullet wound made it hard to breathe. My vision blurred. But I couldn't look away from him. I had to see him, even if it was the last thing I ever did.

He stepped closer, his hands trembling as they reached for me, but he stopped short. The distance between us felt like miles. The love in his eyes flickered like a candle in the wind, threatening to go out, but it was still there. He wanted to understand, but there was no time to explain. No time for the truth to sink in.

"Why?" His voice broke on the word. "Why, Max? Why did you, why did you do this?"

The pain in his voice shattered something inside of me. But I couldn't give him the answers he needed. I couldn't fix what was broken.

"...no choice," I whispered, my voice barely audible, my words slurred with blood and exhaustion.

Grayson's chest heaved with silent breaths, his gaze flicking from me to the bodies on the floor, to the gun by my hand. I saw the storm in him, the conflict, the anger, the betrayal, and then I saw the heartbreak, the kind that could break a man's soul.

His hands curled into fists, and for a moment, I thought he might lash out, but he didn't. Instead, he staggered back, as if the very air between us had become too much to bear.

"Max...I..." He choked on his words, looking at the mess in front of him, at the family he had tried to protect me from, and then at me, the man he loved. "I thought you...I thought you were better than them..."

His voice cracked again, and I felt the last shred of the connection we had begin to slip away, unraveling before my eyes.

"I...I don't know who you are anymore," he whispered, his voice hoarse with pain, more than just the physical kind.

It felt like a slap, but worse. I could feel it deep in my bones. The weight of his words dropped down on me harder than anything I'd ever felt. The man I had loved, the man I'd wanted to protect, was pulling away, and there was nothing I could do to stop it.

I could see him, standing there, frozen in disbelief, the weight of what he had just witnessed crashing down on him. He was lost. I saw the man he was, a protector, a fighter, reduced to something smaller, broken. His love for me, the thing that had kept us together, seemed to drain from him with every passing second.

I wanted to reach out, to hold him, to tell him it wasn't what it seemed. That I'd done it all for him, for us. But my vision was fading. The edges of the room were growing dark, and the pounding in my chest grew fainter, slower. I tried to say something, anything to make him understand, but nothing came out. The words were trapped in the growing void between us.

He didn't speak again, but his eyes, his eyes haunted me. And then, as the world blurred and I slipped into darkness, I saw him take one last look at me, at the blood and the chaos, and then turn away. I wanted to call out to him, to make him stay, but I couldn't. Not anymore.

The last thing I heard were sirens approaching. The last thing I felt was the cold seeping into my skin. And the last thing I saw was Grayson, the love of my life, walking away.

The Sins of the Past

(ALMOST ONE YEAR LATER)

Chapter Eight

RYDER

"How is he today?"

I grabbed the chart from the basket by the door of Room 1207 and skimmed through the overnight notes while the charge nurse added her commentary.

"So, no change, right?" I asked.

"Correct, Dr. Delaney."

I knocked lightly on the door before stepping in. It was pointless to wait for a response. He hadn't spoken since being admitted a few weeks ago.

"Good morning." I tried to sound upbeat, even though his case troubled me deeply. "I hope you slept well." I touched his leg through the sheet. Physical contact was a technique they taught us in med school to build a physician-patient bond. But given that he was restrained, his wrists and ankles tied to the bed frame to prevent him from harming himself, I knew it likely had the opposite effect.

I kept speaking, even though I wasn't expecting a response. His gaze was glassy and unfocused, fixed on some distant point. A pearl of saliva had formed at the corner of his mouth, so I quickly grabbed a tissue and wiped it away.

I adjusted the blinds to let more light into the room, hoping it might trigger some reaction, a murmur, a grimace, anything. His pupils dilated, indicating brain function, but that was all.

I checked his chart again. His medications had already been reduced to their minimum dosages. We weren't the cause of his continued stupor. If he wanted to speak to us, it seemed he could. There was no sign of brain injury from his actions. He just didn't want to, or wasn't ready to. It would take time. That was my professional opinion, but only because I'd exhausted all other options.

I had spoken to his sister. She couldn't explain why he'd tried to end his life. She said he'd struggled with depression for years, but not to the point of harming himself, at least not that she knew of. His meds had been working, and he'd recently started a new job. He had a home in Oklahoma. Responsibilities he appeared to handle just fine. She mentioned some family estrangement, so she couldn't say for sure how he'd been, only what he'd told her.

I checked the bandages on his wrists. No blood. Nothing had seeped through in days, so the wounds would be cleaned and redressed later this afternoon.

"I wish you would talk to me," I said softly. "I want to help you, but you need to let me in."

I brushed his hair back from his forehead. I was only a few years older than him, but I couldn't understand the pain that might have driven him to this point, to want to end it all in such a permanent way. I only knew what I'd been taught.

Footsteps behind me made me turn, but I knew who it was without looking.

"Good morning, Clara."

"How is he, Dr. Delaney? How's my brother today?"

"He's the same as when you left yesterday, unfortunately."

She stepped closer, standing by his side.

Clara Heath was young, fresh out of high school, and somehow left to deal with her brother's struggles on her own. I knew she had other brothers, but their father was deceased, and their mother was absent. Clara lived with an aunt and uncle here in Austin. They were the ones who'd had him transferred here, the ones who'd brought me onto the case before disappearing and leaving Clara to handle everything on her own.

"I thought he could hear me yesterday," she said, her voice barely above a whisper. "Well, I'm sure he could hear me. I just thought maybe he'd respond. Probably wishful thinking. Maybe today…" She took his hand, stroking the back of it with her thumb.

"I hope so, Clara. All of his vital signs are strong. He's responding to stimuli. His reflexes are good. He's just not ready to communicate yet. He's shut inside himself, and we just have to wait until he's ready to let us in."

"I'm not giving up on him," she said firmly.

"I know. But this is a lot for you, for anyone. Have you reached out to the rest of your family? Maybe they can help."

"Jasper's in the Army, overseas. He can't get away. My other brother is even harder to reach. But I'm trying. I've left messages…"

"Well, if there's anything I can do to help, please don't hesitate to let me know. I've got to finish my rounds, but you have my number. Or just ring the button for a nurse if anything changes. I'll check in on you again soon."

"Thanks, Dr. Delaney."

"Please, call me Ryder." I gave her shoulder a brief squeeze as I turned to leave. He wasn't the only one I needed to forge a bond with.

I walked away from the room, wondering what I was missing in his case. I'd spent nights researching similar cases, only to find there was nothing exactly like his. Physically, Clara's brother could get out of bed, could hold a conversation with us, if only he wanted to. But something, some reason, some trauma, was keeping him from engaging with the world. I couldn't figure it out, and it was driving me mad. It was as if he realized he couldn't physically end his life, so he'd decided to emotionally end it instead.

My phone buzzed in my pocket. Another text. Sean. Again. That was twice already this morning. I wanted to talk to him, but this wasn't the time or place, and he knew that.

It had become par for the course since he took this assignment in Paris. It was hard to find the right time or place for more than a few words. My good mornings were his afternoon meetings, his good nights were my evening rounds.

We'd committed to making it work. It was just for a year. But it was harder than I thought it would be. I missed him. I missed rolling over in bed and feeling his warm body next to mine. I missed how he became so invested in those stupid reality shows I couldn't care less about. I missed coming home late from the hospital and knowing he'd be there, waiting for me. I even missed the way his dirty clothes dotted the floor around the hamper, close enough for him, but never quite in it.

But now, missing him had become a distraction I couldn't afford.

I quickly typed back.

SEAN

Is now a good time?

With a patient 🩶

I waited, but no reply came. Which was OK. It had to be OK.

I checked in with my other patients and prepared for the group therapy session I led three times a week. But Room 1207 was never far from my mind.

I passed by his door several times, even when it meant going out of my way, just to see if there were any signs of…anything. But time after time, it was just Clara Heath sitting in the same chair next to the bed, holding his hand, speaking softly to him with that expectant, hopeful look on her face. It was as sad as the Pietà I'd seen at St. Peter's Basilica on our trip to Italy. Grief for the living, I thought, could be just as emotionally draining as grief for the dead.

Before I left for the evening, I stopped to speak with her one last time. She couldn't keep going like this indefinitely. I was starting to worry about her too. She looked much older than eighteen.

"Good news, Dr. Del...Ryder." She blushed slightly, saying my first name. "I got hold of my other brother. He'll try to be here in a few days. I'm not sure what he can do to help, but maybe hearing his voice..." Her voice trailed off, knowing she was grasping at straws for her brother's recovery.

"That's good news, Clara. You need the support. And you never know what might trigger him to come out of this."

It may have been a trick of my tired eyes, but for a fraction of a second, I could've sworn I saw him tense up. It had to be my imagination...

"You should go home, Clara. There's nothing more you can do for him today."

"Soon. I promise."

"I'll see you tomorrow, I'm sure." I left the hospital for the night.

I took the long way home, something I'd been doing more and more lately. Our empty house was the last place I wanted to be these days, but it was the only place I had to go.

It was just too damn quiet without Sean there, and it made me angry. The silence made me feel ugly and abandoned.

My life had once been quietly peaceful, before Sean Cunningham came into it. I had my work, my residency at the hospital, a long-gestating research project, and it had been enough. But then Katelyn had to go and be all big-sisterly and insist I meet the new analyst who had recently transferred to her office from Seattle. She thought he'd be perfect for me.

"And why is that, Katie? Because we're both single and gay? He is single, right? We've been down that road before..."

"In my defense, Greg was either separated from his partner or about to be…I think it was a timing issue between the two of you…"

"Sure. Right. And Seattle Sean is…what?"

"A really nice guy who would get you out of the house, away from work, and having some fun again."

"I do all of those things now, just fine."

"Really? When was the last time you just went out to a nice restaurant for dinner?"

"We went to…"

"NOT WITH ME! You're proving my point. Just let me set the two of you up. If it doesn't work out, well, we'll cross that bridge when it's built…but if it does, I get naming rights for your first child."

"First dog. I'm not raising a daughter named Dana Scully Delaney-whatever Seattle Sean's last name is."

My sister took her job at the Bureau very seriously. She'd wanted to be an agent since she first watched *The X-Files* as an impressionable teen. I didn't know much about her work, for obvious reasons, but I knew it ran through her veins and made her the most trustworthy person in my life. I also knew she only had my best interests at heart.

"It's Cunningham. And fair point."

I agreed to one date, and I still hate the fact that she was right. He was kind of perfect. And he upended my life before I even knew what hit me.

Katie gave him my number, and we exchanged voicemails for several days. Even then, our schedules were at odds. When we finally connected, we couldn't find an open evening for a couple of weeks. His work took him out of town often, and I ran evening clinics for patients who couldn't make daytime appointments. It seemed doomed before it even began.

But the dinner went amazingly well. Maybe I was too tired from my long week to put up my usual defenses, or maybe he was just so damn charming I hadn't even thought to build them up. Either way, we overstayed our welcome at the restaurant. The maitre d' stopped by several times to offer us complimentary drinks at the bar, but we never budged. Neither of us wanted to break whatever spell had been cast upon us.

We bonded over our love for classic films. *The Thin Man* had sparked his appetite to become a detective, while William Powell had sparked his love for dashing men with biting wit and a flair for mixing the perfect cocktail. And even though I was more of a Bette Davis/Joan Crawford devotee, he didn't hold that against me.

It didn't matter the topic, he got me, or rather, we got each other.

We both had older sisters, parents who were still married, and because they were still wildly in love with each other, not just too complacent to get divorced. We preferred red wine, especially if it was paired with Northern Italian food, dogs (the bigger, the better), wildflowers picked by the side of a lake, Black Watch plaid (his Scotch/Irish ancestry drew him to it; I just liked how it brought out the green in my eyes), Caribbean beaches (the whiter and more private, the better), all of the Brontë sisters (even Anne), and Joni Mitchell (he loved *Court and Spark*, my favorite was *Ladies of the Canyon* and we debated their merits for hours). It just went on and on. I struggled to find his flaws, but he was either an expert at hiding them, or they didn't exist. Or they were just normal flaws, like other normal people had.

The restaurant closed, and we finally had to disengage, but neither of us wanted to call an end to the date. We walked through downtown until we reached the Capitol, lit up brighter than noontime Austin. He took my hand, and we circled the perimeter until we were standing on the steps, where he leaned in and kissed me, bathed in the spotlights for the world to see.

I'm sure the fireworks were only in my head, but they were brilliant and explosive. My hands were sweating, my knees were weak.

Sean Cunningham. His name echoed in my head, settling there like it belonged.

"Would you like to come back to my place?" he whispered in my ear, conspiratorially, as if suddenly the whole world was eavesdropping on us.

"I…I can't."

I couldn't believe I'd said it. I did want to go back to his place. I did want to sleep with him. I wanted to wake up with him, didn't want to leave him. But in the dark recesses of my mind, I remembered what had happened with Greg. I'd rushed in too fast, lost perspective, ignored the warning signs, and got horribly hurt in the end. Even Katie didn't know the extent of his betrayal. I'd vowed to go slow the next time, if I ever found myself in a similar situation.

But I couldn't explain that to Sean. The cardinal rule of first dates is never to talk about past relationships, and we hadn't. Now wasn't the time to bring up Greg.

Much later, he told me he could see the reason behind my refusal on the Capitol steps in my eyes. He knew that the next time he asked, he'd get a different answer. He knew I was worth the wait, that the first time we slept together should be when we were both safe and secure with each other. And if I wasn't there yet, I would be soon enough. He allowed me my dignity and didn't press.

He really was perfect.

We continued our walk through downtown, through the historic district to the river, hand in hand. We were miles from our cars, so we took an Uber back to the now darkened restaurant and finally parted ways. We marked our next date on our calendars. From then on, at least for a while, our lives would have to revolve around this new priority.

That was more than two years ago, and things had progressed quickly between us. That first week was filled with flirty texts and a countdown to our next date, which went just as well, if not better, than the first. We talked more about our families and our childhoods, danced around our past relationships. We were both looking for someone to settle down with, build a life with, but we never said out loud that we each thought we'd found that person.

When he hinted at continuing the date at his apartment, I eagerly agreed, sparing him the embarrassment of another refusal and saving myself from the tarnished reputation of being a frigid nun. I was far from that.

As soon as the door to his apartment shut behind us, he let me prove that to him.

I felt even more connected to him after that first night, but that didn't mean our schedules magically opened up so we could see each other more often. Criminals and medicine didn't seem to keep to any sort of normal work hours. It was frustrating.

When his short-term lease came up for renewal, it just made sense for him to move in with me. At least then, the odds of seeing him every day, even if he was still sleeping when I went to work for morning rounds, greatly increased. Unless he was out of town on assignment.

It wasn't perfect, but it was all we had, and we learned to make the most of the time we had together.

Then he was offered the Paris assignment, assisting Interpol on something I wasn't allowed to know anything about. It was a long-term opportunity for him, one that could advance his career in ways staying in Austin never could.

I kept my reservations to myself, mostly because he'd accepted the role before he even told me about it. It hurt, and that hurt lingered, cropping up every time I thought about him being seven time zones away.

What was I to him? I knew he loved me, but everything pointed to him loving his career more. Looking back to that first week of playing phone tag with him, trying and failing to meet up for our first date, those were the signs I had willingly ignored. Without saying the words, he was telling me where I would always fall in the pecking order of important things in his life. Austin would never be enough. I might never be enough.

I knew I couldn't just pick up my career and move to another country with him, temporary or not. My medical license wouldn't transfer, and I'd either have to start my residency all over again or find something else to occupy my time wherever we were. As much as Sean had dreams about how his career should progress, so did I, and starting over at twenty-seven wasn't part of those plans. I knew love and sacrifice often went hand in hand, but compromise had yet to make an appearance.

I robotically cleaned up the kitchen, loaded the dinner dishes into the dishwasher, took out the garbage. I sat in front of the television for twenty minutes before I realized I had no idea what I was watching. I shut it off and went to bed. I set the alarm for one AM and reached under Sean's pillow for the t-shirt I knew was balled up there. I brought it to my nose. It was faint, but I could still smell him on it. I wasn't sure what I'd do when he was completely gone. Most nights, his essence was the only way I could calm my brain enough to fall asleep.

When the alarm went off, I was disoriented. I started to get up, thinking through my day ahead, until I flipped on the bathroom light, saw the time on the clock, and remembered it was still the middle of the night, and why I was suddenly awake. I stumbled back to bed, grabbed the tablet from its charger on Sean's nightstand, and initiated the FaceTime call.

We hadn't planned to connect that morning, so catching him at a café with a coworker, or a friend, or whoever the hell Pierre was, and him being unable to talk? That was on me. But the fact that he wouldn't excuse himself for two minutes to tell me he missed me, that he wished he were lying in bed next to me, that he wanted to fuck me until we were both exhausted? Well, that was on him, and it didn't sit well.

He promised to call me later, that they had to run. I could hear Pierre in the background urging Sean to hurry up, more by his tone than by actually understanding his words. The screen went dark, and so did my mood. I dropped the tablet off the side of the bed onto the rug, balled his goddamn t-shirt into a wad, and threw it across the room. I pounded his pillow with my fist.

I was just fucking miserable without Sean.

I watched the clock crawl toward dawn before I finally gave up on sleep. I made coffee and took a long, hot shower, but when I looked at myself in the mirror before walking out the door, I looked hollow, and I felt the same way.

I had a twenty-minute drive to put my own problems behind me and realign my focus onto my patients. They didn't care about Sean, and by the time I got to the hospital, neither did I.

The day was chaotic enough to make it feel like it passed in a flash. I checked on Clara and her brother several times, but nothing had changed except Clara's outlook. She seemed to be mirroring my own internal darkness. Overnight, it had all become too much for her to handle alone. She'd once mentioned starting at UT in the fall. She should be spending the summer preparing for that, partying with her friends before everyone went their separate ways, not spending day after day in the behavioral health unit of the university hospital. I was failing her. I felt like I was failing everyone.

So, when I left the hospital for the night, I didn't go home. I went to Wrangler's.

I hoped maybe I'd run into a friend, someone I could have a drink with without seeming needy or obviously avoiding going home for some reason. But it was Thursday, so it was just me and about a dozen strangers keeping Donny, the bartender, company. I took a seat at the far end of the bar and ordered a double whiskey on the rocks. One would take the edge off and hopefully loosen the knot that had been growing between my shoulder blades all afternoon, the one Sean was usually so good at kneading out. Half a drink in, and the knot seemed to be growing worse, not better.

"My momma used to say that if you sat hunched over like that, you'd grow a hump like a camel."

He startled me, pulling me back from the brink of another round of 'Poor, Pitiful Me' that had been playing on a loop in my head.

"It's just been a long day," I said, not really wanting to engage with a stranger or explain why my day had felt so damn long.

"I get it. Same," he said, finishing the beer he'd walked up to the bar with and signaling Donny for another. "Let me buy you another," he said, and before I could stop him, he motioned to Donny for another whiskey, too.

"Thanks, you didn't have to…"

"I know. Just doing my good deed for the day."

I glanced at my watch. "You certainly waited long enough to get that done."

"Just waiting for the right opportunity, I guess."

I lifted my glass to thank him again, hoping he'd get the message that I wasn't looking for anything more than a drink and as much peace and quiet as a person could get sitting five feet from a pool table and ten feet from a juke box. I still had a pity party to attend.

"Do you come here a lot?" he asked.

Were we really going to play this game?

"Nope."

"Wanna play winners?" he said, gesturing toward the pool table.

"Not really, no." He was handsome, so I figured these lines probably worked well for him, but suddenly I was becoming a challenge he hadn't expected.

He leaned in closer. "Then why don't we just go back to your place and fuck…"

I choked on my whiskey, coughing uncontrollably. He rubbed my back, grazing past the painful knot just hard enough to make me let out a little moan.

"You're so tight..." he said, pressing harder. I wanted to tell him to stop, but a free massage is a free massage. Soon he stood up, putting both hands on my back, and I began to melt like a stick of butter.

"Now imagine we were naked in your bed, doing this..."

"I'm not..." but I couldn't finish. His thumbs dug in deep, and I lost my breath. He was breaking down my defenses, and I didn't want that. I was mad at Sean, or probably just mad at myself, and I knew that would pass. I wasn't going to cheat on him just because I'd had a bad day.

I pushed my drink away and tried to stand up but wobbled a bit. His arms caught me and turned me around so I was inches from his face. Without hesitation, he kissed me. Hard, passionate, wet...devouring. I could taste the beer on his tongue as it mixed with the whiskey on my own. His hands gripped my shoulders, not that I was fighting him too hard.

My brain surged into overdrive. Sean didn't want me. This guy did. It's just sex. I didn't know what was going on in Paris. WHO THE FUCK IS PIERRE?

The crack of pool balls crashing into each other broke the trance I'd fallen into. I pushed my hands against his chest to break the kiss once and for all.

"I can't," I said.

He seemed to have finally heard me and loosened his grip, stepping aside.

"It would've been fun," was all he said as I passed by, heading toward the door. I wasn't sure if I was OK to drive, but I knew I wasn't OK to stay there. I sat in the dark parking lot for twenty minutes before starting the car and heading back to my very quiet, very lonely home.

I thought about calling Sean again, but I knew it would only be out of guilt, so I shut my phone off instead and went to bed. I reached under Sean's pillow for his t-shirt and panicked when it wasn't there. I remembered the fury with which I'd thrown it across the room that morning. I turned on the light to find it half-hidden behind the dresser. I strained to smell him, but all I could sense was the beer and whiskey still lingering in my mouth.

Sleep was hard to come. I overslept, missing my morning rounds, which would only mean an even busier day than the one before, always playing catch-up, juggling all the balls in the air. No time for lunch, barely time to pee, running from room to room, floor to floor, losing track of time.

It was much later than I wanted it to be before I finally had a chance to check in on Clara and her brother. He hadn't been my priority. His condition hadn't changed, and if he'd had a break-through overnight, one of the nurses would've paged me. I almost dreaded seeing her. I didn't want to see the lack of hope in her eyes, knowing I didn't have much to give her. I was sure she already knew that.

I caught up on the notes in his chart while heading into his room.

"Sorry I'm running late, Clara, it's been a busy…"

I stopped in my tracks.

"There you are, Ryder. I'm glad you're here." Her mood was completely elevated from where it had been yesterday. She was smiling and bubbly, pointing at him. Him. From last night.

"This is my other brother. This is Max."

Chapter Nine

MAX

I t had been a long day of travel, and I was just trying to blow off some steam before facing whatever was coming the next day. Just one last bit of necessity before my world came crashing down around me again, and the ghosts of the past tried to finish what they'd started years ago.

From her first message, and the several that followed, which I'd ignored, I knew I'd eventually end up back with the family I'd worked so hard to put behind me. What I hadn't considered was that I might end up trying to fuck my brother's doctor along the way. That was a surprise for both of us.

He stood frozen at the foot of the bed, a blush creeping up his neck, unable to respond to Clara's introduction. I wasn't ready to explain to my little sister that I'd had the good doctor's tongue in my mouth less than twenty-four hours earlier, so I did my best to break the awkward silence that had settled over us.

"What's up, Doc?" I stuck out my hand, as if I were meeting him for the first time. "Maxwell Heath. I think you've already met most of my siblings."

He seemed to snap to, slowly reaching out for my hand, like it might have secret teeth waiting to bite him. He hadn't been nearly as hesitant at the bar.

"Dr. Ryder Delaney. I've been treating Evan since he was transferred here to Austin."

"Clara's been filling me in…what there is. Doesn't seem like there's been much treatment going on."

"Maxie! That's not fair. Ryder's been doing a lot. Evan's just not responding…"

"Sorry. Didn't mean any disrespect. Forgive me?"

He ignored me, which I probably deserved, brushing past me to approach Evan and take his vitals for the hundredth time since I'd arrived. He was clearly breathing, but that was about all he was doing. Occasionally blinking.

"Does he really have to be tied to the bed, Doc? He's not going anywhere."

"It's more for his safety than any sort of security issue. If he does wake up, he might spasm or act out in a way that could hurt him. They're not hurting him, I promise."

He finished his exam and made notes on the chart, the scarlet blush still creeping up his neck.

"Do either of you need anything? I'm about to leave for the day, but I'll be back first thing tomorrow. Hopefully I won't be as busy."

Clara wished him a good night as he hurried out the door, eager to escape.

"I'm going to grab a coffee. Be right back…" I spotted him at the end of the hall and jogged to catch up, not wanting to shout his name. I ducked into the empty elevator just as the doors began to close.

"Listen," I began, "we should probably talk about…well, you know, what happened last night."

"Nothing happened. If anything had, it would've been highly inappropriate."

"Well, it's not like I knew who you were, or you knew who I was. You were just a random hot guy I wanted to fuck."

And the blush in his cheeks rose again.

"But nothing happened," he repeated.

"Right. That's what I wanted to clarify. Clara doesn't need to know…"

"No! Of course not. No one needs to know anything. Nothing."

He kept pressing the ground floor button, like maybe if he hit it enough, the elevator would finally get there, or someone else would get on and end the agony of our conversation.

"I just didn't want things to be awkward between us. I'm here to help Evan, just like you."

"And I'm glad you're here. Clara needs the support. She's been shouldering all of this on her own."

"I'm not surprised our aunt and uncle are keeping their distance. Clara's the only one they've ever liked. The boys were too much for them. We were too much for a lot of people."

The elevator finally landed on the ground floor, the doors opening up to the grand lobby, where Ryder Delaney made a hasty exit.

"See ya tomorrow, Doc," I said, pressing twelve to go back to my little brother's room.

Clara and I left shortly after. I gave her a ride back to Uncle Ted's house after I found out they'd been making her take the bus to the hospital every day. Not only were they doing nothing to help Evan, but they certainly weren't making it easy for Clara either.

"Why don't you take a break for a while, tomorrow, the next few days? Let me take over, spend some time with him…"

She almost looked hurt at the suggestion, and it dawned on me how it sounded, like she hadn't been doing a good enough job to save our brother.

"I'm worried about you, too, Clara. You've been doing so

much, and you're doing a great job, but you need to focus on you, too. You've got things to do, I'm sure..."

I was giving her permission to be somewhat normal again, at least for a little while. She reluctantly took it. She never realized that what I really wanted was to reconnect with just one sibling at a time, and Evan was my first priority.

The last time I saw my sister, she was ten and oblivious to the nightmare unfolding around her. Pa died. I left home. I'd hoped things would get better for everyone I left behind. That had been the plan, anyway. It was clear now that hadn't happened. My brother, lying in a hospital bed after trying to kill himself, again, was all the proof I needed to know I'd fucked up even worse than I could've imagined.

The family had splintered. Momma sent Clara to live with Pa's brother, Uncle Ted, and his wife, Darlene. They never had children of their own, and from what I could remember of their visits to Oklahoma, they never seemed to care much for us. If Momma sent Clara away, things must've been pretty bad. But where were Jasper and Evan? What about the Oldhams? Why didn't anyone help her?

There were too many questions, and asking them all would overwhelm Clara. And I was sure she wouldn't have the answers I needed.

I'd begged to remove myself from the family, and they'd done just that. To barge back in now and immediately start opening old wounds seemed unnecessarily cruel, even for me. But the reason Evan was lying in that bed had to be connected to everything that had happened after I left.

I pulled into the hotel parking lot. A far cry from the accommodations I'd grown used to over the years, but it was what I saw in my foreseeable future.

When I arrived at the hospital the next day, it seemed Evan hadn't moved since I'd left him the day before. I guess that was to be expected. Arms strapped to his sides, ankles tethered to the end of the bed. It broke my heart, for him and for myself.

I took the chair Clara had been sitting in and pulled it closer to his bed. His hand was cold, and he didn't respond when I touched him, but that didn't stop me. I leaned in and started talking to him.

I told him I was there for him. That Clara was going to college soon. That Jasper was in the army. All bullshit he probably already knew. I didn't know what else to say. I couldn't tell him where I'd been, what I'd been doing, for fear that he really could hear me. I wanted him to come back, not be frightened away.

When the doctor walked in, I was exhausted and had to collect myself quickly while he discretely reviewed Evan's chart.

I felt his hand grip my shoulder. Neither of us knew what to say to the other. We had started this relationship awkwardly, and neither of us was sure how to realign our positions, even after our conversation the night before. He was my brother's doctor. I was just a relative of a patient. We had a common goal, and Evan was lying strapped to the bed in front of us.

"I know this isn't easy," he began.

"It's actually much harder than I thought it'd be." It was the most honest thing I'd said in a long time, and I was actually surprised I'd said it out loud.

"As I've been telling your sister, physically, Evan is healing from his suicide attempt. He'll make a full recovery from that, although we'll need to talk about therapy or counseling to hopefully prevent another attempt in the future. But that's in the future. We can't find any reason why he's otherwise unresponsive now. We've done every test and scan we can, and everything has come back negative."

"I just don't get it..."

"I know, Max. There's something, some block, that we can't get past. He's fighting us."

"Stupid bastard...him, not you, Doc."

"I figured...so, my advice to you, as much as I'm sure you want to hear something different, is to keep doing what you're doing. Hold him, touch him, talk to him, ease his fears, let him know you're here for him, that he's safe."

"Thanks, Doc." Instinctively, I placed my hand over his, where it rested on my shoulder. The warmth of his hand was a sharp contrast to my brother's cold one.

"I'll check back in a little while, see if you need anything."

He left me there, right back where I started, hoping Evan could hear me and that something I said would get through to him.

Three hours later, he returned to check in before leaving for the night.

"You should go, Max. It's really shaping up to be a marathon, not a sprint like we'd initially hoped."

"I don't really have anywhere to go…just a lousy hotel room not far from here."

"You're not staying with Clara?"

I chuckled and shook my head. "No, my aunt and uncle aren't my biggest fans. They probably wouldn't have me even if I asked, and I'm doing us both a favor by not asking."

He hesitated. I could see the wheels turning in his head.

"Let me take you to dinner, then."

"Doc, I'm not going to sleep with you out of pity." I tried to make it sound like a joke, but after a long day, I put very little effort into it, so it came out sounding serious. From the look on his face, that's how he took it. "Just kidding, Doc. Dinner, sounds nice."

Relief passed across his face, and I gave Evan's hand a final squeeze before leaving. "Sleep well, baby brother."

We went to a small Italian restaurant not far from the hospital. The older woman at the door gave Doc a hug like he was family, then gave me a look like I might burst into flames at any moment. I didn't blame her. It wouldn't have surprised me if I did.

"She sure likes you," I said under my breath as we sat down, and the woman walked out of earshot.

"Carmen? She's great. Sean and I used to come here…a lot."

Ah. A penny the size of a husband, or ex-husband, or late husband, dropped right in the middle of the table and just sat there like a dead husband. I wasn't sure how to address it, and by the way Ryder grabbed his menu, he wasn't about to touch the subject. But I started to understand his behavior at the bar the other night.

We ordered, linguine for me, veal piccata for him. I had a glass of red wine, he had club soda. It was all very proper. He talked about the path that brought him to Austin, and I, of course, lied about what I'd been doing with my life. It was second nature at this point. I wasn't sure I could produce the truth if I had to.

Regardless, it was almost nice to just sit with another person. Someone who didn't need anything from me, someone I wouldn't have to owe a piece of myself to.

"Please, call me Ryder. I'm not your doctor."

"Are we friends?"

"We have a common goal, so we're more like co-workers at this point, I guess..."

"You guess?"

"I don't know what we are, Max, but I think we're past the formality of titles."

It didn't take much to recall the feel of his tongue in my mouth before he started protesting...

"Ryder it is then." I finished my wine in one gulp, feeling the pleasant burn as it went down, wanting another but not trusting myself.

"So, Ryder...today was more intense than I thought it would be. I don't know how Clara's been doing this on her own all this time."

He nodded thoughtfully. "She's probably stronger than you think, at least from what I've seen."

"I'm sure she's told you that we haven't seen each other in a while..."

"Only bits and pieces. I was curious how she got to Austin, and she mentioned your father's passing and your mother's, um, issues."

Issues? He knew more than I did, but I nodded as if what he was saying wasn't news to me.

"Yeah, it's pretty fucked up, but aren't all families?"

"To some degree, probably. But that doesn't rule out what happened to Evan in the past, how he dealt with various traumas that may've been going on around him, as a possible cause for what he's going through now."

"Are you saying this is my fault?" I could hear my voice rising, my defense mechanisms kicking in. "I've done nothing but try to…"

"Max, calm down." He reached across the table to me, but I recoiled. "No. I'm not blaming you, or anyone. It's more complicated than that, I'm sure. There's no blame to assign."

Maybe I was just feeling guilty because I knew it was my fault. My string of bad decisions, leaving everyone else to face the consequences.

Neither of us spoke. Ryder mimed for the check. I withdrew, flashes from the past flickering behind my eyes. Pa's striking hand. The blast of the gun. The clang of the cell door slamming behind me.

"Can I ask you a question, Max?"

"Can I stop you, Doc?"

He seemed amused by that.

"I'd like to set up an informal session…"

"Therapy!?" I almost shouted.

"Informal. More of a conversation, kind of like this. I'd like to find out more about Evan and his past…I don't feel comfortable doing this with your sister. I think, as the younger sister, she may've been shielded from some of the experiences Evan may've had growing up."

"I don't know, Doc. I need to think about it. I wasn't ready to have my head examined when I agreed to come here."

"I get it. It may or may not lead to anything, I'm just trying to come at it from a different angle. I'm missing something…"

A smoking gun, perhaps?

"Let me sleep on it."

"Fair enough. Thanks. And for the record, I know you want to help. You wouldn't have come if you didn't. No matter what your answer is, I believe that."

He drove me back to the hospital so I could get my car. The hotel loomed large in my mind, and I wasn't thrilled about it. I'd rather be bending the good doctor over, getting balls deep inside of him until I heard him scream my name, but that wasn't going to happen. Instead, I was going to be left alone with my demons, sweating through another sleepless night, watching my life pass by on repeat.

I realized I was following him. I drove past my turn for the hotel, watching his tail lights up ahead, turning when he did, slowing when he did. When he pulled into a driveway beside a dark, single-story Craftsman bungalow, I discreetly drove past and pulled over down the block. I killed the lights and the motor, still unsure of what I'd been thinking. I caught my reflection in the rearview. I was kidding myself. I knew what I was doing. I had the doctor in my sights. He had become my prey.

I got out of the car, careful to dim the interior light so I wouldn't be noticed. I approached his house. I stood in the shadow of an oak across the street, biding my time. I had no other place to be, and I knew how to be patient.

I watched him through the front windows, moving between rooms, switching on lights as he entered each one, bringing his home to life with every flick of the switch.

When he started to move toward the back of the house, shutting the lights off and checking the locks, I crossed the street and made my way around to his backyard. I had to hope he didn't have motion-activated lights. I moved slowly through the darkness, cloaking myself in it.

I rounded the corner into a surprisingly large backyard. A stream of light filtered out from an open window. There were no homes beyond the yard, just undeveloped woods giving off a false sense of privacy that I hoped to exploit. I approached a window, careful to stay outside of the light's perimeter. I knew I'd found what I came for.

Ryder stood there, his back to me, engaged in what sounded like an increasingly heated phone conversation.

"I know it's early there. It's always either too early, too late, or just too much for you to take five minutes to talk to me." There was a long pause while he listened to whatever rebuttal came from the other side.

"I know your job is impor..." He was pacing now, getting more agitated with each step. "We just need to..."

"Well, when would be a good time for me to come?" Apparently, he didn't like the answer he got.

"Fine. Call me when you have time for us," he snapped, disconnecting the call and tossing the phone onto his dresser. He let out a guttural moan of disgust. He stood motionless for a moment before stripping off his shirt and walking into the en suite bathroom. I heard the shower start and waited.

Steam began to drift out from around the door as the night air around me cooled. I waited, patient. Finally, there was silence, and Ryder emerged from the bathroom, a towel wrapped loosely around his waist. The water still beaded on his smooth broad chest. Rivulets trickled down between his pecs.

Frustration rose inside me. I fought my primal urge to lick him clean, to swirl my rough tongue around his tight, pink nipples, to bite them into hardness. But I couldn't do any of those things. He was out of reach. All I could do was watch.

He turned on a small bedside lamp, killing the overhead light on his way back to the bathroom. Moments later, he emerged completely naked, backlit for a second before he shut the bathroom light off.

While he climbed into bed, I felt free to approach closer to the window. I figured the brief glimpse I'd already had would be all I was going to get for the evening.

But Ryder had other thoughts.

I pressed up against the bedroom wall, peering in through the corner of the open window. Even in the dim light of the bedside lamp I could easily make out Ryder lying prone on his bed, legs akimbo, hand stroking his already hard cock.

My breath caught in my throat. I was afraid I might choke and give away my presence.

I'd been intrigued by the doctor since our lips first met in the bar. I was only hoping to get a clearer picture of who he was, what he wasn't revealing to me in our conversations. This was an unexpected bonus.

His strokes were long and slow as he settled into his rhythm. Whatever fantasy was playing out in his mind it didn't involve whoever he'd been on the phone with earlier. He was calm, methodical.

My own dick was distracting me from what was happening before me. I undid the button on my jeans and quietly pulled the zipper down.

My cock felt heavy in my warm hand. I had no trouble imagining Ryder's mouth around it. I was soon keeping tempo with him, stroke for stroke. When his hand went between his legs, it was my cock that was poised to enter him. When his back arched and his head thrashed, it was my mouth that was biting his neck, lapping at his running sweat.

I could hear myself panting, powerless to control it but hoping that Ryder was so lost in himself that he was oblivious to what was happening ten feet from him, outside his bedroom window, in the dark early summer night.

He exploded onto his stomach, the dim light catching flashes of cum shooting, landing on his chest in creamy puddles. I bit my lower lip and crossed my own point of no return, unleashing my cum into the bushes next to me, wishing I was inside of him.

I closed my eyes, tried to center myself, aware of the quiet night, the stillness of the air and the fact that Ryder had somehow stood and walked over to the window. He was standing naked just a few inches from me. I could smell the ripeness of his cum. I watched as his fingers played in it.

He opened the window wider to let in whatever breeze might arise in the night then he walked away. I glanced in to watch his smooth, muscular, ass as he strode into the bathroom. It still begged for attention, needed it. I imprinted the image on my brain.

I heard the water running from the tap. I crammed my still leaking cock back into my jeans and quickly zipped up. I needed to make a stealthy exit from his property before I was discovered, either by him or a nosy neighbor out for a late-evening stroll.

I couldn't lie to myself. I knew I'd be back.

The next day, Ryder stopped in to see Evan, as usual, but this time when he walked in I had a brief but distracting flash of him jerking himself off the night before. He asked if I'd given any more thought to what he'd asked. I told him I had and whatever he needed, I'd do it.

"That's great to hear," he said, opening his calendar app. "Looks like I have an opening tomorrow at ten."

He cocked an eyebrow, anticipating an answer.

"It's a date," I said, taking great pleasure in watching him begin to blush again.

Chapter Ten

THE CONVERSATION

Ryder

I knew everything from here on out would be a long shot, but it was worth the time and effort to try to release Evan Heath from the prison of his subconscious. Whether or not Max would be the key I needed remained to be seen.

Max was an enigma, not just to me but to his sister as well.

When she first mentioned her two brothers, she went into great detail about Jasper, where he was, what he was doing, his relationship with Evan. But when it came to Max, I barely got more than a name. She said she was barely ten when he left, around the time their father died. It wasn't until later that she mentioned their father had been killed. Even later, I discovered that Max had been convicted of the crime. Most of her recollections were based on things she'd been told as a child. Her father was "with the angels." Her brother had "gone away." Words like "murder" and "prison" were never used to describe the events that had changed all of their lives. For all of her good intentions, she was an unreliable witness to whatever trauma Evan might've suffered, both in his youth and in the years since.

Max had similar blind spots. His disappearance from the family meant he couldn't fill in the gaps of the last eight years or so. But at least he could paint a picture of a younger, hopefully happier Evan. He could create a baseline, and the rest, well, we'd have to figure that out when we got there.

There was a knock at my door at exactly ten. He was either afraid to be late or too nervous to be early. No one was ever exactly on time. I opened the door to let him into my small, cramped office. The larger therapy areas were reserved for groups of actual patients with real needs. My office was more intimate, just a desk, two chairs, and a ficus that was on life support.

"Hi, Max, come in. Thanks again for agreeing to this."

"Like I said, anything for Evan."

I motioned to one of the chairs. As he passed by me, his scent brought back the memory of our encounter at the bar. Our inauspicious introduction that, luckily, hadn't gone further than it did. Things were tenuous enough with Sean. I didn't need a guilty conscience on top of everything else.

"I saw Evan earlier this morning. I don't know if you've had a chance to see him yet...?"

"No, not yet. Clara texted. She's coming by this morning to sit with him. I'll go when we're done here."

"Clara cares a lot for him."

"Clara cares a lot for everyone. That's always been Clara."

"You mean Clara as a child, right? You haven't really known her as a young woman, have you?"

He squirmed uneasily in his seat.

"I suppose. But I doubt she's changed much."

"Do you not think that people have the capacity to change, have the free will to become other people if they choose to?"

"People, yes. But not my sister."

"Tell me about Clara as a child..."

"I thought we were here to talk about Evan."

"I'm just trying to get a sense of the family dynamic that Evan and the rest of you were raised in."

He grew pensive. His eyes started to dart around the room, landing on nothing for any length of time. I couldn't tell if he was thinking about or avoiding my question. Finally, he locked onto the dying ficus and began to respond.

"What you're probably wanting to know, but are too professional to ask, is how anyone as sweet and kind as Clara managed to survive in a house that was constantly terrorized by my father."

I knew better than to respond. He was asking and answering his own questions, questions I wasn't sure I had the nerve to ask so boldly. He was oblivious to my presence or maybe it was just easier to talk about the past if the present wasn't staring you right in the face.

"Evan and I are barely a year apart in age. I always thought it was great, having a brother that close. We went through everything together, good and bad. It wasn't until I was much older that I thought about how difficult it must've been for my mom, one not even crawling and already pregnant with another. But that was Pa's doing, not hers."

Inside, I winced, wondering how old Max had been when he'd started to understand the sexual dynamics within his parents' relationship.

"Jasper's five years younger than me, but there was another, at least one other…before him…"

He paused. I waited. This was his story to tell in his time.

"There was a fight. There was always a fight. I don't know if he meant to do it or not. He'd probably been drinking. But Momma ended up going down the staircase backwards. I'd say she was lucky he didn't kill her, but was she? Evan and I were both there. I barely remember it. I'm not sure he knew what was happening. We never spoke about it. They took Momma away in an ambulance, and we went to stay with the Oldhams across the farm."

I couldn't help myself. I had to say something, express my concern, my compassion. "I'm so sorry, Max. That's horrible."

"No. What's horrible is that he knocked her up straight away and then there was Jasper and then Clara. By then I was seven and in my father's crosshairs. Never doing anything right. SMACK! Lazy fuck. SMACK! Worthless, like your mother. SMACK! I didn't understand what I'd done, not really, but when he started going after Evan, I did everything I could to stay one step ahead of him."

I reached behind me and grabbed a bottle of water from the mini fridge. I could see that Max was getting upset and wanted him to regain his composure, stay calm.

"I'm assuming your father focused most of his anger on you and to some extent Evan? Were Jasper or Clara ever targets?"

"Never. I'm not sure they were ever in the room when any of this would happen. It was like Pa was specifically trying to shield them or remain the good guy in their eyes. And that was fine by me. But his death must've been a confusing shock to them."

"Do you want to tell me about his death? How he died?"

"I'm sure you already know that answer, Doc. A simple Google search will tell you all you need to know about that. I'll just say, I'm glad he's dead."

He was right. I knew what had been reported at the time. I saw the pictures of an eighteen-year-old Max sitting stoically in court, staring blankly ahead while the adults around him decided his fate. There wasn't reason to delve into it further.

"When you got out, why didn't you go back home? You'd worked so hard, sacrificed so much, to protect them, to bring some semblance of peace to that house. Why turn your back on them then?"

Max

I hadn't intended to talk about any of this. It wasn't that Ryder had tricked me, I hadn't been hypnotized against my will, but once I started talking, it all just seemed to fall out. It didn't feel good to unleash those words into the world. There was no relief, no catharsis. They were just words. It felt like I was telling someone else's story. A completely different Max. One that no longer existed.

That Max had been a victim, powerless, until it was too late to stop the dam that was holding everything back from breaking. It had only been a matter of time, but that day, I think, was when I truly came to life. Everything that had happened before then had been the prologue to my story. That day, a killer was born.

But I didn't know how to answer his question in a way that would make him understand why I couldn't go home again, not without mentioning Bobby Oldham. Just the thought of seeing him, seeing the disappointment in his eyes, would've been too much to bear. Even today, with everything I've done, I still don't think I could do it.

I'd long convinced myself that I'd forbidden my family from coming to see me in the detention center, but the truth, the truth that was almost too painful to admit, was that they just never came. I wasn't going to tell Ryder that. I had sacrificed for my family, and they had abandoned me for my trouble. So, I chose to ignore them as well. But Bobby? That hurt more than anything.

Bobby Oldham broke my heart. Slowly, painfully, as deliberately as I'm sure I broke his.

I surrendered to the cops as soon as they arrived at the house. I was taken into custody immediately. There was never a formal investigation into the shooting. I offered myself up to them and sat in the local jail until I was sentenced. It was a blur, but I never regretted what I did. I only regretted not being able to explain to Bobby what had happened. After that night in the barn, I never spoke to him again.

But I thought about him, a lot, especially in those first awful days in detention. What he'd felt like in my hands, tasted like in my mouth, what he looked like when I left him, promising to see him the next day. The day that never came.

What might've become of us if things had gone differently? Would we have left Choctaw together, or would that fucking town still have found a way to keep us apart? What might our future have looked like? I replayed that encounter over and over, hoping there might still be an outcome where we could end up together. One where I was released, and he was waiting for me at the gate, car idling, ready to take us away, far from the farm.

The first time I was attacked, I tried to pretend it was Bobby inside of me. That plan backfired. The guy was rough and it hurt, as did the second and the third. My feelings and emotions got all jumbled up, and it became Bobby who was hurting me. Every time it became Bobby holding me down, Bobby pulling at my clothes, Bobby leaving me aching and sore.

It was Bobby who turned me cold, who deadened my feelings, but who ultimately helped me to survive.

I fought back. I fought Bobby. I turned the tables. Like the rest of my life, I'd finally reached a point where I stopped being the victim. But by then, the only feelings I had left for Bobby were hatred and anger. I had no desire to ever go back to Choctaw to see him. I let him fade away. Bobby was never going to be in my life again.

As irrational as it was, and I knew it was irrational, it was how I survived for two years. It was why I went east when I left, and why my life turned out the way it did.

And now, in the last thirty minutes, Dr. Delaney had brought him back into my life for no fucking reason. There was no connection between Bobby and Evan. Bobby had been my friend. Evan had come with us when we went hunting, but he had school and his books. I couldn't imagine them doing things together after I left the farm. But I didn't know for sure. I didn't know anything for sure anymore.

"I just didn't see a future in going back to the past," was all I told Ryder, which, I guess, was partially true. I remembered my training: stay as close to the truth as possible.

"I understand that. But did you have any contact with them? Did you know what was happening there?"

"Look, I'm not proud of it. It was never my intention to erase them from my life permanently, or erase me from theirs. It just happened. Evan had my contact information, or else I wouldn't be sitting here now. They weren't calling me back to the farm, and I wasn't calling looking to go."

I realized my voice was escalating. I was agitated by his question. The truth of their dismissal of me was bubbling just under the surface, ready to boil over. I took a deep breath to calm myself.

"If they needed me, they would've called. And when Clara called, I came. I guess it's true what they say…"

"Blood is thicker than water?" he guessed.

"You can't escape your past."

It was blunt, but it was true.

The stupid chair was becoming more and more uncomfortable. The room had become too warm, claustrophobic. I didn't try to hide the fact that I was looking at my watch. We had to be almost finished. Evan's life was a mystery to me from this point forward. What more could I add?

"What was your coming out like?"

That was unexpected, and none of his fucking business.

"What was yours like, Doc?"

"Max, this isn't about me, you know that. It's OK if you don't want to answer my questions. It's just that sometimes those events can have ripple effects throughout a family. It's personal to you, but parents and siblings have reactions too. I was just curious, given what you've told me about your father…"

"Who I fuck is my business."

"Really? You tried to make it mine the other night," he answered quickly.

"It won't happen again."

"Sorry. That was unprofessional of me. You've been very helpful, Max. I'm very sorry. I want you to know I appreciate what you've shared with me."

"Are we done, Doc?"

Ryder

I'd clearly hit a nerve, but I'd needed to push him. I couldn't get past the idea that he was hiding something, or perhaps just outright lying to me. The pieces weren't aligning. I wasn't expecting a complete picture of the Heath family dynamic from one conversation, but for a kid to shoot his own father, no matter how tyrannical he might've been, there needed to be an inciting incident. Something had to have lit that fuse and caused that explosion of violence.

But everyone was entitled to their secrets. I have mine, Sean has his, and Max Heath definitely has his. Those piercingly dark eyes pulled everything in while simultaneously blocking out the rest of the world.

My phone vibrated in my pocket. It had been going off for the last twenty minutes. They'd page me overhead if it was a patient. It was probably Sean. He'd have to wait. I'd been waiting for him for a while now.

"When did you last speak to your mother, Max?"

"Long time ago."

"Are you aware of her current situation?"

He broke, just for an instant, but long enough for me to gather that he wasn't up to speed with Katherine Heath's condition. His non-answer said everything.

"For the past six years, she's been living in a facility just outside Enid." I waited for a reaction, but now there was none. He'd put up his defenses. I needed to tread carefully, or he'd bolt from the office, and probably the hospital, and I'd never see him again. "I'm sorry if this is new information for you, but I think it's important you know."

His focus once again drifted to my dying ficus. I carefully detailed his mother's condition and living arrangement, as much as Clara had relayed to me.

"There was a series of minor strokes, with accompanying aphasia and disorientation. She was moved to a care facility when she couldn't safely stay in her home any longer. Evan had been trying to take care of her basically on his own. Jasper was young. Clara was sent here to your aunt and uncle."

Max listened silently, dispassionately.

"I really hope you're not suggesting that any of that was my fault…"

"Absolutely not, Max. Trust me. None of this is on you or any of your siblings."

I reached across and put my hand on his knee, trying to reassure him. He didn't brush it off, which seemed like a good sign.

"From what you've told me, you've done what you thought was best for your family and paid the price for your actions. I can't say I condone everything you've done, but you…your family's situation might've just continued to get worse had you not acted when you did. There is never going to be a way to predict anyone's future. You had to act in the now with the information you had. It was brave, and I can see the cost you've paid for it."

There was stillness in return. Silence. I took my hand off his leg awkwardly, breaking the connection I think I failed to forge.

"Are we done here, Doc?"

I wasn't sure if we were, but I knew I couldn't keep him there any longer. It was clear he wanted to bolt.

"If you want to be. I'll be down to see Evan in a while." We stood in unison, accidentally knocking our heads together in the process. I instinctively grabbed Max by the arm, just trying to keep him from falling backward. He flexed under my grip, his eyes flashing with fury at me, then, just as fast, he relaxed, his composure regained.

He left without saying another word, just as my phone began to vibrate again.

"Is now a good time?"

It needed to be. I'd been wanting to talk to him for days. I'd been dying to hear his voice, but for some reason, it felt like he was intruding on the moment Max and I had just shared.

"I only have a few minutes…"

"You always only have a few minutes…"

"It's the middle of my day, Sean. I'm busy. I have patients…" I was trying not to sound as annoyed as I was, but it was creeping into my tone despite my efforts.

"We need to talk, Ry."

"You don't think I know that? But you're never around when I'm free, or you're having coffee with Pierre or someone else."

"Pierre has nothing to do with this…"

"I didn't say he did," but his sudden defensiveness was startling, and noticeable.

"Well, when will you have time for me?"

"Don't make it sound like it's all my fault we're not connecting…" I wasn't even trying to hide my annoyance now. I hadn't intended to start an argument, but it seemed like that's where we were heading yet again.

But Sean wasn't taking the bait. Instead, he'd gone quiet, perhaps counting to ten before saying something he'd regret. I took a deep breath, considered apologizing for taking my work frustrations out on him. But then the beeping in my ear pulled me out of our familiar cycle. I checked the display, and my heart started to race.

"Sean, I have another call I have to take. I'll try to free up some time later today. Bye," and I clicked over to the other call before he had a chance to say anything, or before I could let him drag me back into the familiar cycle we always fell into.

"Ryder Delaney," I announced, "thanks for calling me back…"

By the time the call ended, I'd almost forgotten the foul mood Sean's call had started to put me in. I made my rounds, checking on my other patients, before heading to see Evan Heath. I wasn't sure how the news I had to share with Max would sit with him.

I knocked gently on the closed door before entering, but apparently, it wasn't heard. When I stepped into the room, Clara was there, and she and Max were engaged in a heated exchange that they quickly ended when they noticed me.

"Sorry to interrupt, but I wanted to check in on Evan…Clara, it's good to see you again. I hope a few days away did you good. I'm sure Max kept you informed about your brother. There's still no change. He's in good condition, his vitals are strong, he's just…" I was at a loss for words as to how to describe his condition in a way that didn't sound hopeless. They knew what we were facing.

Clara looked on the verge of tears, and Max looked like he was ready for a fight. I was even more nervous to share my news now than when I walked in, but I had to, for my patient.

"I just got off the phone with the facility in Green Lake… where your mother is living." That got both of their attention. "With your permission, I'd like to go up there, speak with your mother, see if she can shed any light on the time she and Evan spent alone on your farm, after…"

There was silence.

I didn't actually need their permission to go see Katherine Heath. The sanitarium where she'd been living had already given that. They'd also just told me she'd been having a string of really good days, alert and conversing, but they didn't know how much longer that would last. History told them it wouldn't be much more than a couple of days before she withdrew back into her world of fantasies and delusions. She was possibly my last hope at unlocking Evan from his self-imposed exile. I didn't want to take hope away from either of them, but I felt a sense of urgency. Going to Green Lake seemed imperative.

"I'm going to drive up there tomorrow morning. I hope to see her in the afternoon…"

Max didn't let me finish. "I'm going with you."

Chapter Eleven

MAX

I'd never wanted to return to Oklahoma, but I couldn't ignore what Clara had told me. I had to take care of something long overdue, and Ryder's wild goose chase was the perfect excuse to do it.

When I told him I was coming along, Clara grabbed my arm, scared of what I might do but not sure why or knowing how to express her concern. Ryder wasn't sure about me joining, maybe he doubted how I'd help, or maybe he just didn't want eight hours in a car with me. Either way, he agreed reluctantly.

He picked me up the next morning with a large black coffee and a sticky bear claw. The gesture was a peace offering after our tense conversation the day before. I should've apologized to him, but I wasn't ready to.

I wasn't sure what to think about Momma's condition. I hadn't asked about her, just like she hadn't come to see me in lockup. She'd washed her hands of me, and I'd done the same. But hearing what Ryder said made me think I had misunderstood. The fact that Clara was sent to Texas should've been a clue, but there were a million reasons we got cut off. None of them involved strokes or sanitariums.

And I wasn't good at apologizing.

We drove through Austin, heading north on the interstate. Ryder hummed along with the radio. Neither of us knew how to start a normal conversation, one that didn't sound like therapy.

I still had the image of him from the other night stuck in my head, and it was making my cock twitch. I shifted in my seat, trying to focus on the passing scenery, but there wasn't much to look at, just wide-open spaces and the occasional farm until we hit Waco or Dallas.

"Tell me about Sean." He'd mentioned him at dinner but never brought him up again. I hadn't seen him at the bungalow, and I assumed he was on the other end of the argument so I figured I might as well ask.

He looked surprised. "How do you know about…oh, right. Dinner."

"Plus, there had to be another man in the picture if you didn't want to sleep with me the night we met." I grinned, hoping to ease the tension.

"Is that the only reason someone wouldn't sleep with you?"

"The only good reason. But even then…"

"Damn. This is a side I haven't seen before."

"Confident?"

"I was thinking more arrogant."

"But there is a Sean, right?"

"There is. FBI agent. Works with my sister, that's how we met. Currently in Paris with Interpol. What else do you want to know? Aries. Left-handed…"

"I'm still processing the fact you have both a sister and a partner in the FBI. I need to get on your good side, if I'm not already."

"You're fine, Max, unless you've been committing federal crimes in your free time."

I let the comment slide. "Paris is a long way away. Has he been gone long?"

"Five months and four days. Not that I'm counting."

I whistled. "That's a long time."

"I know. And it's supposed to last a year. The Bureau tends to operate on their own timeline, regardless of agents' personal lives."

Bingo. The angry phone call.

"And here we are, complicating your life with our little problems..."

"Evan is not a complication. He's my patient, and I care about him. I care about you and Clara, too. I'll do whatever I can to help him..."

"Clara's done nothing but sing your praises since I got to Texas..."

"Where were you coming from, Max?"

It was a fair question, but damn, I'd walked right into it.

"Miami," I said, hoping it sounded convincing, though it felt like a lie. People believed what they wanted to believe, right?

"What were you doing there?"

"Managing a club in South Beach." It felt like something a different version of Max Heath might do. Besides, explaining a gunshot wound seemed like over-sharing.

"Do you like it there?"

"It's fine. I tend to move around when I get tired of a place. Haven't found the right place to settle down yet." I glanced at Ryder. He nodded, the settled doctor with a steady job and a house in the woods. He seemed the picture of stability.

"Well, maybe Austin will be your next stop. I'm sure Clara would love having you nearby, and Evan, once he's better..."

"Is he going to recover?" I asked, harsher than I intended. "That seems questionable. Not every story has a happy ending, Doc."

"I try to stay optimistic whenever possible. It makes my job more bearable. There are too many hard days, Max. I need to believe every patient has hope."

But that had never been my experience. Nothing good stayed

that way for long. Something always fucked it up, usually because of me.

I saw a rest area up ahead and told Ryder I needed to piss, though really, I just needed a break from the conversation.

I offered to drive, and surprisingly, he let me. I changed the radio to a college station from Waco, playing music I'd never heard of. Ryder closed his eyes and was soon asleep, leaving me alone with my thoughts.

By the time we passed Dallas, he hadn't stirred. Around noon, we crossed into Oklahoma, and his breathing was still deep and steady. His hair had fallen over his forehead, nearly covering his eyes. He looked peaceful, unaware of what I was about to drag him into. I wanted to kiss him, apologize, but more than that, I wanted him to kiss me back and tell me everything would be okay. But I knew neither of those things would happen. No man as kind, as thoughtful as Ryder would ever choose me, at least not if they really knew me. I had to let that thought go. Once Evan was better, I'd disappear, and everyone's lives would be better for it.

We passed Oklahoma City, and I nudged Ryder awake. I wasn't sure exactly where we were headed, so I needed him to navigate. I also needed to set my plan in motion.

"I've been thinking," I began, hoping he was listening but not wanting to look at him. "I may have been too impulsive coming with you. Momma might have an adverse reaction to seeing me. It could hurt your chances of getting any information out of her if I'm there."

"It might," he said, "but it might also trigger memories that'll help me understand Evan."

"Are you willing to take that risk? We've come this far. Are we really going to risk it all on a maybe?"

"So, what are you thinking?"

"I think I should drop you off at the facility and let you spend the afternoon with her. I'll find a hotel for us, because I am not driving back to Austin tonight. That was bad enough in daylight…"

"If that's how you feel, then I'm okay with it. I don't want to overwhelm your mom. You know her better than I do."

"And I don't want to be the cause if she has a setback and can't help you. I know you're running out of options. Even if Jasper gets leave, I can't imagine he'll be more helpful than Clara or I were."

It was that simple. Ryder would be out of the way for a few hours, and I could do what I'd come home to do.

Green Lake, Oklahoma wasn't much to speak of. It was only twenty minutes from Choctaw, and I'm sure I'd driven through it before, probably on the way to the livestock auctions in Enid, but I'd never veered off the main road to actually see the town. The facility where Momma was living sat off Route Nineteen, and from a distance, it looked like it could be quite nice. Acres of well-maintained land surrounded the main building, which looked more like a private residence than a medical center. As we got closer, it only looked more like a large private home, a southern plantation ripped from Georgia or South Carolina and dropped into the middle of bumfuck Oklahoma, rather than the sanitarium it really was behind the genteel facade.

I pulled up to the front to let Ryder out, but he hesitated before opening the passenger door.

"Please don't get your hopes up, Max."

"Please don't doubt yourself, Doc."

I squeezed his shoulder, trying to reassure him, or maybe myself, that he was doing the right thing. He was doing the only thing. He casually covered my hand with his for a brief moment before the wall between us went back up.

"I'll call when I'm done," he said quickly, slamming the door behind him.

I watched him walk up the front steps, his rumpled white shirt, wrinkled from the trip, loose jeans riding low on his hips, well-worn loafers. He looked more like a college student than a doctor. He turned briefly to wave me off, his blonde hair blowing across his face in the light breeze. I absent-mindedly played with the ring hanging on the chain around my neck. Why did these good men keep coming into my life, only for me to ruin them with my evil?

I drove off the property and headed back to the main road. As much as I wanted to drive on to Enid, find a nice hotel, relax for the afternoon while Ryder undoubtedly uncovered our family secrets, exposing me for the fraud I was, I turned the other direction, back in time.

Choctaw had changed almost as much as I had in the ten years I'd been gone, but I knew there was still a wrong side of town. That's where I was headed.

Hollis Auto Repair was exactly the dump I knew it would be. It had never seen better days, and its future looked just as bleak as Petey himself. Ryder's BMW looked out of place among the wrecks parked around the lot. I'd told Ryder we could take my car on our road trip, but he'd insisted on driving, so here we were. I parked in the back, out of sight, in case anyone passed by.

For the number of cars around, no one seemed to be working there. That was good, made my job a lot easier. I walked into the shop, the bell clinking in the back, announcing my presence. It only took a moment for Petey to appear, looking much worse for wear. Time hadn't been kind to my Uncle Petey, and that didn't bother me at all.

"How can I help you?" he asked, craning his neck to look out the window. I assumed he was trying to spot my car's value, so he could adjust his prices accordingly. Not seeing anything, he finally looked at me, and the half-smile on his face disappeared quickly.

"Son of a bitch…" he muttered. "I didn't think we'd ever see you again around here."

"Hey, Petey. Can't say I missed seeing you either, but I was just passing through and thought I'd stop by…"

I started walking around his godawful shop, picking up and putting down things caked in dust. It was clear nothing had been touched in a long while. This place certainly wasn't how he earned his living.

"Quite the operation you're running, Petey. But I hear you've got a little side hustle…to help make ends meet."

"I don't know what you're talking about, Max. Say what you came here to say, then you can go on your way. Going out to that so-called farm of yours?"

"I wanna know why you were supplying my brother with drugs, Petey."

He deflected, stupidly defiant. "I wasn't supplyin' him nothing. He bought, just like everyone else around here."

"Don't get fucking smart with me, Petey. It doesn't suit you. You know what I mean."

From the second Clara told me about Evan and Petey, I knew it would end like this. I'd warned him once before, back when we both knew I couldn't make good on my threats. But he still should've listened. He was about to find out that I was no longer the boy I used to be. I always made good on my promises now.

"No one was forcing him to do nothing he didn't want to. I can't help it if he can't handle his junk."

My anger flared. "Or was getting him hooked your pathetic way of getting back at the rest of my family?"

"I don't give a shit about you or your family, Max. Never have. Whatever happens to them, I'm sure they deserve it. So, if you're done, there's the door…you can fuck off through…"

I grabbed the hard steel ball of the dirty trailer hitch and hurled it straight at Petey, hitting him square in the chest. If I'd hit him in the head, I'd have killed him outright. But the chance of missing, of making a bigger mess of his shop, wasn't worth it. Besides, I wanted him to suffer. I wanted him to know it was me who ended his miserable existence.

I heard his ribs crack. By the way he hunched over, I could tell he was struggling to breathe. It would be so easy from here.

I took my time walking over to him, picking up a pair of

jumper cables lying on the counter. They wrapped easily around his neck. He offered little resistance as I pulled the ends tight.

"I warned you once that I'd kill you if you ever came near my family, and I'm a man of my word, motherfucker."

His hands scratched at his throat, trying to find air. One of his feet slipped sideways, and he lost his balance. His own weight worked against him as I pulled tighter. A minute passed, maybe two. Time barely moved in my mind. Blind rage had taken over. Was this how my Pa felt when he whipped me with his belt?

I ignored Petey's flailing arms, his kicking feet. They stopped soon enough. Eventually, he was just dead weight, crumpling to the shop floor where he'd never hurt anyone again.

There are a lot of places to hide a body in an auto shop: car trunks, lift bays, burn pits. I chose a metal drum, probably meant for discarded car batteries that Petey would bury illegally. The fact that Petey wasn't a big man made the job easier. He fit without me having to remove any limbs. By the time I replaced the lid on the drum, there was no sign of a struggle. The owner of Hollis Auto Body just wasn't receiving customers anymore.

I scanned the shop for any security systems, cameras, or recorders Petey might've installed, likely more for the drugs than the junked cars. But I knew Petey was too dumb to think he'd ever need them. Stupid, dumb fuck.

On my way out, I replaced the jumper cables and the trailer hitch, exactly where I'd found them among the other useless junk.

I climbed into the BMW, my adrenaline pumping. But after a few deep breaths, I casually drove away, making sure not to draw any more attention than I already had. I checked my watch. I'd been there less than thirty minutes, but I'd remember the thrill of taking his life for much longer.

The subconscious is a strange, powerful thing. It was strong enough to imprison my brother deep within himself, while mine had led me down the rural route toward the farm where it all began. And I let it. There was something about that house. I suddenly needed to see it. I'd never really escaped it, no matter how much I'd wanted to, or thought I had. I needed to put it behind me.

I stepped out of the car and just stared at the old facade, overcome by the onslaught of memories. The window Evan had broken that I'd taken the blame for. The front door I'd almost slammed off the hinges countless times, swearing I'd never go back in that house, never face that man again. Even the dirt path where they'd wheeled his body away while the cops stood by, bathed in the blue flashing lights, unsure what to do with me, looked the same. And yet it was different. I wasn't scared of it anymore. The voices were muted. It, he, couldn't hurt me.

"Can I help you with something?"

I hadn't heard him approach, which was dangerous and unlike me. I turned, adrenaline surging again and ready to fight. I didn't know him. What was he doing here, at my house? I glanced back at the place, but it wasn't my house anymore. Suddenly, it looked different. New paint. A mowed yard. Curtains? We never had nice curtains.

"Who are you?" I snapped before I could stop myself.

"Hugh McIntyre. This is my home." His voice was low, measured, but I could tell he was wary, defensive, wondering if he was going to have to protect his home from me.

"Sorry. Your home? I thought…"

His voice came from my opposite side, and for the second time in a minute, I was blindsided.

"Oh my God," was all he said, but that was all I needed to hear. I'd never forget that voice, no matter how much I tried. The hate I'd created in my head disappeared, and as if by a miracle, I was wrapped in his arms again. "Max. I never thought I'd see you again."

I was eighteen again, and the world was perfect and full of possibilities. He smelled the same. His arms felt like they could protect me from anything. He'd been mine for only an instant, but

I'd been his forever. I wanted to kiss him, but he pulled away, and I was back in the present. I felt every one of my old scars again. The weight of the years that had come between us.

"What are you doing here, Max?"

It was a good question, one I didn't have an easy answer to.

"I don't, um, I'm not sure. I came to see Momma…"

"Oh, Max, she's not here," he thought he was telling me bad news.

"No, no, I know. I'll see her over in Green Lake. I know she's not here, but I didn't know you would be."

"Hugh and I live here now. Running the farm. Together."

I'd forgotten he'd been standing behind me, watching, wondering. Hugh. Did I want to know about Hugh?

Hugh was a knife in my heart. Hugh was living the life I'd thought I'd be living. Hugh had Bobby now. My Bobby.

"Hi. Max Heath. I used to live here. A very long time ago." I awkwardly shook his hand. It was rough, firm. It was the hand that held Bobby's now, the hand that smoothed the cowlick in his hair before they went out, that rubbed his back at night when he was sick, that held him down on the bed when they had sex.

I knew it was irrational, but I hated him.

I wasn't sure I could stay standing much longer. Less than an hour ago, I had nerves of steel when I killed Petey Hollis, but seeing Bobby Oldham was about to bring me to my knees.

"Do you want to come in, or…?"

"No. I don't want to see inside there ever again. No offense."

"No, I understand. I wasn't thinking…"

I saw him give Hugh a look, the kind couples who've been together a long time give one another, the 'I'll explain later, trust me' look.

"I should go, actually. I need to get over to Green Lake. Looks like rain, and they'll be wondering where I am."

I hadn't thought to expect to see him when I drove in. He should've been at his parents' place, if he still lived here at all. But I guess it made sense that he needed a place of his own now. He and Hugh. There was still so much I wanted to say to him, but I knew this wasn't the right time, and I didn't have the right words. Bobby looked happy, and that was all that mattered. It was what I'd always wanted for him. It was what he deserved. Everything else was just a fantasy of mine that I hadn't even realized I'd been harboring all these years. He was never going to be happy with me.

"Hugh, it was nice to meet you." I almost meant it. I hated him, though, and I wanted to tell him that. I wanted to say, like I'd told Petey years ago, that if he hurt Bobby, I'd end him without thinking twice. But I didn't. Their lives were theirs to live as they chose. I had to accept that.

"I wish you didn't have to go so quick."

If he asked me to stay, I was afraid I would. I was already in too deep, and I had to find some way to the surface so I could breathe again.

I gave Bobby a final hug goodbye. I knew I'd never see him again, I *couldn't* ever see him again, and I wanted to remember everything about that moment. My hand found the back of his head, and I held him to me. It was only seconds, but it felt like forever, and it still wasn't long enough.

"I'm sorry…for everything," I whispered in his ear as I pulled away. I turned and got into the car without looking back.

I felt like I'd been kicked in the gut. Numb. In pain. I couldn't stop the tears if I tried, so I didn't try.

Chapter Twelve

RYDER

Katherine Heath was never going to recover.

She would never leave the Green Lake facility where she had been a patient for the last four years, nor would she see her farm again. If she ever saw her family, it was doubtful she'd recognize them fully. There might be glimpses of familiarity, but the life she once knew was gone forever. Whether that was a blessing or a curse, well, that was open to debate.

Dr. Travis Paul had spent the last four years piecing together Katherine's life. The file he'd compiled was inches thick and told a grim story, one of serial abuse at the hands of her father and husband, the loss of a child, the incarceration of another, and even a murder. The police report included in the file stated that Katherine had been knocked unconscious by her husband moments before he was killed. She didn't witness her son pulling the trigger, but when she regained consciousness, she knew. He had saved her, and the rest of the family, from Walter's final, violent outburst.

She tried to rebuild, to reconnect with her family, but her efforts were in vain. The farm was profitable, and it continued to fund her care, but she couldn't manage it anymore, not even with help. She sent her two youngest children to live with their only remaining relatives, even though they continued to blame her for Walter's death. If she'd been a better wife, if she hadn't burdened him with that damn farm, maybe things would have been different. Her sins were endless, at least in their eyes.

Katherine's life changed irrevocably one final time on a sidewalk outside a local beauty salon. After an argument with the owner, she suffered her first stroke. The decline was swift, and within a few months, she was transferred to Green Lake to spend the rest of her days.

Her middle son, Evan, was her only visitor of record. But Dr. Paul had noted the increasingly long gaps between visits and his growing suspicion of a drug addiction. His rare appearances were probably for the best, at least for Katherine.

The details in Dr. Paul's notes were insightful, but I wasn't finding any answers. All I'd gathered was that Evan's decline had been gradual and that he probably hadn't had anyone close to help him fight whatever demons had taken over his life.

I'd spent the last two hours poring over Katherine's chart, trying to make sense of how the pieces of her life intersected with her children's. I was looking for some thread that might explain Evan's breakdown, some deeper connection beyond the obvious. In the back of my mind, I heard a voice telling me I was grasping at straws, that I was never going to find the answers I was seeking. Maybe Evan was untreatable, maybe his troubles were his own. Not everything had to be cause and effect. But the scientist in me held onto hope. Maybe I'd find something in these pages, or maybe, just maybe, Katherine herself might hold the key.

Dr. Paul knocked before entering, even though it was his office I was camped in.

"Have you found the needle in your haystack yet?"

"I think I'd have better luck with that. Your file is incredibly thorough, and it's filled in a lot of the gaps for me, but nothing is connecting the dots to Evan Heath's current condition."

"I wish I could tell you that she's divulged secrets to me and sworn me to silence, but no such luck. In the years she's been here, her bad days have far outnumbered her good ones. Only recently has she become more communicative, but even then, it can be more confusing than helpful. It's hard to tell what's fact and what's fantasy most days. She'll say things that never happened, or relive the same events over and over. So go in with an open mind, but be on guard."

"Might be easier said than done, but I appreciate the advice."

"Well, she's in the solarium. Are you ready to meet Katherine?"

I was nervous. As much as I'd warned Max about managing expectations, I knew mine were all over the place. I struggled to temper them with each step I took. I saw Clara and Max in my mind, and I didn't want to disappoint them. I didn't want to see the disappointment in their eyes. And Evan...Christ. What if, fuck, I didn't even want to begin thinking about the 'what ifs' surrounding his future, not before meeting his mother. He'd been her only connection to the past for so long. I didn't want her to suspect that she might never see him again. My visit with Katherine had to be upbeat, positive. I was just a friend coming to see her for an afternoon chat. Nothing more.

I saw her in the corner of the solarium as soon as we walked in. She was unmistakable. Her light hair was pulled back from her face, her eyes staring out into the room. She looked a lot like Clara, or probably the other way around. I knew she was barely in her fifties, but she looked much older. Life had ravaged her, that much was obvious. But as we approached, I felt an aura of deep sadness that seemed to change her features. I could only imagine how Evan must have felt, coming here to see her like this. The toll it must have taken on him each time.

"Katherine?" Dr. Paul's voice had taken on a calm, gentle tone that I tried to mimic when I spoke. "Hi, Katherine. I want you to meet a friend of mine. This is Ryder."

I waited for her to look my way before extending my hand. She didn't attempt to take it, and I realized it was a useless gesture. So, I reached a little further and gently touched her arm, trying to make some form of connection.

"Hi, Katherine. How are you today? Do you mind if I sit with you for a few minutes?"

I knew Katherine could speak if she chose to. Her aphasia from the strokes had been mild, and according to her chart, therapy had improved her speech over time. It might be halting or slurred if she got tired, but she was communicative. I just had to get her to want to talk to me. She was a lot like her son in that way.

"I'm a friend of your daughter's, Clara. I saw her yesterday, and she wanted me to tell you hello when I saw you. She loves you and misses you."

It wasn't the icebreaker I'd hoped for, but there was a slight glimmer of recognition in her eyes. That was all. By her own admission, Clara hadn't been to Oklahoma to see her in a long time. The mother/daughter bond might not be as strong as I'd hoped.

"And Evan. He's doing really well…"

"Where…is…he…?"

"Well, um, he's…he's in Texas, visiting Clara right now. That's where I'm from."

"Sorry…"

"I'm, what? What was that, Katherine?" I wasn't sure I'd heard her correctly.

"I'm sorry…"

"Why are you sorry, Katherine? Did you and Evan have an argument?" Was that what sent Evan over the edge, trying to take his life? What could Katherine even say to do that? I was desperately grasping at her words and I knew it.

"Good boy. Not…his fault."

I tried to remain calm. I looked at Dr. Paul, hoping he'd have an answer, but he just looked back at me blankly.

"What wasn't his fault, Katherine? Your argument?" I was trying to put together a jigsaw puzzle and all of the pieces were blank.

"Walter…" Her husband. I was more confused, and the mere mention of his name seemed to agitate her, which was the only thing that made any sense. I stroked her arm gently to try to soothe her. I wanted to ask more questions, but I didn't want Dr. Paul to shut down our conversation if Katherine became upset.

"Walter's not here, Katherine. You're safe here, with Dr. Paul, and with me."

She looked at me like I didn't understand, which, I had to admit, I didn't really. But I wanted to.

"Evan…coward…"

The conversation was picking up speed just by mentioning Evan's name. She clearly had him on her mind. It had been weeks since he could've been here to see her. Weeks for her to stew about an argument they might've had, waiting for him to return so she could maybe apologize? Or continue it? Did it involve her late husband, Walter?

"It's OK, Katherine. You can tell Evan you're sorry the next time he comes to see you. I'm sure he already knows, though."

I looked to Dr. Paul for help. I didn't want to leave her in a worse state than when I'd found her, but it seemed like that's where we were headed. He mouthed the word "Clara" and shrugged. Worth a try.

"You'd be real proud of Clara, Katherine. She's going to the University of Texas in the fall. She's smart, very responsible."

"Jasper?"

Her hand reached up to my face, her eyes searching mine. Did she think I was her son? Did she think I was Jasper? I'd never seen a picture of him, so I wasn't sure if there was a passing resemblance, maybe the blonde hair? She was just confused. This conversation had been a lot to ask of her.

"Katherine, no, this is Ryder Delaney. Jasper's in the army. You know that. He's not here."

"Good. Jasper...safe..."

"Everyone is safe, Katherine, even..."

"Maxwell. My...baby."

She was looking past me now, and I turned to see Max standing in the doorway, taking in the scene, clearly unsure if he should interrupt. I motioned for him to come over. Katherine had already seen him. He couldn't leave now.

He approached her slowly. I wasn't sure when the last time was that they'd seen each other, but I assumed it was around the time of his trial. I felt like an intruder. I got up, at least to step aside so Max could sit with his mother, but he grabbed my shoulder, holding me in place.

"Hello, Momma."

"My boy...is home."

"I'm not home, Momma. I'm visiting. I don't live here anymore."

It sounded cold, but I couldn't imagine what Max was going through. I was still surprised to see him. I thought he would wait for my call.

"Sit...by me...please."

I felt his grip loosen, only then realizing how tight it had gotten.

"We'll be over there," I told Max, following Dr. Paul's lead as he stepped away to the other side of the solarium, where we could observe from a distance.

I wasn't sure who I worried for more, Katherine, who hadn't been expecting the bombardment of visitors and was clearly getting more and more confused, or Max, who still carried years of hurt and anger inside of him, much of it aimed at the mother he felt had abandoned him when he was sent away for killing his father.

I debated asking Dr. Paul to intervene, to stop their conversation before it caused Katherine more distress. But then my phone rang, disturbing the fragile peace in the solarium. I'd forgotten to silence it and regretted it when I saw Sean's name on the screen.

I hadn't liked the way we'd left our last conversation, and I knew if I sent him to voicemail, it would only make matters worse. In a split-second decision, I hit "answer" and whispered, "Hold on a second," motioning to Dr. Paul that I was stepping out to take the call and would be right back.

I stepped through the French doors onto the patio, leaving Max and his mother behind in their own awkward conversation.

"Sean, hi. I need to be brief. I'm with a patient's family…"

"Then I'll be quick. You never have time to talk, but I need to tell you something. I've been offered a job with Interpol, in Berlin. I've been wanting to talk to you about it, but you're never available, and now I need to give them an answer. It's too good to pass up…"

His words faded, and I lost track of what he was saying. All I heard was "job" and "Berlin," and I couldn't breathe anymore. It was my worst fear coming true. I was going to come second to his career, one last time.

I found a chair and sat down hard. "Why…" was all I managed to say.

"Ryder, I love you, you know I do, but this is a dream come true. A posting like this is why I became an agent in the first place."

"Maybe I can move to Berlin…" I wasn't sure what I was saying. My thoughts were a jumbled mess. I was blindsided, but I also knew I had to get back inside the solarium.

Sean's voice refocused in my ear. "And do what? You told me yourself you'd have to start over if you moved here. Could you do that without resenting me? Could you?"

He was right. I pictured the arguments, the hurt, being alone without a support system. I knew how that would affect my clients, and I wouldn't be immune to those same feelings.

"I don't know what to say, Sean."

"Say you understand." But I didn't.

Instead, I said, "I have to get back," and disconnected the call.

The sun disappeared behind a dark cloud, as if on cue.

I felt as confused as Katherine must have felt. Ambushed by someone I loved, someone I thought loved me in return.

Was it over? He seemed set on moving, and equally set on me not coming along.

Voices drifted out from the solarium, raised voices. Max's voice.

"I had to, Momma, I had to protect him. It was my job, mine!"

I rushed back in as Dr. Paul quickly approached from the other side of the room.

"Max, calm down," I said, trying to soothe him. He was agitated, clearly, and stood up, glaring at her for whatever had been said, glaring at me for bringing him here. He pushed past me, shoving me out of his way as he made his way to the door.

I wanted to follow him, but I knew my professional duty was to Katherine. I had brought this disruption into her life, and I needed to calm her, not just walk away and leave it to Dr. Paul to handle. Sean was right. My patients, even those in my temporary care, came first.

I sat and took Katherine's hand in mine, telling her everything was OK, that whatever had just transpired wasn't her fault, it was surely just a misunderstanding. I knew she already carried the weight of an argument with one son, and now another was stacked on top of that. The situation was volatile. Katherine was poised on the brink of a setback. Whatever had just happened between her and Max might have driven one son to attempt suicide, and I was deeply concerned where it might lead the other.

A nurse approached knowingly with a cup of tea and a piece of cake, which thankfully calmed Katherine, or at least distracted her long enough for me to say my thank-yous and goodbyes. I told Dr. Paul I'd check in with him later, and he assured me Katherine would be OK.

Then I had to find Max.

I glanced out of one of the front windows as I passed by and saw movement in the distance. Max was running across the property like he didn't intend to stop until he reached Texas. I ran to the front door and chased after him, calling out for him to stop. I could only imagine the scene we were creating for the other residents inside the facility.

He must've realized he was nearing the edge of the hospital grounds, because he stopped abruptly at one of the large oaks that dotted the property. I was out of breath when I finally reached him. He looked like he was going to punch the tree, his feet planted in a boxer's stance, fists clenched and drawn up to his chest. Just when I thought he was going to strike out, he unleashed a scream that seemed to come from miles deep within him, building, gathering force, until it exploded with such rage and velocity that it could've toppled the surrounding trees.

I let him finish before I closed the space between us.

"Max?" I was quiet, tentative. I didn't want to startle him or bring him back to reality faster than he was ready for. "Max, it's OK. I'm sorry I brought you..."

"No. I should've known better. I told myself years ago to never come back, and I forgot why I made that promise. I'm so stupid to think..."

"Max, this isn't solely on you. This whole situation is fucked up, pardon my French." I thought I saw him shudder, but then realized he was laughing.

"Everything that's happened, and you're worried your words might offend me? Fuck, Ryder. Fuck. Fuck. Fuck. Better?" I laughed along with him, thankful the tension had been broken, regardless of how it happened.

"If you're done attacking the landscaping, let's get out of here."

"Yeah, Doc, I'm ready. I got a couple of rooms in Enid for the night. I even stopped and bought you a toothbrush and some deodorant for the morning."

"Great. I'm too exhausted to sleep all the way back to Texas." I winked at Max to make sure he knew I was kidding, but it was unnecessary. He was already grinning at my lame joke.

The first raindrop hit my face when we were only feet from the tree, and we were soaked by the time we got back to the car.

"Well, this is a fitting way to end this shitty day," he said.

I put the key in the ignition but paused before turning it.

"Max…" I knew I had to be careful with my words. "Max, I'm not going to say I know or understand all the family dynamics at play here, but I'm pretty sure I can appreciate that you did something pretty selfless today, to possibly help your brother. I hope you can see that."

He just looked out the window at the facility we'd just left, distorted through the pouring rain. "Can we get the fuck out of here?" It was more of a demand than a request, and I started the car, pulling away from the facility, leaving Max's past behind us.

Enid was twenty minutes away, and the hotel Max had booked us into was nicer than I expected, considering where I'd picked him up that morning.

He must've been reading my mind. "I figured you were going to pay, being the doctor and all."

"Well, you did buy me a toothbrush, so it seems pretty even…"

It was only seven, but it felt much later. It had been a long day for both of us. I told Max I'd see him in the morning, grabbed my bag of new toiletries, and went down the hall to my room. I needed a hot shower to clear my head. What Sean had told me earlier weighed heavily on me, and I didn't like the way I'd ended our conversation. I needed to call him so we could talk about it calmly, not leave things in such a precarious place, even for a night.

But I was even more unsettled after my shower. I kept replaying our conversation: Him blaming the lack of communication on me. Him telling me what was best for me, my career. Him telling me the Interpol offer was all but sealed. I wasn't sad about it; I was frustrated and angry. And hungry. I ordered a pizza and some beer from room service and put on the same clothes I'd just taken off.

I watched the clock, knowing it was the middle of the night in Paris, debating whether or not to make the call. Room service arrived, and I ate half of the pizza and drank a beer, still flip-flopping on whether to dial his number. Before I knew it, I found myself reaching for the phone.

There was a series of clicks before the ringing started. After four rings, I thought I might be sent to voicemail and began mentally crafting an appropriately worded message. Then, he answered.

"Oui..."

I'd clearly woken him up, and was about to apologize when I realized it wasn't Sean on the other end.

"Who is this??" I demanded. "Who are you?"

"Pardonnez?"

Then I heard Sean, talking to whoever was answering his phone in the middle of the night, telling them he'd mixed up the phones again.

My mind raced, jumping in a million directions, but quickly returning with one conclusion: Sean was sleeping with another man.

We'd talked before he left about what being apart would mean when it came to sex. Neither of us was interested in opening up our relationship just because of the distance. His posting was supposed to be temporary. We were going to figure it out, and we thought our relationship would ultimately be stronger for it. What a fucking fool I'd been. I had been jacking off, fucking myself with a dildo, whatever it took to satisfy my needs. He, apparently, had gone another route.

I hung up the phone and threw it on the bed like it had been burning my hand. If I'd been on the verge of anger before the call, I was now over the edge, moving right into furious.

Had I really been considering leaving my position in Austin and moving halfway around the world to be with him? I wanted to scream, at him, at myself. I paced around the room, talking to myself, admonishing myself for being so blind, so fucking stupid. Was this Pierre from the café? Had it been going on longer than a few weeks? Did they work together? The questions stacked up, and I was sure I knew the answers to all of them.

I realized Sean wasn't calling back. He must have seen it was me who had called and woken them up, and yet he wasn't calling.

A bizarre calm settled over me. He knew I was angry, and he knew he had to come up with some plausible story for why another man had answered his phone in the middle of the night. I knew that whatever he had to say didn't matter. It was over. I'd been down a similar road with my last boyfriend, Greg, and I wasn't going down it again. I couldn't.

I didn't want to hear from him, didn't want to hear his lies. I needed to be as far from my phone as possible. I grabbed the half-empty pizza box and my room key and padded down the hallway in my bare feet. I needed to check on Max anyway. His day hadn't been any easier than mine, and sometimes it was true: misery did love company. And pizza.

The *Do Not Disturb* sign was hanging from his door, but I ignored it and knocked anyway. When there was no answer, I knocked louder. It hadn't crossed my mind that he might've already gone to bed, it wasn't even much past nine. But when he opened the door, wrapping a towel around his waist with one hand while running the other through his hair and face, I knew I should've respected the door sign.

"Jesus, Max, I'm so sorry. I didn't think you'd be asleep this early. I, uh, brought pizza…"

He didn't say anything right away. It seemed like he was trying to make sense of the words I'd just spoken. He must've been deep asleep. I felt really bad.

"I'll just leave it. You can have it in the morning…or whenever…"

He shook his head, finally engaging his words. "Might as well come in," he said, letting go of the door and walking back into the room.

The light from the hallway illuminated clothes strewn on the floor and the unmade bed he'd clearly just been pulled out of. He picked up his jeans and stepped into the bathroom, emerging a few seconds later with them on. I flicked the switch by the door as I pushed it shut, and he covered his eyes from the bright overhead light.

"Turn that off," he said. I did, plunging us into darkness. A click followed, and a bedside lamp came on, low wattage, less harsh.

"Much better. You have pizza?"

I remembered the box in my hand and held it out to him. "Bacon pineapple. It's not everyone's favorite, sorry."

"It's fine. Thanks. I didn't eat." He sat back on the bed. "I was just going to lay down before I took a shower, and, well, now you're all caught up."

"So, here we are…" I found a chair just outside the periphery of the light and watched while he quickly finished two of the remaining slices. "I had a couple of beers left, I should've brought them. Wasn't thinking…"

He got up and walked to the minibar, pulling out two cold beers.

"Jeez, those are probably twice the price of the ones I have, Max."

"That's OK. I'm not the one paying." He gave the first hint of a smile since I'd entered the room, handing me one of the beers.

"Thanks, but I probably owe you more than just an overpriced beer."

He said something about how we were both probably disappointed with the way the day had gone. He had no idea just how much of a shit show this day had really been.

He sat back on the unmade bed. Shirtless, his pecs moved slightly each time he brought the beer to his lips. It was distracting.

He had a tattoo on his shoulder I hadn't seen before, a black, intricate design, some sort of bird. And the silver chain with the ring that hung around his neck, usually hidden beneath his shirt. The bedside light made his dark eyes appear blacker, more intense. For the first time, I was really looking at Max, not just as my patient's brother.

My mind drifted back to that night at Wrangler's, which, if I'm being honest, I hadn't stopped thinking about since we'd agreed to put it behind us.

It wasn't behind me, at least not yet. I still thought about his mouth on mine when I was home, alone. What might've happened if I hadn't walked out of the bar? What if I'd said, *yes, let's go fuck?* I shook my head. That was just my feelings of rejection talking. I knew that.

I wasn't listening to what he was saying. The numbing effects of the cold beer were starting to take over. I needed to go. My head wasn't in the right place to be there anymore.

"...so, that might be a good thing, you think?"

The sudden silence while he waited for a response snapped me back to reality, but I was clearly lost as to what he'd just asked.

"I'm sorry, my mind drifted...what did you say?"

"I said, Clara heard from Jasper. She left a message this afternoon. He's in line for a compassion leave to come see Evan. He might be in Austin soon. Do you think that's a good thing?"

"Max, honestly, right now, I don't know. I thought you showing up might be the catalyst we needed, but, no offense, that didn't seem to be true. I wouldn't hold out much hope that Jasper might be the key either. I'm sorry. I know I'm not giving you the good news you want to hear. I...I should go."

I put the empty beer bottle on the end table and stood to leave. As I passed by the bed, Max lunged forward and grabbed my wrist.

"Don't go."

I'm sure part of me knew that, as soon as I walked out of my room, I could find myself in this position. That part of me propelled me down the hallway to Max's room, without regard for the consequences. Anger, hurt, and desire knocked on that door repeatedly. Revenge stared Max in the eyes and told him I didn't want to leave.

He used the weight of my body to pull himself up to his knees, then paused. His eyes locked on mine, unblinking, judging me, measuring my seriousness. He tried to captivate me as if I wasn't already his.

His lips were soft, the kiss light, testing. Then his tongue insistently forced itself into my mouth, and his hands were on my back, pulling me into him. I pulled him to me in return, letting him know I wasn't going to run off this time.

His bare skin was warm beneath my touch. Sweat was beading up. The muscles of his back danced as his hands moved to rip my shirt off. No time for buttons. We were both panting, staring at each other like hunters. We quickly attacked each other.

I pushed him back onto the bed and fell on top of him. My full body weight pressed into him. My hips ground urgently against his. He tasted like beer and pineapple. I held his wrists over his head and licked down his bicep, through the dark mass of hair under his arm. The musky smell of his long, arduous day went straight to my head and turned me feral. I needed this man.

He managed to roll me onto my back, returning the favor of kissing down my neck, my chest. He licked and bit at my sensitive nipples until they were rock hard and raw. Distress signals were straight to my cock. I writhed beneath him. Goosebumps covering my body. My hands gripped his shoulders, pushed him downward. If he didn't free me from my pants immediately, I thought I might explode.

His tongue swirled around my navel. My hands clawed at the bedsheets, twisting them into knots in my desperation.

Finally, after what felt like an eternity, I felt him release my jeans and pull the zipper down. He slid them off my hips, taking my underwear with them. I was free at last.

There was no teasing, no gentle flicks of his tongue around the ridge of the sensitive head, no prologue. His mouth engulfed me. He swallowed my shaft until he gagged on it. Fucked it with his mouth. Hot spit like lava ran down the sides, onto my balls, wetting the crumpled sheet beneath me. It was everything I'd been missing for several months. I'd tried to go without and now I wanted it all back.

His name fell out of my mouth. Max. My god. Max.

He sucked on my balls, rolling them, tonguing them, pulling on them, torturing them. He pressed his hands against my inner thighs, spreading me open wide. I pulled my knees up to my chest. He spit on me. I wanted him to eat me alive. His tongue licked me. I needed him. His fingers played with me. I lost control.

And then, suddenly, he stopped. I gasped. No more fingers, no more mouth. I was left an empty hole with nothing there to fill it.

I opened my eyes in time to see him peel off his jeans. His bottomless eyes stared back at me. His beautifully thick cock was standing at complete erection, jutting from a thick mass of black hair. Glistening precum dripped from the end. Waiting.

"Suck my dick," he growled.

Once again, it was a demand, not a request.

Before I could respond, he was on me, quickly straddling my face. His knees were on my shoulders. He pinned me down. I opened my mouth in anticipation, my tongue lolled out to lick his length as he entered. I couldn't control him. I didn't want to. His thrusts were short, pulling out long enough for me to breathe, to suck on his thick, purpled head, to drink in the precum that continued to seep. He slapped my face with it, made me beg for more of it. He was so hard, I thought he'd come in my mouth. I braced for it, silently begged for it. But he, again, had other plans.

He pulled his cock from my mouth while I hopelessly chased it with my tongue. He fell onto me, our naked bodies wound around each other, dripping with sweat. He roughly grabbed my face, brought it to his. His tongue went deep into my mouth. I wrapped my legs around him, clawed at his ass. I tried desperately to feel his cock against my needy hole.

"Fuck me, Max. I want you, I *need* you, to fuck me…now."

I waited to feel him graze my hole as he guided himself into me, but instead he pulled himself off me, completely, leaving me once again confused. Suddenly he grabbed my ankles and flipped me onto my stomach. He pulled me, roughly, to the end of the bed, almost off of it, until only my chest was still on the mattress. I pulled myself open wide for him, bent over, aching, desperate to feel him inside of me.

His fingers spread me open. He buried his face into me again. His rough stubble drove me to the edge. His spit, his tongue, lubed me as best as possible. Neither of us could wait any longer. He grabbed my hip with one hand and pushed my head down onto the bed with the other. I heard him spit one last time and felt the wetness slip down over my hole.

He began to enter me. Slowly, surprisingly patient. He spit again. He went in further. I took deep breaths and did my best to relax even though his cock was stretching me unbelievably wide. He paused when he was fully inside, allowing me a moment to enjoy, to be overwhelmed, and allowing himself to admire his complete domination of me.

My brain reached a crescendo and then shut itself off. I was lost under the tidal wave.

I wasn't thinking about Sean. I wasn't thinking about Evan, or Katherine, or even Max. I was thinking about me. Exquisite pain swept through me. His cock was perfect. He hit me in all the right places. Quickly, there was much less pain, much more pleasure. I heard a deep moan and realized it was coming from me.

He picked up the tempo, got rougher, more forceful. Thrusting. Pounding. His hips loudly met my flesh.

My brain floated elsewhere, somewhere far, far away. Lights flashed, sounds ricocheted. I could hear him grunting as he fucked into me, like an animal rutting. It only turned me on more. I didn't want it to ever end. I was in a daze.

"Get on your back," he ordered. I silently obeyed.

I laid on the bed, my legs bent, my feet in the air. I begged to be filled again. He quickly did.

My ankles came to rest on his shoulders. He leaned over me and drove himself in deeper. New nerves fired as his cock slid past my prostate. I opened my mouth in pleasant surprise and found Max's mouth suddenly there, covering it, licking it, kissing it. His hair fell around my face. The silver ring he wore around his neck dropped into the hollow of my throat and laid there heavily.

His mouth on mine, his cock sliding inside me, my arms around him pulling him deeper into both orifices. His hips gyrated. My cock rubbed between us. The friction of his body, flesh and hair, brought me to a surprising, teeth-gritting, orgasm. My balls drained themselves, pumping load after hot load onto my stomach and chest while Max continued to pound himself into me. Frustration, aggression, whatever he was feeling, he was taking it all out on me. The feeling was intoxicating, endurable, overwhelming. I owed it to Max, and to myself, to take it.

He settled back, watched himself penetrate into me while I writhed beneath him. He slowed as his own climax neared as if he were deciding where to finish. He gradually pulled out and, simultaneously, swept his hand down my belly, collecting the cum that was still cooling there. He stroked his cock with it, two or three was all it took, and he came in a howl. Long streams of his cum shot across my stomach and chest, mixing with my own. I felt the sting of droplets hitting my cheek.

And then it was over. I was sore, exhausted, and relieved. And I had zero regrets.

Max dropped onto the bed next to me, panting. His heart pounded in his chest like my own. I lay there quietly, unsure of what to do next.

I knew that what we'd done hadn't changed any dynamics

between us. It would only get awkward if we let it. We were both grown men, capable of compartmentalizing sex as just a physical release. We weren't suddenly in love, and we certainly hadn't magically become boyfriends. We'd both needed this for our own reasons, I only knew my own. And now it was done. I needed to go.

But I didn't. I let Max get up to grab a towel. He came back with two bottles of water from the minibar, which I took to mean he wasn't kicking me out, at least not immediately.

"What a gentleman," I said with a sincere smile. "Thanks." I took the water and the towel. He made no move to put any clothes on, comfortable in his nudity and this new level of intimacy between us. When he lay back on the bed, he turned onto his side to face me, his arm casually behind his head, his hair wild where I had grabbed it.

"So, what changed?" he asked. His dark eyes had softened. His fingers casually ran down my arm. He didn't look like he was going to attack me anymore.

"What do you mean?"

"We could've done this the other night at the bar, but something, or someone, was stopping you. What changed?"

It was a fair question, but one I didn't want to answer. Telling him about Sean felt like it would ruin the moment. I had enjoyed getting fucked by Max in spite of Sean, not because of him. To tell Max that my relationship had suddenly imploded wouldn't tell the whole story. So, I lied and said, "Nothing. It's just sex, after all, right?"

He seemed to accept that, at least for the moment, which was all that mattered. We still had a long car ride ahead of us. He might use that time to dig further, he might not. Maybe by then, though, I'd have a better answer, even for myself.

My eyes drifted across his body. The tattoo had been a bit of a surprise, and up close, it was quite striking. It was an ominous black bird wrapped in barbed wire, looking seriously dangerous. It made me wonder if there was a story behind it, and if it had anything to do with the scar on his belly, just to the left of his navel.

Unconsciously, I reached out and ran my fingers over it. He didn't move away but instead let me trace my fingers around it, across his stomach. It wasn't fresh, but it didn't look old either, maybe within the last year or so. If I had to guess, it looked like he'd been shot, and at fairly close range.

I looked into his dark eyes, wondering what he was thinking, and found nothing there but blackness.

"What happened?"

"Exactly what you think happened."

We both had our secrets.

The clock on the bedside table behind him showed it was past eleven.

"I should go. We have a long drive tomorrow, and your brother is arriving…"

I waited for him to protest, maybe suggest I stay, but no protest came. I got up and redressed while he watched me. It had been fun, it had been necessary, but it probably wouldn't happen again, and that was okay. The morning would bring all the same problems into focus. This diversion was only temporary, for both of us.

As I turned to head for the door, he once again lunged down the bed and grabbed my wrist to stop me. He pulled my arm, bending me towards him, wrapping his free hand behind my neck to bring my mouth to his one last time. Soft, wet, brief.

"Good night, Doc," he said as he released me from his grip, a wry smile crossing his face.

"Good night, Max." I couldn't help but smile in return.

I returned to my room, stripped off my clothes, again, and made a beeline for the empty bed. My mind was near blank, but the taste of his kiss still lingered in my mouth, and the feel of his… and then nothing but black.

I fell into a bottomless darkness, but somehow, I wasn't scared. I felt like I landed in the palm of a giant hand that kept me safe.

Then I was flying. I was a bird. My wings were black and strong. I was surrounded by hundreds of other large black birds, just like myself. Our sound was deafening. My sharp black beak opened wide to let out my call.

Then suddenly, the other birds flew at me, attacked me. They somehow knew I was different, that I wasn't really one of them. I fell to the ground, and they descended upon me. I opened my mouth to scream and...

The pounding on the door jarred me awake.

"Doc! Get up, Doc."

Max. I looked at the clock. It was almost nine. I was sweaty, the sheets clammy and damp, pulled from the corners of the mattress. I'd slept long, but I didn't feel rested.

"Yeah, alright," I shouted back. "Gimme ten minutes." I hoped that would be enough for a shower to bring me around. We had a long day ahead of us, and we were already running behind.

I drove the first few hours in near silence while Max stared out the passenger window at the farmland and oil fields. Was he saying his final goodbyes to his past, once again? I knew better than to ask. We crossed the border into Texas and stopped for gas, after which Max once again insisted on driving. If I'd learned anything on this trip, it was that Max liked to be in control.

I resigned myself to more silence and closed my eyes as we got back on the highway.

"I think I know why Evan tried to kill himself."

My eyes flew open. Had I really heard what I thought I had, or had I fallen asleep and it had been a dream?

"Max?" I said cautiously. "What did you say?"

"I think I know...no, I'm pretty sure I know."

"What makes you sure now? Do you want to tell me?"

"What Momma said yesterday. I've been thinking about it ever since we left the hospital." He paused, his eyes still staring straight ahead, hands gripping the steering wheel tightly. "She all but blamed me, not necessarily for Evan's suicide attempt, I don't think she knows he tried to kill himself, but for all of his other problems."

"Why would she do that? Is it…" and I knew I was about to venture somewhere dangerous, "is it because you killed your father?"

He shook his head slightly, not responding to my question. I was about to tell him to pull over; we shouldn't have this conversation on the highway. He continued to shake his head, fighting with himself, knowing he needed to say what was locked up inside of him but not wanting to do so. He took a deep breath and slowly let it out. He looked at me and said, "It's because I didn't."

It hung there between us. Neither of us uttered a word. I was sure he was waiting for me to acknowledge what he'd said, but I wasn't sure if what he'd said was even true. How could it be? He'd been convicted, sentenced. He served time.

"Max, I'm confused. What do you mean, you didn't?"

"Evan did it. I walked in, Momma was on the kitchen floor. Pa must've hit her, at least that's what I assumed. Evan had the gun raised, pressed up against his shoulder like I'd taught him, and…he just fired."

I saw the scene in my mind. The chaos. The split-second reactions. Young Max, in control once again. I took it in. "Then why did you…" but I already knew.

"I had to protect him. I always protected him. I took his punishment when I could. I knew he could never survive whatever was about to happen. He was too sensitive, too broken."

"Oh my God, Max." My heart broke for him, what he had done and what he had endured, for someone else. My hand went to his shoulder, trying to offer some form of comfort, but he withdrew like I'd burned him.

"I told him, made him promise, to never tell anyone what had really happened. I took the gun. I pled guilty. I did the time."

I was still confused, though. Why was he telling me this now?

"What did your mother say to you yesterday, Max?"

"She said he'd never be a man, like me. She called Evan a coward."

"She…"

"And it wasn't the first time. I left him behind. I thought he'd be safe, and she's been calling him a coward all these years. She thinks I'm a hero. He's the fucking hero. He's the one who saved her. Saved all of us. I think he just reached his limit."

I could see his knuckles turning white, the muscles in his forearms bulging. His eyes were brimming with tears.

"Max, pull over. Please. This is too much. It's…I don't know, it's fucking horrible. You've kept this a secret for so long. That's such a tremendous burden you've carried, that you've both carried. What you've both gone through…"

Thankfully, he listened and pulled off to the shoulder. He threw the car into park and got out before I could get my seatbelt unbuckled. By the time I rounded the car, he was behind it, bent at the waist, bellowing a scream he'd been holding in for far too many years. It drowned out the sound of passing cars, going on past the point of his exhaustion. I didn't know how to help him. We'd been so close only hours earlier, and now I was almost afraid to touch him, afraid he'd run off or, worse, shut down completely.

"Max. It's OK," I said softly. "It's not your fault. You didn't know…"

Cars continued to pass by, oblivious to what was happening. Max knelt down on the shoulder, continuing to scream, he had years of it built up inside of him. His hands grabbed at the stones on the pavement. His voice grew hoarse, his body shook violently. When he finally slowed, gasping for breath, I slowly knelt next to him, tentatively wrapping an arm around his shoulder, letting him know I was there.

"You didn't know, Max. You were just a kid." I kissed him softly on the temple, impulsively, and felt the tension release from his body. "I'm here, Max. It's going to be OK."

Without speaking, he turned and wrapped his arms around me,

burying his face in my neck. His tears fell onto me. It was more intimate than anything we'd done in his hotel room the night before. I had no words to help him. I just let him cry, for his family, for himself, for the future he'd sacrificed a long time ago while trying to do the right thing.

"I caused all of this," he finally said.

Fault and blame are concepts I try to steer clear of in my work. It does no good to go down those rabbit holes. No one wins, and nothing ever really gets resolved. But I know it's always easier said than done. I fall victim to it myself. Often. But I feared that if Max went down that hole, I might never get him back.

"Look at me, Max."

He hesitated, so I took his tear-soaked face in my hands and forced him to look me in the eyes.

"We'll talk about why you may think this is all because of something you did as a kid, but hear me now when I say, there are so many factors at play here, not the least being that Evan is a grown man capable of making his own, complicated, decisions based on a myriad of things. Your relationship with him may be a part of it, it may not, but you don't own the blame. Let that go. Please."

"You don't understand…"

"You're right, I don't. But you don't either. You made a rash, impulsive decision ten years ago. You couldn't predict that we'd be here, years later. You did what you thought was best, given the facts at the time. You may've done the right thing. Maybe not. We can't change the past, but we can learn from it. You are not that one act, and neither is Evan."

We sat on the side of the highway for some time, not speaking. The hum of passing cars was a distant, irrelevant noise as Max's breath slowed, and his body began to settle. The weight of what he'd just shared hung between us, heavy and real. It was as if the world around us had been muted, just the two of us in that small space, trying to make sense of the chaos inside him.

Max didn't seem ready to leave the moment yet, and neither was I. The silence wasn't uncomfortable, just necessary. I had no words to fix what he'd carried for so long, no comforting platitudes that would erase his past. I just stayed, offering him the space to breathe, to begin to let go.

Finally, after what felt like an eternity, Max stirred, breaking the stillness.

"Let's go. I need to see my brother."

I nodded, starting the car and pulling back onto the road. The drive back to Austin was longer than it should have been, the weight of his revelation still thick in the air between us. When we reached the hospital, I dropped Max off at the front door, wanting to give him the space he needed. As I parked the car in my usual spot, I couldn't help but feel the enormity of what had just been shared. Max had carried that secret for years, and now, like a dam bursting, it was spilling out in fragments. It was more than a burden,it was his life.

By the time I entered the hospital, Clara was standing in the hallway outside Evan's room. Her posture was stiff, like she was waiting for something, or maybe someone, to tell her everything was okay.

"Ryder, what's going on? Max came storming in and kicked me out. He said he and Evan needed to have a talk?" Clara's voice had a soft edge of concern, but there was something else in her eyes, something guarded. It made me wonder if she knew more than she let on about what was happening.

I glanced into the room. Max was sitting with a chair pulled up close to Evan's bed, his head bowed. I couldn't hear the conversation, but I didn't need to. Max's body language said it all. He was finally confronting the weight of what had happened all those years ago, the guilt, the responsibility, the family he had tried to protect.

"He's talking to him," I said softly, my voice low. "They've got a lot to work through."

Clara's gaze flickered toward the door, but she didn't move. I could see the internal battle in her eyes, torn between wanting to help and needing to give Max and Evan the space they deserved.

"Let's go get a coffee," I suggested. "He may be a while."

Clara hesitated but then nodded, her shoulders loosening just a fraction as she turned toward the elevator with me. As we walked, I could sense her relief that she wasn't alone in this. There was something more to her quiet demeanor, a heaviness I hadn't seen before. Maybe she, too, was carrying secrets, maybe even the ones Max had kept from everyone else. But for now, we both remained silent, giving Max and Evan the time they needed.

The Course of True Love

Chapter Thirteen

MAXWELL

The line between sinner and saint can blur fast, turning jagged before you even realize it. Right and wrong, those clean, black-and-white concepts fit for church sermons and bedtime lessons, aren't always easy choices in the heat of the moment. More often than not, life lives in the grey space outside the margins.

The deaths of Paloma and Spencer Donato weighed heavily on me for a long time. They weren't the first people I'd killed, far from it, but theirs hit different. It made sense. Operation Falcon had been unlike any other job I'd ever been involved in. It was more immersive, emotional, and their deaths, while necessary for my success, were harder to process than any of the others. Because of Grayson.

I hadn't been honest with the DA or Captain Harris for a while. I was in way over my head, and I knew it. My feelings for Gray had been real. And when it was all over, knowing how I'd hurt him, how deeply I'd hurt him, left me with a wound that went far beyond the one in my belly. It was one I didn't think I'd ever be able to heal.

I was choppered from the Donato estate to a private clinic in upstate New York, admitted under an assumed name in case anyone had an idea to finish what Spencer Donato had started. When I was released, Dixon had me flown to his estate on Maui to recover. The hole in my gut slowly healed over, and within a few months, I was left with a scar that only a few would ever notice. But the hole in my soul, that one would take a lot longer to close.

For months, I sat alone on lounge chairs on the expansive lanai. The staff made sure I ate, often against my will. I'd stroll the manicured grounds and stare out at the never-ending Pacific Ocean, wondering where he was, what he was doing, if he still hated me. When I was discharged from the hospital, they handed me a plastic bag with the few belongings I'd had when I was admitted. At the bottom of it was the ring Grayson had given me that afternoon by the lake. I'd worn it for less than a day before I betrayed him and showed him who I really was. Now, it hung on a chain around my neck, a reminder of the price I'd had to pay for my sins.

It took months, but eventually, I started searching for him.

I scoured the internet for any scrap of information, anything that would tell me he was okay. But all I found was that he'd left *Joshua* and sold the loft on North Moore, the place where we had "accidentally" met and where we'd fallen in love. Now, they were gone. Someone else was living amongst my memories, and Grayson had become a ghost. He'd disappeared behind the vast Donato fortune that was now his alone, at least what hadn't been confiscated by the Feds.

The crimes of his family were exposed, the syndicate they'd successfully run for years unraveled and disappeared. Only I knew it had mostly been absorbed into Dixon St. James's vast empire, just as had been planned all along.

While Operation Falcon was deemed a success, and I even received an accommodation *in absentia* for my "heroic efforts," I knew it had all been a fiction from day one. I was never really a cop. I'd been sent in to eliminate Spencer and Paloma Donato by any means necessary. Grayson was just a footnote for everyone involved. The NYPD labeled him an expendable means to an end, Dixon knew he wouldn't fight for control of his family's operations. But to me, to me he was a good man who'd done nothing to deserve any of the pain that had befallen him. His only crime was in trusting me.

Dixon checked on me periodically, patiently wondering when I would return to work. I never had a solid answer for him beyond "I'm not ready yet." I knew what going back would entail. He said he understood, and I believed him, but after almost a year on the island, Bear arrived, unannounced. I knew the moment I saw him that he was Dixon's messenger and the message was clear: my time was quickly running out.

Since I first met Bear and he brought me into Dixon's unique circle of employees, we'd seen each other only a handful of times. Bear's role was much more behind the scenes, corporate espionage, cybersecurity, Trojan horses. He hibernated deep within a company's structure until the time came to wake up and take control. Bear was a genius with an angelic, baby face that no one ever suspected of being up to no good. He destroyed companies right under their noses, allowing Dixon to swoop in and peck at the carcass, taking what he wanted. He was all finesse. I, on the other hand, was a magician. My sleight of hand eliminated problems permanently when all other methods failed.

I was known as The Rook. Dixon had named us all after animals he thought suited our character or role. We were his little menagerie, and I was his omen of death. I'd been given two passports: Maxwell Walter Heath for personal use and Raphael Vincenzo Cook for business. Dixon's telltale wordplay. I had more entries in Raphael's passport than I had in my own.

"You don't have to go back immediately," Bear told me. "But you need to set a timeline. Dixon understands what he put you through in New York, but he's also a businessman trying to maintain an empire. He needs you, and he doesn't want to replace you."

"I just don't know if I can do it anymore, Bear."

I'd been wrestling with leaving the organization, but Dixon had been very good to me. The thought of leaving him behind for good left me scared, unmoored. I was outrageously well-paid for my services, and I knew I could never find another job that would pay me that well. I'd barely graduated high school before entering the system. The best job I could ever hope for in the real world would involve a fast-food apron or a reflective highway department vest. Everything I'd grown accustomed to would be gone. Everything I had belonged to Dixon. And even if I wanted to leave, I wasn't sure Dixon would let me. The information I had, the harm I could do to him and his businesses, it didn't seem possible that he'd ever run that kind of risk.

"I get it, man. This is the most intense job imaginable, and there's no room to be in it only halfway. That's why Dixon's been letting you have this time to get your head straight."

"He really has been great. I owe him so much, I know that. But am I going to do this forever? Or just until I get caught or killed?"

"Dixon would never let you do time. There are so many favors he can call in without even sweating. He had to do it for me once. I was in big trouble, looking at serious time, then suddenly it just all went away. I had to lay low for a while, create a new identity, but I was safe. He kept me safe. He'd do the same for you."

"But I assume there was someone before me doing this job. What happened to him?"

"Her. He called her his Dove." He hesitated, clearly unsure if he should tell me what had happened to her, but then it struck me on my own. Knowing Dixon and his love of wordplay...

"Jesus, fuck me, Bear...in Spanish, dove is..."

"...Paloma. You were the one stone that took out two very inconvenient birds, literally. No one betrays Dixon, not if they want to live a long life."

I had my answer. I thought I was going to be sick.

Dixon hadn't confided in me all the reasons for infiltrating the Donato family and their home, why Spencer and Paloma both had to die, but about my own precarious fate if I didn't rejoin his team, that message was received loud and clear.

"Don't you want more someday, Bear? A partner? A family?"

"Dixon is all those things for me. I give him my mind, my body, whatever he needs or wants, and he gives me everything I need in return."

"Except normalcy."

"Depends on your definition of 'normal,' I guess. Would you say you came from a normal background?"

"Fuck, I hope not. But that doesn't mean there aren't aspects of normal out there, somewhere. I love Dixon, I do. When we're alone together, he makes me feel like I'm all that matters. But I'm sure he makes you feel that way too. And Kit. And Buck. None of us are truly special. All of us are disposable."

Bear stayed with me in Hawaii for a couple of weeks, and we talked a lot about what we each thought our options were in life. But in the end, I still wasn't sure what to do.

When he left, I told him to let Dixon know I would be back in New York by month's end. I had until then to think about what my endgame looked like, and to try to figure out how I could achieve it without ending up like Paloma Donato.

I was in the pool one afternoon when my phone started to ring. I assumed it was Dixon calling to discuss my return, so I let it go to voicemail while I swam my laps. The quiet time in the water felt like meditation, and I wasn't ready to let the outside world disturb me just yet.

I swam until exhaustion set in, then pulled myself from the pool and laid on the hot concrete apron, letting the sun evaporate the water from my naked body. There was no need for modesty on the estate, and I often wore nothing but Grayson's ring around my neck. It was the only thing that gave me any real comfort, and now, the feel of the metal growing hot on my chest, branding my skin, gave me the sense of the punishment I still felt I deserved.

The ringing dragged me back from the edge of sleep, and I

cursed Dixon's impatience for calling twice in one afternoon. I reached for my phone, only to be more annoyed when I saw the call was coming from an unknown number. I dropped it back onto the chaise. The caller could leave a message if they wanted. I probably wasn't going to listen to it anyway.

My peace sufficiently shattered, I wrapped a towel loosely around my waist and headed back up the hill to the house, taking in the view of the ocean for the millionth time, asking the same unanswerable questions about my past and my future.

"Fish for dinner, Mr. Maxwell?"

"That's fine, Rose. Thank you. I'll be down at six, as usual."

Another night, alone at dinner, alone in bed. Maybe this was my future. Maybe my questions were already answered.

Sleep was hard to come by, and when I was awakened by the damn phone that I'd forgotten to silence. I was ready to kill. I regretted the mistake.

"WHAT?!" I yelled at the unknown caller. "What do you want?"

Silence, and then a small voice said, "Maxie?"

There had only ever been one person who'd ever called me that, and I hadn't heard it in a lifetime.

"It's, it's Clara," was all she said.

My first response should've been to ask if she was okay. Instead, I asked, "How did you get this number?"

"Evan had it in his phone. I...I didn't know if it was good anymore or not. I've left messages..."

Why was she going through Evan's phone? I sat up in bed, the sheet falling to my waist. I suddenly became very conscious of being naked.

I tried to remember what had prompted me, years earlier, to text Evan. I think I had a premonition that he was in trouble, something irrational like that. I still felt protective of him, even if I couldn't really help him anymore. "Is Evan okay? What's happened?"

"No, he's not okay, Maxie, and I don't know what to do…"

My brain jolted awake, and I tried to do the mental math. Clara had been seven, maybe eight, when I went away? She'd be a young woman now, but I didn't know who she was. She certainly didn't know me, or what I'd become, or where I even was.

I ran my hand through my hair, massaging my scalp, hoping the physical stimulation would clear the fog from my head. "What's happened? Where are you?"

It took her a long time to get the story out. She bounced between fact and fiction, and I had to keep stopping her to get clarification about things I had no idea about. Why was she in Texas? Where was Jasper? What had happened to Momma? But after what felt like an hour, I still wasn't sure what she wanted me to do. Evan was clearly in a bad way, but he was under a doctor's care. There wasn't anything I could do. I felt bad for her, I did, but eventually, I told her straight out that I was the wrong person to be calling. She needed to just give it time and lose my number. I hung up annoyed at her for thinking I was going to swoop in and save Evan, and at myself for being a complete dick to her.

For months, I'd been trying to reconnect with one part of my past, and when another finally appeared, it was the wrong fucking part. I pounded the pillow with my fist.

"Fuck." It was just the complication I didn't need at the moment.

I laid there until morning came, waiting for the rising sun to brighten the room, but it never did. When I finally got up and opened the curtains, I saw why. Ominous black clouds filled the sky. Thunder rumbled in the distance. It was going to be a day to match my mood, or vice versa.

I threw on a pair of gym shorts and the same t-shirt I'd been wearing for a few days, then went to the kitchen to see if Rose would make me one of her special omelets. But there was a note saying she and Brock, her husband who took care of the grounds, had gone back to their home. The coming storm threatened to wash out the road, stranding them on the estate, far from their children.

I pouted for a moment before remembering that their children's welfare was certainly a higher priority for them than me. I'd survive for a day or so without someone making my meals and changing my sheets. If I was seriously thinking about leaving Dixon's employ, I'd better get used to taking care of myself again. Besides, I wasn't that many years removed from the farm. I'd be okay.

I checked the sky again. This definitely wasn't a normal Hawaiian squall. When the rain came, it was going to come hard.

I began to peel a banana as I made my way back to the bedroom. I kept thinking about Clara's call, but more so, I kept thinking about Evan. I'd always tried so hard to protect him, but I'd dropped the ball. I thought once Pa was out of the picture, their lives, *all* of their lives, would be better. But Clara had certainly popped that childish bubble. It was too late to change any of that now. I couldn't go home and magically fix everything. We were past that.

I laid on the bed, listening to the rain hitting the window, then pelting against it harder. Lightning periodically lit the room, and the thunder grew louder as the strikes got closer. If I had thoughts of falling back to sleep, that's all they were. I got up and began wandering through the house, ostensibly checking the windows to make sure they were all closed and keeping the rain out, but realistically, I was just adrift, overwhelmed by my thoughts.

Was I actually thinking about going back there? Going back to my family? Jasper was in the service, stationed overseas, and Momma was still in Oklahoma. But Evan...Evan was my closest family. I couldn't deny that the bond we'd forged growing up was still there, still felt strong to me now that Clara had nudged it awake.

The power went out that afternoon. I lost cell service that evening.

The storm raged. I was cut off from everything except my own thoughts. I was drawn out onto the lanai. Palm trees bent in the wind. The ocean was boiling. I was quickly soaked through, my hair plastered to my face. It all just seemed so damn absurd. For no reason, I began to chuckle, which soon turned into a full-throated roar. There was no peace in my life. I'd given everything, and still they wanted more.

"WHAT ELSE DO YOU FUCKING WANT FROM ME?!" I screamed into the darkness.

I didn't have to wait long for my answer. A bolt of lightning pierced the sky, striking a date palm in the corner of the yard and sending a plume of sparks and flame skyward. The concussive shockwave knocked me backward, but not down. I was stronger than that. I had withstood worse, and whatever might be facing me, I would withstand that as well.

I pushed my doubts aside and tried to think about how I'd left things with Clara, the apology I'd need to make to her. I'd need to plausibly explain to Dixon why I was going to have to delay my return to New York once again.

The storm raged through the night and well into the next day. The windows rattled in their frames, and the furniture from the lanai blew across the property. The date palm smoldered. The sun came out just in time to set on the second day, bringing with it a hopeful promise of blue skies on the horizon. We wouldn't get the utilities back online for a few more days. I spent that time trying to figure out what to say to the woman my sister had grown into that wouldn't get her hopes up. I was done disappointing members of the Heath family.

"Clara, it's Max. I'm sorry…" was the simple, effective approach. It seemed she'd spent the time since our last call thinking about her expectations of me as well, and we met on common ground: Evan. I told her I needed a few days to tie up some loose ends, and I'd be in Austin by the end of the week.

Then I had to tell Dixon I was going to extend my leave yet

again, unsure how he would take it. Family wasn't a topic he liked to talk about.

I knew the people in Dixon's employ all had different skill sets and personalities, but we shared one thing in common: no family pulling us away from our work. Dixon had known before I ever met him that I'd left my family behind. I'd be his completely, and for years, that had been true. To tell him now that I was going back, even if only temporarily, felt like a betrayal.

The call was tense. He said he understood, but the edge in his voice reminded me that the leash, though loose, was still there. I packed my few belongings into a duffle, thanked Rose and Brock for taking care of me, and left with the morning light breaking over the horizon. I wasn't sure where this next step would lead. It felt like I was walking into the unknown yet again.

I landed in LA and made my way straight to Dixon's Bel-Air estate, choosing the least extravagant car I could find - the Viper. Dixon didn't exactly do understated. After tossing my duffle in the back, I hit the road for Texas, not bothering to look back.

Austin wasn't home, that made my return a little easier. I could breathe without the weight of expectations. It took two days to get there, and I'd hoped I could stretch it into three, but that didn't happen. I checked into the cheapest hotel I could find. If Dixon's indulgence was slipping away, I needed to get used to living without it. Funny thing, though...I hated it.

Lying on the uncomfortable mattress, listening to the couple next door go at it like teenagers, I couldn't shake the feeling of being trapped. I wandered the hotel room for a while, trying to talk myself into something resembling peace. There was no use pretending. I'd crossed too many lines already. I hadn't wanted to come back, yet here I was. I couldn't escape the pull of family, even if it was a past I'd buried for so long.

I needed to clear my head, get out. So, I found a bar nearby.

Grayson was the last man I'd had sex with. Between my lengthy hospitalization and recuperation and my subsequent Hawaiian self-imposed exile, there hadn't been an opportunity, other than the week Bear came to stay, and I couldn't begin to imagine having sex with Bear, though I'm sure he would've if I'd made a move. It had been a long dry spell, and I needed it to end before I got buried in the avalanche of family drama that I knew was headed my way.

I should've known from the name, but the guys at Wrangler's weren't what I typically went for. I guess I thought it'd be more collegiate, less older cowboy cosplay. But then I saw him, sitting alone at the end of the bar, staring at a drink like it was his only friend in the world. I knew the feeling. I ordered a beer and stood back to watch him, see if he was with anyone or what he did if anyone else dared approach him. It only took a few swigs of my beer to conclude that he was alone, and everyone was steering clear of him. Probably the scowl on his handsome face, but I remembered once liking a bit of a challenge.

I approached and made some lame icebreaker comment to test the water. It didn't fail miserably, but it wasn't a huge success either, so I tried the never-fail, "Let me buy you another," hoping the booze would lower his defenses and he'd let me into his pants. I just wanted to get off. I wasn't looking to marry the guy.

He was appreciative, and I could've sworn he cracked a smile at one point. But then the wall went right back up, and he tried to brush me off. So, I took my shot.

I leaned in so he wouldn't miss a syllable, and he'd feel my hot breath on his ear. "Why don't we just go back to your place and fuck?"

It got his attention, but no immediate response. Okay, phase two: contact. I put my beer down on the bar and began massaging his shoulders. Every guy in the bar could see how tense he was. Probably why no one was paying him any attention. He was too much work. I was down for it though, massaging deeper and deeper until I heard him moan unconsciously.

"Now imagine we were naked in your bed doing this…"

I didn't give him time to turn me down again. I dug in deeper, releasing the knot between his shoulder blades. He was putty in my hands, or at least I thought he was, until he tried to stand up and push past me on wobbly legs. Time for phase three.

I gracefully angled his face up towards mine, just then realizing he stood a few inches shorter than me, while quickly adjusting my own angle so our lips would meet as planned.

I'm not a guy who would force himself on anyone, and I would've pulled back if he'd indicated he wasn't willing to go along for the ride. He didn't indicate that. In fact, he grabbed my waist, pulled me closer, and opened his mouth, messing around with my tongue. I moved my hands down his back, and that seemed to break whatever spell he was under. He put his hands on my chest and lightly pushed me.

"I can't," he said, but the hard cock throbbing against my thigh indicated otherwise.

I was about to protest, but decided to admit defeat instead. He was cute, but way too much work for what I needed. I cut bait and let him swim away. I made some "Your loss" kind of comment as he left, but my eyes were already scouting the room. My missed opportunity with the cute stranger had turned my mood from horny to feral, and I no longer wanted some long, drawn-out passion play. Someone there certainly wanted to suck me off, and I didn't care if it was in the Men's room or out back behind a dumpster. I needed to unload in someone, soon.

I was about to order another beer when a cowboy hat from across the bar caught my attention. He raised an eyebrow and nodded toward the door. I understood him quite clearly. We were in the front seat of his truck in a matter of seconds, zippers down, cocks out. He blew me, I blew him. It was quick. It was messy. We both came, put our dicks away, and I was back on the road to my hotel. Mission accomplished, with only one minor blonde-haired detour along the way.

I lay in bed for a while, wondering what sex with the handsome stranger might've been like. His kiss was certainly memorable, but I was serious when I said it: Not sleeping with me was his loss.

Chapter Fourteen

RYDER

T he mind protects itself from what is too difficult to face.
I remember reading that sentence in medical school, and it's something I've often returned to since then, trying to make sense of particularly opaque situations.

The trip to Oklahoma had been illuminating, just not in the ways I'd imagined when we set out that morning. Katherine Heath had been the key, or a key, but it unlocked something in Max, not Evan. At least, not directly.

After Max's bedside apology to his brother, a decade too late, we all hoped that somewhere in the recesses of Evan's mind, he might've heard those words and could begin to forgive himself enough to free his body from the prison it had become. But that didn't happen. Life isn't like the movies, and the mind is more complicated than that. Still, there was renewed hope, a sense that something positive had occurred, even if it couldn't be named.

Max slowly worked through his own demons. I offered my professional services, which he predictably declined. What had happened between us in that Oklahoma hotel room silently hung between us, much like our kiss that night at Wrangler's. Neither one of us brought it up, not even in jest. It hadn't brought us closer. In fact, it had done the opposite.

That night, the line between the professional and the personal had blurred, if only for a moment. But it was long enough for each of us to see the other from a completely different perspective. I saw a man who was passionate, direct, and careful, not the rough, taciturn man who had been showing up at the hospital every day. But I'd allowed my professional judgment to become compromised, and there was no going back to change it, no matter how much I might've wanted to.

Ten days passed. Summer was in full swing. Texas was warming like an oven, and it would stay that way for the next several months. Clara and Max were at Evan's bedside every day, putting aside whatever responsibilities they had outside of the room, at least for the time being. I knew Clara would be starting university in the fall, but I didn't really know where Max had come from. His story about Miami seemed off, for some reason. But that was his business. He seemed committed to Austin, and to Evan, for now.

The relationship between Max and Clara had clearly changed since that first day. I often found them deep in conversation, Evan a nearby, silent witness to their slow but steady reconnection. Ten years of estrangement couldn't just vanish overnight. Rebuilding a relationship takes time, but they were getting to know each other again, gradually erasing the lost years they'd spent apart.

"Jasper's got a seven-day compassionate leave. He's flying in from Germany tomorrow." Max stopped me in the hall as I passed during rounds.

"Max, that's great, but I think we both know not to get our hopes up. That doesn't necessarily mean anything for Evan. We've been down this road already. Your being here has been great, but probably more for you and Clara than anything. I'm sorry." I reached out to place a hand on his shoulder, hoping to offer some measure of support alongside the harsh dose of reality. He pulled away reflexively.

"I just thought you should know," he said before turning back toward Evan's room.

I debated following him in. I'd already checked on Evan earlier that day. No change, except maybe a slight improvement in his coloring. His skin looked less waxy, or so I thought. I made a mental note to keep monitoring it. It might be a positive sign, or it might just mean the room was getting too warm. I was ready to consider any possibility.

Just as I was about to push the door open, my phone vibrated in my pocket. I checked my watch: four on the dot. Eleven in Paris.

It had taken a couple of days, but Sean finally called to discuss his bombshell announcement. It seemed the offer wasn't as final as he'd initially said, and he was still hoping for some sort of compromise. He felt trapped, caught between the two things he wanted most in the world. At least I was now part of the equation, but I couldn't see how this would end without one of us sacrificing our ambitious career.

"Hey, babe. How's Texas today?"

"Hot. We need rain. The landscaping's turning brown. It's not Paris…"

"The city without A/C, a garbage strike, and a super crowded Metro…"

I laughed. "This is how you sell me on moving to Europe? It's a good thing you're not in Sales."

"But we'd be suffering together, Ry."

"Well, there is that." I paused before stating the obvious. "I miss you."

"I miss you too. I'm lying here in my boxers, wishing you were next to me…"

"Stop it! You know I'm at work! You can't get me all worked up just because you're horny."

"It's just been so fucking long."

"You don't think I know that? You know sex isn't the issue or the answer, right?" I glanced up through the window into Evan Heath's room and saw Max staring back at me. I was flooded with guilt.

Sean had explained that Pierre had been kicked out of the flat he shared with his girlfriend, and he'd been crashing on Sean's couch for a few days while they worked through their problems. He used them as an example of how to deal with big issues when the foundation between two people was love, and all I could think about was my misinterpretation of an innocent situation and the aftermath that followed.

I shouldn't've slept with Max.

I thought about it every time I saw him. His kiss. His touch. His power. He was so rough yet vulnerable that night, and I was sure he never would've unburdened himself of his long-kept secret if we hadn't been that intimate together. Despite how he acted toward me now, I knew he felt that connection too. Unfortunately, strings had been attached to our hookup that neither of us had anticipated.

"...so what do you think?"

Ugh. I was still looking at Max and not listening.

"Sorry, someone just handed me a form to sign. What did you say?"

"Come to Paris. Make the time. We can train to Berlin, see if we can even imagine living there. I mean, we might hate it..."

"I know. We need to do that. But there's a lot going on here right now. I can't just pick up and go. Not for a while, at least."

I knew that wasn't the response he was hoping to hear, but it was the truth. Besides all my other patients, until something definitive happened with Evan, I couldn't imagine just leaving the country, even if it was to see Sean.

To his credit, Sean's tone was even, measured. "Well, just keep it on your radar. I can push off my decision for a little while longer, but not forever."

"I know. I'm sorry. I want to. I'll make it happen somehow…" even if I wasn't sure how I'd do it. "I need to go. Go get some sleep, or jerk off thinking about me…I like that scenario more. I love you, Sean."

"I love you too, Ry. I miss you…"

The line went dead, and I just…continued on with my rounds. We were maintaining a thin connection, but no closer to a resolution, as usual. My feelings were all over the place. It was a good thing I was seeing my therapist later.

Every man should be lucky enough to have a big sister who makes him feel like a safe and protected little boy, regardless of the situation. I was just that lucky. Katelyn had always watched over me like a second mother, even though she was only three years older, and I had always been able to tell her everything that was going on in my life.

When I was fifteen, I thought I might be gay because I had a terrifying crush on Trip Hooperman, my Biology lab partner. He was so handsome and he made my stomach tighten, hurt in the best possible way every afternoon when he walked into class. I told Katie and she didn't make me feel like a freak. She also convinced me not to confess my feelings to Trip because she could tell he was as straight as they come, and it wouldn't turn out the way my nighttime fantasies dreamed it would. She was right, of course. Trip got Stacy Leigh Myers pregnant our senior year, and, last I heard, he was on his second marriage and still living in Redmond, working for his dad at his car dealership. Still handsome, though.

In med school, when I was struggling with deciding on a specialty, Katie laid out the pros and cons of each one I was considering. It was her comprehensive list that led me to Neurophysiology and Behavioral Science. I've never doubted that choice because she's never doubted me.

But I hadn't spoken to her in a while. She didn't know about Sean's job offer unless she'd heard it from him or through the work grapevine, but I knew she would've called me immediately if either had been the case. I needed to tell her. I needed her advice.

She was already sitting at the table when I got there, rising to greet me with one of her signature hugs, firm, purposeful, and motherly. As an FBI agent, I wouldn't want to get on her wrong side, but as a big sister, she was soft and comforting.

"Mom wants to know why you haven't called her or Dad in weeks. I told them you were probably just busy, and that I hadn't heard from you either, but this is not like you. So, what's going on, little brother?"

"Can I at least order a drink before we get too deep into the therapy portion of the evening?"

"I've already ordered one for you…here it comes now. Get ready to start spilling."

I took a long drink and waited for the burn to subside before starting in. Katie's jaw dropped when I told her about Sean's Berlin job offer. She hadn't heard anything about it at work, but she knew what a big step that would be for him, career-wise. She also immediately connected the dots to form the complete picture. It wasn't exactly good news for me, or us as a couple.

"Oh Ryder, no…"

"Yeah…this time apart has been bad enough. I wasn't planning on it becoming permanent." I took another long drink, grateful for the warm buzz. "Katie, I feel so selfish not jumping on board with this. I'm thrilled for him, I really am. I know staying in Austin wasn't his forever dream. I've always loved his drive and determination, and I guess I always knew this could happen, someday. I just didn't expect it to happen this quickly."

"Ryder, you're not selfish…you're the least selfish person I know. I've seen and heard stories about the lengths you go to for your patients. And I can't imagine Sean has used that word in any of this."

I admitted he hadn't, but I was pretty sure he'd thought it once or twice, stopping just short of hurling it at me, knowing it would hurt too deeply.

"What am I going to do, Katie? I don't want to lose him, but I don't want to lose me either…"

"Well, whatever you do, don't call Mom until things are more decided. She'll be down here packing your house up before you know it. She moved to six different states with Dad, following his career. It was fine for her. It was a different time. You were too young to really experience all the upheaval before we settled in Redmond. You didn't really uproot yourself until you came to Austin, and I was already here. Germany. Wow. That's a whole new ballgame."

"I know. I'd know no one, have no career…I'd be home baking strudel all day, waiting for my man to return at night so I could sit attentively and listen to how exciting and fulfilling his day was."

"God, you'll probably start having missionary sex!"

I gasped and waved my napkin as if I were about to swoon. "I just can't…although it would be better than not having any…" I didn't want to tell her that I'd slept with Max. It didn't factor into the bigger picture, and I knew she'd want all the details. She'd end up jumping to some false conclusion about what it meant 'in the big picture,' how it spoke volumes about how I really felt about Sean and staying with him. That would be unfair, to everyone.

"Do I need to take you shopping for some sort of sex toy? I find that…"

"No, nope, stop. We're about to cross a line that I have not had enough to drink yet to cross." We talked about *almost* everything.

"Joking aside, I'm not sure how to help you this time, Ry."

"I know. There really isn't a viable compromise for either of us. One of us will have to make a huge sacrifice if we want to stay together."

I could feel the tears welling up, and I didn't want to cry in the middle of the restaurant. I took a deep breath and blew it out, regaining a semblance of composure.

"Change of subject. How's my adorable niece?"

"She's a little bitch these days. Whoever coined the Terrible Twos never met a three-year-old."

"I don't know how you do it, all of it. Career, family, maintaining your sanity…"

"Well, I'm not getting job offers to move to Germany. I've had to make my peace with my career plateauing, which was a pretty bitter pill to swallow. But Dan really steps up when I have an opportunity to travel, and Pippa isn't as bad as I make her out to be. You know that. She rolls with the flow pretty well. And she misses her Uncle Ryder."

"I know. We need to have an Uncca Wyder and Little Miss Pippa solo outing ASAP. Dammit, see, that's another huge con to leaving Austin. I don't want to miss out on her growing up."

"She'll be fine. You focus on you. Besides, I'd have no problem shipping her off to Europe for a summer when she's older."

"So you're saying I should go?"

"Only for purely selfish reasons."

"Maybe I should ask Dan what he thinks."

"Oh, he'll definitely want you to stay. He'd have to cultivate a new gay friend, and I'm not thrilled thinking about him at Wrangler's, taking interviews."

"Oh, he'd be very popular there."

"That's what I'm afraid of. I'm too old to deal with a husband having a sexual identity crisis!"

We laughed, drank, and ate off each other's plates until her maternal guilt kicked in and she declared it was time to head home. Pippa would be long asleep, but she had to see her, lying peacefully in her new 'big girl' bed. I longed for those carefree days, those nights, and envied her for them. Katie had, uncharacteristically, not brought me any closer to a decision, but I knew it was unfair to think she could. Still, she had taken my mind off things just long enough to make me feel more human again, and for that, I was thankful. If I could just add in a good night's sleep like Pippa, I might be able to think clearly about things tomorrow. And maybe, by our four o'clock call, I'd have an answer for Sean, at least about going to Paris for a visit. I really did miss him...

I got home and poured myself a cold glass of Sauvignon Blanc from the near-empty bottle in the fridge. I wasn't ready to lose the heady buzz I'd been carefully cultivating all evening, and I wasn't quite ready for bed yet. Besides, I knew the alcohol would help me sleep, once I got there.

I stepped out onto the patio and decided that if I stayed in Austin, I'd invest in some backyard landscaping, maybe cover this patio, add a fire pit over there by the trees for the cooler fall nights. And maybe finally put up a fence to block off the expanse of woods that sat behind the yard, dark and ominous. The animals that lived out there didn't need free entry to my space. They had theirs, I had mine.

As if on cue, a rare cool breeze blew out from the woods, reminding me that they would have a say in any potential changes I was considering. A shiver ran down my spine, and I felt my nipples spring to attention under my shirt. My hand subconsciously rubbed across one. I missed how Sean would walk up behind me in moments like this, his hands cupping, massaging my chest, pinching my nipples, knowing exactly how turned on that made me. We often ended our petty arguments that way. He knew I couldn't stay mad at him once he started playing with my chest, one of my many, well-known, weaknesses.

"Oh, Sean," I muttered aloud. "What are we going to do?"

I waited to see if the wind had an answer for me, if the gods of the forest wanted to weigh in on the situation. But other than a few crackling branches and the rustling of leaves, there was silence from the dark woods.

I felt the first drop of rain as I emptied my glass. I stood there and let it come. I unbuttoned my wet shirt and pulled it off. The drops pelting my bare skin stung briefly, reminding me of their power and my small place in the universe. I unzipped my jeans and tossed them back into the house in a damp heap. I stood in the pool of light from the living room in my soaked boxers and let out a primal, cleansing yell like I'd watched Max do in Oklahoma. It came from deep in my soul, rattling my bones on its way out. I hoped it would loosen whatever was blocking my brain from making any decision about my future. I didn't care if the neighbors heard. They'd think it was just thunder, or a coyote, or some other feral creature on the prowl, and they wouldn't be far wrong.

I stalked back into the house, pulling off my boxers as I made my way into the bedroom. My cock was already semi-hard. I'd worked myself into a horny frenzy of desire without even trying. I glanced at myself as I passed the mirror over the dresser, one hand massaging my chest, the other wrapped tightly around my dick. They should've been Sean's hands on my body. He should be the one taking control of me, leading me to the bed, taking me into his mouth. It wasn't fair that I was there alone.

I fell backwards onto the bed, my cock arching up towards my belly, full and hard. I stuck my fingers into my mouth, coating them with my spit so they would slide into me easier. The hollowness within me needed to be filled. One, then two, then a surprising third. No matter how many I tried to force into me, it wasn't going to be enough.

Barney was in the back of the nightstand drawer. Purple, thick, about nine inches long, and ready for emergencies just like this. I tore through the drawer and pulled him from his hiding place along with the bottle of lube. I slathered it, spread myself open, knees to my chest, and zeroed in, pressing in slowly, to start, and then pushing in deeper and deeper. My vision blurred.

I loved having a dick in my ass, even Barney if that's what it had to be. Tonight though, I wanted it to be Sean. I saw him hovering over me, sliding into me, telling me he loved me, his hands tangled in my hair and his sweat dripping onto me. I wanted to feel his lips on mine, his strong back muscles flexing beneath my hands as he thrust into me.

I worked Barney in and out, each stroke eliciting an unconscious moan of delight.

I got on my knees, squatting over Barney, letting my free hands
stroke myself. In and out, up and down, riding and stroking. I
looked down at the bed and saw Sean, a smile across his beautifully
complicated face, taking pleasure in watching me, as I tried to take
care of both him and myself at once. I closed my eyes, threw my
head back. I twisted my hard nipple until it pained me. I knew I
could be coming at any moment. I was overcome by the frenzy of
sensations. The flashes of light in my mind, images of Sean,
images of Max...Sean, Max...blending together, until they
blended into one. I was coming. My muscles clenched around
Barney, my cock erupted, and cum sprayed across the spread. I
continued to stroke myself over and over, long past the point where
there was anything left in me. I collapsed onto the bed landing in
the streams of cum I'd just made, still warm and slick. I slowly
removed Barney and dropped him onto the floor. Satisfied but
confused, and empty inside once again.

I lay there, exhausted. It wasn't the first time I'd thought about
Max, but this time had been different. For the first time, I hadn't
been able to separate him from Sean. They felt like two halves of
the same person. Maybe it was because I'd avoided mentioning
Max to Katie earlier when we were talking about Sean. Maybe it
was because I hadn't really processed what had happened between
us in Oklahoma. Maybe because I knew it hadn't just been sex
between us. Maybe because it had been more. No. That was the
delusion. It had been more. I had lied to Max.

I stripped the spread off the bed and tossed it into the washer,
the mundane task grounding me, even if only briefly. By the time I
crawled back into bed the earlier rush of emotions had faded,
leaving behind only the familiar weight of my thoughts. I was sober
now, but my anxiety hadn't subsided. My mind wouldn't stop
racing, looping between Sean and Max, between the life I'd built
here and the life I'd nearly lost. I needed to stop obsessing over

Maxwell Heath. He hadn't given me a second thought in weeks, and I wasn't even sure what we'd been. Was he just a mistake, or something more? It didn't matter. I didn't want to matter to him.

I let the rain against the window become white noise, let it drown out my thoughts. The steady rhythm of it softened my racing heart, reminded me of how far I'd drifted from the answers I'd been hoping for. I couldn't fix this tonight. I couldn't fix *anything* tonight. I closed my eyes, willing myself to forget everything for just a few hours.

Sleep finally began to pull me under and I let it take me, grateful for the quiet that would follow.

Chapter Fifteen

MAXWELL

S pying on Ryder had become my nightly obsession.

I didn't like to think of it as spying, or stalking. I told myself I was just gathering intel. I'd spent years doing this: learning someone's habits, observing their routines, calculating when the perfect opportunity would present itself. But Ryder wasn't a target. He was different.

It wasn't just about watching him when he thought he was alone. I'd study him from my hideaway at the edge of the woods that bordered his property, taking in the whole of his life outside the hospital. I knew which hook by the door he always used to hang his work bag. I knew he had an alarm system he never bothered to set. I knew which chair in the living room he never sat in, probably because it was his. I knew he always washed his dishes right after eating, never leaving them to pile up. I knew he preferred to sleep on the right side of the bed.

He was a creature of habit, and away from the grind of the hospital, where the demands on him never stopped, he exuded a quiet sadness. I'd watch him roam through his empty bungalow, moving through the space like he didn't belong in it, like the solitude had worn into him over time.

Each night, before he went to bed, he'd jerk off. Like so many men without a partner, it seemed almost mechanical, a way to satisfy himself without needing anyone else. And when he did, I wanted to break in and join him. He deserved more than just a release. He deserved to be taken, to be pleasured, to experience something that would leave him gasping, craving more. I could do that for him. I had done that for him once before.

But I kept my distance. I'd exposed myself to him in Oklahoma, let my desires slip in a moment of weakness, revealing a truth about myself that no one, not even Evan, had ever known. It terrified me. Being that vulnerable, giving in like that, was something I wasn't ready to do again. Especially not with him. Part of me wanted to keep that truth locked away. I knew, though, that the deeper reality was that I wanted more. But he wasn't available. There was someone else, a mystery man I knew I could never compete with.

So, I watched. Stolen glances at the hospital when I thought he wasn't looking. From the woods behind his house at night. From just outside his bedroom window when he thought he was alone. I was always there. Watching. In the dark.

Then, last night...he almost caught me.

He was late arriving home. Usually, by the time I'd get there, he was well into his nighttime routine. I'd park my car a half mile away, then meander through backyards, careful to avoid motion-sensitive lights and neighbors who liked to keep their dogs outside. But last night, when I got to his place, the house was dark.

I thought he'd stopped by Wrangler's again. I was afraid he'd come home with some stranger, maybe even fuck him in his bed while I watched from the shadows. I wasn't sure how I'd react to that. No, I knew exactly how I'd respond.

I stood in the middle of his backyard, my mind running through scenarios, when the first light flickered on. I moved closer, jealously, as the patio door opened and he stepped out, alone, thank God. I darted back to the tree line, breathless, watching him.

He was restless, agitated. When the rain started to fall, he didn't move. He stood there, letting the drops soak into him, as if he were trying to work something out. Something must've happened with the boyfriend.

He peeled off his wet clothes, his skin shimmering under the dim light coming from inside the house. I almost ran to him, unable to stop myself. Watching him there, in nothing but his wet boxers, was almost too much. He was so close.

Then, the howl. The gut-wrenching sound that nearly brought me to my knees. The pain he felt was something I knew well, something I had felt once too. It was the kind of feeling that couldn't stay inside any longer, that had to escape in the most violent way possible.

I prayed he would find the release he needed. But even as I watched, I knew it wouldn't come so easily.

Then, he stormed back into the house. The light in his bedroom flickered on. I sprinted to the window, pressing myself against the wall, frozen in place as I peered in and watched the scene unfold before me. He was a man possessed, and I was nothing more than a riveted voyeur.

I couldn't tear my eyes away. His naked body, slick with rain and sweat, moved with raw intensity. The way he rode that purple dildo, I longed for it to be me he was on top of. My wet hair fell across my face, but I didn't bother pushing it back. My hard cock strained to be set free but I couldn't be distracted. I was too absorbed, too mesmerized by the way he moved. I wanted to commit every second to memory, the way he breathed, every thrust, every desperate motion.

I couldn't look away.

When he came, I opened my mouth and pretended the summer rain was his warm cum, letting my mouth fill until I almost choked.

I had to get out of there before I gave in and stormed in to fuck him the way he truly needed to be fucked. But I knew it wasn't me he was fantasizing about. It wasn't me he needed inside him. I was never going to be that man again.

The long, painful walk back to the car in the pouring rain did nothing to clear my head. I knew that seeing him at the hospital the next day would bring all those thoughts rushing back. But that's all they were, thoughts. I couldn't afford to have serious feelings for Ryder Delaney. I couldn't. I had lost the ability to truly feel anything for another man when I lost Grayson. I was certain of that. Nothing felt right anymore.

The next day, when I arrived at the hospital, everything seemed as it always had. Evan lay tethered to his bed, Clara sat by his side, her face a mask of quiet expectation. I wasn't sure how much longer I could bear it, the false hope, the crushed expressions when nothing changed. Day after day. Adding Jasper to the mix might just push me over the edge. For a decade, I hadn't had to shoulder the weight of this family, my family. Now, it felt like I was being pulled back in against my will. Every second in that hospital room felt like it could be my last. I had already done my part. What more could I give?

Clara and I took turns getting coffee. It still felt strange seeing her as an adult, like she'd aged overnight. In the snap of a finger, the little girl I remembered, who loved playing in the mud around the sty, was now a grown woman. I knew seeing Jasper would have the same disorienting effect. In an instant, the boy who had once run wild with me on the farm would be replaced by a soldier, a man.

When Ryder walked in around lunchtime, I could hardly bring myself to look at him. I could see the smile on his face, but it didn't reach his eyes. I knew there was darkness behind it. I wanted to hold him, kiss him, comfort him, but it wasn't my place. In the hospital, he was Evan's doctor. Only at night, when I silently watched him from the shadows, could he become someone else, someone I could want. But the fight against desiring him? That was constant. The only way I could keep my feelings in check, to not betray myself, was to keep things short between us. The fewer words, the better.

"When is your brother arriving?" he asked.

"Later."

Clara shot me a look, like I should know better. "His plane lands shortly after two, Ryder. Knowing Jasper, he'll head straight here and worry about where he's staying later."

"Oh, won't he be staying with your Aunt and Uncle, with you?"

"There really isn't room. They barely have space for me there."

I looked at Clara, sensing something in her tone. We'd talked about a lot of things in the past few weeks, mostly old memories, life on the farm that she barely remembered, awkward questions about Pa that I did my best to answer without shattering the image she had of him. We'd talked about her life in Austin, but not much about her relationship with our Aunt and Uncle, who had taken her in. I assumed they treated her well; Clara was always sweet, then and now. The thought that they might not have treated her like their own child never crossed my mind. But maybe they had. Maybe Uncle Ted was more like his brother than I realized.

I tuned out of their conversation and looked down at Evan. He looked peaceful, like he was lost in a deep sleep, one he wasn't ever waking up from. I muttered to myself, "What did we do?" as if I had given him any choice all those years ago but to follow me down my reckless path. He would've followed me to the ends of the earth and never asked why. I knew that. I tried to protect him, but maybe I only did so temporarily. What was the lifetime cost to everyone else?

And then, I could've sworn I saw a slight twitch.

"Doc," I said, hesitantly. I didn't want to alarm anyone, especially not Evan, if this was a sign that something, anything, was happening. "He moved. His face, his cheek...I swear I saw it move."

The conversation stopped, and everyone stared, first at Evan, then at me.

"Maxie, I'm not doubting you, but it might've just been a play of the light," Clara said, her voice measured as she ran her finger down Evan's cheek, testing for any reflexive response. There was nothing. "I think it was just wishful thinking, Maxie."

"I know what I saw, Clara."

I leaned closer to Evan, my voice barely above a whisper. "Come back to us, Evan. Come home." I took his hand, but it just hung limp in mine. I let it go. "I know what I fucking saw..." I turned and stormed out of the room, leaving Clara and Ryder's disbelief in my wake.

My days at the hospital were spent either sitting in Evan's room or killing time in the depressing cafeteria, and I was fucking sick of both. I walked the halls, passing floors I'd never been to, raising more than one eyebrow from the nurses. I could tell a few of them were seriously considering paging security, but I didn't care.

The rain the night before had cooled the air and driven out some of the humidity, so I stepped outside, hoping for a little peace. I found a bench, as far away from everyone as I could get. If only I could get away from my own thoughts.

Every time I closed my eyes, I saw Ryder grinding down on that dildo, and my mind raced with thoughts of him grinding down on me.

"Ryder..." His name tasted different in my mouth.

I shook my head, trying to push the thoughts out. There was already one lost cause in that hospital, I didn't need to make it two. I needed to focus on my brother. I needed to get him well. And then, I needed to get the hell out of Austin.

I looked up and saw him approaching from the parking lot. Even if he hadn't been wearing his olive green fatigues, I would've recognized him anywhere.

"Jasper Heath! Jesus fucking Christ. Look at you..."

He was as tall as me, but broader across the shoulders and

thicker through the chest. His dark blonde hair was shaved short, but his blue-green eyes, identical to Clara's and Evan's, were a perfect blend of the best parts of Momma and Pa. I was the only one who'd inherited Grandpa Pete's dark, hateful eyes, a fact Pa used to take a sick pleasure in pointing out.

He wrapped his arms around me in a hug so tight I thought he might break me in half. He held me longer than I thought comfortable, but in less than a minute, he'd broken down whatever defenses I might've still had.

"I've never been sure I'd see you again," he said, pulling back. "You look like shit."

I laughed. "That's about how I feel. Asshole."

"That's Sergeant Asshole to you, civilian."

"Careful. I can still whoop your ass. You don't even want to try me, little brother."

I initiated the next hug. He'd barely been a teenager the last time I saw him, and now, here he was, a full-grown man. I'd missed so much, all because of that one reckless, split-second decision I'd made.

We sat back down on the bench. I needed to tell him what he was about to walk into upstairs, though I was sure Clara had filled him in as best she could. Still, as the oldest brother, I felt the responsibility to protect all of them, even though I knew I was years too late to the job. They'd had to protect themselves for so long already.

"...so don't get your hopes up. We're not sure what we're doing. We're just...there for him."

"I can do that. I can be there. He was always there for me, after you were gone. That's why I needed to come. He'd be here if the situation was reversed."

I knew exactly what he meant, but his words still hit me like a knife to the heart. Evan had been there for him. I hadn't. It was the way it was, the unfortunate truth. He wasn't saying it to hurt me, it was just a fact. But that didn't make it hurt any less.

"I'm glad you two had each other," was all I said, standing up, hoping to break the tension building in my chest. "Let's go see Evan. And I know Clara's up there pacing the floor, waiting for you to get here."

"She'll never not be impatient."

"Yeah, some lucky guy's going to have to figure out how to deal with that one day."

Clara threw herself into Jasper's arms the second he walked into the room. I still couldn't fathom Momma deciding to send Clara to Texas alone, separating her from her brothers. I understood the circumstances, but I knew what a horrible scene that must've been. Clara still had scars buried deep inside her, scars she'd alluded to in the past few weeks. She hadn't come right out and blamed me yet, but I could tell I was one of the reasons she felt torn, one of the reasons she felt stolen away from her brothers, no longer the little sister but a *de facto* only child, overnight.

I hadn't told Clara the truth about Pa's death yet. I wanted to wait until Jasper got there. I was only going to tell that story one more time before locking it away again in the dark place I'd been hiding it for the last ten years. But they deserved to know the truth, even if it shattered their image of the father they thought they knew. I wasn't trying to rehabilitate any image of me, the monster with a gun who killed their father in cold blood, but they needed to understand the risk Evan took, not just for himself or Momma, but for them as well. It was only a matter of time before Pa started lashing out at them. Evan and I both knew that.

But I'd give Jasper time. Time with Evan. Time with Clara. Time to settle in before I dropped that bomb. I stood back and watched them reconnect. Their easy conversation told me they'd been keeping in touch. Jasper asked about Clara's college preparations, if she'd gotten into the dorm she wanted, if her friend Margie had decided to enroll or go to beauty school instead.

I'd been here for weeks and this was the first time I'd heard Margie's name. I hadn't even thought about where Clara would be living in the fall. I'd thought we'd been connecting, but I realized just how superficial it had all been. I was here, but I wasn't really a part of her life, not yet.

I hadn't heard Ryder enter the room until he was standing right behind me, his presence at my shoulder, silently watching as Jasper and Clara carried on like they were the only ones in the room.

"Why aren't you over there with them?"

He asked it like he already knew the answer. I was too tired to lie.

"I sort of feel like an outsider within my own family," I said softly, mostly to myself, though I knew he could hear me.

His hand settled heavily on my shoulder, strangely comforting. "I'm here if you want to talk about it, Max. Always."

He left it at that before stepping fully into the room to introduce himself to Jasper. I watched how easily he took charge of the situation, answering questions and calmly explaining Evan's condition as he currently saw it. Compassionate, but realistic. His focus was on protecting Evan, preparing Clara and Jasper for whatever might come next. I knew Ryder was struggling with his own personal demons, yet he carried on like it was nothing. I wasn't sure how he did it. I didn't feel capable of doing the same.

"I'll leave the four of you to it, then," Ryder said, his voice gentle but firm. "Just be natural. Include Evan in your conversations. Touch him, whatever. I'll be in and out, but you can always page me if you need me."

"Thanks, Ryder."

The door had barely swung shut when Jasper began poking fun at Clara. "Ryder? You're on a first-name basis with the young doctor? Clara and Ryder..."

"Jasper, stop," she giggled. "He's Evan's doctor, and he was just being sweet, He was just tired of having me call him 'Dr. Delaney' all the time."

"Clara has a crush, Clara has a crush..."

"Stop it, you two. He probably asks everyone to call him Ryder.

It just puts people at ease. Clara, don't get your hopes up. He might be married, for all we know."

"I didn't see a ring…"

"Jasper, stop," she wailed.

"Although, it would be nice to have a doctor in the family…"

"Not you too, Maxie!" She laughed, enjoying the teasing and the break in the tension.

"But a brain doc?" Jasper laughed. "It may be what we all need, but it's a little too on the nose…"

"You two are…are…"

"What?" we asked in unison.

The tears weren't entirely unexpected. Teasing Clara had always ended this way when we were kids. But instead of a plaintive wail for Momma or Pa to come to her rescue, she held her arms out wide, pulling us all into the moment.

"We're going to get through this," I said, my voice thick. "All of us." I reached down and took Evan's hand, completing the circle. We were finally together for the first time since we were kids, and it was still my job to protect them.

I broke the circle. "I'm gonna go get coffee. Somewhere that isn't this hospital. I can't handle their battery acid swill any longer. Anyone want one?"

They took me up on the offer, and once again, I left the three of them on their own.

While waiting in the coffee line, I pulled out my phone and, on a whim, did the Google search I'd been putting off since we left Oklahoma.

According to the *Enid Star-Tribune*, they'd found Petey's body three days after we left. Guess someone finally missed him, which, honestly, was surprising. But even more surprising was the mention of a silver BMW with Texas plates seen in the area, and that the police were looking into it. There was a hotline number.

Fuck.

Immediately, my mind went to Dixon. I thought about asking

him for help making this all go away, but I knew he'd be pissed about my little extracurricular activity. I'd avoid that conversation if at all possible. My job, and by extension, my life, was already skating on thin ice with him. His good graces only stretched so far, even for his precious Rook.

I'd been trained not to panic in tight situations, but this one felt like it could tighten up fast. Even though we'd been back in Austin for a couple of weeks, that didn't mean we were in the clear. There were a lot of Texas cars in Oklahoma, so that wasn't the problem. But seeing a BMW in that neighborhood was probably what caught someone's attention. That image had settled into someone's memory. The car couldn't be traced directly to me, but I didn't need Ryder caught in the middle of this. If they found him, he might innocently mention that I'd had his car while we were up there, he might inadvertently place the noose around my neck. I needed to act quickly.

As I saw it, I only had one option.

I paid for the coffees and called Bear on my way back to the car. By the time I got to the hospital, I'd told him everything, well, everything I thought he needed to know. He said he'd be in touch within a day, and I cautiously left things in his hands. I wasn't sure what I'd do if Ryder got pulled into my mess. I was certain that would be a problem too big to fix easily.

The afternoon dragged. Jasper and Clara took turns talking to Evan, recounting world events and detailing every little thing from some TV show they'd recently watched. I almost wished I could join him in his coma. When Ryder stepped in and they started giggling like kids, he glanced at me in confusion. I rolled my eyes and shook my head. If they only knew how wrong they were.

I debated following Ryder home again. The images from the night before still burned in my mind, but watching him interact with Clara and Jasper today made me feel guilty about invading his privacy. It didn't stop me from getting hard every time I saw him, though.

I didn't hear from Bear the next day like I'd expected, which made me a little nervous. I knew I'd asked a lot of him, and it might've taken longer than anticipated, but I still bolted when my phone finally rang the following afternoon. I pulled the door shut behind me as I stepped into the hall. I saw Ryder at the far end, on his phone, and quickly turned, heading the other way.

"Bear, what took you so long?"

"Sorry, Max. Ran into a bit of a hiccup."

"Shit. What does that mean?"

"Well, the Oklahoma thing was fine, easy, almost. The PD's firewall was a joke. There was a video of the Beemer driving away, but it's completely corrupted now. The evidence log had a few details erased, scrubbed right off the server. It was all pretty routine. I wouldn't go back there for a while, just to be safe, but you and the doctor should be in the clear."

"Jesus. Thank you, Bear. I owe you…"

"Not so fast. Here's the hiccup. I was doing my due diligence… Do you know a Sean Cunningham?"

"I don't think so…"

"Partner of your doctor friend?"

My eyes shot up, searching for Ryder at the end of the hall. He was still on the phone, oblivious. "Fuck. OK. Didn't know his last name, but I've heard of him. Why?"

"He's a Fed. Working with Interpol in Paris right now. Guess who they've been sniffing around?"

"Fuck. You're joking, right?"

"I wish. Kit's been in deep on this one for a while. From what I'm hearing, he's about to pull the trigger."

I knew Kit's specialty, and my palms started to sweat. Kit liked to blow things up.

I was usually brought in for a single target, someone who needed to be taken out quietly. Kit, however, was called in when entire groups needed to disappear, small teams that needed to vanish without a trace. He was brute force. If he was on this, Dixon wanted the entire investigative team eliminated in some "accident" that wouldn't raise suspicion - a private jet crash with everyone on board was my guess. Kit was a master at making these things look like mechanical failures. Coincidental, but oh-so-convenient. Meanwhile, Bear would probably be planting malware on servers, erasing entire investigations. Dixon would get years added to his life. We all would.

And Ryder would become collateral damage. I knew he and Sean were having issues, but I was sure Ryder didn't want to see him dead. That would completely devastate him.

"Sean can't die," I whispered into the phone. "Kit has to find another way."

"Max, you know how this works. The planning, the precision, these ops take time. You can't just stop everything and reroute. Kit's been in play for a while now. It's probably too late."

"Bear, I'm begging. I can't let Ryder go through this. He's done too much for my family, for me. I can't stand back and let him get hurt."

"Your time away has made you soft, Max. Dixon's not gonna like it."

"You let me handle Dixon. Do what you can to stop Kit. Please."

The line went dead before I could beg him again. I looked back toward Ryder. He was putting his phone back in his pocket, walking in my direction. He saw me and gave a nod in recognition. I returned it, but mine was heavy with the knowledge of what was coming for him, another innocent life I'd have a hand in ruining.

I returned to Evan's room with a heavier weight than when I'd left just minutes earlier. Bear's final words echoed in my head.

I wasn't soft. I knew that. I'd dispatched Petey without breaking a sweat, and I'd do it again without thinking twice. But I had developed a soft *spot* for Ryder. I could admit that now. His purity, his spirit, it had changed something inside me. When he entered my life, he altered my genetic makeup. Being with him, in him, made me want to protect him, at all costs.

My nightly visits to his backyard may have started out with different intentions, but now they were about more than just sex. I was desperately searching for a way into his life. I knew that being even remotely responsible for his partner's death would end any chance of that forever. Grayson would never forgive me. Even if he never connected the dots, it would still change things between Ryder and me. I would never be the man he needed if Kit went through with his plan.

I told Clara and Jasper I had a massive headache and needed to take the rest of the day off. Unfortunately, it was closer to the truth than I wanted it to be. I went back to the hotel, trying my hardest to resist the urge, but by ten o'clock, I was back. I was skulking through backyards again, making my way to my usual vantage point in the trees, watching him. I couldn't stop myself.

Ryder was restless, pacing from room to room, his hands moving wildly as he had some animated argument with himself. It was clear he wasn't winning the fight. When the phone rang, he answered, immediately picking up where he'd left off. When he stepped out onto the patio, his phone on speaker, everything became clear.

"I just don't know how you could take the job and not think about me. We were supposed to discuss it first."

The voice from the phone was loud and sharp. "You never wanted to discuss it. You just pushed it away like it wasn't happening…"

"I was going to come to Paris…"

"When? When were you coming? You kept saying you would, but you never made any plans!"

"It's not that easy. I've told you…"

"You've told me all the reasons that come before me."

"You're a fine one to talk, Sean. You just accepted a job that'll mean the end of our relationship."

"It doesn't have to…"

"I can't go on with you halfway across the planet. That's not a relationship!"

"If we end this, that's on you, not me."

"Don't make a unilateral decision and then blame me for the consequences."

"Ryder, I don't know what else to do."

"Me either. I guess I'll send your shit to Berlin. I can't do this anymore. Goodbye, Sean."

He ended the call, holding the phone in his hand like he might throw it into the woods, releasing a low, mournful groan. He dropped down onto the concrete patio, cradling his head in his hands. I watched as his heart broke in real time, and there was nothing I could do to help him without exposing myself.

His body shook with sobs, and I felt my own tears stream down my face in empathy. He sat there for what felt like an eternity, and I didn't blame him. My fingers toyed with the ring I wore around my neck. I knew that pain. A year later, I still wasn't completely over losing Grayson. I wasn't sure if I ever would be. The tears still came easily when I thought about him.

When Ryder finally got up and went back inside, I left him alone. It was going to be a long night for him, and my being there wouldn't help either of us.

The next day, I made sure to get to the hospital early, hoping to catch Ryder on his morning rounds. I needed to make sure he was okay, but a different doctor showed up instead. They said Dr. Delaney had called in sick.

He was gone for three days.

I tried calling, but he didn't pick up. My after-hours visits found him lying on the sofa. He must've moved at some point during the day, but I never saw evidence of it. I knew he needed time for his broken heart to start healing, so I reluctantly gave it to him.

In the meantime, Clara and Jasper settled into their bedside routines. We only had Jasper for a few more days before he had to head back to Germany. The clock was ticking, and I still hadn't found the right moment to tell them what I needed to. Then I realized, it wasn't going to come out naturally. I had to dive in and hope for the best.

"I need to tell you both something that's been weighing on me...and Evan...for a long time," I began. The words got their attention immediately. With Evan by my side, I opened the floodgates, letting the truth pour out. I finally told them about Pa's abuse and its steady escalation, about the way Evan and I had worked to keep them unaware, and about Pa's death and the terrible secret I'd made Evan carry for the last decade.

"I took the punishment because I thought I was helping, that I was protecting him...protecting you," I said, my voice heavy with regret. "But I made him feel like a coward in the process, even though he did the bravest thing I've ever seen. He protected you from Pa, not me. And he's had to live with the guilt of knowing I went away, that I did the time he should've done. I think that's the root of his drug use, his depression, the suicide attempt...why he's lying here today. It's my fault. I'm so, so sorry..."

I couldn't say anything more. The room was painfully silent. I needed someone to say something, anything. Tell me what a fucking piece of shit I was. They didn't know who I was. I was a monster. They hated me. I could handle whatever came next, but I couldn't handle the silence. It was too much to bear.

"I knew Pa was horrible to you guys," Jasper spoke quietly, thoughtfully. "And to Momma. I heard him from my room. I saw him when no one knew I was there."

"In some way, I think I knew too, Maxie," Clara said softly. "I never heard or saw anything, but things were just...different when Pa walked into a room. I didn't know what it was though. I'm sorry." Tears brimmed in her eyes.

"Clara, don't be sorry. We didn't want you to know. Either of you."

"Max, did you think we hated you for killing Pa? *Do* you think that?"

"Jasper, out of context, I'm a monster in this situation. I didn't...I *don't* blame you if you hate me for it."

"I never did," Clara said, her voice steady. "I'm not sure why. I guess I always knew there were things I didn't know anything about. I think that's part of why Momma sent me here, to keep me unaware."

"I never hated you either," Jasper added. "But Momma wouldn't let us visit you, and when you got out, you never came home. I blamed you more for that than killing Pa. And I certainly don't blame Evan, now that I know the truth."

Clara grabbed Evan's hand, squeezing it tightly. "I don't blame him either. My God, no. Evan, I don't blame you. Thank you... thank you for saving us."

She held on to him tightly, repeating her thanks, her tears flowing steadily now. Jasper came over to pull me into another one of those Army-approved bear hugs. "I'm sorry, Max, if you thought we hated you all these years. I love you. What you both did was brave. You gave up everything for us."

I clutched at his back, never wanting him to let me go. The years that had separated us were finally melting away.

Clara's voice cut through my thoughts, her words forgiving, her hands holding on to Evan's like she was trying to anchor herself to something real, something good. Jasper, too, his hug tighter than before, his words warmer than I ever expected. They loved me. They really did. And I realized loved them as well.

But how could I reconcile that love with the man I had become? How could I look them in the eyes and pretend that I wasn't still that broken man. How could I accept their forgiveness when I knew everything I had done?

I wanted to be the brother they deserved, that they needed, but I couldn't shake the shadow of the man I was. That darkness still clung to me, no matter how much light they tried to offer. Every time I looked at them, I saw the faces of the children we used to be, the ones I couldn't protect, the ones I failed. The pain of their love felt like salt on old wounds, and every moment of peace, every second they might give me, I didn't know how to take without feeling like I didn't deserve it.

And then there was Ryder. He was the one person who might see the real me, the man I hid from everyone else. With him, there were fewer lies, fewer pretensions. But even that was a risk. He didn't know everything I had done. If he did, if he ever found out, how could he ever look at me the same way again? How could I let him in when I was so broken, so tainted by the past?

Yet, as I stood there, feeling the weight of their forgiveness and love, I realized something. Maybe the only way I could move forward was to accept what they were offering, to accept their love, even if I didn't deserve it. Maybe it wasn't about earning it anymore. Maybe it was about being worthy of it.

And that terrified me more than anything. Because I wasn't sure I could ever be worthy.

Clara's shriek broke the moment. "EVAN!"

Jasper and I turned to look at her, alarmed.

"Clara, what...?"

"He squeezed my hand."

I rushed to her side. "You know what Ryder said. It's probably just a muscle spasm..."

"He did it again! Look!"

His fingers moved, slightly, but they definitely moved. And it wasn't just a spasm.

"Evan, bud, can you hear me? It's Max. Clara and Jasper are here too." I reached across the bed, grabbing for his other hand, but then I remembered he was strapped to the handrail. I ran to the other side and grabbed him, squeezing his hand as hard as I could. "Evan...can you hear me? Squeeze my hand if you can feel me..."

It was faint, but there was movement.

"Jasper, get Ryder...fuck, he's not here today. Fuck. Get some-one! Evan, it's going to be OK. Hang on. Come back to us. We're all here..."

His lips quivered. It was as though his body was coming back online, piece by piece. Unintelligible sounds began to come from him. Doctors ran into the room, pulling us away from our brother so they could work, they could bring him the rest of the way home.

Chapter Sixteen

THE NEXT NINE WEEKS

Week One - Ryder

I couldn't let myself believe everything had changed so quickly.

I returned to work, only to hear that Evan Heath had somehow regained consciousness and was showing signs of a full recovery. At night, I came home to the realization that Sean Cunningham had somehow disappeared from my life, and wasn't ever going to be a part of it again.

Clara Heath called what happened with her brother a miracle. I don't believe in miracles. Sure, the scientific explanations were a bit thin, but there had to be a physical reason behind Evan's recovery, even if no one could explain it. One colleague suggested that Evan's subconscious had been waiting for his family to surround him, even going as far as to say he willed himself back to consciousness when they were all there. It seemed like a stretch, but I couldn't say she was wrong. When Max recounted the events leading up to Evan's awakening, it did seem like Evan had been listening all along, waiting for his family to heal before allowing his own body to follow suit. I couldn't argue with that theory. In fact, I wasn't sure I wanted to. I'd always believed the mind protects itself from what's too difficult to face, and when that difficulty eases, that's when supposed miracles happen.

I waited for my own miracle. Like Pavlov's dog, each day at four o'clock, I reached for my phone, expecting Sean to call. I convinced myself it would happen again eventually, only to be disappointed, day after day, when it didn't, and I remembered, yet again, that it never would. That cycle played out for days.

I constantly wondered what he was doing, where he was, if he was thinking about me, and if he regretted his choice. Surely, he'd rethink taking that job in Berlin. Surely, he'd call. Surely, we'd get past this hurdle. Surely, I'd hear from him. Surely.

But there was nothing. Just silence.

Evan Heath was a success story, but one I didn't feel I could take much credit for. He would soon move out of my direct care and into rehab and therapy. His recovery would be a long road ahead, but he was making remarkable progress. His mood was improving. The issues that had led him to attempt suicide seemed to have vanished. Whatever had brought him back, whether science or miracle, there was no question he was here to stay.

My other patients barely missed me while I was out. The covering physicians performed seamlessly, and I began to wonder if fighting to stay in Austin hadn't been the fight I thought it was. When he calls, I'll tell him that. I'd just been stubborn. I'd felt overlooked, not like an equal partner. It had all been a misunderstanding. When he calls, I'll tell him that.

But there was nothing. Just silence.

I couldn't believe this was happening, that he was doing this to me. Why was he doing this?

Week Two - Max

We lost Jasper back to the Army, but his short time in Texas had been crucial to Evan's recovery. Maybe. Probably. No one could say for sure, not even Evan. His memory was foggy, at best. He could recall hearing voices, but he couldn't make out who they were or what they were saying. All he could remember was a feeling of being incomplete, like he was trying to solve an unfinished puzzle. I didn't quite understand what he meant, and he couldn't explain it any better. It didn't matter. He was back with us. There were months of therapy ahead, where he could dissect the details with his doctors. But for now, I was just glad he was alive.

I rented an apartment on a short-term lease, somewhere for Evan to return to when he left the hospital, which would be soon. Ryder confirmed Evan could continue his therapy, both physical and behavioral, on an outpatient basis as long as he was living in a safe, supportive environment. I guess that meant me, though those weren't two words I'd ever use to describe myself.

Clara would be heading to UT in a few weeks. Even though she was staying in Austin, she'd decided long ago to live on campus, away from Aunt Darlene and Uncle Ted. I wholeheartedly endorsed that decision. I also made her promise she wouldn't come running back to us every time she had a free moment. She needed to focus on herself, making new friends, figuring out who she was, who she wanted to be. Evan and I weren't going anywhere. At least, he wasn't. Not for a while.

My future, however, continued to weigh on me, almost as much as my past had for the previous ten years. I couldn't hover over Evan forever. I needed to take my own advice and figure out who I wanted to be, which I had to keep reminding myself was easier said than done. Dixon needed me to return, and he wasn't going to take no for an answer.

Week Three - Ryder

How fucking dare he! He blew up our relationship and then wanted to blame me for it? Fuck him.

Our last conversation was stuck on repeat in my head, and I couldn't stop fixating on that one part. My anger grew each time I cycled through it. I lay awake for hours every night, tossing and turning, getting tangled in the sheets, throwing pillows across the room, swearing at the ceiling. I hadn't heard from Sean in weeks. No attempts at reconciliation, not even a word about when he could expect his things to arrive in Berlin. I assumed he was there by now, but then I reminded myself that I didn't know, and I didn't fucking care! Sean Cunningham could fuck right off. Prick.

I ought to burn his things. That would show him. Unless he never asked for them, then the joke would be on me.

Fuck you, Sean. Go to hell.

I raged through the house, touching anything that reminded me of him, stopping just short of shattering everything into pieces. Every object seemed to mock me, a reminder of yet another failure. But then, after these moments, I'd remember: I was the most angry with myself.

It was my fault Sean chose Berlin. If I hadn't been so closed off to the idea from the first mention of it, if I'd gone to Paris, given it a real shot, if I hadn't been blinded by Max Heath, maybe things would've turned out differently.

Max had clouded my judgment. Those dark eyes that bore through me, the rough hands that touched my naked body, the broken heart I couldn't forget. I fantasized about being with him while reality slipped further and further away.

And now I had neither of them. Sean wasn't coming back, and

Max would leave as soon as Evan was settled and stable. I was living in a nightmare of my own making.

Week Four - Max

The Rook needed to cease to exist, but that was easier said than done. Now I understood Dixon's unspoken policy: *Till Death Do Us Part.* I needed to find a loophole that worked for both of us. Dixon hadn't gotten to be the man he was by leaving loopholes exposed, loopholes that could be exploited by his enemies. It had been my job to eliminate those threats. Now, I needed to avoid becoming one of them. I wasn't his enemy, and I needed him to believe that, if for no other reason than it was the truth.

The news of the crash of a charter plane traveling from Berlin to Nice barely registered in the *Austin American-Statesman*. Section B, page fourteen. But I had been looking for it. Waiting. Expecting it to happen eventually. I'd been buying a physical newspaper every day to avoid leaving a cyber footprint. When I saw it, I knew what it meant, I knew the cause. What I didn't know was who was on board. The paper didn't say. I'd have to wait a while longer for that news.

I hadn't heard a word from Bear, but I still held onto the hope he'd done what I'd asked. In time, I would know if I was right. So I kept waiting.

Evan was released from the hospital, and two days later, he and I helped move Clara into her dorm. Well, I helped Clara while Evan sat and supervised. He was on strict "no exertion" orders from his doctors, and I made sure he followed them.

I'd been avoiding my Aunt and Uncle since I'd arrived in Austin, and judging from the near-hostile reception I got, it had been a smart choice. To Uncle Ted, I was the man who'd killed his brother and hadn't paid a high enough price for the crime. He would never know the truth. That stayed between the four of us, and Ryder, who'd somehow broken down my defenses and gotten it out of me.

I could handle their icy glares and thinly veiled comments. I'd heard worse. But Evan wasn't as strong as me, not yet, and every harsh word Uncle Ted muttered about me, every barbed comment, Evan felt them too.

Clara was loading the last of her things into the Viper. It didn't seem like she planned to ever come back, which made me happy. I told Evan to get in the car. We were leaving. But before I joined them, I grabbed Uncle Ted by the elbow and shoved him into the back corner of the garage. I had a message to deliver.

"I appreciate that you took Clara in when my Momma was struggling. I don't give a fuck if you like me or not, but if I ever hear you say another foul thing in front of my brother, I'll find you, and I'll end you. You're just as nasty as Pa was, and we all know what happened to him."

I left him standing there with his mouth agape. He knew I was serious, and he knew I'd follow through. Clara and Evan were both staring at me when I got in the car, but neither of them said a word. We drove to campus in silence.

The Rook still lived in me. That was the message I sent to Dixon. It wouldn't be a full retirement. It was more like a hibernation. I wasn't a threat to him or his organization. I'd given almost ten years of my life to serving him in every way he needed. I had been loyal, and I still was. I just wasn't focused anymore, and that was dangerous for both of us.

"I need assurances, Maxwell. I can't just let you walk away like my little dove tried to do."

"No one understands that better than me, Dixon. I know the price I'd pay, that my family would pay, for betrayal. I would never do that to you. I owe you everything. I'm not forgetting that."

"Then I need you to do one last thing for me."

I listened as he explained exactly what needed to be done. I understood the assignment and accepted without hesitation. I knew I needed to, to give Dixon the assurances he required. If the Rook was going to disappear, he needed to make one last appearance first.

Week Five - Ryder

I decided to ask Dr. Schmidt, my department chair, if she knew of any possible exchange programs with a medical center in Berlin, or if she could help me research one. I don't know why I hadn't thought of it before. Maybe there was a way I wouldn't have to start over in Germany. There was no guarantee Sean's posting in Berlin would be anything more than temporary. In fact, it was quite possible it might last only a year, maybe two, not long enough for me to finish an entire residency program. But an exchange? That could act as a stopgap while I worked toward something more permanent.

I was almost manic when I burst into Dr. Schmidt's office, spilling out the reasons why I had to go to Berlin, why I desperately needed her help. I think she agreed to help me just to get me to shut up and leave her in peace.

I started making bargains in my head. What was I willing to give up? What would I need in return? The lists morphed into what I'd have to sacrifice, and what I might get in return. It grew unwieldy. Ugly. Very quickly. I saw my life, my career, being dismantled, disintegrating before my eyes, replaced by promises and dreams too easily erased.

The worst realization? I was actively letting it happen. I was sabotaging my own life.

I went back to Dr. Schmidt and withdrew my request for her help.

Darkness settled in.

Week Six - Max

I owed him something, or at least I felt like I did, and I always paid my debts.

I knew Sean was alive. While his whereabouts were unknown, saving his life wasn't enough. Ryder didn't know I had an invisible hand in keeping him off that private plane so I needed another way to show my appreciation for what he'd done for my family, for me. I needed to remain in his orbit, but I knew he'd never want to accept anything for his services.

Since Evan's discharge, I hadn't really seen much of Ryder. Occasionally, when I took Evan to his therapy appointments, I'd spot him in the hallway, conferring with a nurse or ducking into a patient's room, but we never interacted. And with Evan and I living together now, I couldn't just leave at night for no reason. Lurking in Ryder's backyard, lusting after him from afar, had come to a halt as well.

Then one afternoon, when Evan was in physical therapy, trying to regain his muscle mass and coordination, I walked the hospital corridors as usual. I tried hard not to remember the times I'd passed through these halls while Evan lay motionless in his bed. Those memories needed to fade, along with everything else.

I heard him before I saw him and realized the doctor's lounge was up ahead. I slowed my pace, taking out my phone and pretending to focus on it while listening to his soothing voice. He was talking with a co-worker about finally having time to tackle some backyard landscaping he'd been putting off, hoping to increase his home's resale value. It sounded like the perfect distraction. I had an idea.

While I hadn't thought about Carlos Delgado in ages, the skills I'd picked up working for him that summer were far from gone. If Ryder had a plan, I had the know-how. All I needed was for him to agree to put the two together. I'd solved harder puzzles.

I heard chairs scraping across the floor and knew someone was about to exit. Head down, I walked forward with purpose, hoping for the best. Within seconds, I was walking right into Ryder, just as I'd hoped.

"Sorry...oh, Max...um, hi...are you here with Evan?"

I looked at him like *why else would I be here?*

"Yeah...sorry, I was just looking for some landscaping jobs...I need something to keep me occupied other than taxiing Ev back and forth to the hospital every other day..."

"You never told me you were a landscaper..."

"I guess I never told you a lot of things," I replied, and that was the most truthful thing I'd ever said to him. "Do you know anyone looking to get some work done before winter sets in?"

"Funny enough, I was just talking to Sarah, Dr. Malcolm, about doing some work..."

"You don't say." I gave him one of my best performances. "Maybe we could help each other out..."

"How do I know you do good work?"

"Hmmm...good question. I used to do this professionally, but it's been a while...What do you say I do it on spec? You tell me what you want, I build it, and if you hate it, I'll tear it out and put everything back like it is now. No cost." It was a gamble.

"You're awfully confident..."

I stared into his blue eyes. "I want to leave you satisfied."

He stared back, unsure of where this conversation was headed.

"Why don't you think about what you want and we can discuss it later? You've got my number. And don't hold back just because you think I can't handle it." I turned and walked away while he stood there, still searching for his words.

Week Seven - Ryder

Work kept me busy, thankfully. From the planning in the morning to my mental review at night, I barely had time to think about Sean and the hole he'd left in my life. There wasn't anyone new to take his place. The thought of trying to meet someone, those horrific first dates, the assured disappointments...I wasn't ready. I wasn't sure I ever would be.

I came home at night, thankfully exhausted. I'd pour a glass of wine while my dinner warmed in the microwave, then go out back to check on the progress Max had made that day on the new pergola. It was the same every day. Life on repeat.

It became harder and harder to face the empty bed each night.

For months, while Sean was in Paris, I'd endured sleeping alone. The promise had been that it was only temporary, but now it had become permanent. I'd thrown away Sean's old t-shirt, bought new sheets, moved the bed against a different wall, and yet, it still felt like a prison sentence each night. I'd been found guilty of wanting too much and sentenced to die alone.

I couldn't remember the last time I'd masturbated. I had no desire. I was afraid that any fantasy I might have would still have Sean lurking at its edges, which would only leave me feeling worse.

I told myself the same thing I told my patients: *It will pass.* There are things that will spark joy within, but they won't be as obvious as they once were. Joy was hiding now, and it might need to be actively sought out. It would take work. And suddenly, I understood why my patients sometimes rolled their eyes at me, some even telling me to "fuck off." When you're at the bottom of the pit, it's hard to believe when someone tells you there's daylight above.

But I endured. Work. Home. Work. Home. Then, one day, there he was, standing on my doorstep like he still belonged there.

"What are you doing here?"

"I didn't feel like I could wait inside…"

"No, Sean. Not here. Outside my house. Here…in Texas, for a start."

"Can I come in? Can we talk?"

"You haven't wanted to talk in months. Why now? No. You know what? No. This is my house. You have no right to just show up here without warning."

"I know, I'm sorry. It's just, I…"

I'd been waiting for him for months, but now, standing there, I realized I didn't feel like waiting for him anymore. I didn't have the urge to run into his arms, overjoyed that he was back, like I once thought I would. I was wary of him, of what he had to say. Something was different, and it wasn't just me.

"I lost my job…"

"Oh, that's why you're back! Priority number one's not there anymore, so time to move down the list to priority number two, or was I three?"

"Ry, it's not like that."

"Really? Because you weren't here when you still had a job. So what am I supposed to think?"

"It's complicated…"

"Bullshit, Sean. Complete and utter bullshit. It's always been simple. You chose to make it complicated."

"I almost died, Ryder. Well, sort of…"

"How do you 'sort of, almost' die? You know what? I don't care. Whatever happened to you, whatever caused this great epiphany that you somehow experienced, whatever brought you back to Austin…rethink it. I've moved on." It was a lie, but only I knew that.

I heard a sound inside the house and glanced around until I saw Max's car still parked up the street, in front of what must've been Sean's rental. Max was still here, inside, listening.

Max. I knew he wasn't the joy I'd been searching for. He was another heartbreak just waiting to happen. But he was someone who found me attractive, who once wanted to sleep with me, who wanted to build me a goddamn pergola just to thank me for doing my job. He respected my work, unlike Sean, who thought I could just follow him around the world. I realized, standing there on my front lawn, that I was the one having the epiphany. I was going to be alright without Sean.

"Ryder, we can work this out. I swear…"

"Sean. You need to go. If you don't have your job with the agency anymore, then there's no reason for you to stay in Austin. Go. See the world. Go back to Seattle. Go somewhere, anywhere. Just don't stay here. This is my home. You didn't want to be a part of it before. You're not going to be a part of it now."

I pushed past him and slid my key into the lock, pausing only for a moment to think if there was anything I'd left unsaid. I was never going to see Sean Cunningham again. I shook my head and stepped inside, shutting the door behind me with a final click of the latch.

Where had those words come from? An hour ago, I was lost without Sean. And now, I couldn't imagine him in my life again.

I looked around, expecting to see Max, but he wasn't there. I dropped my keys and work bag by the door and listened for Sean to leave. It took longer than expected, maybe he was debating knocking again, trying to continue our conversation, but eventually, he walked to his car and pulled away for what I hoped was the last time.

I heard hammering from the back. I stopped in the kitchen, poured two glasses of water, then stepped out onto the patio to see what had changed since yesterday, besides me.

Max was up on a ladder, sweat pouring down his bare back,

soaking the waistband of his jeans. He was nailing one of the last pergola crossbeams into place. The muscles of his shoulder and back bulged with each swing of the hammer. Oklahoma had been months ago, but I continued to discover that that night had been about much more than just sex. It had reminded me of my self-worth, something Sean had slowly whittled away, though probably not on purpose.

I walked over and offered him one of the glasses of water as he stepped off the ladder. He drank it so fast it spilled from the edges onto his sweat-soaked chest. The cold water brought his nipples to attention, and I could only imagine taking each of them into my mouth, biting them gently. The early evening sun glinted off the silver ring around his neck, nestled between his strong pecs. I could feel myself starting to get hard and quickly refocused to avoid embarrassing myself.

"You're almost done..." I said, a mix of excitement and sadness in my tone.

"Another couple of days, probably. I need to treat and stain the wood, but otherwise, this is what it'll look like."

"Max, it's really beautiful. Exactly what I was imagining."

He couldn't help but smirk. "I told you I'd leave you satisfied."

The twist in my gut started again, and I quickly walked away, circling around the pergola, inspecting his work, running my hands across the smooth wood he'd spent hours sanding to perfection. My mind recited the bones of the hands and feet to distract me from the thoughts I was having about Max. I knew it wasn't Max himself. I knew it would pass.

He stepped up onto the raised platform with me, surveying his work. We moved around each other like orbiting planets, but I was always aware of his precise location. I could feel the heat coming off his body, smell him nearby.

"I don't want to pry..." His words snapped me back to reality. I turned to look at him.

"But...?"

"I didn't want to leave while he was standing out front...just in case..."

"In case?" I chuckled. Had he thought I might be in some kind of danger that he was going to have to save me? It certainly fit his pattern. Maxwell Heath, Protector of All. "I wasn't in any danger, at least not physically. That was Sean. My ex."

It was the first time I'd referred to him that way, privately or publicly. I wasn't sure how I felt about it. It felt heavy, odd. It would take time to get comfortable with that label.

"I'm sorry," he said, but I knew what he meant. Sean had always hung between us, like the wall of this pergola. I'd once used him as a shield to keep Max at a distance. Then he asked, "Are you okay?"

"I think so. I think it's for the best. He's leaving Austin..."

We stood in silence for a few more minutes, each of us pretending to inspect the fine details of the new pergola, the new fire pit in the far corner, the two new Adirondack chairs he'd crafted.

"I should go," he said. "I'll be back tomorrow."

And then he was gone, grabbing his discarded tee from the lawn on his way out.

I said goodbye, but I was already alone.

Week Eight - Max

I knew Sean hadn't left Austin like Ryder thought. I also knew he had no intention of leaving. He'd rented a house not far from Ryder's, and I'd seen him driving by while I worked. I wasn't sure if he was trying to find Ryder at home or what his endgame was. Was he trying to win him back, or was he there to do him harm?

Sean Cunningham had become another obsession of mine, but this one had much more riding on it.

I'd finished the pergola and no longer had a reason to be at Ryder's every day. Evan was seeing other doctors now, so I didn't even see him at the hospital unless I sought him out. So, I began my trips to his bedroom window again.

Ryder was a man of routine, and I knew it by heart. I'd watch him from the woods, eating dinner or enjoying a cocktail under the pergola, in one of the chairs I'd crafted just for him. I knew that soon his nightly routine with his purple dildo would begin. More and more, I wanted it to be me who filled him, who brought him to orgasm. But every time I thought about making my feelings known, I remembered that his last lover had left him, breaking his heart. I didn't want to do the same, because I knew I'd leave him too, eventually.

So I watched and jerked myself off into the bushes, only imagining it was me inside Ryder.

Until the night Sean arrived to do the same thing.

That's when I realized what my imagined rival was up to, and Ryder wasn't as safe as he'd assumed.

I knew I'd complicated Kit's careful planning when I'd asked him to spare Sean's life. But he did it, and I owed him for it. Still, Sean hadn't gotten the message. Bear planted damning evidence of intelligence leaks to the Russians, sealing his professional fate and hopefully sending him into hiding to avoid prosecution. Again, the message went unheeded. Instead, he'd come running back to Ryder, begging for forgiveness. He'd been given more opportunities than he deserved, and I was done giving him any more.

The irony of his spying on Ryder being the last unforgivable sin wasn't lost on me. But I wasn't going to let irony stand in my way. Sean needed to go. I just wasn't sure how to do it, short of killing him, which I still didn't necessarily want to do.

I stewed on it for a couple of days. Evan kept asking what my problem was, as if it were that easy to tell him. It wasn't, but I needed to tell him something else.

Coming out is different every time you do it. Reactions vary. Sometimes you care a lot, sometimes less. With Evan, it was the former.

Back on the farm, Evan and I had been as close as two brothers could be. But I'd only just figured out my feelings for Bobby when everything changed, and I left. Now I knew exactly who I was and who I wanted to be with. I'd traded sex for protection in the youth center and used it to gain entrance into Dixon St. James's world, but almost none of it had been against my will. I was, and still am, as much of a predator as any man I've ever seduced, or been seduced by. But I also have strong, complicated feelings that lie just beneath the surface, and I constantly risk getting hurt, especially by Evan. For the first time in a long while, I was actually frightened.

I couldn't look at him while I did it. I wanted to hear his words, not see his eyes, which might say something different. I focused on the stove, concentrating on dinner, when I heard him enter the small galley kitchen behind me.

"Do you need help?"

"I've got it…It'll be ready soon."

I could feel him standing there, hovering over me, expecting something. "Who knew you'd be the one with the cooking skills?"

"There's a lot…"

"Then just tell me already, Max."

My breath caught in my chest. He knew. How did he know? Or had I just read too much into his words?

"Well…" I was at a loss. I hadn't been ready for this to be the moment. Now I was giving it too much power, turning it into something bigger than it already was. Evan didn't say a word. I couldn't sense if he was moving at all. I could only hear my own heart pounding in my ears.

I stopped stirring the vegetables on the stove and carefully set the spatula on the counter. I closed my eyes and said the words.

"I'm gay."

His arms engulfed me from behind, strong and swift, despite their months of disuse.

"Thank you for telling me," he whispered into my back. "I needed you to trust me."

"I do trust you, Evan. I do. It's just…"

"It's OK." His arms squeezed tighter. He wasn't letting go.

We stood like that for a while longer, until Evan could feel my heart slow to a steady rhythm. Then he released me, and I turned to look at him. His eyes didn't betray anything other than love and support, which, deep down, I guess I always knew they would, despite the small inkling of doubt I'd let overtake my thoughts.

"Did you know?" I had to ask.

"More like *strongly suspected*," he said. "I saw how you were with Bobby. And I saw him after you were gone."

Of course.

"And his partner, Hugh, well, he's what I always imagined you'd turn out to be like. And you are. Bobby never really got over you, I guess."

"There wasn't much to get over, really."

I turned back to finish cooking, lost in thought about Bobby and the *what ifs*. I hadn't noticed Evan still standing behind me until he spoke again.

"I hope you've been happy. That leaving was worth it."

I knew he didn't mean it in a cruel way. He was genuinely concerned that I might feel like I'd sacrificed everything and got nothing in return.

I hand went to my chest, toying with the ring there, the happiness I'd built, only to burn it to the ground in an instant.

"Yeah," I said. "I've been pretty happy…"

I plated the vegetables and pulled the roast chicken from the oven, relieved the conversation had happened but also glad it was over, at least for now. I didn't want to think about Bobby, or

Grayson, anymore. I needed to think about Sean and how to make sure he disappeared from Ryder's life permanently.

Evan's therapist had told me I needed to let Evan have his independence, to trust him to not fall back into old habits once I wasn't around. It would give him a chance to test his coping mechanisms without me acting as a safety net. I told him I was going to a bar on the nights I went to Ryder's, and now I told him I was going camping for the weekend, that I just needed to be alone for a while to clear my head. It was another lie.

Thanks to a loose screen, I waited for Sean inside his house when he returned from his nocturnal trip to Ryder's bedroom window. It would be the last time he ever did that.

When I heard the front door open, I pulled the black ski mask down over my face. He would survive this evening, but I needed to as well. I stepped into the darkened bathroom when he passed by, walking down the shadowy hallway to his bedroom in the back. Sean matched me physically, but I could tell his physique was built in a gym, not through hard work, and certainly not from fighting. I had the edge on him there. I'd been boxing since Bobby showed me how all those years ago, in the back of the barn, and I'd picked up other skills inside detention. I was ready for this fight.

I stepped out, took three quick steps, and landed two furious blows to Sean's kidneys, knocking him into the wall. His head smashed into a picture frame, shattering the glass and knocking it off the hook to the floor. He was down on one knee, refusing to concede, trying to rise. He wanted desperately to take a swing at me. He turned to look back at me. I saw blood starting to pour from a cut on his temple.

"Stay down," I growled, landing a blow to his face, once and then twice. It took a third shot to finish the job. All in all, it was far easier than I imagined it would be.

I tied his hands behind him and his ankles together, gagging him with a t-shirt from his room just to be safe. The next ten minutes would be crucial.

I had to leave him alone while I went to get my car. I didn't need him trying to be a hero while I was gone. That wasn't going to end well for him, and he seemed like the type who'd try just that.

I backed the car into the driveway, thankful for the cloudy night. I blindfolded him with another t-shirt and covered his head with a pillowcase. Carrying his dead weight to the car was the hardest part of the night. I slammed the trunk, sealing him in.

Now came the part I struggled with the most. I needed to appease Dixon, which meant going against everything I'd learned over the years. I went back in the house, back down the hallway, and took off one of my gloves.

"I hope you're happy, Dixon," I murmured as I pressed my palm into Sean's pooled blood, leaving a partial print on the wall.

"I'll make sure Bear makes the evidence disappear," Dixon had told me. "But if you ever make a move against me, it'll come to light, and I'll have you by the balls. Understand me?"

It was crystal clear. An attack on a former federal officer wouldn't mean much, but it would be the tip of the iceberg, sending me away for life. I looked at the print on the wall and knew it marked the end of my freedom. I was Dixon's for life, even if I wasn't part of his menagerie anymore.

I tossed a few things around to make it look like a random home invasion, not a targeted attack. Wrong place, wrong time, Sean Cunningham. But his disappearance would draw attention, so I had to move fast.

I drove through the night, east through Texas, then into Louisiana, heading south into the bayou. It was almost dawn when I stopped. Sean had been awake for hours, pounding on the trunk until he wore himself out or realized the futility of it.

When I finally opened the trunk, he tried in vain to wriggle free. It wasn't going to happen.

I pulled him out and dumped him on the ground. I took my pocket knife and began slicing through his shirt, and then his pants. I debated leaving him in his underwear and then remembered that he hadn't allowed Ryder that bit of modesty. Off came the expensive designer briefs, tossed into the trunk with the rest of his clothes. I slammed the lid to get his attention, as if I didn't already have it.

I knelt down next to his face and whispered, "You didn't understand our first message. We saved you from that plane crash. You were supposed to be a good boy after that, but you weren't. So you lost your job, brought down. But somehow, even after that, you persisted. You have to go. This is your last warning. Get lost. Don't contact your family. Don't contact your friends. We're watching. We will know."

Even in the humid bayou heat, he shivered. But I needed to know he heard me. I stood and kicked him in the side, hard.

"Do you understand me?"

He nodded. Good enough.

I left him there, on the edge of the bayou, where his fight wasn't with me anymore. It was with nature.

Week Nine - Ryder

I had to start with *I'm sorry*.

My emotions had been all over the place for months. I'd been short with co-workers, over-involved with patients, and, worst of all, hot and cold with Max.

I'd hidden behind being Sean's boyfriend and then being Evan's doctor until those impediments disappeared. Then, it became the assumed fact that Max would be leaving eventually that kept him at arm's length. Oklahoma had somehow allowed me to dream about what being with Max might be like, but that was just a fantasy. I never wanted to admit I was actually attracted to him. That had always seemed too dangerous.

My new favorite place to be alone was the pergola he'd built for me. My end-of-day glass of wine, my erotic thoughts, everything was set free out there, out of sight from the neighbors, and out of touch with the world.

The weather had been too warm for a fire in the fire pit, so I'd lined the railings with citronella candles to keep the bugs away. But tonight, with a sudden chill in the air, combined with the end of the long week and a new bottle of Sancerre, I was in the mood to light the first one.

The kindling caught fire, and I added a couple of the small logs Max had chopped and left in a neat stack nearby. I turned my chair to face the dark woods. I imagined my future lay out there, somewhere. The past was fading. Sean hadn't contacted me, and my urge to hear from him had long receded. I still had some regrets about the words I'd used the last time I saw him, but not the sentiment. I'd finally put myself first, served my own needs. But to what end?

I was alone, which was OK. I might make mistakes, and that was OK too. Maybe Max was one of those mistakes, or maybe not being brave enough to explore my feelings for him was the mistake. I took a drink and implored the dark woods to send me a sign. A childish wish from someone who should've outgrown making them.

I waited in vain. I finished the glass of wine and poured another from the bottle that was quickly warming. A flock of dark birds crossed the sky in front of the moon, reminding me of the haunting tattoo on Max's shoulder. The dark bird with the hooked beak, the sharp, dangerous barbed wire that protected it, yet also made it fiercer.

"I thought I might find you back here. I rang the bell..."

I started, torn from my thoughts. I hadn't heard him approaching, and for a second, I wasn't sure if he was real or a figment of my drunken imagination. I turned just as he stepped up into the pergola.

"What are you doing here, Max?"

271

"I haven't seen you at the hospital in a while, and I wanted to tell you I'll be leaving once I get Evan settled into a permanent home."

"Oh," was all I could manage at first. It wasn't a huge shock. I'd known it would happen, but it still seemed sudden.

"Yeah, he's doing great. Clara's here, so he doesn't need me hovering…"

"It just seems so quick."

"I've already been here a lot longer than I thought I would…"

"Oh, right, I'm sure you need to get back to…"

"I just wanted to say thanks again, in case I don't see you at the hospital before I leave. I owe you a lot…"

"No, Max, you don't." I almost left it at that, but there was more to be said. And he was right, this might be my last opportunity. "I think I'm the one who owes you." I motioned for him to sit in the partner chair he'd built, the one destined to remain empty for a while yet.

"We got off on the wrong foot from the start, had missteps along the way, but ultimately, somehow, I hope we've become friends, of sorts."

"I'd like to think so…"

"…but lately, I've…I've been avoiding you at the hospital. I've seen you and gone the other way."

He looked shocked by my confession. "Why?"

I knew I was teetering on the edge now. My liquid courage was beginning to fail me, and I couldn't read anything in Max's face. The firelight threw shadows across him, and it terrified me.

"I…I can't stop thinking about what happened in Oklahoma…"

"You mean between us, right?" I nodded, unsure if he could make it out in the dim light. "I thought we'd decided that was just a one-time thing. We were both emotional about the day we'd had…"

272

"I thought that was all it was…"

"But…"

"But now I think it was, is, something else."

I couldn't look at him, and he didn't say anything. He let my words hang there between us. I expected him to get up and leave me there the way he'd found me, alone. He'd just told me he was leaving Austin; he hadn't come here to hear any of this. What was I expecting him to say? That he was suddenly going to change his plans because I had a crush on him? Sean and I were in love, or so I thought, and he hadn't changed anything for me.

"I'm sorry, I shouldn't've…"

"Stop," he said. "Don't speak."

I bowed my head, unwilling to face him as he left.

His hand on my shoulder was heavy and firm. It reminded me of the way he'd held my arm when I tried to leave his hotel room in Enid. His touch spoke for him.

I slowly turned to look at him. Now I had to see his face. Now it was going to tell me everything I needed to know.

His face had softened, even if his eyes hadn't. They were still bottomless black voids. He slipped quietly off the chair and knelt in front of me. He took my hands in his, and I realized how cold I'd suddenly become compared to his warmth.

"Ryder, I never wanted to pressure you. It wasn't my intention coming over here tonight…"

"I know…"

"But you're partly the reason why I need to leave."

I cocked my head. I didn't understand.

"I've been fighting feelings for you, too. Feelings you weren't, you aren't, able to reciprocate."

"I wasn't…you're right, but…"

He leaned forward and kissed me before I could say anything else.

He'd kissed me before, hurriedly when we'd first met at Wrangler's, forcefully in the hotel in Oklahoma, but this was different. He was softer, more tentative and careful than before. He was testing me, making sure I was alright with what he was doing. I took his head in my hands, ran my fingers through his hair to hold him firmly in place, while I opened my mouth and let his tongue meet mine. It felt perfect.

And yet, a part of me wanted to stop him, to ask if he was sure of what he was doing, what his intentions were. I didn't want to go forward if he was only looking for another hook-up. I wasn't sure I could handle that. But then the moan that came up through him, the passionate turn his kiss took, reassured me. I had very little to be concerned about, and I relaxed into him. His plans to leave might just change.

He pulled me down onto the pergola floor with him, laying me on my back, resting his weight on top of me. It felt perfectly familiar. My leg wrapped around him, holding him tightly in place. His eyes stared into mine, the flames from the fire reflecting in them, making him appear as if he were burning from the inside. I wanted to burn with him.

Time slowed. He lowered his face to mine and kissed me again, biting my lips, pulling my hair. His saliva filled my mouth and I gulped it down. I wanted all of him in me. Between kisses, he whispered my name again and again., each one tattooed itself upon me.

His hand worked its way up my shirt, slow at first, teasing me, then quickly until he found my hard, sensitive nipple. He toyed with it, making me squirm with pleasure. My tongue worked feverishly in his mouth, my hands dug into his back. His cock pressed into me, hard, insistent.

Suddenly, he sat up and pulled his shirt over his head while I quickly unbuttoned mine. I wanted his skin on mine. Then I saw it, the silver ring on the silver chain, dangling between his furry pecs, catching the firelight. My hand went to it.

"Not now," he whispered, pulling my hand away. When he laid back down on me, the ring fell onto my chest, resting there. Its weight only faded when he began kissing me again.

I had been imagining this for weeks, months, and my excitement almost overwhelmed me. He kissed down my chest. His hand finally found my erection, stroking it through my shorts. His tongue swirled across my belly. The fire crackled in my ear. I looked up and only saw the moon. I was lost at sea, excited and terrified.

I could feel his fingers twisting the button on my shorts, and I longed to be free of them. I pushed them down while he pulled my underwear off, leaving me naked, exposed. Instinctively, I knew I was safe with him. Somehow, I always felt like he was protecting me in a way I couldn't quite explain.

I opened myself to him, but he had other ideas. He licked my hips and stroked my thighs, kissing his way down my legs and massaging my feet, nipping at my toes as he put each one into his mouth. He was savoring me, eating me like a banquet, and saving the main course for last.

His hands opened his jeans, and he shucked them off, throwing them off the pergola. We were naked together, finally. I took in his magnificence. The hairy chest that tapered down his belly into the explosion of black hair, his thick, hard, cock that strained upwards, searching for a home. I reached and took him in my hand, stroking him softly, remembering the heft and the girth and the pleasure his cock had already brought me.

He got up on his haunches. I wasn't sure what he needed me to do.

"Let's go inside," he said, standing up and extending his hand to me. It seemed almost cruel to interrupt everything, but then the penny dropped, and I remembered there was lube in the drawer next to the bed. He knew it was there, and he wanted to make the experience as pleasurable as possible.

He took my hand and led me, naked, across the yard and into

the house. He walked us straight to my bedroom as if he'd been there before.

I knelt before him at the foot of the bed and took him into my mouth, down my throat until I gagged. I pulled him out then went down again. I tongued around his engorged, purple head, felt it pulsate and swell as I did. His precum seeped out and I sucked it in like nectar from a ripe peach.

I played with myself, fingering my hole with his cock sliding in and out of my mouth. When he noticed he said "Let me".

I got on the bed on my hands and knees and let his tongue begin to work its way into me. He licked, bit, and sucked like the expert I knew he was. His mouth alone could send me over the edge. My hands grabbed at the comforter, I gritted my teeth against an orgasm that ebbed just in time.

"Fuck me, Max." It was *my* command, not a request. I couldn't take another minute without him inside me, where he belonged.

He pulled the drawer free from the nightstand, spilling its contents onto the floor.

He grabbed the bottle of lube, I rolled onto my back. He covered himself and coated my aching hole. I was open, relaxed, and ready for him.

I rested an ankle on his shoulder, my knee pressed against my chest. Max's face was inches from mine. Our eyes locked.

He easily found my entrance and pressed himself inside, inch by glorious inch. I took deep breaths. He stretched me wide but the pain quickly subsided once he was in deep. I could feel his balls nestling warmly against my ass.

He leaned down and whispered my name before kissing me. The ring at the end of his chain fell into the hollow of my throat, reminding me of the secrets yet to be discovered about this man.

"You're so fucking beautiful, Ryder."

My heart burst open. It was what I'd been longing to hear from him. I felt the same, and I told him so.

He was gentle, methodical. Neither one of us wanted this to

end. We weren't in a hurry. We had all night. His pace gradually increased like a train slowly leaving the station.

His hips pulled back slowly before working himself back inside of me. Stroke after stroke he plunged into me, hitting all the right spots with each and every thrust. I was afraid he'd cum, not that I didn't want him to, I just wasn't ready for it to be over just yet.

I pulled his hips into me and, in one well-choreographed movement, he rolled onto his back and I sat myself on top of him. We never lost contact with each other.

I began lifting myself and then quickly taking him in again, using his chest as resistance, his hands on my hips and then under my ass. His fingers dug into me. I twisted his furry nipples. His cock throbbed deep inside of me. Our eyes never strayed from each other.

My face stung from the stubble of his beard. I wanted to scream his name, tell him I was falling for him, that I never wanted him to leave. But those thoughts could wait for another moment.

I slowly rocked back and forth, tightening my grip around him the best I could but feeling exhausted and ready. My cock had been dripping onto his stomach, begging for permission to release itself. I leaned over and kissed Max deeply, giving him the signal that I was ready.

His hips bucked up into me, I grabbed my cock, and together we exploded. I felt his warm cum coat my insides, paint me, while stream after stream of my own landed in the great expanse of his chest hair.

As the euphoria subsided, and his cock slipped away from me, reality set back in. Had anything changed? I nestled into the crook of his arm as he wrapped himself around me. The cum from his chest was now on me while his slowly trickled out of me. I didn't care. I could lay there like that forever. Whatever would happen between us, I was going to be OK with it. I resolved to respect his decision if he still chose to leave once Evan was settled. My heart was open again. Someone would hold it one day, if it wasn't going to be Max. I wanted it to be Max.

He kissed my forehead and threaded his fingers through my hair. There was a delicate tension between us.

Finally, he said, "Can I stay?"

"Of course, Max. I want you to stay."

Chapter Seventeen

MAXWELL

Autumn

I drunkenly opened my eyes, letting them adjust to the dim light slowly creeping into the bedroom. Rolling onto my side, I peered at him, admired him in the early morning light. As usual, I needed to confirm that the warm body next to me wasn't a dream.

His blonde hair was messy and wild from the night before, just like mine probably was. It fell across his eyes, shielding him from the realities of the world. I wanted to reach over and brush it aside but didn't want to wake him. He deserved his rest.

As if on cue though, he stirred, rolling onto his side, turning away from me. It wasn't personal. Last night, he couldn't get enough of me, begging for more of me, his hands grabbing at me, pulling me in deeper. He gave himself to me and I took him, gladly.

The sun caught the faint scratches on his back where I'd raked him with my nails. The memory of his moans still echoed in my head. The vision of his throat as his back arched with pleasure. The feel of me releasing within him, the chain reaction of events that followed. His cum was still in my beard.

Every time felt like the first with him. He surprised me in ways

I never anticipated. Sometimes passive and receptive, sometimes aggressive and dominant. While he mostly let me take control, there were times when he wanted to explore my body, take me from behind, bend me to his will. And I let him. I trusted him completely.

Almost completely.

I inched closer to spoon him, my arm crossing his chest, my hand resting softly on his pec. His skin was still sticky with our dried sweat from the night before. Consciously or not, he relaxed into me, letting me protect him and his dreams. I struggled to feel worthy of the honor. His heart beat slow and steady beneath my hand. Finally, peace. A cool autumn breeze blew in from the open window, the same window where I used to hold my nightly vigil, never letting myself imagine I could one day be on the inside, looking out.

But I knew: there were predators out there. And in here.

It had only been a few weeks since he'd first invited me into his bed. It was still odd how natural it had quickly become, leaving Evan alone, spending the night with Ryder, waking up with him in my arms, but knowing it could all be taken away in an instant if I wasn't careful.

I used to be very careful with Ryder. Kept him at arms length. But no longer. Now I couldn't get close enough.

I buried my nose in his hair. The smell was already familiar, intoxicating. I kissed the back of his head gently, closing my eyes, trying to keep the dream alive before the alarm began its shrill wail, signaling the start of another day in this new unknown. The only sure thing in my future was another night wrapped around Ryder Delaney, at least for now. And that was enough.

I must've drifted off, because the next thing I knew, the radio blared, and Ryder was staring at me.

"What are you doing?" I mumbled, hoping my morning breath wouldn't send him running.

"Just watching you."

"That's not creepy at all," I muttered, even though it was exactly what I'd been doing to him just an hour earlier.

He ducked in for a quick, chaste kiss. Just a taste. Enough to start the day.

"I was thinking, why don't you, Evan, and Clara come over for dinner tonight? I can invite Katie and Dan. You can meet the darling Miss Pippa…"

I must've given him an odd look because he quickly followed up, "It's not like they don't know about us, and I'm not his doctor anymore, if that's what you're worried about…"

I kissed him, mainly to get him to stop talking for a minute, while I wrestled with the idea of my brother, my sister, and my… And there it was, the thing I was stuck on. If we were going to present ourselves to other people, labels were going to get tossed around. What the hell was Ryder? Fuck buddy seemed rude. Boyfriend felt way too premature. Lover made me want to take a shower. Gentleman friend? If only this was the nineteenth century…

And meeting his sister and her family already? It seemed too soon. He was barreling ahead at a hundred miles per hour, and I didn't blame him. I wasn't giving him any reason not to. I loved our time together, when we were alone. The thought of going public, of building a real relationship, scared me. I still had dreams of Grayson, his wounded eyes, the look of betrayal when he realized I'd been so utterly dishonest, when he turned his back on me. I felt like I was heading down that same road, with no way to change the eventual outcome.

I reached down, caressing his ass. Instinctively, he pulled his knee up, exposing himself so I could run my fingers over his recently fucked hole. Conversation diverted.

"I know what I want for dessert…"

He groaned slightly at my touch, enjoying the sensation of my fingers. "That's only on the secret menu. Good thing you know the secret though…" A quick kiss on my chest followed as he reluctantly pulled himself away. "I have to get ready. Think it over. Ask Evan and Clara. I'll ask Katie. It'll be very casual. I don't want to make them uncomfortable; I just want them to know they're welcome here anytime."

"I don't think either one will turn down a free meal. Evan's gaining back all the weight he lost in the hospital, and then some."

"Just ask them, or I can. You choose." He was smiling way too much this early in the morning, but I couldn't ruin his mood. He stood there, motionless, long enough to let me take in one last look of his naked body before bounding off to put on far too many clothes for my liking.

"I'll ask and let you know."

He walked into the bathroom, starting the shower. I heard him brush his teeth while I pulled on yesterday's clothes and slipped out of his life without saying goodbye. I'd see him again soon enough.

The apartment Evan and I lived in had been shrinking by the day. It was to the point where I didn't feel like his companion anymore, more like his jailer. It wasn't healthy for either of us, so we'd sat down and made a plan.

The farm back in Choctaw wasn't doing any of us any good. Momma would never go back, and neither would any of us. If we sold it, we could each use our share to create a future instead of being tied to the past. I told Evan I'd combine my share with his to buy a house here in Austin for him. He would pay me back, something I was dead serious about. Debt would mean he'd have to get, and keep, a job, and his monthly payments to me would be my assurance he was staying on the right path.

I told Evan and Clara that I wanted Bobby to own the farm, and they agreed. We contacted a lawyer who made the offer to Bobby and Hugh. It was too good for Bobby to turn down. If he ever sold, he'd make a nice profit, and they'd have a future. It wasn't *our* future but it was all I had to give him.

Evan took my car to clear the house of his things, which wasn't much. He packed it all into the back and left for good. I prayed he'd left the sins of the past behind, where they belonged.

That had been a few weeks ago. Today, he had an interview for an IT job with the university. If he could land it, he could finish his degree while working. Every step he took seemed precarious, with so much riding on it. I knew he felt the pressure, but I also knew he was determined to build a better future for himself, one he hadn't thought was possible before.

I didn't have to worry about Clara. She was already fully immersed in college: new friends, new experiences, a whole new life. I was pretty sure she'd have a boyfriend soon enough, and he'd be perfect for her, not gay and sleeping with her brother. She'd been a little shocked when I told her about me and Ryder. Jasper hadn't been wrong; she had developed a pretty strong crush on him, almost as strong as my own. Her initial disappointment almost made me regret telling her, but she quickly sorted everything out. If she couldn't date Ryder, she was happy that I would be. She made it seem so simple, so uncomplicated.

As I drove back to the apartment, I realized I had time with Ryder. Nothing needed to be decided that day. Sean was out of the picture. Even though I didn't know exactly what had happened to him, I'd made peace on my drive back to Texas. He'd had several chances, and that was the best I could do for the man. If he did show up again, I'd deal with it. Ryder wasn't going to be hurt by him again, and that was all that mattered.

"Back from whoring around?" Evan said with a smile as I walked in.

I started to say something back but then realized I hadn't seen him genuinely smile since he'd gotten sprung from the hospital, so I took the hit. Sort of.

"And here Ryder was nice enough to invite you over for dinner tonight. Should I tell him you don't approve of his loose morals and you won't be joining..."

"No way, man. I've got nothing against him. He was my doctor, after all. Without me…"

"Careful, little brother…I'm not sure that's the credit you really want to take."

"Yeah, I know, but Dr. Lewis says if you can make light of the past, it loses some of its weight."

"Well, I hope Dr. Lewis is right. What time is your interview?"

"One."

I walked toward my room, where the shower was waiting, something I knew I needed. "Leave here around noon, then?" I said over my shoulder.

His silence pulled me back into the room. "Ev? Noon? OK?"

He looked nervous, stumbling over his words. "I, um, I…don't get mad…"

"Why would I get mad? What's up?"

"I…I think I want to take the bus. Go on my own."

I was a little stunned. I'd taken him everywhere, been by his side in almost everything he'd done since leaving the hospital. I knew it wouldn't last forever, but I hadn't expected it to happen today.

"I know the buses, the transfers, the times…"

"No, I'm sure you do. Are you sure? The interview will be stressful enough…"

"I've got to start doing things on my own. I know I can do it, but I need *you* to know I can. Besides, you've been leaving me on my own every night. If I was going to start using again, I'd have had plenty of other opportunities…"

"No, hey, it's not that I think you'll relapse suddenly on the bus. I trust you, obviously. Ryder's been telling me to let you go places on your own. I know it's time, especially if you feel ready for it. Just promise you'll call if you need me to pick you up. I'm here if you need me."

"I know. I will. I think we both could use a little independence though…"

He was right. This was the next phase of his recovery, the one where I backed further and further away. But where did I back to?

Evan left for his interview, and I called Clara to invite her to dinner, which she eagerly accepted. She said she was "absolutely desperate" to see all of us. Oh, to be eighteen again, when everything felt like life or death, but it wasn't, not usually. I hoped she'd never know that kind of real desperation. I hoped I'd protected her from it.

I e-mailed Jasper to update him on Evan's progress before I received another "What the fuck is going on?" e-mail from him. I'd spent so many years on my own, not worrying about anyone but myself, and Dixon, that I was still getting used to having three siblings who actually wanted to be a family. And now there was Ryder in the mix...

My left hand unconsciously went to the ring, my finger slipping inside it as usual. I knew this was the problem. Grayson was the problem. I had to put things right with him before I could move forward. He was the wall I couldn't get past. The only issue was, I still had no idea where he was. Every time I tried to find him, I came up blank. He was still a ghost with enough money to stay that way forever, if he wanted. And here I was, stuck in limbo, unable to think about a real future with Ryder until I knew I hadn't completely ruined the last man I'd loved. I couldn't live with myself if I did that to Ryder too, not after everything he'd done for Evan, and Clara…and me.

At the very least, I needed to finally tell Ryder about Grayson. I'd put off all his tentative inquiries about the ring, always telling him "later," hoping later would never come. But how do I tell him I murdered my fiancé's family right in front of him? How do I explain that I'd been paid by a billionaire, a man who had me on a leash like a pet, to do just that? I couldn't. The only way would be to lie, to tell him the truth by lying to him. And the cycle would begin all over again.

I had no way out, and no one to blame but myself.

I waited for Evan to get back from his interview. I might've been more anxious about it than he was. I just wanted him to do well, to rebuild the confidence I'd mistakenly stolen from him years ago. The university would be lucky to have him.

My phone pinged with a text.

RYDER

Leaving work early. Hope everyone can make it for dinner 🍷

The Heath's will all be there and extremely hungry for everything you have to offer 😈

It was almost three. I would've thought Evan should be back by now. What if they rejected him, and he did something stupid? I fought the urge to get in the car and go looking for him. My need to protect him, after everything, would never go away. I was heading to my bedroom to grab my keys when I heard the door open behind me. The tension in my shoulders eased, almost. I'd feel better when I laid eyes on him.

He was smiling.

"They offered me the job." He wasn't even fully in the apartment, but he was clearly over the moon. "I met the team, went around...I wasn't expecting it...The salary is great...I need to buy a car..."

I let out some noise that was a mix of support, relief, and thankfulness. We met in the middle of the room for a tight hug, something we'd become more accustomed to in the past few months, unafraid to show each other how much we meant to each other. He was finally, fully, back on the path he should've been on ten years earlier.

"I knew you'd do it," I said as we broke the embrace. "I knew it. You better call Clara and tell her."

"I already did..."

"Wait, you told her before me?"

"I had to tell someone, and I wanted to see your face when I told you..."

I cocked an eyebrow at him, letting him know he was off the hook, for now.

"Go change. Let's go surprise Clara. We have a couple of hours before we need to be over at Ryder's..."

"Your boyfriend's..."

"Shut up."

"Well, he is, isn't he?"

"It's way too early for that kind of talk. We're still getting to know each other..."

"Is *that* what you're calling it?"

I followed him back to his room. "It's complicated. He's not long out of a really serious relationship, and I'm, well, I'm me..."

"What's that supposed to mean?"

"I just don't have the best track record."

"Well, maybe lighten up on yourself. He's as lucky to have you as you are him."

"Oh, is that right? And now you're the expert?"

"I am. And I'm the only one here with a job, so what I say, goes." He hung his new suit back in the closet. Standing there in just his t-shirt and boxer shorts, his lanky frame finally filling out, he wasn't the same Evan I remembered from ten years ago, or even earlier in the summer when I first saw him again. Lifetimes had passed. And maybe he was right. Maybe I was lucky.

"Finish getting ready. Let's go surprise Clara. We can head over to my boyfriend's together..." I smirked at him, watching to see if he was satisfied. He was.

As we got closer to campus, I took a detour through what looked like a neighborhood with younger families. It was the kind of area I could picture Evan living in, close to work, hopefully friends, eventually. Safe and peaceful. I spotted a For Sale sign ahead, almost as if I'd willed it into existence. I wasn't one for fate, but I needed to rethink that.

We stopped in front of it. Evan clearly knew what I had in mind, and we stared at the house critically. From the front, I could see nothing wrong with it. I told Evan to write down the realtor's contact info from the sign, and I'd call first thing in the morning.

"After you get home from whoring?"

"Yes, after I get home from whoring, dick."

"Whoring dick...sounds about right."

"Get it out of your system now. I don't want to hear you saying that in front of Ryder, and definitely not in front of his sister and niece."

"Roger, boss," he smiled at me. "You know I'd never do anything to hurt you...your chances..." He turned serious, and I knew he wouldn't.

I pulled away from the curb, feeling like I'd checked another thing off the list of things I had to do before stepping away from my role as protector.

"Call Clara. See where she is. She might not want us surprising her in front of her friends."

"Her junkie and ex-con brothers?"

"Ex-junkie..." I laughed.

"Work in progress, brother. Work in progress."

We pulled up to Clara's dorm just in time to see her walking toward us with a friend, laughing at something one of them had just said. Her wide, carefree smile spread across her face. From afar, there wasn't a trace of the turbulent life she'd grown up with. If there was one thing I'd learned about Clara, it was that she could almost always find the positive in any situation and focus solely on that. She never gave up on Evan, and in her way, she never gave up on me.

We got out of the car as they approached. The young woman with Clara appeared older, more poised, not the awkward freshman I was expecting.

"Evan! Maxie!" Clara shouted, even though we were only a few feet away. "This is Fawn."

Her hand shot into mine, and she stared at me with an intensity that made it hard to look away.

"Fawn Dixon," she said, in a clipped, posh British accent. Her grip tightened around my hand like a vise.

My blood almost froze in the autumn heat. Her upper lip quivered slightly, her only tell. She was Dixon's failsafe. My blood wasn't enough. She was the insurance policy he'd put in place to keep me honest. As she embraced Evan with a hug much too tight for a first encounter, I knew the message: step out of line, and they die.

My hand instinctively went to my shoulder. I could feel my tattoo beneath my fingers, and I knew somewhere on her, she had one too. We all did. I would never be free of Dixon. I would always be his fucking Rook.

Clara was saying something about Fawn being a last-minute addition to their suite, someone else had decided not to enroll. I knew Bear was behind that, altering transcripts, denying admission, all part of Dixon's latest game.

"We should go," I said.

Clara frowned. "What's the rush?"

"I just want to get there early. Help Ryder out if he needs it." A lie. I knew Ryder would have everything handled. The person who needed help was me.

Clara said good-bye to Fawn, who gave Evan another warm hug. I walked back toward the car, offering a curt good-bye over my shoulder.

Clara climbed into the car, slightly miffed.

"You could've been nicer, Maxie. Fawn's really sweet, and she doesn't know anyone here yet."

"So she doesn't have a boyfriend?" Evan piped in, clearly amused.

Clara reached over the seat and punched him in the shoulder.

My urge was to tell them everything. The truth was the only thing that could truly protect them from what they were now part of. But it could also be the thing that got them killed. My palms started to sweat on the wheel. I had to let them go. They'd be safe as long as I kept my word, and I had every intention of doing just that.

But then it dawned on me. If Dixon could get to Clara and Evan, he could get to Ryder as well, if he hadn't already. My silence was all of their protection now. I would never be able to be completely honest with any of them. Dixon wanted me for himself, and Dixon always got what he wanted.

"When are you going to clean all of this stuff out of your car, Maxie?"

"It's all Evan's from the farm. Hey, Ev, tell her about the house…"

Hearing his excitement about the house, his interest in dating, his new job…these were the reasons I came back. I loved being in this car with Clara and Evan, and maybe, one day, Jasper would join us here too. I could safely lock the past away and begin a future with a man I could, at least to myself, admit I was falling in love with. Ryder was in my life for a reason. I needed to believe that and stop trying to sabotage it with second-guessing. I didn't want to leave. I didn't have to leave. Life was going to be peaceful from here on out.

I turned down Ryder's street, past the vacant lots that were prime for development one day. Maybe we'd buy the one next door, expand the house, make room for kids and a dog or two.

I pulled into the driveway. The garage door was up, and Ryder's car was inside with the trunk open. The first sign that something wasn't right. Home or away, he always closed the garage door. He didn't like how it looked from the street with it open, exposing the mess behind the neat exterior.

"That's weird…" Evan's voice snapped me from my thoughts. He was pointing at the front door. It was partially open, and the window next to it was shattered, jagged glass dangling at odd angles.

Evan started to get out of the car, but I grabbed him by the shirt and yanked him back in.

"No." I thought for a second. "Stay here with Clara. I'm sure it's fine. He probably just locked himself out..." But I knew that wasn't what happened. "Give me five minutes. If I'm not back out, call the cops. Stay here!" I ordered again, before getting out of the car and approaching the front door.

There was blood on the glass, and a small pool lay just inside the door. Droplets led the way to the back of the house. My rage built as I tried to make sense of what I was seeing, and there was only one conclusion I kept coming back to: Sean had found his way back to Austin, and this time, I was going to kill him.

I wanted to call out Ryder's name, hear his voice, hear that he was okay, but I didn't want to alert Sean to my presence before it was necessary. I walked into the kitchen, finding it a mess, groceries spilled on floor, broken glassware, blood smeared in the countertop, and bloody footprints that pointed toward the back door, which was standing wide open.

He didn't come to talk, that was for sure. Ryder was in trouble.

I hurried out into the backyard, expecting to find them there, but it was empty, which could only mean one thing. I looked into the woods but couldn't see them from the house. I knew they were in there. I'd spent enough time shadowed in their darkness to know how quickly the trees could close in, as Sean would know as well.

I bolted across the yard, past the pergola, into the first rows of trees, heading deeper into the dense growth that had once protected Ryder's home and property. Now, it might be masking something far more sinister.

I had to fight the urge to scream Ryder's name, to let him know I was coming. That I would save him. Truth was, I wasn't sure I wasn't already too late.

Up ahead, there was a flicker of movement, and I could finally hear voices, at least one.

I stepped into the small clearing and froze when I saw him.

"What are you doing here? How…"

"Hi, Max. I knew you'd find us, eventually."

I took in the scene. Ryder was slumped against a tree. His hair was matted with blood, plastered it to the side of his head. His neck struggled to keep his head from falling sideways. His shirt was torn open, and he was missing a shoe. A gun was pointed down at him.

"What are you doing, Grayson?" The words came out as a question, a demand, a plea. I couldn't understand what was happening.

He didn't answer. He just stared at me.

I needed answers. "How did you find me?"

"When you rented that apartment. My man was finally able to track you. Maxwell *Heath*. Fucking liar."

Ryder moaned softly, but it hit me like a shout.

"You know I didn't mean to hurt them, Grayson. You were fucking there. I was fighting to save myself, to save you…Don't do this…" I was losing control. This wasn't the Grayson I knew. The one I loved. That man would never be standing here with a gun, threatening to kill someone.

"Shut up! You were nothing but lies the whole time. I know who you are now. I know the truth."

Did he? Or did he only know the truth he'd been fed to conceal something even worse?

"Whatever you think you know, he had nothing to do with it. If you want to hurt someone, hurt me." The words were out before I could stop them. The thought of witnessing Grayson's revenge exacted on Ryder, seeing him harmed right in front of me, broke something deep inside of me. I let out a scream, raw and desperate, releasing the rage and fear that had been building inside.

I dropped to my knees, pounding my fists into the ground. My necklace, his ring, fell from inside my shirt and dangled in the early evening light.

"How fucking dare you still wear that!" Grayson's voice was

now shrill with fury. "Take it off. You don't deserve to have that! Judas!"

"I loved you, Gray. You know I did."

"You're incapable of love. You used me to get to them."

I saw Ryder's eyes flutter open, scanning the area, unfocused and scared.

"I was trying to protect you."

"You killed them…" The gun in his hand shook, and I knew the lack of control made the situation even more dangerous.

"Don't hurt him, please. Don't…"

"But that's exactly what I came here to do. I've been watching you. I know…"

"TAKE ME. KILL ME. PLEASE." The words I'd been holding back for so long finally slipped out. "I love him…"

The first bullet tore through his shoulder, slicing through muscle and nerve. He let go of the gun, and it fell to the ground, resting among the leaves and dead branches.

The second shot was the kill shot. It hit the center of his chest, and blood erupted. His eyes widened. He collapsed to the ground without a sound.

"No! No. No…" was all I could manage to say.

I turned and saw Evan walking into the clearing, his hunting rifle, the one he'd packed into the car weeks earlier, dangling at his side. Behind him was a woman I didn't recognize at first. She passed me and ran straight to Ryder, pulling out her cell phone and calling for help. She identified herself as FBI agent Katelyn Delaney, demanding immediate assistance for her brother.

I somehow managed to get to my feet, stumbling toward Evan. He stood frozen, looking at the man he'd just killed. I took the rifle from him, dropped it to the ground, and wrapped my arms around him tightly.

"I'm sorry," he whispered, his voice breaking.

I held him tighter, feeling the tremors in his body. Then I looked up and saw Clara walking tentatively toward us, her eyes wide in shock.

"Don't be sorry. You saved me...again," I said softly. "You saved us all."

EVAN WAS TAKEN INTO CUSTODY. I got him a good lawyer, who, after hours of questioning, asked me if I thought Grayson was capable of murder. Did I think he'd actually pull the trigger? For Evan's sake, I said yes, but the truth was, I wasn't sure. The Grayson I'd met and fallen in love with, the one I'd agreed to marry, would never have hurt me. But my actions, my deceit, had changed him into a monster like me. That Grayson was possibly capable of anything. I'd never know for certain.

Grayson's death was ruled justified, it wasn't the word I would've used, and Evan was thankfully released.

I buried the necklace, and the ring, in the woods where Grayson died.

Ryder was in the hospital for three days with a concussion, a few deep cuts, and several broken ribs.

When he was ready, I told him the truth, or the version of it that was as close as I dared get, for everyone's sake.

I told him about Carlos and the fear, the mistrust, that experience had left me with. I told him I worked for a billionaire, for a while, as a sort of assistant. I told him about my time on the NYPD and the case that led me to Grayson, Spencer, and Paloma. I explained how I got shot and almost died. I apologized for lying to him in the past and I answered his questions as best I could, but when he asked again about the tattoo, the rook wrapped in protective barbed wire, all I told him was, "It's just art."

Shortly after he returned to his home, we were lying in bed together, my body gently spooning his from behind. He was still processing everything that had happened in the woods. His ribs wouldn't be the only things that took time to heal. I stroked his hair and quietly kissed the back of his neck. Grateful wasn't a word I used often, but that was how I felt in that moment. For this man, for my family, for my life.

Ryder broke the silence, something he'd have to get used to doing when I was around.

"Did you mean what you said?"

I knew exactly what he was referring to. My confession in the woods when I thought I might lose him forever. "I did. I do."

My hand moved down his body and rested on his bare thigh. He let out a small, contented sigh and relaxed into me.

"I love you, too," was all he said before his breathing steadied, and I knew he'd finally faded into a restful sleep.

Epilogue

TWO YEARS LATER

"Austin and I are going for a run!" I called up the stairs, knowing Ryder was still sprawled naked in bed, just as I'd left him twenty minutes ago. "I've got my phone if you need me!"

By the time we were out the door and heading down the drive, I thought I heard him reply, something like, "Don't get lost," or maybe, "Hurry back."

We'd been here a week already. I wasn't worried about getting lost. And, honestly, I was always in a rush to get back to him, even when we were on vacation.

We turned left at the bottom of the drive, out the subdivision gate, and toward the quiet streets of Palm Desert. The dry wind stung my face as it swept through the air, evaporating my sweat almost instantly. Austin panted heavily but stuck with me.

The sun was a welcome burn against my face, warming my chest. Vacation sat comfortably on my tanned shoulders. My lungs filled with the dry desert air, while tiny grains of sand pelted my skin in the wind. It felt familiar...It reminded me of Casablanca.

I'D BEEN on the yacht for a few months, sailing the Canaries, the Algarve, the Costa del Sol, seeing to all of Dixon's needs, in and out of his bedroom. The time and distance between me and my past had long since settled in. I barely thought about Bobby Oldham anymore, about what could've been if I hadn't taken that gun out of Evan's hands that day.

I knew Evan was safe now. He'd look after Jasper and Clara. I'd done what I needed to do, protected him, all of them, when it counted. I'd given them the opportunities I never really had.

Meeting Dixon had been the first real chance I'd ever had to make something of myself, something that was only mine. Turning him down had never really been an option, and it still wasn't, even after I flew to Europe on his jet. Dixon St. James owned me, just like he owned the others - Bear, Kit, Piper, Buck, Paloma, Leo... Captain Leo Harris of the NYPD. We were his menagerie of soldiers.

I managed the staff, organized the dinners, coordinated transport on land. I made sure Dixon was satisfied before he went to bed at night, whether with me or with someone else, man or woman, someone new who caught his eye. I made all the arrangements. I relied on him for everything, and he relied on me. I could've sailed the Mediterranean, or circled the globe with him, forever, without complaint. But Dixon had bigger plans for me.

It was as we were leaving Tangier, preparing to cruise down the Moroccan coast, that he told me what he really needed from me.

I'd unknowingly revealed more to Bear than I'd thought on our initial trip east. The way I dispatched that deer, without hesitation, without fear, the surgical precision with which I wielded that knife, had caught his attention. Bear knew Dixon would appreciate that. I killed without remorse, like it was just a job to be done.

We went to the aft deck, watching the sun dip into the North

Atlantic as we did every night. His warm hand rested on the small of my back, the waves lapping quietly beneath us. And then he simply told me: when we reached Casablanca, I was to kill a man named Seurat.

He said it didn't matter exactly how I did it, just that it was done within the twenty-four-hour window of our stay. I had to execute Seurat and get back on the yacht, unfollowed, or I'd be left behind to face the consequences. All matter-of-fact.

He took me to his cabin, showed me Seurat's picture, and laid out an array of weapons to choose from. A list of locations, places Seurat had been seen before, spots he frequented.

I remember I had surprisingly few questions for him. Dixon had saved me, and for that alone, I was loyal. If it meant a life of his choosing, not mine, so be it. He had the power to protect me. Whatever he asked of me, including murder, I'd do it. I had nothing left to lose. Bear's words came back to me, he'd do anything for Dixon without question, and for the first time, I understood what he meant. I wasn't the first assistant Dixon had sent to kill, and I wouldn't be the last. However, I would be the one that didn't let him down now.

I memorized Seurat's face: round, thinning hair, beady, narrow eyes. I planned my attack, but I knew luck and chance would play a large part. When we docked in Casablanca, Dixon kissed me good-bye. "Don't worry," I told him. "I won't disappoint you." I wrapped a keffiyeh around my head and face until only my dark eyes were visible, then set off. I didn't look back.

For hours, I walked the narrow, twisting streets of the old town, through the Casbah, past aromatic stalls of spices and rotting meats. I slipped into the cafés where Seurat had been spotted, careful to stay on the edges of the crowds, marking off each place in my mind. By dusk, I still hadn't found him, and the pressure was mounting. The adhan, the call to prayer, had just concluded, signaling the start of the night prayers.

The wind kicked up from the Sahara, sand stinging my skin,

making my suntanned complexion darker under the moonlight. I approached The Bourgogne just as a limousine pulled up to the curb. I froze, stepping deeper into the shadows of a nearby alleyway, waiting as the scene began to unfold.

A black stiletto heel and the shapely leg it was attached to emerged first from the back of the limo. The beautiful blonde in the white silk dress barely registered in my mind. But the man following her, slowly stepping out of the car, was my focus. He was my target. François Seurat.

I knew little about him. Dixon had simply said he was 'in the way' and needed to be 'removed.' That was enough for me.

I had to act fast. No telling how long they'd be in the restaurant or whether I'd get another chance like this when they left at the end of the night.

A half-dozen people milled about on the sidewalk, walking in and out of the pool of light spilling from the restaurant doors. They'd get in the way if they wanted to. I needed a distraction.

I drew the dagger from my boot, my steps deliberate. The thin blade found its mark swiftly, sinking into her chest with little resistance. It pierced her heart before she even had time to process what was happening. Through the knife, I could almost feel her life fading away. Blood spread across the white silk of her dress as she collapsed to the ground. The ensuing chaos was all I needed.

I pulled the Walther PPK from my waistband, hidden in the folds of my robe. The weight of it had been a constant reminder of my mission, a pressure against me all day. I jammed the silenced muzzle under Seurat's ribcage, squeezed the trigger three times. The recoil shuddered through my hand. His eyes went wide for a moment, and then the light drained from them as he crumpled backward into the limo. If anyone had been watching him and not the woman in the pool of blood, they'd have thought he fainted from the shock of the attack.

I quickly walked away, blending into the night, shedding the keffiyeh and my robe, discarding them into a nearby dumpster. It was the best I could do to distance myself from the murder I'd just committed.

For the next three hours, I walked aimlessly through the streets of Casablanca, checking over my shoulder every few steps, making sure I wasn't being followed. Then, I made my way back to The Menagerie II. My skin was alive with heat, my body buzzing with an adrenaline high. My mind was a whirlwind of exhilaration. I wanted to run, to dance, to soar. I needed to see Dixon, to tell him everything while he undressed me and took me to bed. I wanted to make him feel as magnificent as I did in that moment. I wanted his approval, to feel his pride. I felt invincible. And part of me, and not a small part, wanted to do it again.

IT WAS DIXON, his money, his connections, that got me onto the NYPD. Bear forged the credentials I needed. Dixon turned me into the cop my Pa probably always wanted me to be. Where Seurat and the others that followed had been quick in-and-out jobs, Spencer Donato required more planning, more subterfuge, more cunning. I would need every skill I'd honed since that night in Casablanca.

At first, it was exciting, but I hadn't anticipated the consequences of falling in love with Grayson. When I close my eyes, I still see that night in the study at the mansion. The look of betrayal he gave me will haunt me forever. I still don't blame him for what he tried to do to Ryder, to me, really. I've done much worse, for much lesser reasons.

Austin slowed his pace, signaling it was time to head home. Hopefully, Ryder would be up and ready to join me in the shower when I got back. My adrenaline surged at the thought of him, of us together...

My phone rang, cutting through my thoughts. But it wasn't the familiar three chimes I'd assigned to Ryder. Instead, it was the single, unmistakable Chinese gong I'd set long ago for Dixon St. James. I hadn't heard it in years.

I stopped running just outside the gate. Passing through it would take me back to Ryder, to the life we'd built; his thriving private practice, my landscaping business, our plans for children, our future. If I answered, all of it would change.

But if I didn't...what would happen to the people I loved? Protecting them was still my priority.

My finger hovered over the phone. Austin looked up at me, cocking his head, sensing something was wrong. I knew what the call meant. I knew where it would lead. And I knew I'd made a promise, not just to myself, but to Dixon.

Somewhere in the pit of my stomach, a part of me was glad he was calling. I felt dirty, but I missed it. God help me, I needed another fix. I loved Ryder, desperately, but deep down, when I was honest with myself, I craved my old life just as much. Maybe, at times, even more.

If Ryder found out, he'd never understand. So he couldn't find out. All of our lives depended on it.

I pressed the green 'Answer' icon and stepped back into that world of lies, deception, murder.

"This is The Rook. What have you got for me?"

About the Author

Carter Christensen grew up in Rhode Island as the third child of two English professors, which meant books and stories were part of daily life. After a detour through the world of finance, he returned to his first love, writing, and hasn't looked back. He now lives in Manhattan with his dog, Kingsley, who takes his role as "good boy" very seriously.

You can contact Carter at carterchristensen.author@gmail.com or through his website, Carter-Christensen.com

X x.com/CarterC_Author
⃝ instagram.com/CarterChristensen_Author
♪ tiktok.com/@CarterChristensen_Author
ⓑ threads.com/@CarterChristensen_Author

Also by Carter Christensen

The London Boys

A Prince of a Man

Frost on the Ground

Lucky in Love

After the Wedding

Thank you for reading this book. I really hope you enjoyed it. If you did, will you please leave a review on Amazon? You don't have to write anything if you don't want to—a star rating is plenty. I really appreciate your time. Carter.

www.ingramcontent.com/pod-product-compliance
Lightning Source LLC
Chambersburg PA
CBHW021406110726
47901CB00008B/2079